Glenfiddich Inn

Glenfiddich Inn

A Novel

Alan Geik

SONADOR PUBLISHING • BOSTON, MA.

Sonador Publishing
16 Maple Park
Newton Centre, MA. 02419

First Printing, 2014

ISBN 978-0-692-34565-8 (pb)
ISBN 978-0-692-34561-0 (ebook)

www.glenfiddichinn.com
Visit us on Facebook   www.facebook.com/glenfiddichinn
Follow us on Twitter www.twitter.com/GlenfiddichInn

Cover art © 2014 Brianna Harden and Alan Geik. All rights reserved

Interior book design by Alissa Rose Theodor
Set in Goudy Oldstyle Std

For Nina Lenart, Sheila Amos, and Susan Cox
Three great ladies who left us too soon.

AUTHOR'S NOTES & ACKNOWLEDGEMENTS

World War One (1914-1918) was the defining event of the 20th century. Everything that followed had its roots in those few disastrous years—the Russian Revolution, radio and television, the Great Depression, the rise of Fascism and World War Two, the Atomic Age, and specifically in America, prohibition and the women's right to vote movement.

Perhaps the greatest current global threats are also a result of decisions made by the colonial victors of that war—the random division of the Middle East into countries to be ruled for the next one hundred years by kings, sheikhs and generals.

The war deeply affected those who were to most dramatically shape culture and politics well into the 20th century—Churchill, Marie Curie, Dwight Eisenhower, Eleanor Roosevelt, Ernest Hemingway, F. Scott Fitzgerald, Charlie Chaplin, Albert Einstein, Edith Cavell, Walt Disney, Mary Pickford and Irving Berlin to name just a few.

My own interest in this period led to this fictionalized account of two American families, who despite their distance from the raw brutality of the fighting, were changed forever by the conflict.

I hope this story takes the reader on a rewarding journey through this terrifying, yet exciting, time.

I would like to thank my editor, Pamela Guerrieri-Cangioli of Proofed to Perfection. I am also indebted to the following for their support and guidance during the writing of this work— Yvette Palomo Perales, Iris Geik, Johanna Geik, Mike Policare, Lida Gellman, Gary Eisenberg, Howard Dratch, Ken Topolsky, Gary Cox, Eileen LaRusso, Deborah Cayetano, Anthony Christopher, Bret Levitt, Ryan Levitt, Joe LaRusso, and Eddie Lopez.

The newspaper warning from the German embassy in chapter 5, the magazine article regarding President Wilson making a radio address in chapter 19, and the executive order affecting radio transmissions in chapter 25, are all quoted from their original sources.

Please contact me at www.facebook.com/glenfiddichinn if you would like more detailed information.

The dialogue, as well as many of the characters and sometimes locales, such as hotels, in this work are fictional. As in most historical novels, they are used to frame the real events and historical characters that hopefully propel the story forward.

I would also like to thank the Library of Congress for the images used in our cover design.

Alan Geik
November, 2014

PROLOGUE

JANUARY 20, 1919
THE WARFIELD HOTEL
NEW YORK, N.Y.

THE NEW JERSEY SHORELINE poked through the late morning mist over the Hudson River, revealing a line of vessels tethered to their piers. Some ships destined, William Morrison guessed, for a Europe still gasping from the devastating war that had just ended with only a faint whimper.

He snapped open the oil-splattered leather case resting on the windowsill, lifted out the binoculars and quickly appraised them; their once glossy black finish was now blemished with bald spots, exposing a dull bronze underbody.

William recalled spying on the frenzied gamblers in the stands at Fenway Park laying World Series bets with one of Joe Finnerty's guys. Yes, that was the last time he handled the binoculars he had bought Byron for his birthday. He had borrowed them off his brother-in-law's neck that day—was it just four years ago? *Damn things look like they've had a century of wear.*

William twirled the focus ring on each lens, sharpening his view of the stevedores on the distant ships grappling with cargo and luggage, ignoring the frigid harbor wind. They moved with the same slow steadiness as did the dockworkers on Pier 54 down the street below his hotel window.

Joe Finnerty, that son of a bitch, was right, William now told himself. "When this war ends," Joe had said so many times, "the United States will be the center of the universe, not the goddamn Brits anymore."

William slipped the binoculars back into the case and jiggled the window, loosening a thin overlay of pale green paint bonding it to the wooden frame. He nudged the window up, leaned out, resting his palms on the concrete ledge, and breathed in the chilled January air.

Four years prior he had stood in the grand transit structure stretching across the pier on the other side of the wide street now filling with traffic and energy in anticipation of the flood of disembarking passengers from another ocean liner.

That drizzling day his sister Louella, and her fifteen-year-old daughter Sarah, set off for England. They would be safe there. At least that was what everyone thought. It made sense at the time; after all, the fighting was in France, on the other side of the English Channel, not in London or Glasgow—and the fallacy of that belief had gripped him ever since.

How many others had swarmed around him that day to watch that ship slipping into the current of the Hudson River, nudged along by a few tugboats? Waiting hours to wave to strangers on an ocean liner! Imagine that, hundreds of strangers waving to each other.

Teamsters maneuvering horse-drawn carts through the crowded streets, rumors of German spies mingling with passengers, and the marching band at the foot of the gangplank. All that was gone now.

Today, only purposeful movement. No idlers or brass bands in sight, and no thoughts of German spies either. Even those few horse-drawn carts had disappeared from around the pier, now replaced by internal combustion engines buried under the hoods of trucks capable of hauling anything that would fit into a ship's hold.

A knock on the door drew him back into the warmth of his room. Still too early for housekeeping William decided as he opened the door.

A bellboy stood in front of him balancing a tray supporting a whiskey bottle and two glasses. "I saw you leaning out the window, sir, and thought I should stop by before I ended my shift." He spoke, hesitantly—it wasn't the manner of a Warfield Hotel employee to engage a guest so personally. William was amused by the hotel's attempt to claim superiority to the flophouses for sailors and dockworkers that spotted the surrounding streets. It would be impossible to imagine Margaret, or anyone else he knew in Boston, staying in any of these places, he thought.

"Can I help you?" William asked, assuming the whiskey was not likely for him. Maybe the room next door. He had heard muted laughing and the squeaking of rusty springs well into the night.

"I'm Ruggiero. I work the night shift here. I saw you leaning out the window." He cast an ingratiating smile up at William, who stood over him.

"So you said."

"I didn't think you would remember me, but I wanted to thank you anyway."

William waved him into the room. "No, I don't remember you, but there must be a reason for a round of Glenfiddich this early in the day."

Ruggiero removed a brown bowler he had clamped with his fingertips to the bottom of the tray. He looked at William for a sign of recognition. None surfaced.

"You gave me this hat four years ago when you were staying here, sir. You said you had just bought it the day before, and that you had great luck that day. Something like that. I saw your name, Mr. William Morrison, last night in the register and thought it must be you. Same address—Glenfiddich Inn, New Bedford, Massachusetts."

"Then you saw me leaning out the window—I know."

"This hat has been lucky for me also, Mr. Morrison."

William had never thought about it, but now he dimly recalled giving a new bowler to a bellboy. That's right, he had met Joe Finnerty's guys the day before and still another rigged stock promotion was set in motion. Anytime he delivered for Joe it was a good day. It was that simple back then, wasn't it? He also remembered thinking that Margaret would have called the color of that new hat "fawn," or something other than simply "brown."

Ruggiero set the tray onto the pockmarked writing desk near the bedroom door. "So I wanted to bring up a bottle of Glenfiddich for a short sip. I borrowed it from the bar. Nobody will miss it till later. Not too many people here would order it anyway, sir."

"Ruggiero, that bowler still looks new—as if it just came out of the haberdashery. J.J. Hat Center, wasn't it?"

Ruggiero nodded, turning the hat over to display the store name and address scripted onto the dark brown silk lining. "I've only worn it a few times. I keep it in my locker downstairs. It's just like new."

"And it has been a lucky hat for you, you say?" William knew he would have to hear the story.

"That's right, sir. A few days after you gave it to me, another guest gave me a ticket to the Polo Grounds. I wore the bowler to the game. I saw Babe Ruth hit his first home run ever. You heard of Babe Ruth, haven't you? You must be a Boston Red Sox fan. Coming from Massachusetts and all that."

William laughed. "Yes, I heard of Babe Ruth. More than you might want to know, Ruggiero."

"Two days later, I went to MacPhail's Tavern—it's down the next street, past that bucket of blood, the Strand Hotel," Ruggiero said, cocking his head over his right shoulder toward what William assumed was the general direction of the bar. "I also wore it that day. I bet two bucks on Regret in the Kentucky Derby. I got seven-sixty back. She was the first filly to ever win a Derby. Do you remember that Derby, sir?"

"I sure do." William nodded his head slowly. *It was the worst day of my life. The worst weekend of my life. Without a doubt.* "Yes, I remember Regret. I read about the race."

"I also wore it—"

"That's wonderful. You've done well with it."

Ruggiero sensed William's impatience. "A lot has happened since I last saw you, Mr. Morrison," he said, flexing the bowler with his wrist.

"A lot has certainly happened." William nodded once again. Yes, it was the Great War that happened. That's what some idiots were calling it—the Great War. What was so great about it? A question William had asked himself many times since the war ended a few months before.

Ruggiero assumed William's vacant response an invitation to continue. "Some people did say it wasn't going to be too good for us."

"Yes, they did say that, didn't they?"

"It's getting a bit chilly in here, isn't it, Mr. Morrison?" Ruggiero looked past William to the still opened window. "Shall I close it for you, sir?"

"Yes, please do." William followed Ruggiero across the room.

"Are you expecting someone's arrival today, Mr. Morrison? A lot of our guests stay here for arrivals and departures from these piers."

Activity in front of the docked RMS *Mauretania* refocused William's attention down the street toward Pier 54. The weathered ship was settling into its berth after its long journey across an ocean finally free of German U-boats.

Amongst the repatriated would be the reason for William's return to the pier. Maybe the reunion would help peel away the rigors of the past few years.

He imagined the excitement, or maybe just relief, enveloping its weary passengers, two thousand souls returning from Europe. Soon they could touch native soil again and scrub away the horrors of the trench warfare so many of them had endured.

"Yes, Ruggiero, I am expecting someone." He glanced again toward the street.

"Oh, the *Mauretania*. It'll be awhile more." Ruggiero pulled on the window. It slammed shut harder than he intended. William drew back.

"Sorry, Mr. Morrison."

An image encroached—a punch driven by his big fist through a young man's ribcage just a half a year before. It was as if he had struck deep into a threadbare burlap bag filled with dried twigs—there was so little resistance.

He knew the poor bastard was going to die when his ribs splintered that easily. The receipt for that one punch was a murder charge. The punch. The murder charge. None of it would have happened if not for that damn war. It just didn't end soon enough.

"You won't believe this, sir. When I saw your name in the register last night, I knew I should give this hat back to you. Maybe you can have some good luck with it again."

"These have been difficult years, Ruggiero. Wouldn't you say?"

"Yes indeed, sir. I lost two nephews in one of those slaughters in France." Ruggiero looked down at his buffed black shoes.

William placed his right hand on Ruggiero's shoulder, covering the dull brass epaulets on his dark blue, tattered-at-the-cuffs uniform jacket. He took the derby from Ruggiero. "I guess a little good luck can't hurt now. But I'll pass on the Glenfiddich, thank you."

Yes, Margaret. Byron. Helen. All four of us, he remembered. We each had so much we wanted to do—then everything changed quickly. Our futures went down with that ship that so effortlessly inched away into the Hudson that day. Who would have guessed that it would never berth alongside a pier again?

I

"...ships searching for survivors now...."

Four Years Before

1

APRIL 15, 1915
THE NORTH END DOCKS
BOSTON, MASS.

DAMN THIS DEVIN KEANE. The elevated train rattling above them and the clips of horse-drawn carts against the cobblestones smothered Keane's patter. William Morrison struggled to hear every word. Of course Devin would do anything to screw him with Joe Finnerty. William knew that. At least anything Devin could get away with—and who knew what Finnerty would believe anyway?

Devin Keane drove his Packard onto the peninsula of unpainted, roughly tacked together warehouses and a muddle of overlapping trolley tracks. William hated Keane's driving; he had no inclination to smoothly work the three pedals on the floor of the car or to avoid small obstacles. Devin just barreled over them. Even the piles of horse shit.

By then, William had been at Finnerty's bank for three years, ever since he graduated from Yale. But now that he was a newly promoted vice president, he should be, he reasoned, further up the ladder than Keane—he shouldn't still have to watch his back from this snake.

Keane lacked Finnerty's phony charm. Margaret dismissed Devin but had long savored her contempt for Joe Finnerty. William smiled, imagining his wife's freckled face, when flushed, either angry or excited in bed, would match the crimson of her long, thick hair.

Why was he so sensitive to this transparent Finnerty hanger-on? Keane shouldn't matter right now. *After all, the day did start off with—um—gusto; Margaret did roll on top of me. She slid me easily inside of her. She must have thought about it awhile before she awakened me.*

"You are so reliable, Mr. Morrison," she had whispered afterwards.

Surely, not everyone gets a compliment like that first thing in the morning. He doubted Devin Keane would ever hear something like that.

William grinned to himself, remembering that Margaret had also said, stroking his cheek, "And ohh, those root beer eyes work every time, my dear." Aunt Agnes had always just called them "brown eyes."

"Finnerty is talking about a deal with these guys over here at Purity." Keane swiveled his head toward William and then back to the wide street with no road markings, the horse carts and trucks avoiding each other by their own design. "He's looking a few years down the road. He probably wants to buy Purity. You know Joe will never tell us the whole deal until the time is right." William ignored Keane's speculation.

There is no reason for Keane's suit not to hang right, William concluded. Finnerty paid him enough. And Keane pocketed a good piece of change on the side from everything he did for Finnerty. Even the bay rum on his neck didn't smell right.

"Finnerty thinks there's still money to be made in whiskey no matter what happens with those temperance assholes." Keane drove past bales of hay and loading docks attached to one-story warehouses. Slow moving workers loaded and unloaded wooden casks from barges moored at the water's edge. "He wants to use the molasses for rum. Who cares about the industrial alcohol they've been making with it?"

An awkward steel structure rose high above the docks, towering over the nearby crumbling tenements. It was out of place. It would have been out of place anywhere. William had not taken his eye off the huge metal tank since it came into view one mile back. *It's the damnedest thing. It looks like a cooking pot.*

It would have been the biggest cooking pot in the world. Fifty feet high. Fifty feet exactly. William knew this from looking through the Purity Distilling Company files at the bank. The tank schematics reminded him of Uncle Isaac's diagrams of his own crazy inventions; nonsensical to anyone but Isaac and perhaps to his often equally befuddled friend, Hans Stitler. William had often wondered if even Hans understood them.

The tank was ninety feet across at the top. Ninety feet! It even had a conical cover mounted on top. Just like a cooking pot. Coarsely contoured sheets of steel girdled by irregular seams of rivets rendered its shape.

Keane parked alongside a narrow gauge railroad track. A layer of dust quickly feathered down onto their suits as soon as their shoes touched the parched gravel.

William inhaled a curious combination of smells. He couldn't quite place them. Perhaps a merging of horseshit and a candy store—a sweetness reminiscent of McConnell's Candy Store right down the street from where he grew up. *McConnell's always smelled sweet. It still does.*

William turned toward the source of the sugary scent; laborers steered thick, brown molasses from a rusted cargo ship into vats on flat carts hitched to aged horses, their sagging hides pocked with pinkish-red sores. William imagined there was probably enough molasses to supply all the rum makers and distilleries that had rooted around the Boston harbor since the first Pilgrims landed nearby.

The peninsula also stank of horseshit. The decaying Boston Public Works barn overpowered Morrison's sweet childhood recollections. That raggedy barn hadn't been cleaned in years. William didn't need to be a farm boy to know that.

Keane nodded toward five men sleeping on bales of hay piled next to the barn door. *Lifeless.* Like those giant flannel rag dolls set out for the summer party William was so thrilled to go to every year at the Guinn farm.

"Those wretched Irishmen are on the mayor's dole. Believe it or not, that's a hard job to get these days. But only my Micks could sleep so soundly on a shit pile." Keane laughed at his own joke and then motioned toward the listing, shingled tenements on the other side of the elevated train screeching around a sharp turn in the elevated track. "When the wind blows in, you can smell the Italians over there. I don't know what the fuck they're cooking. Most of them don't even speak a goddamn word of English, but they manage to be anarchists anyway. Nobody trusts them."

Keane stopped, collecting another thought. "William, did you know these Italians bombed a few places nearby already? They sided with the Germans. I can't fault them for going against the British— there's not an Irishman in Boston who would fault them for that. But they could never fight a lick in any war. They could all go back to Italy as far as I give a damn."

Keane motioned toward the two men standing under the distant faded sign, **PURITY DISTILLING COMPANY**. "That fat guy in the brown suit is Jell. He's Purity's treasurer. He's got the best deal of all. He gave the storage tank contract to Haram Iron Works without a bid. The skinny guy with him is Abelson from Haram. Jell takes a few bucks off the top from Haram's invoices and then overcharges Purity on the other end."

The men watched Devin Keane and William approach. Jell muttered a few words to Abelson as he half-turned away in a motion he probably thought discreet.

"Ships are already on their way up from Puerto Rico with molasses. Jell's anxious to get this tank filled," Keane said.

"Margaret would say that this storage tank is not a candidate for a good design award." William visualizing his wife flicking her hand dismissively. He was sure though she would find the tank 'fascinating.' That's what she would call it. Fascinating.

William remembered how, soon after he had met Margaret, she also found the story of the small, three-inch crescent scar over his left eye 'fascinating.' He had reaped it, he had told her, from a knife wielded by a drunk in a barroom brawl near these same docks. The target may have been someone else but it landed on his brow nonetheless. "It just missed your eye," she had said solemnly at the time, gently running the course of the wound with her index finger.

Her concern had compelled him to confess. "Actually, I got it while ice skating at the pond near the inn one winter. I fell and one of the other boys got tangled up with me and slashed me with his skate. It's just not as exciting as the barroom story."

"Nonetheless, the scar and your oak tree stature do make you rather imposing, despite how you received that wound." She had said it so firmly, and gently.

He had taken her response to be a sign of interest—her first such sign at the time.

"—William, your wife didn't have to go to art school to know this tank looks like crap." Keane peered up to the top of the tank. "But it holds two and a half million gallons of molasses and that can make a shit load of rum. Who knows how that war over there is going to go and what if we won't be able to get molasses any more? Also if those temperance laws get passed, the price of rum will go up and we can make a killing."

The birthday present. William had forgotten about it. The party for Margaret and her twin brother, Byron, was just two weeks away. He had to stop at Duncan's Jewelry. His sister-in-law, Helen, tipped him off that Margaret would—how did Helen put it? —"absolutely love" a particularly smart string of pearls in the window display.

For Byron—it would be powerful binoculars—the perfect accessory to have in the press boxes around the American League baseball circuit when he covered the Boston Red Sox for the *Boston Examiner,* his father's newspaper. Particularly useful, William thought, for ferreting out players trying to go unnoticed in the dugout, napping off the previous night's drunk.

Keane nodded a greeting to Jell and Abelson, now coming alongside William.

"Jell, this is William Morrison. He works closely with Finnerty and me." Keane waved his hand toward the two men.

"So Mr. Morrison, you'll be handling our account for the bank," Jell said, amused, or perhaps condescending, William concluded. He noticed the two open buttons on Jell's soiled shirt above his belt, well hidden beneath his ample stomach.

"Close enough for him to get a cut, Devin?" Jell asked, eyeing William cautiously.

"No, Morrison doesn't take that kind of action yet."

Jell squinted into the sun. "I'd rather work with people who like to get their beaks wet." He jerked a thumb at the man standing alongside him. "This is Abelson from Haram Iron Works. He's also here for the pressure test. He's the guy I deal with most of the time."

William quickly evaluated Abelson; more sophisticated than Jell perhaps—but just another small-time grifter nonetheless. Finnerty likes doing business with these kinds of men, doesn't he? The tank has already lined a few pockets, and not even a single drop of molasses has been poured into it. *Now this really is the New Age of Commerce the newspapers are writing about.*

"How do you test a tank like this?" William asked. "And what are you testing it for?"

"Well, we want to see if it can hold its liquor," Jell said, looking toward Keane and Abelson. They laughed. William nodded, indifferently acknowledging the joke.

William knew the routine. He had been through it before. Finnerty would write himself into a deal and then turn the job over to William for "oversight," as Joe liked to call it. William couldn't complain. Finnerty always gave him a piece of the action. Finnerty told him not to tell Keane about his skim. Who knows what bullshit went on between them? Who cares anyway? Maybe to Margaret's family, working at a bank is a boring job. *They're rich; they don't have to do much of anything. It doesn't matter what they think anyway.* He knew that nothing he did at the bank could ever be boring—he needed to be alert all the time.

A horse-driven fire wagon rolled out of the barn disrupting William's thought—the horses' hooves tapping out their approach. A plume of white steam funneled out of the brass chimney on the engine. A silver-haired, red-faced fire captain stood on the sideboard, grasping the handrail.

"The pump house we built by the dock still isn't working," Jell informed Keane and William. "So Finnerty arranged for the fire department to fill the tank with water. It probably cost him a couple of cases of whiskey—Haig Pinch, I'll bet."

The solid white draft horse and its jet-black mate treaded to a stop next to the storage tank. Both were carefully brushed. They had a real groomer, William speculated. Probably a country boy from Ireland—someone not yet accustomed to sleeping on hay bales all day.

9

Horse-drawn fire wagons still raced around the city, but they would disappear soon enough. William was certain of that. An engine needed neither food nor groomers. Gasoline was more efficient. It was a simple dollar and cents calculation.

The indolent workers stirred from their leisurely postures alongside the barn. A few straggled over to get a better look. Others strained to see, waiting for the show. Anything to interrupt the monotony of their day.

Two firemen combined lengths of hoses into one snaking unit along the ground. The trail extended from the river behind the wharves to a thick brass connection at the side of the wagon. The younger of the two firemen climbed the narrow ladder welded to the tank, hoisting over his shoulder a hose attached to the other side of the fire wagon. He held the shiny nozzle over an opening at the top of the tank.

Captain Schultheiss surveyed the preparations and nodded to his lieutenant nearby. A gush of brown water shot into the tank, followed by a few weak bursts of water, and then nothing.

"One of the force pumps crapped out on us again," the fireman called down to his captain. "We'll get one from another firehouse."

The captain walked closer to the gauges on the wagon, leaning in as if to make an evaluation. William guessed that the captain had no idea what the needles indicated. A political hack probably. In a nice uniform though.

Jell waved his hands. "Not necessary, that's enough water." The captain quickly agreed.

"Abelson, break the tank's cherry. Crack open that tap and let the water out." Jell pointed toward the bottom of the tank. Abelson crouched down, cranking open the manhole. A bathtub 's volume of rusty discharge splashed onto the cement foundation.

"What kind of test is this?" William looked around for an answer.

"How do you know it can hold two and a half million gallons of molasses?"

Abelson shrugged his shoulders. "How the hell should we know? We never built one of these things before. I could have pissed in the tank and saved Finnerty a few cases of good whiskey. Don't you think that would have been smarter?"

"Yes, real smart," William said. "Then you would have been kneeling in piss instead of dirty water." He pointed to Abelson's soaking pants and shoes.

Break its cherry. William guessed that Jell heard Finnerty say that.

"You broke your cherry already, William," Finnerty had announced triumphantly after William narrowly escaped being arrested along with the Burr brothers when he first started at the bank. Finnerty had sent William to Philadelphia to visit the Burr Brothers, a shabby stock brokerage; paint chipping off the walls in a few spots, threadbare carpets around the entrance. Finnerty wanted to use them for one stock fraud or another.

When William left the office, seven or eight men raced up the narrow winding marble stairway from the lobby, bumping him out of their path. He never made eye contact with any of them. He knew immediately they were government agents. He opened the brass front door to the street and hastened his step.

The next morning William read that the brokerage office had been raided and the three brothers arrested for postal fraud. They had been peddling the stock of non-existent companies, or so the government claimed. They would probably be released for $10,000 bail each. If he had lingered for just a few minutes earlier he could have shared a cell with the Burr brothers.

Even now William wondered how Margaret would have reacted back then if he had been arrested—just for being there. It would have taken days to sort it out. His name would have jumped out to the writers on the crime desk at her family newspaper. *What would I have said? "I just happened to stop by to say hello to the Burr brothers."* The Townsend household would not have been sympathetic—even if it had been just a case of wrong time, wrong place.

2

APRIL 27, 1915

RADIO STATION 1XE

TUFTS COLLEGE

MEDFORD HILLSIDE, MASS.

MARGARET RUSHED THROUGH THE transmitter room into the crowded audio laboratory. Harold Power clasped the peach-sized glass bulb, rolling it slowly on his fingertips, examining it with squinted eyes. Sunlight filtered through a patina of grime on the window near his workbench, schematics scattered on top. He held the bulb above his eyes, angling it so that the light reflected off the wire elements fused to its base. Three technicians gathered around him peering at the bulb.

Margaret understood that no one would examine this bulb more intently than Power. Everyone accepted that Power possessed a unique insight into the project —he was from the very beginning the mentor and leader. She often struggled to decipher the cryptic dialect he shared with the electrical engineers—but it didn't matter. Margaret was thrilled just to be in their presence. She knew that despite what her father or the other newspaper people thought, the experiments in this laboratory, and others like it, would one day profoundly change the world.

The hiss of a welder's torch in the courtyard distracted her. She leaned over her bench to get a better view through the window. Pungent fumes from the searing metal seeped inside. It was a welcomed smell, at least for Margaret: it bestowed their work with an aura of progress.

She recognized Helen hunched over the welder, her face covered by a metal mask to prevent the sparking, white-hot particles from scorching her alabaster skin. The mask also restrained Helen's long blonde hair, while sagging work clothes muted her curvaceous figure.

The lanky steel frames stacked around Helen prompted, for Margaret, a fleeting recollection of the Eiffel Tower's beautiful lines and crisscrossing skeletal shapes. Margaret remembered the photograph on the front page of her father's newspaper when the Tower had been inaugurated in 1889. She was eight years old then. The Tower had looked so odd—so functionless.

"What is it for?" she had asked her father.

"It's a beacon for progress," he had replied simply. "A new era of invention and technology is before us."

It sounded so thrilling.

Power leaned over the desk and handed the bulb to Margaret.

Here, there was no use for an Eiffel Tower. They were erecting an antenna that would transmit sound waves as far as twenty miles, maybe further. Their mission was to send the human voice, through the antenna, into the air. Without wires. The vital element was now in Margaret's hands. The Audion tube. Even Power referred to it just as 'the bulb.'

Who, except small groups like this one, Margaret thought, could understand how important these experiments were? A *wireless voice transmission is more impressive than the Eiffel Tower could ever be.*

"Did you ever have a bulb that size in your hand before?" Helen asked breathlessly, slipping onto the stool next to Margaret. "Maybe

I can get one for your birthday. You can hold it all day. Even slide it between your legs. Now that could be exciting—wouldn't you say?"

"You're leering again, my dear," Margaret responded, feigning exasperation. She turned the bulb slowly, examining it from all sides. "Perhaps your closeness to that torch has set you a-flutter once again."

"It's the torch I have to bear."

"I see." Margaret agreed, as if a profound observation had just been shared.

Sexual banter bonded Margaret and Helen since their first encounter at the Boston Museum Art School three years before. "Good work is neither masculine nor feminine," had been a school tenet. Except for life drawing classes, which were segregated by sex. A woman studying nude males was still too uncomfortable for the museum trustees.

Helen, Margaret, and a few other female students, ignoring the school's attempts to protect them, often set themselves up in the back row of easels, eager to impress onto their canvases the charcoal image of the male body on display on the raised platform at the front of the sunlit studio. Few of the male models escaped Helen's often humorous, sometimes deprecating, critique.

"Give me a cigarette, darling," Helen said, removing her face protector, revealing streaks of sweat and matted hair. She pulled lip rouge and powder from her canvas shoulder bag and moved toward the bathroom. Her transformation from dust-covered to elegant required, as Margaret had witnessed many times, just a few careful strokes.

"Oh, Helen, thanks for directing dear William to Duncan's Jewelry for that *stunning* string of pearls," Margaret called out. "One of the salesgirls, Lydia, I think her name is, told me that he bought them yesterday. Lovely, isn't it?"

"Think nothing of it," replied Helen, deftly coloring her pursed lips. "Last year, didn't you hint to Byron how much I would appreciate that divine watch? Left to himself, he might have bought me one of those old leather gloves those fat-assed baseball players spit into all the time."

"I wonder if my brother ever mentions that those idiots spit in their gloves in those baseball stories he writes. Wouldn't it be grand if we could one day broadcast a baseball game and describe what *we* see?"

"Sorry, It sounds rather dull to me," Helen said. "Byron and those writers are frightened that nobody would buy a newspaper if people could listen to those sporting games on the radio. I'll be back in a minute." She continued on her way to the bathroom.

Margaret raised her voice. "Oh, Helen—they are not called 'sporting games.' They are either 'games' or 'sporting events,' darling—I think."

"How interesting," Helen responded over her shoulder.

Harold Power gestured toward the uniformed naval officer walking into the room just as Helen exited. "Margaret, this is Chief Warrant Officer Andrew Henderson. The Department of the Navy assigned him to be their liaison with us, as well as with several other radio stations on the Eastern seaboard." He seemed to have addressed the introduction to just Margaret. Curious, she thought—or maybe the others had already met him.

"Margaret Morrison is one of our excellent draftsmen. Along with Helen Townsend"—Power looked around—"who just left the room."

Chief Henderson smiled, acknowledging Margaret with a slight bow of his head.

A bit stiff, she observed, but actually quite striking. Grayish eyes and sandy-haired; erect and alert in his tailored blue uniform—a striking resemblance to Admiral Peary, whose photo her father ran in the newspaper a few years before. Admiral Peary also had a thick moustache, curled out into symmetric circles on either cheek, just as did this Henderson gentleman.

Margaret recalled how Father scoffed at Peary's claim that he had discovered the North Pole. "This Peary character is an opportunist, a transparent one," Father had said, and he made certain that each of the many explorers who agreed with him had their opinion printed in the newspaper. *Father does so enjoy defrocking public figures.* Those "pretenders," he called them with a sputtering indignation which always amused both Margaret and her brother, Byron.

"Margaret, Chief Henderson is curious how you became involved with these radio experiments," Power said. He seemed so *unathletic* next to Henderson, as he did the few times he stood next to William. His slight frame lent no trace of any hint of physical exertion. Both Margaret and Helen had concluded early on that Power probably had never spent a single day in the sun—or in bed with a woman. They were certain that he never had an interest in anything but the latest technological innovation. Now it was only wireless voice transmissions that captured all of his attention.

Margaret understood this to be Power's cue for her to recite her story—once again. Was the officer curious how any of the men in the room became involved in these radio experiments? Obviously not. But what did it matter?

"It was quite serendipitous, actually." Margaret had by now refined a tightly worded chronology. "Three years ago Helen and I went to the Boston Museum for a lecture by Nora Stanton Blatch."

The name did not seem to register with Chief Henderson.

"Nora Stanton Blatch comes from several generations of suffragettes. Her grandmother even spoke to Congress after the Civil War." Margaret did not see any reaction to the word 'suffragettes'—the women's right to vote movement did not evoke in Chief Henderson the slight wincing sometimes evidenced in some men when the subject arose.

"One would think that women's suffrage and radio would not be part of the same lecture." Chief Henderson seemed interested.

Good point, Margaret thought, and there was a connection. "Nora told us that the museum's hallways reminded her of her life with her former husband, Lee DeForest. A life filled with wooden boxes. The museum that day was unloading art from huge crates."

"Lee DeForest? I read about him." Henderson turned toward Harold Power. "One of the inventors of this tube. Wouldn't you say?"

Margaret didn't wait for Power's response. "Yes, Mr. DeForest developed this about ten years ago. It has been improved a lot since then."

Helen, returning to the table, took the bulb from Margaret and held it up. She continued Margaret's narrative. "Nora was so excited when she talked about the possibilities of actually transmitting voices without wires. She said it would be the most exciting technological development of our lifetime. And she wasn't talking about wireless telegraphy—Morse code either. They had just conquered that."

"That's right," Henderson said. "The *Titanic* already had wireless Morse code and that helped get the rescue ships to the site. Otherwise nobody would have survived. Not a single soul would have been telling their story now. And, as you know, the newspapers are still running the *Titanic* survivors' stories. The public will never tire of them."

Yes, the *Titanic* rescue, Margaret remembered; those faint distress signals heard at stations along the Eastern seaboard throughout that night. The world waited for every bit of information—any detail. Her father Donald's first headline for the morning edition had been the stricken ships' first desperate signal—*Come quickly. We have struck a berg.* The family newspaper printed thousands of copies more than its usual press run for many weeks after.

"And that Lee DeForest gentleman? Wasn't he convicted of fraud?" Henderson asked. Power casually monitored the exchange, looking back and forth between Margaret, Helen, and their guest.

Helen corrected him. "Actually, he was found innocent—apparently Mr. DeForest has been in more courts than audio laboratories. He and his partners were on trial for stock fraud once. Lee was the only one acquitted. The others went to jail."

"Nora Stanton Blatch told us that every wireless engineer sues every other one for patent infringement," Margaret added. "Everyone claims that every idea is just an improvement of one of their own."

Henderson laughed. "So much for a noble experiment." He looked at the bulb, still in Helen's hand. "Actually, I'm certain that you appreciate its importance more than do I. I'm just beginning to learn about radio. It will be part of my life for the next several years. Perhaps you can tell me more about what is so *terribly* exciting about this bulb."

Margaret had an explanation by now well honed into its barest essentials. "If you think about Morse code, the dots and dashes are no more than breaks in a strong electric circuit. A shorter break for a dot, longer breaks for dashes. All tapped out on a keypad by a telegraph operator. Of course you know that already, I'm sure."

Chief Henderson smiled. "My experiences with Morse code in the naval academy could only be described as grim."

"Morse code was, in its time, ingenious," Margaret continued. "But to transmit a human voice, a continuous signal is needed. There can be no breaks in the current. This may be new to you." She arched her eyebrows into a question.

"More or less," Henderson replied. "I have been studying the subject—with some success, I think."

Margaret nodded. "The real difficulty is to make the faint signal from a microphone into a strong signal that can be transmitted by antenna over a distance. Then that strong signal needs to be made into a faint signal again so that it can be heard in headphones or a small receiver in someone's living room."

"It will be an extraordinary achievement." Henderson looked around the room. "And to think that perhaps dozens of similar groups are working on this— wireless transmission of a voice."

"Not just a voice, but also music. A weather report. Maybe even news stories," Margaret said, enthusiastically listing her favorite possibilities. "And, not just one person would be able to hear it. Hundreds of people maybe. It's not a telephone. The signal is like a farmer throwing seeds into the air. That's why we call it broadcasting. It can be heard wherever there is an antenna and a receiver."

Henderson nodded, then looked at his watch. "I expect to be coming back here on many occasions. I have to leave now—but I do want to thank you very much for your time."

Helen once again retraced the story as she had heard it so many times in this laboratory—the newer version of the Audion tube was far more advanced than DeForest's original design ten years earlier. Scientists discovered that the faint electric signals in the glass tube could be amplified by creating a vacuum and by reconfiguring the tiny wiring. They realized that this newer Audion tube could provide every function needed to broadcast a real audio signal. *Transmission. Amplification. Reception. All in one tube!*

With small vacuum tubes at the core of transmitters and receivers, a voice might then be heard clearly miles away, maybe one day even far out into the ocean. Unrestrained by wires, anyone would be able to broadcast and anyone could receive the signal. The engineers at the laboratory speculated about the changes in warfare that would result if the armies in Europe could use voice transmissions. They talked about it a lot.

Margaret and Helen imagined music recitals at the Tufts theater that one day might be heard in a farmhouse a mile or two away. A family could gather in the warmth of their sitting room and never miss a note of music—and avoid having to travel on a brutal New England's winter night.

"Thank you for coming, Chief Henderson," Helen called after him as he left the laboratory.

Harold Power, regaining his focus, quickly unfurled a ragged diagram and tacked it on the wall. He spoke purposefully, as if weighing conflicting thoughts simultaneously, each one competing for his attention. He had only one interest though—audio. Nothing more.

His single-mindedness had so impressed the trustees at Tufts College that they donated the building, dilapidated as it was. A summer job as a wireless telegrapher on J.P. Morgan's yacht a few years before gave Power the chance to convince the financier to put up money for this adventure. At least that was the legend.

"Are we all aware that in one month we will be transmitting a music program?" Power asked, gazing casually around the room, certain of everyone's attention. "We expect that it may be heard as far as twenty miles from here. Ships at sea equipped for this transmission will also receive it. The antenna outside will be at its full two hundred-fifty foot height in ten days. Transmission is now set for June 16 at three in the afternoon. As you know the Department of the Navy still maintains jurisdiction over these transmissions. They will probably send representatives from Washington. If they are as befuddled as usual, I'm sure you will take the time to explain everything—slowly, of course."

Harold Power paused, then he smiled. "May I assume that none of you will miss the transmission?" He knew there could be only one answer. An answer to a question that needn't have even been asked.

An excited murmur scattered amongst the engineers and volunteers he had carefully groomed for that transmission, and for the adventures still to come.

3

APRIL 27, 1915

THE THREE BELLS SALOON

BOSTON, MASS.

"I DON'T KNOW IF he's just an idiot, or maybe a new beast of burden? I laughed for days. I bet the elevator operator is laughing about it right now," Nick Flatley said, still amused.

Ralph McMillan leaned on the oval table, straining to hear Nick through the amalgam of boozy fellowship and insults shouted randomly throughout the saloon.

Nick, feeling hands pressing onto his shoulders, turned around. "You're a little late, Byron. But we'll still buy you a birthday drink. What do you say, Ralph?"

"Happy birthday, asshole." Ralph slid down the bench, pulling Byron Townsend into the tiny space he created.

Byron, judging any attempt to evade Ralph's sweaty arm encircling his shoulder would be futile, succumbed to the embrace. At least, he decided, it wasn't as disgusting as at Fenway Park when they sometimes sat sealed together through nine tortuous innings on steamy Boston summer afternoons.

"Nick, who's the idiot you're talking about? Or is it a beast of burden?" Byron asked, gesturing for a hint. "Have you guys decided yet? Or were you waiting for me to get here to help you figure it out?"

"Nick was just talking about the hotel in St. Louis the other day," Ralph said, not waiting for Nick's eyewitness account. "Nick comes out of his room and he's walking toward the elevator. It stops, and the elevator door opens. Babe Ruth pops his head out and stares, sort of sideways, at Nick coming towards him. Babe turns and looks the other way down the hallway, then back at Nick. He asks Nick real seriously, 'Are you going up or down?' Nick points down and gets on the elevator. Babe stops at the next floor and plays with the handle to get the elevator exactly even with the floor, then he opens the door. He looks out both ways and closes the door again. He stops at every floor on the way to the lobby."

Byron laughed.

"But that's not the end of it." Nick picks up the narrative of his own story, first looking down to insure that he shredded the butt of his cigarette into the sawdust with a quick twist of his heel. "I look at the elevator operator standing in the corner. I've known him a couple of years. Jimmy, I think his name is. You know him, Byron— he takes bets from the players and gets them whores, even in the middle of the night. Anyway, Jimmy, he looks at me and shrugs his shoulders. I see he has a stack of bills in his hand. What's he going to say? So I just laugh and get out at the lobby."

"But not before Nick hears Babe asking the people getting on the elevator, 'Are you going up or down?'" Ralph finished the story, cackling as if he had never heard it before.

"By God, that calls for a drink," declared Byron, joining in the camaraderie. He motioned to the waiter easing his way between the tightly arranged tables. "That's a great story. I can tell you that Ruth gets my vote as the slowest-witted barnyard animal in the league.

No doubt about it. In Philadelphia I saw him wrestle Pennock and Baker to the ground in the clubhouse—at the same time, one with each arm. He wouldn't let them up until he farted on Pennock. Real loud. He giggled like a fucken' schoolboy."

Byron, finally getting the waiter's attention, pointed around the table indicating refills for everyone.

Ralph waved his hand over his empty glass—he'd had enough for the afternoon. "I gotta finish a piece that new son-of-a-bitch editor assigned me yesterday." Then he reminded himself of another story. "Oh yeah, Pennock told me that Babe was shocked when he heard that the Pirates fixed a game the week before to get enough money to make it to their next paycheck. He said Ruth looked like a child who had just heard a nasty secret about his mother."

"We should give thanks every day that we have someone like him to write about." Byron raised his glass to toast the absent Ruth. "He's going to be one of the greatest pitchers we've ever had in Boston—and none of us have ever seen someone hit a ball as far as he does in batting practice. Ruth will even hit a home run or two this year. I'll bet on that."

"Ruth hasn't changed his underwear since he joined the team last July. You've heard that, haven't you?" Nick looked around the table. "That's what Baker says. He should know—they've been rooming together since they both came to the team."

Byron wiggled out of Ralph's embrace. "To hell with Ruth! What do you fumbling skirt-chasers have to say to a guy on his twenty-fifth birthday? Any words of wisdom?"

"Yeah, here's something—how come your sister Margaret is so beautiful and you're such a damn mutt?" Ralph grinned, wiping his brow with a soaked handkerchief. "She walks so gracefully and you drag yourself around like a club-footed old man. The only thing that screams twins about the two of you is the red hair you both have. And Byron, yours looks like a baboon's ass—and don't forget to give her my fondest birthday wishes."

"Sure, you old prick. I'll give her your message, but I doubt she remembers who you are."

"Of course she'll remember Ralph. Who can forget this bald-headed lecher?" Nick ruffled the three or four strands of hair Ralph had artfully swept across his bare, glistening skull. Then he wiped his fingers on Ralph's sleeve with a theatrical attempt to remove the residue of sweat.

Furtive movements at the far end of the engraved mahogany bar distracted Byron. He peered through the fog of cigar smoke veiling every feature in the room. Maybe it had been the squeal of a chair that first caught his attention. A gambler, lunging quickly over the card table, grabbed a drunken adversary by the throat. The table tipped onto its side, bills floating to the floor. The two combatants rolled out of sight; lost behind shadowy figures surrounding them, straining to get a better view.

Byron recognized Helmut, the aged but still masterful typesetter at his newspaper, the *Boston Examiner*. Helmut raised two fingers toward another spectator, placing a bet on which one of the brawlers would disfigure the other's face more convincingly, and thusly be considered the winner.

Byron anticipated another long baseball schedule ahead of him, with these same companions in saloons in every American League city. The same whiskey-fueled arguments, and strangers falling off barstools. But there was always a possibility of the grand prize—the World Series. If the Red Sox were in it again, Byron would be one of just a few reporters covering the biggest sporting event of the year. This would make up for the stifling, overcrowded trains shuttling from city to city.

Byron knew that the promise of a close pennant race excited even these old bastards. Then at least, they wouldn't have to invent bull-shit to entertain their readers. And could they invent bullshit! Byron learned that quickly when he joined them on the road two years be-fore. That first year he read their stories and couldn't believe he was at the same game they were writing about.

They had ignored him back then—especially Nick, who consid-ered himself the dean of Boston sportswriters. Maybe it was worse for Byron because his father owned the *Boston Examiner*. That made him different from the others in the press box; they always had to look over their shoulders and kiss their editors' asses. It took Byron awhile to get them to just say hello. But touring American League cities for two years, sitting in ballparks on endless summer afternoons, and hopping on trains rolling out of stations, finally bonded them into a peculiarly cynical clan.

This was a good time to announce his plan, to let them break his balls a little, and then they could all have another drink before they stumbled home. Byron wasn't sure if he even liked whiskey. But it was hard to spend time with these guys and not drink. Especially when they were with the team on a road trip. They loved being away from home.

"Gentlemen, there is something I want to tell you," Byron an-nounced, and then paused. Ralph looked up from his aimless stare into the tabletop. Nick's gaze wandered the bar. Byron had as much of their attention as he could expect. "I'm trying to go to France to cover the war. I've been talking to some of the wire services. There are a lot of writers who want to go over, but I think I have a good chance."

"What's wrong with you, Byron?" Nick asked sharply, turning quickly towards him. He took Ralph's cigarette to light the one in his mouth. "You can do whatever you want right here. Right here in Bos-ton. I mean your father owns the goddamn newspaper. I wish I had a lifetime job like you do."

"That's right, Nick." Ralph agreed. "I hope this isn't some romantic crap, is it, Byron? I understand guys going over there freelancing stories, hoping it gets them a real job, but what the hell does our Byron know about trench warfare? Have you been following this thing? They are killing each other by the thousands. Every goddamn day."

"Yes, I know, but I need to get off the sports beat," Byron insisted. "Sure, I can write cute articles about the Red Sox, but the war is the big story. It may even become the story of our lifetime."

"Why don't you just have daddy take you off sports?" Ralph asked. "You can do whatever you want. That isn't our war over there and nobody here gives a damn about it. Those assholes have been killing each other since someone started keeping score. By the time you get over there it will probably be over anyway. I mean the way they are killing each other, they have to run out of soldiers sooner or later. What the hell are they going to do then?" He shrugged his shoulders as if expecting an answer.

The question amused Nick. "That's right, Byron. What will you do if they can't find any more soldiers—and call the war off, like a rainout at Fenway?"

Byron had expected less antagonism. "The big story is on the other side of the ocean. Not following men playing a kid's game."

"That's crap," Nick said, his thick hand waving away Byron's dismissal of the sport that provided their livelihoods. "Writing about this kid's game is going to seem like a blessing once you're really in the middle of a war. Believe me. I thought being a war correspondent in Cuba would be exciting until I got down there. It was fucking awful. The first time someone explodes into a spray of turd nuggets right in front of you, you'll wish you were home under the covers, in between your sweet wife's legs. And remember that isn't Cuba you are going to.

France is on the other side of the ocean–and they're killing each other with weapons nobody has ever seen before."

Ralph leaned in, sweating. "Byron, take a close look at this food we're pushing into our faces." He pointed at the greasy plates forming a porcelain shell across the rickety table. "Are you ready to eat your breakfast porridge next to a corpse? You'll be happy to eat even this slop. And you'll be happy to eat it in that shit-stinking toilet over there." He gestured over Byron's shoulder toward the door at the side of the bar. Byron didn't need to turn around; the stench from the john was potent enough to lead even the most falling down drunk in the tavern toward it.

"Another thing to remember, young Byron," Nick added. "For us it's great to get out of town on the road trips. We get to leave our wives and kids. How many saps in this world can say that? And it's great to poke a whore in another city, and don't tell me you haven't done it too. I know you like a colored girl once in a while, and don't lie. But your wife Helen is beautiful and you have no screaming kids. Why the hell would you want to leave her alone for that?"

Byron had weighed it all before. Mother and Father would not be pleased. Neither would Helen. Helen and Margaret together would be torturers, like the ones in China, or somewhere like that. *They won't let me forget they think I'm a fool. Not even for a minute.*

Byron had thought, like everyone else, that the war would end quickly. Just soldiers in those funny uniforms shooting each other— like they have always done. Nobody believed they would still be killing each other like this eight months later. How could anybody not want to cover this story? Who cares about moldy breakfast porridge in the trenches? *This is the story of a lifetime.*

4

APRIL 28, 1915

CRYSTAL LAKE

NEWTON CENTRE, MASS.

WILLIAM MORRISON EASED HIS year old Dodge to a stop under the elm tree next to the path winding around the side of Donald and Beatrice Townsend's house. He swung his legs out of the car and flexed his right one, relieving the cramped pain that always accompanied a long drive to the Townsends.

William started along the path; gravel crunching under each step. He passed through the white, arched arbor embroidered with cascading clusters of purple wisteria. He picked one and laced it through the white ribbon binding the small box in his hand.

A late afternoon sun warmed the red trim on the freshly painted porch. The painters' gear was stacked neatly alongside the wall, assembled for the final touches of the house's interior the next day. William imagined his mother-in-law, Beatrice Townsend, pointing imperially at corners and crevices still lacking a satisfactory finish.

He noticed, through the large bay windows, the mound of colorfully wrapped packages arranged on the sitting room table. He decided that it would be better to slip the pearls around Margaret's neck as she dressed one morning—on that long graceful neck—rather than just burying it amongst the pile of other birthday gifts for her and Byron. He had already given Byron the binoculars two days before.

The path opened onto a neat lawn ending abruptly at a small bluff above a jagged lake rimmed in thick green and brown foliage. One afternoon at Langley Books, William had noticed the cover of a mystery novel Margaret had just designed. It was an image of the skeletal tree inexplicably shooting out of the lake; it had always appeared to William to be drowning as it stretched its long, mossy fingers skyward. Inexplicably, the tree had not even the smallest of islands to sink its root into. He never understood why Margaret was surprised that he recognized it on the book cover. It seemed so obvious. How many lakes have a tree growing out of it?

He continued toward the edge of the lawn, each step revealing more of the sturdy wooden table and benches dominating a small alcove at the water's edge beneath him. He had spent many evenings at that table drinking wine with Margaret. He stepped onto the short, uneven stone staircase leading down to the lakeside.

"Uncle William, look what Aunt Margaret bought for me to take to Scotland." Sarah ran toward him, her long arms and legs flying in different directions. The women at the table turned toward him.

"It's a Kodak camera." Sarah raised it in front of her excitedly. "Take a picture of us, Uncle William. It will give mother and me something to remember everyone by. I'll miss you so much."

"I thought it was Aunt Margaret's and Uncle Byron's birthday party, not yours, Sarah," William said, delighted by his light banter with his only niece. "Why is Aunt Margaret giving you a present today?"

"Oh, it's for our trip, not for my birthday, Uncle William. My birthday is not for another month." Sarah pulled his arm, leading him toward the table. "Take a photograph of all of us."

"I'm just teasing you, Sarah." William took the camera. "I know your sixteenth birthday is next month. Have a wonderful party in Scotland and send us lots of photographs."

Sarah ran back to the women arranging themselves around the table. Margaret invited Sarah into her extended arms.

"Uncle William, all you have to do is press the button on the top." Sarah reached out to demonstrate which button to push. William gently stopped her hand.

"Yes, I know, Sarah dear. I don't think it is especially difficult. It's this button—right?"

Sarah nodded vigorously and looked over at her mother. Louella laid her fork on the table and gently waved her hands up and down, attempting to dampen her daughter's excitement.

Uncle Isaac had given William a camera when he had been a few years younger than Sarah. It arrived in a cardboard box covered with cartoon characters. It was the first Brownie. Every boy wanted one. It cost one dollar. The camera William had in his hand now looked so modern compared to that one. A latch on the side attracted his attention.

"What happens if I open this little spring door?" William asked, examining it. "Will it ruin the film? I never saw this before."

"No, Uncle William. It covers a slit that allows you to write on the film without exposing it." Sarah looked at Margaret to see if she had explained it correctly. Margaret agreed, sweeping Sarah's long auburn hair off her shoulders.

"Writing on the film while it's in the camera? Now that's impressive." William turned the camera over in his hand, looking for other new features. "Very interesting indeed."

"They just started to make them." Sarah put her arm around Margaret's waist. "It's new. Take the picture now—*please*."

William motioned the women closer to each other. They posed around Beatrice Townsend, Margaret's mother, sitting at the end of the table. William noticed the women were dressed leisurely. Gone from the table were those figures enforced by bustling petticoats and labyrinths of fasteners. He recalled his aunt Agnes's laborious dressing procedures. Even Beatrice now wore these new garments that signaled a woman with her own life, not merely an appendage of her husband.

He pressed the button and wound the handle advancing the film. The women relaxed their pose.

"Let's have one more for insurance," William suggested. "This time, Sarah, move around to your mother's side."

Louella pulled her playfully struggling daughter against her.

"I wish the two of you didn't have to go and leave us," Beatrice addressed Louella and Sarah. "It is so unfair. I have come to adore this young lady. Of course I adore you too, Louella. But I'm sure you will agree that your daughter is special."

"I understand, but our place is with Gilbert right now. Even though I do treasure living near you and having you in our lives everyday." Louella smiled at Beatrice and then looked down. Nobody at the table could disguise their discomfort with Gilbert's long absences.

"Can you send Sarah back every few months if we miss her too much?" Beatrice asked.

"A *delightful* idea, Mother," Margaret said.

"It's not just the distance." Beatrice had thought about this before. "This war is bestial. I am not at all comfortable with you two crossing the ocean. I don't care how far you are from the conflict—'Only the dead have seen the end of war'—Plato said that many centuries ago. It is still true today."

Sarah, more engrossed in her camera than with Plato, coaxed it back from William so that she could admire it again.

"We'll be safe in Glasgow," Louella assured Beatrice. "Gilbert told us that it is not as frightful as London is right now—and Sarah will profit from being abroad at her age."

"And best of all," Louella added, attempting to further divert Beatrice's concerns, "we will, of course, be traveling first class. Gilbert arranged that. It's part of his agreement with the company. Now that is exciting. Isn't it, Sarah?"

"Yes, Mother. This will be *truly* marvelous. I want to go to art school like Aunt Helen and Aunt Margaret. I think I would like to be a sculptor. I can hardly wait to see the museums in Scotland and England."

Beatrice smoothed the pleats on her white dress. Gilbert! A dolt of a man. She reminded herself once again. Leaving his wife and daughter just to manage a business in Scotland. What could be more important than being with his family? Especially now with a frightful war raging on. Donald would never have done that to his family when the children were young. These three women all should have men devoted to them— men like Donald.

But unlike him also, she smiled. He could be a bit of a windbag at times but he was always ready to engage in the "good fight," as he called it. And he always had time for her—*he was so lusty when we were younger.* She smiled again.

And why, Beatrice asked herself still one more time, isn't Byron writing about all of the medical breakthroughs that always interested him when he was younger? Or else he could, at least, show interest in running the newspaper. Donald couldn't do it forever.

"I hope we don't get lured into this war." Beatrice reached for the wine glass offered by William. "The Germans and Brits are trying their very best to get us involved. Luckily President Wilson seems to be working just as hard to keep us out of it."

And yes, William too, Beatrice couldn't ignore her disappointment with her son-in-law. Even if his uncle Isaac was a bit daft, he gave William an appreciation for building. And inventing. He could be doing that right now. Why did he need disreputable men like Joe Finnerty? *He can be so much more for my Margaret—*

Beatrice turned as her husband stomped out of the bramble, shaking off brownish muck from his thigh-high rubber boots. He balanced his fishing pole on the edge of the table and took Beatrice's outstretched hand.

At first, William found it curious that Donald and Beatrice parented Byron and Margaret. Unlike their two lanky but graceful children, the parents shared a similar stout body structure. Both short and compact, much like the smaller students on William's Yale wrestling team—hard to knock off balance. Whenever William tried to visualize the Townsends' youthful sexual couplings only large, writhing bowling balls with limbs occasionally poking out would come to mind.

"Catch anything, Donald?" William feigned a sincere, hopeful tone. Margaret, Helen, and Beatrice looked away, amused. They believed the patriarch's fishing forays a waste of time. They were certain that in all the years Donald Townsend spent knee-deep in the lake, he had never felt even a single feeble bite on his line.

Donald acknowledged William's sarcasm with a faint smile. "So, where is Byron?"

"Dr. Carlson called," Helen said. "He's having trouble with his car. Byron went to pick him up."

"Oh good." Donald looked around the table, settling on Louella and Sarah. "I'm glad that William is able to go down to New York to help your departure."

He patted Sarah on her shoulder affectionately. "This isn't the best time for a trans-Atlantic voyage. I wish you could just stay here with us. This war will be over soon enough. Then it would be a wonderful time to go."

"Actually, Mr. Townsend, I intend to volunteer and use my nurse's training over there," Louella said, attempting to reassure him—once again. "I've heard that the seriously wounded are almost beyond count. Of course I would have to convince my husband to allow me to work in those horrid conditions. But that is what nurses are for, is it not? I may be a bit rusty, but I'm sure I can help."

"William thinks it's just fine if the war goes on as long as America gets the contracts from the Germans and the Brits," Margaret said, measuring William's reaction. "They are buying up everything here, are they not, Father?"

"Why is it required for you to portray me as a mercenary?" William asked, displeased. "I didn't start the war. Nobody consulted with me. They managed to start it on their own. Now they are all coming here for supplies. Why not sell them everything they need?"

"After they buy everything they will be looking for American boys to fight the war. Both sides want them. It's disgraceful," Helen said. "Those soldiers dying everyday are just a few years older than Sarah."

Sarah shuddered. Louella pulled her daughter closer.

"I just hope the Brits can turn this around fast," said Margaret, laying two slices of seared whitefish on her plate. "The Germans are acting savagely. Bayoneting nuns and children in Belgium—disgraceful."

"So, William, you will be going down to New York two days before the sailing?" Beatrice introduced a more practical matter.

"Yes, I have to see a few bank clients. I scheduled a few meetings the day before the departure."

William noticed Margaret's hat—a floppy black Rembrandt beret. He pointed at it. "I like the red trim. Very colorful. It almost matches your hair."

"It's claret, not red. But thank you for noticing, darling."

"I thought claret might be a possibility," William said. Claret? Red seemed close enough.

William had another mission in New York. Joe Finnerty wanted him to meet the stockbrokers who were "pumping and dumping," as Joe liked to call it. It was so simple. Finnerty bought a stock and then he paid for phony publicity and had his brokers start rumors that the company was going to do something grandiose. Almost any story would do. "Everybody loves a little excitement," Joe Finnerty would say. After Finnerty pumped the stock up enough, his brokers just as quickly unloaded it on naïve investors who, soon after, would watch the price plummet.

William knew this sidebar mission in New York was best left un-disclosed to Margaret. He would save himself from her diatribe against Finnerty and the other "amoral scoundrels," or whatever she called them. Why bother discussing it anyway? Investors were not forced to buy stock. Nobody puts a gun to anyone's head. It was just business.

Byron appeared at the edge of the lawn above them, leading a woman toward the steps. He pressed a blood-splashed towel to her eye, a young man supporting her other arm.

Margaret moved toward them. "Byron—what happened?"

Byron and the other man guided the woman to the closest bench.

"I was driving back with Doc Carlson," Byron answered. "We saw these two when we stopped for gasoline at Campbell's. Doc saw the blood on her face, and so we brought them here. This is Patrick and Anne."

Edward Carlson came down the steps followed by Suzette, the Townsends' servant, holding an armful of wet towels.

"Yes, but what happened?" Margaret asked again.

"My brother Patrick and I went to the women's right to vote ral-ly on the Commons this morning." Anne's voice had more than a tinge of Ireland in it. "Almost as soon as it began the police came and pushed into us, throwing us backward. They said it was unlawful, that we should leave. They jumped on one lad who spoke up and they hit him with their sticks."

Beatrice stood up. "That is an ugly cut. Who hit you?"

The young woman dabbed at her eye with two fingers. "I'll be all right, ma'am—a copper grabbed at my hair and I pushed his hand away. He pulled me away from the crowd toward the wagons. He asked my name. I smelled whiskey on his breath. I told him Anne O' Reilly. He said, 'An Irish Catholic girl, eh?' I could see he was as Irish as I am. He was hurting my arm. He said, 'What's a fresh-faced colleen like you doing here with these troublemakers?' He had as much an accent as I do, I tell you.

"He said, 'If my daughter was part of this rabble, I would push her off a cliff.'

"If an ugly Mick like you were to be my father I would jump off the cliff, I told him. He punched me in the eye."

Beatrice leaned forward, squinting, getting a closer look at Anne's eye. "That's a brave comment for a young lady to make to a drunken policeman."

"Sis never misses a chance to speak her mind, ma'am," Patrick said, a trait he seemed to wearily accept.

"Patrick, keep pressing this against her eye," said Dr. Carlson, nudging a clean damp towel toward him. "Suzette, please get my bag from Bryon's car—thank you."

Beatrice regarded Patrick's concern for his sister. She had seen the likes of him many times before—one of those Irish boys with black, black hair and a very white face. Either a priest or a revolutionary, she concluded—the island didn't seem capable of producing anything else.

"What right do those bastards have to prevent a demonstration?

There is a Bill of Rights, isn't there?" Margaret's face reddened, still a few shades lighter than her hair. "Is there not freedom of assembly? That covers women's right to vote gatherings, doesn't it?"

William decided not to respond. For Christ's sake, he thought, sure, women should vote, but they have meetings about everything. They even have meetings about whether the colored girls should be in the back, or at the front of the march. Righting these injustices is a luxury of the rich. The rest of the world, like the one he grew up in, had to just 'make do,' as Aunt Agnes used to say.

Margaret moved next to Dr. Carlson. "They're such cowards. Hitting a woman."

"Yes, they are," Beatrice said. "You wouldn't think they are scared by looking at them, but they are. They don't want their lives changed. They are, well, let us say, small people. Plato summed it up rather succinctly, I believe—'the measure of a man is what he does with power.'"

William looked out toward the lake. He was certain that if the sun burned itself out Beatrice Townsend would still quote Plato. Jesus Christ! She must have invented a few of the quotes. Who would know if she did? Maybe that was Beatrice's private amusement.

Suzette hurried toward them, clutching a worn black leather bag. Dr. Carlson opened it and knelt on one of his long legs in front of Anne. He removed an iodine ointment and dripped it onto a clean patch of the now reddish towel. He held Anne's chin gently, moving it side to side, evaluating the injury.

He had such a delicate manner, Helen reminded herself. She and Margaret had often gossiped about Dr. Carlson. He never discussed women. He seemed so energized whenever his friend Dr. William Welch was in town, as he was now on his lecture tour. Yes, the two doctors were surely *artistic types*, a polite designation for the men and women drawn to the anonymity of a big city where they could dis-

40

creetly live their lives. Not like her Denver, where there was no place for them to hide.

Margaret grasped William's hand, pulling him from the table. "Now that help has arrived," she announced, "I'm going to show William the new wallpaper and painting we did inside. I know he'll love it." She quickened her pace, gesturing for him to stay close behind.

"Too bad I can't go with you to New York, Will," Byron called after William. "I'm still working on that Babe Ruth feature with the sports desk. We'll be printing it next Sunday." He looked at his father to make sure the date was still correct. Donald nodded without looking at Byron.

"Which newspaper, sir?" Patrick asked.

"Our newspaper—the *Boston Examiner*," Byron answered. "Are you a Red Sox fan, Patrick?"

"Yes, I am a fan, sir—and I also work for them. In the locker room. I tend to their equipment."

"Oh, yes. I thought I recognized you," Byron said. "I've seen you around the locker room, Patrick. Why aren't you on the road trip with the team?"

"I don't travel, sir. I stay behind and take care of the locker room and do other things around the park."

"I'm missing this road trip also, thanks to my birthday and the feature story," Byron said, sitting down at the table. "I would have liked to have been with the team in New York. Do you think we will win the pennant this year, Patrick?"

Patrick was relieved to be in a conversation as an equal participant. "If the pitching holds up we can beat Detroit or Philadelphia easily. Ruth is pitching great. So is Shore."

"You said it. And Ruth is hitting the ball into the stands all over the league," Byron said, eager to share his opinion about the Red Sox.

"Too bad it's just at batting practice. One day he's going to hit like that in the game."

"That's what the players think." Patrick nodded enthusiastically. "Babe has hit the ball farther than any of them have ever seen."

"Well, you can see that you are among a clan of Red Sox fans, young man," Donald Townsend said. He leaned over Beatrice to lift a baked potato crusted with singed cheese from a small wooden bowl.

"That Ruth is causing quite a stir. Even I've heard of him." Beatrice sliced off a piece of Donald's potato and raised it to her mouth.

Byron introduced everyone at the table to Anne and Patrick—ending with his father. "And last but certainly not least, my father, Donald Townsend, publisher of the *Boston Examiner.*"

Patrick's eyes lit up. "Pleased to meet you, sir. I read your newspaper every day. I don't suppose you get out to Fenway Park, do you, sir?"

"No, Patrick. I went the first year it opened. That was, what, three years ago? Haven't had time to be back since. Byron is our official representative."

Byron smiled, pleased with his father's pronouncement.

WILLIAM OPENED THE FRONT door to the Townsend house and motioned Margaret to enter. A canvas tarpaulin marked with strokes of paint still covered the sitting room sofa.

"The smell of paint always reminds me of once when I was a young boy at the inn," he said. "Aunt Agnes and Uncle Isaac painted almost every spring." He coaxed her into an embrace. "One day I was running on the second floor and slipped. I tripped over an open paint can. It was full of paint. It fell through the railing and hit the banister on the staircase. It sounded like an explosion. That's what it looked like also. I've always remembered the name *orchid* since that day. That was the color all over the staircase. I still cringe every time I see orchid."

"My poor darling. Carrying such memories," Margaret said, cupping her hand around his neck. "That mustn't have endeared you to Auntie and Uncle. Let me try very hard to make you forget."

She didn't wait for a response. She wriggled free of his arms and ran toward the staircase. William followed her up to the second story. She pulled him into the first bathroom. He lifted her onto the tiled counter alongside the sink. She unfastened his suspenders.

"That's quite an impish smile, Mrs. Morrison." William slid his hand under her white cotton dress into her bloomers. She rolled her hips around his finger that she pressed inside her.

"Yes, there is nothing like making love in the late afternoon and being able to watch Mommy and Daddy at the same time." She peeked through the curtained window. "Don't forget to take a good look at the wallpaper in case Mother gives you a quiz."

"You can be a naughty girl sometimes, darling."

She unbuttoned his pants and gravity forced them toward his knees. "Please take them off, darling. It appears to be oh, so rushed with your pants all bunched up like that. Like groping teenagers in a schoolyard at night."

"THE GIRL WILL BE all right," Dr. Carlson announced, gently swabbing Anne's bruise with the red-orange ointment. "We need more ice to keep the swelling down. This ugly abrasion is probably from a ring that drunken swine was wearing. They can be so brutish."

"It hurts even more knowing that it was an Irishman who hit me. Don't they know how many of us are dying in France for the British?" Anne looked around the table, at nobody in particular.

"They're doing a good job censoring the news in Europe, Anne."

Donald said. "I don't believe a thing I read from the wire services. We only know that it is a war that is getting worse with each passing day. "

"Is it true that your newspaper had over a thousand telephone calls last month during the Johnson-Willard fight, sir?" asked Patrick, returning the conversation to sports. "That's what I heard at the ballpark."

"Yes, it is true, Patrick. Our switchboard couldn't put through all the calls. But the *Chicago Tribune* was worse. Cyrus McClellan tells me they had over ten thousand calls that one afternoon alone."

"It pays to have a fight between a colored champ and a Great White Hope," Byron said, putting his arm around Helen's shoulders. "Everyone wanted Johnson to lose. At least the promoter did well——about thirty thousand dollars, I heard."

"Mr. Frazee from those Broadway shows promoted that fight, sir." Patrick was quick to engage Byron on common ground. "And he will be buying the Red Sox, I heard."

"Yes, there is that *rumor*," said Donald Townsend, amused that Patrick thought he had inside information. "Frazee has wanted to buy the Red Sox for the past three years."

"Patrick, soon nobody will ever have to call a newspaper when they want information about a sporting event," Margaret declared confidently. She and William were now at the bottom of the stone staircase, stepping onto the grass. "Soon there will be a reader at a radio transmitter who can keep the listeners current on everything."

"Maybe even someone describing a boxing match as it is in progress," Helen added quickly.

"And how will someone hear it, Helen dear?" Byron asked. He glanced at her, expecting his wife to react to his reference to the sparse sales of radio equipment. Instead, she ignored him.

"I think we have been through this before, dear brother Byron.

Haven't we?" Margaret responded. "We are manufacturing receivers at Tufts—you know that. People are beginning to buy them. We are getting orders from far away. Someday anybody will be able to listen to this kind of news. Even to something as boorish as a boxing match."

"That's wonderful, Margaret." Donald said. "Then nobody will ever need to buy a newspaper again." He leaned toward young Sarah, urging her to try the chilled shrimp on the platter Suzette had just placed on the table. "The day after that Jack Johnson fight our circulation went up fifteen percent, remember that? Everyone wanted the details. That is what we do for a profession—we own a newspaper. That is our livelihood, our legacy. You are aware of that, are you not, Margaret?"

"When they can hear the news instead of buy it, all of us will need to find other work. Real work, as some people might say." Beatrice looked over at Donald. He mustered a resigned grunt.

"Look at these lovely pearls. William just put them on me in the house." Margaret rolled out the string of pearls from under the open collar of her blouse. "Are they not beautiful? He picked them out himself."

"Did *you* give *him* anything in the house?" asked Helen, feigning curiosity. "You look a bit flushed, darling."

"Why should she give him anything? It's not his birthday." Sarah looked toward her mother for an explanation. Louella shrugged her shoulders innocently, glancing at Helen.

"I suppose you are right, darling," said Helen, embracing Sarah. "Why would Aunt Margaret want to give him anything today?"

"Sometimes people just give each other presents for no reason other than that they care for each other," Louella said, hoping to stifle her teenage daughter's curiosity.

"I think that's quite enough, ladies, don't you?" Beatrice asked, suppressing a smile, peering over her eyeglasses at Margaret and then towards Helen. She tugged at Donald's shirt and pointed at a bottle of cabernet at his elbow. He scanned the table for a corkscrew.

"Do you work at the newspaper also, sir? If I may ask?" Patrick looked across the table at William Morrison.

"No such luck, Patrick. I'm a vice president at the Columbia Trust Bank of Massachusetts."

"Isn't that Mr. Finnerty's bank?"

"How do you know of him, Patrick?" William asked, surprised a locker room attendant would know Joe Finnerty.

"He has whiskey delivered to the locker room for some of the players. I think he sends some to Mr. Lannin also."

William understood. Finnerty's father had bought the distribution rights in America for Haig Pinch when it was first blended in Scotland in the 1870s. Joe knew how to use whiskey as currency with politicians and anyone else he often shamelessly sought favor.

"Where do you work, Anne?" Margaret evaluated her, a slight woman, who Margaret was nonetheless certain could quietly endure the suffering that seemed to be the eternal curse of the Irish.

"I was working at the Stigler foundry, ma'am, till I got fired after the strike ended two weeks ago."

Margaret slid onto the bench and draped her arm lightly on the girl's shoulder, and ran her other hand gently through Anne's matted brown hair. Anne reacted with a start, never expecting such a display of comfort from a stranger—especially one belonging to that house.

Beatrice watched Suzette, carrying the bloodied towels, making her way back up the steps towards the house. She turned to Louella.

"Suzette is returning home to Scotland on the same day as you and Sarah are sailing," she said. "She is leaving on the *Cameronia*. It's also a Cunard liner. She wants to be home with her family while the war is on. The poor dear, two of her brothers are somewhere in those Western Front trenches and her family is having a difficult time."

Beatrice thought for a moment more. "Anne—maybe you should stay with us? Work for us until you find another job."

"I don't know, ma'am. It seems so—" Anne moved her hand from her eye to her chest, surprised by the offer.

"You can work here until you feel better," Beatrice said, a simple, logical solution offered. "That *is* all right, isn't it, Donald? That bruise is frightful."

"A lovely idea, Mother," Margaret said, regarding Anne next to her with kindness. "It makes perfect sense."

Anne self-consciously touched the wound over her eye again.

"Don't worry, Anne, you will heal quickly," Beatrice said, patting her hand. "But you may, in the future, want to stay away from these ugly confrontations, my dear."

"Now everything is settled," said Donald, familiar with his wife's summary judgments. "And now, Anne, that your wound has been tended to"—he waved his hand over the table—"Beatrice has set out a feast for our birthday twins. You two must join us." He motioned for the young visitors to take plates.

"Well, it is my birthday, so I have an announcement to make." Byron said firmly, glancing around the table—he had everyone's attention. "If I have my way, I will soon be a war correspondent on the Western Front. Actually, I hope to get an assignment at the beginning of the year."

"Byron, are there not enough reporters over there already?" Donald asked. "Anyway, we could never afford to send our own correspondent over there. We already have a far too expensive wire service for war feeds, and everything is censored, so whatever we do receive is nonsense anyway."

Byron braced himself for the inevitable negative family input. "I wasn't thinking about writing for our newspaper. I want to talk to the services. Maybe write featured articles. I'm not sure."

"Byron, that's a dumb idea." Margaret's verdict was rendered instantly. "Honestly. You read the reports from Europe. We all do. Thank God we are not involved, otherwise you would probably have to fight, not report the news. It's just a dumb idea."

"It's the story of the century already. If it gets bigger it will be history making. I want to be part of it." Byron knew there would be little enthusiasm at this table for his vision.

His mother surprised him. "If you really need to do this, Byron, I will approve. I think it is foolhardy, of course." Beatrice turned to Helen. "What do you think, dear?"

Byron looked at his wife, then back to Beatrice. "I haven't told her yet, Mother. I haven't told anyone before this. I just don't want to be on the sports desk forever."

"You know you won't be on the sports desk forever," Donald said. "It should be obvious that we have greater plans for you. At least it's obvious to everybody else at the paper. For a journalist you missed a lot of signs, as the baseball players would say." He nodded, pleased with his use of an appropriate sports metaphor.

"This is all so sudden. I could meet you in Paris. I would love to see the fashions." Helen's cheerful response didn't hide her surprise—or disappointment. "Perhaps we can talk about this privately, dear."

"Of course," Byron said cheerfully, reaching for the wine. "Patrick, do you know William used to be play baseball? His last game was especially exciting."

Margaret moved next to Byron. She placed her arm on his shoulder. William observed their resemblance. Not just their agile movements and lean frames topped by striking red hair, but also their conspiratorial smiles when they teased someone, as they were teasing him right now.

The incident had passed into Townsend family lore, with minor embellishments added with each telling. In the last baseball game William Morrison ever played, Byron had played on the Harvard starting team against William's Yale club. Even though William was not born into Townsend privilege, he attended the same private schools with Byron, and they were teammates many times. Now, in college, they were on opposing teams.

In the third inning William slid hard into second base and felt his right knee rip. His teammates carried him off the field on a canvas stretcher. After the game Byron came to see him. He brought Margaret into the cramped clubhouse. William, his bloodstream filled with morphine, mumbled incomprehensibly. He had not seen Margaret for seven years and would have never recognized the now graceful beauty looking down at him.

"You certainly arrived at second base with gusto, my dear man," she had said as she lit a cigarette. Her easy manner interested him. He told Byron later that he would be seeing her again. When and where he didn't know.

"And so, that was your last game?" Patrick asked. "I saw you walk down those steps just now with a bit of a limp, sir. Was that the injury from the game?"

"Yes—but more likely from the botched medical attention afterwards," William said dryly.

"Maybe the limp wasn't *just* from the game," Helen suggested.

Margaret feigned disbelief. "I hope it wasn't something *I* did."

5

MAY 1, 1915

PIER 54

MANHATTAN, N.Y.

THE SHIP'S FOUR RAKED funnels pumped bursts of smoke into the spring morning drizzle. Porters hurried on the streets and through the transit building on the pier, pushing and pulling dollies stacked high with baggage. Carts hitched to horses lined up, their teamsters waiting their turn to unload provisions. Trucks puttered in between the growing crowds on the streets.

Longshoremen wrestled dozens of odd-shaped wooden crates onto lifts to be deposited deep into the holds of the ship.

Three tugboats surrounded the edge of the pier, their crews working towlines to the RMS *Lusitania*, the pride of the Cunard Line. William Morrison flipped his cigarette between the ship and dock. He examined the expanse of metal plating and welded bolts above him. So sleek! Every bolt driven precisely into the keel. A magnificent design. What a difference, he thought, from that horrid molasses storage tank—that mess of steel he had just seen for the first time only days before.

The departure of trans-Atlantic liners was still the greatest show in town. Crowds lined the area just beyond the docks, and at the end of the pier, cheering and waving aimlessly at passengers on the ship they did not even know. They were just there to watch the *Lusitania* pull away from its berth.

Fireboats spraying salty water high into the air added to the carnival atmosphere. The ship's brass band, stationed alongside the gangway, played "Pack Up Your Troubles in Your Old Kit Bag," now a popular song in America, having made its way across the ocean from Britain.

William surveyed the spreading skyline of Manhattan. He recognized the Singer Building from a visit to New York seven years before. Then it was a forty- one story iron skeleton growing out of the street, and now that skeleton was fully fleshed out into an engineering marvel, a magnificent skyscraper, as these colossal structures had come to be known. Its nerve center was an elaborate elevator system. A ground floor dispatcher communicated with every elevator operator by telephone—a vertical railway station. Uncle Isaac had read about it and wanted to come to New York just to stand in the lobby and watch the orchestrated arrivals and departures of the elevators.

William felt the change in New York as soon as he stepped into the concourse of the Grand Central Terminal—a cavernous, enclosed marble courtyard bordered by dozens of gated ticket windows, many with lines of passengers awaiting their turn, suitcases resting at their sides. Margaret had once stared for minutes in stunned wonder at the celestial nocturne rendered in great detail across the concourse's immense concave ceiling. Huge chalkboards listed the platforms for the dozens of daily arrivals and departures to faraway cities. The sprawling station laid convincing claim to New York as the vault, the heart, and the piston of America.

Now just a glance at the harbor told the same story; New York was pressing forward as the center of the universe. Its wharves teeming with ships, a few still with billowing white sails, most now driven by steam spouting out of metal chimneys. The city's vibrancy pulsed beneath his soles as he walked through the narrow streets facing the long line of berths that morning.

"Uncle William."

William turned towards Sarah's voice. Today would begin a great adventure for her. He heard the excitement in those first two words. She seemed to have grown since just the other day. He looked down and confirmed his impression; she was balanced on tiptoes on the thick wooden planks of the pier.

"Uncle William, did you see that?" Sarah pointed behind him. William turned toward a wide escalator conveying luggage upward into a hold. Dozens of pieces at a time. "Isn't that wonderful? Nobody has to carry them onto the ship."

"Very handy for old-timers like me," William said.

"You are not *old*, Uncle William. You've heard that the sailing has been delayed for a few hours, haven't you?" Sarah even invested their departure delay with excitement.

"The ship is taking on some of the crew and passengers of another ship that's being changed into a troop carrier—that's the scuttlebutt," she reported breathlessly.

"Don't use such a vulgar term, child," Louella said, shaking her head disapprovingly. Then she laughed. "Where on Earth did you ever hear that word—and that rumor?"

"Ah, let her be, Louella," William said grinning, unable to contain his own amusement. "It's a beautiful day to sail out of New York—even with this bit of drizzle." He extended his hands, palms up. He motioned them to move into the transit building that was constructed for just such eventualities as rain and snow. Both Louella and Sarah ignored his suggestion as they absorbed the frenetic action around them.

"I'll miss you very much, William," Louella said, restraining Sarah from backing into a porter maneuvering a dolly through the crowd. "Do tell Uncle Isaac and Aunt Agnes how much I will think of them everyday. They have been so good to us."

"Margaret wanted me to remind you to try to look up Dr. Fleming." William had almost forgotten this request. "The one who is suing that DeForest fellow about some kind of radio patent infringement. Fleming's audio laboratory is in London. I know she would like to hear about what he's doing."

"I'll try, Will. But you know how consumed those radio fanatics are with their work. I think they speak a foreign language. I'm not certain I understand a single thing Margaret or Helen, or any of them, are talking about. I'm sure Gilbert doesn't either."

William nodded vigorously. "Nor do I."

He had sponsored Louella's husband, Gilbert Newell, to manage a division of a Scottish whiskey consortium. Gilbert soon worked his way into the Glasgow home office as the head of North American operations. William hoped Gilbert could one day work out of one of the skyscrapers he was admiring that morning. Then he would have his sister and darling niece close by—not across an ocean.

A straw hat landed at William's feet.

Sarah pointed towards the deck of the *Lusitania*. "It came from there. Somebody just threw it. For no reason!"

William looked down at the straw hat. He remembered that just the night before he had given his new brown felt derby to one of the bellboys at the Warfield Hotel across the street. The little man had admired the hat and William felt lucky after his meeting with Finnerty's stockbrokers at the Belmont Race Track clubhouse. He laughed again, recalling the hat slipping down over the bellboy's head when he tried it on.

"Shall we go aboard now, William?" Louella asked, edging toward the gangplank. "Let's make certain our accommodations are satisfactory."

"That's why I'm here, dear sister."

He turned to his niece to include her in the adult conversation. "I've seen a lot of photographs of this ship. I read about it when it first came to New York a few years ago. Sarah, this is certainly the way to travel across the ocean. I am jealous indeed."

William had sensed tension on the pier as soon as he had arrived; plainclothes security guards had surrounded a moving picture news crew photographing the departure. Offering no discussion, the guards quickly escorted the crew off the pier. There had been rumors that the Cunard Line had taken precautions to identify suspected German agents intent on proving that British passenger ships secreted munitions in their holds and shouldn't be considered neutral vessels.

Revelers opened a path for a shiny white touring car easing its way forward in front of the entrance to the transit building. A few of the more curious stood on crates to get a clearer view. A man stepped out of the car—many in the crowd turned in his direction, others moved toward him. Alfred Gwynne Vanderbilt. William recognized him—he was fabulously wealthy and certain to attract attention. Margaret had once said that he was the most photographed man in America. Yet William sensed a refined simplicity, and perhaps even gentleness about him. Attributes William rarely observed in his own business world.

Sarah picked out Suzette, the family maid, in a group moving hurriedly past them. "There's Suzette. Grandmother Townsend said she would be leaving today also." Sarah disappeared and then reappeared with Suzette at her side.

"Hello, Suzette. Mrs. Townsend told us that you were sailing on the *Cameronia*, wasn't it?" Louella asked.

"Yes ma'am. But I was transferred to the *Lusitania* with many other passengers." Suzette glanced nervously toward the street. "They say the *Cameronia* is going to cross as a troopship. I hope my baggage gets here safely."

"I'm sure it will," William said, lightly patting her shoulder. "Have a good trip, and leave secure with the knowledge that you did a wonderful job for the Townsends."

"Thank you, sir." Suzette curtsied. "That's very kind of you to say."

"What berth are you—?" Sarah asked.

"Sarah, please don't keep Suzette from her business." Louella gently scolded her. "She wants to make certain her luggage arrives safely. Let her tend to these personal matters."

"Thank you, ma'am," Suzette said, moving quickly toward the truckloads of luggage now arriving on the pier.

William leaned over toward Louella. "How do you suppose a Scottish girl got the name Suzette?"

Louella suppressed a giggle. "I have wondered about that also."

William pulled the *New York Times* from under his arm.

"Did you see the German ambassador's letter, Louella?" He tried to sound relaxed. She shrugged her shoulders, unwilling to be concerned. William read aloud, hoping not to frighten Sarah:

> "Travelers intending to embark on the Atlantic voyage are reminded that a state of war exists between Germany and her allies and Great Britain and her allies; that the zone of war includes the waters adjacent to the British Isles; that, in accordance with formal notice given by the Imperial German Government, vessels flying the flag of Great Britain, or of any of her allies, are liable to destruction in those waters; and that travelers sailing in the war zone on ships of Great Britain or her allies do so at their own risk."

6

MAY 6, 1915

THE LENOX HOTEL

BOSTON, MASS.

DONALD TOWNSEND HAD ANTICIPATED this evening for the past three weeks—his reception for George Creel, a journalist from Denver, now on tour promoting his new book, *Child Labor*. Donald had chosen his favorite dining room at the Lenox Hotel. He personally selected the trays of food, drinks, coffee, and desserts to be served by circulating waiters. No need for his guests to sit for an entire evening at a dinner service when they could be moving about in a more leisurely fashion.

New England's newspaper publishers and editors had, for years, been his allies in the vicious circulation wars—and they required little formality. Many of them had battled the Hearst newspapers for dominance, some even for their own survival, in every part of the country. The Hearst managers were predatory invaders and these men were their able adversaries.

Creel's colleagues listened to him in a silence punctured only by the faint chiming of long-stemmed glasses and the occasional rattle of a serving dish. Creel glided around the perimeter of tables at the front of the room. His voice and cadence discharged a practiced excitement with each word.

Margaret recalled a Hungarian violinist, maybe he was Romanian, a few years before in the same room at another of her father's receptions. He had strolled between the tables, leaning over his seated audience, reeling one person and then the next into his exuberant melody. Creel had the same hypnotic effect. He indicted every industry stained by child labor. He saved his wrath for the guiltiest, the *most contemptuous* he called them: the zealous low-level government bureaucrats who fight progress with their clumsy attempts to censor the press and who are well practiced in muzzling any regulations designed to protect working people, especially children.

CREEL JOINED THE TOWNSENDS at their table, sitting opposite Margaret, partially obscured by a red floral display. She watched as he lit a thin, light brown cigar and turned to talk to a man she had never seen before at the next table. A handsome profile, she decided. His black hair combed straight back, just long enough to straddle the collar of his tuxedo jacket. He joked with Creel and then turned away. Margaret looked over at Byron, who understood her wordless question. He shrugged his shoulders. Not someone from the Boston newspaper world.

She evaluated George Creel. Pompous, but not as overbearing as others in the room. She knew her opinions were of no particular interest to most of them—except to the few who had the wild fantasy of bedding her. It amused her that she would be a prize conquest in this male newspaper world—her father's world. They were so manageable individually for her, but a dreadful lot when they were in a pack.

Creel enjoyed his new celebrity. He had become a force for social reform, a movement that had momentum a few years before, but was slowly being pushed off the front pages of the nation's newspapers by the new lead story—the war in Europe.

"The British left the Germans at a decided disadvantage when they cut their trans-Atlantic cables last year," Creel pronounced. Margaret hadn't heard what preceded that comment. "All five of the German cables were cut soon after the war began—a brilliant stroke. That may even prove to be the Brits' most important strike against the Germans. German dispatches now filter through the British and French. Of course, they are distorted or ignored. Our war news is now totally one-sided. If you include the non-stop British propaganda machine in this country, then it is only a matter of time before public opinion tilts toward the Brits."

Creel relaxed amongst his colleagues; it was his evening. He motioned for the man at the next table to join them. The stranger moved his chair between George Creel and Donald Townsend. He nodded to everyone at the table.

"I can't imagine this country getting involved in that mess. Anyway, whose side would we be on?" Byron asked, shrugging his shoulders. "Our big cities are mostly German or Irish. Neither will support the British. That should be enough to keep us out."

"You are absolutely right, Byron," Creel said, shaking an index finger into the air. "No doubt here in the Northeast there is some support for the British. But in cities all over the country, the Irish and Germans would love to see the British lose—"

"If the Germans had developed wireless audio capabilities they could have sent their stories out to the world without cables," said Margaret, unable to prevent herself from interrupting Creel. Her mother would have once admonished her for such a graceless intrusion, Margaret thought. She continued. "Then the British would have no cables to cut. That is the way news will be delivered in the future."

"Then we will all be out of work, wouldn't we?" Creel's friend asked, looking around the table. He put down his whiskey glass and lifted a cigar from the lacquered box just at the extent of his reach.

"That's what our father believes." Byron said, taking a cigar from the box the stranger edged toward him.

"Mr. Townsend is probably right, but I think we are still far away from the demise of the newspapers," Creel's friend said, nodding toward Donald Townsend, intent on scooping out poached salmon from an engraved serving dish.

"Vincent Chelios," George Creel began the introductions. "You know Donald Townsend of course. This is his daughter, Margaret, and son, Byron. Byron is a fine reporter. He's on the sports desk and Margaret does brilliant, *absolutely brilliant* design. If I were a book publisher I would want her artwork on my releases."

Despite his bursts of self-importance, Creel had never, in their few encounters, regarded Margaret as anything other than Donald's daughter. Perhaps even as the talented artist he claimed. Never an appraising glance.

"Byron, both your Boston teams have a good chance of winning this year, do they not?" Chelios lit Byron's cigar, then his own.

Byron nodded as he puffed his cigar to life. "I've been writing about the Red Sox for the past three years. Larry McNulty follows the Braves for us. I like the Red Sox's chances. Great pitching."

"I saw the wire at the *American* that Babe Ruth hit a home run at the Polo Grounds today," Chelios said. "Nobody has ever seen a ball hit that far there. Was that his first home run?"

Vincent was not an avid baseball fan, Byron concluded. Everyone knew Ruth had yet to hit a home run before. "Yes, it was his first. I can't believe I missed the road trip. Of all games to miss. A lot of people are talking more about his bat than his pitching."

"Vincent is in town from San Francisco. He works for Hearst."

George Creel filled in the few necessary details. "I thought I would invite him along tonight."

"The alternative was a grim evening alone in a hotel room. Thanks again, George." Chelios nodded his appreciation to Creel.

"Hearst?" Margaret asked stiffly. "Are you starting another newspaper in Boston? Filled with your standard murder stories, no doubt." She paused only to form another question. "Tell me, Vincent, do your reporters in San Francisco still have a shirt and tie in a closet at the morgue to dress the bodies before you photograph them for the front page? It's really quite a charming presentation."

"No, actually we gave up that practice fifteen years ago—before I started there," Chelios answered, amused.

"Oh, don't misunderstand me," Margaret said. "Your design and layouts are first-rate. I actually enjoy looking at some of them." It was a grudging concession.

"Thank you. I'm glad an artist like you can appreciate them."

Sarcasm? Margaret wasn't certain. He was handsome, she decided. Vibrant black eyes, matching his hair—and probably a social reformer if he traveled in George Creel's circle.

"It is just that your artwork is in the service of such nonsense," Margaret said—it was so hard for her to resist. "Will you be trying to suck up the circulation here in Boston soon with sensational headlines?"

"No, we have no intention at the moment of another Boston daily. The *American* will do for now." Chelios lightly shook his empty glass at a waiter who nodded and turned away to fulfill the animated request. "I think if you read our editorials you may notice that we want America to stay out of Europe—we maintain that this is not our war."

He shrugged his shoulders. "Hardly sensational, is it, Margaret?"

"America feels indebted to the Brits." Donald Townsend paused as a waiter relit his cigar. "It's their money, and also Dutch and Belgian money, that financed us over the past fifty years. Not the Germans. Don't forget that. We also speak English here for a reason. We would probably be best to stay out of the war entirely. We should support the Brits—but it is not an obligation worthy of our boys' lives."

So he had stated in his editorials since the war began the previous August; his stance didn't surprise anyone at the table.

"You are right, Father—it is the Germans who are cutting off the hands of Belgians and raping nuns," Margaret said, her voice rising in pitch. "They have acted despicably."

She turned to Chelios. "Your Mr. Hearst is pro-German. He doesn't report these atrocities, does he?"

"You can call him anti-British, but not pro-German," Chelios said, calmly correcting her— his tone suggesting that it should have been obvious. "Those stories about German atrocities are manufactured by the British. Without real news from Germany, the Brits can write their own fiction. They will do anything to drag us in on their side. Not everyone in this country, by the way, cares about the Belgians."

Chelios stopped to assess whether to continue—he did. "The coloreds here know the Belgians only as brutal colonialists in the Congo. They used the Africans as slaves to extract rubber and then ivory for fifty years, at least. Tens of thousands were killed and mutilated. Only the colored papers wrote about it. You do read the colored newspapers, don't you? You do know there are colored newspapers, don't you?" His sarcasm was no longer restrained.

"Yes, we do know there are colored newspapers," Byron said, his naturally reddish face flushing even more. "We don't need you to tell us that."

Creel, who had stood up a few minutes before to chat with another guest, leaned over. "I don't think Vincent meant any offense, Byron. This war is going to change everything in this country whether we get involved or not. I just hope the damn thing—oh sorry, Margaret—is over soon."

"Yes, I am sorry. I didn't mean to offend anyone." Chelios reached up to intercept the drink the waiter was putting on the table.

"Why don't you have another drink then, Mr. Chelios?" Margaret suggested derisively. "Maybe you can think of another condescending comment for us."

She stood up, excusing herself.

"Margaret, there is something I wanted to ask you about," Chelios said, attempting to reengage her. She turned toward him. "You mentioned wireless audio. I heard about it. Do you really think it will change—?"

"You are welcome to see our audio laboratory tomorrow—if you wish," Margaret responded coldly. "An AT&T technician is coming in the afternoon to inspect our new antenna. We will be transmitting a music program in the middle of June. Ships may even be able to receive a signal at sea. Byron, why don't you give him directions to the laboratory?"

"Margaret and my wife, Helen, will be at the laboratory tomorrow," Byron said. "I'm writing a feature about wireless radio, so I'll be there also."

"Your wife?" Vincent asked. "Doesn't she come to Mr. Townsend's receptions?"

"Not often. Neither does William, Margaret's husband. They don't have their arms twisted by Father the way we do." Byron glanced toward his father, reassuring himself that Donald was too distracted to overhear him. "We have to endure these evenings. The family newspaper, that sort of thing, you understand. I don't mind them as much as Margaret does."

"My brother has a lovable honesty, doesn't he?" Margaret said, turning toward a small circle of guests, gesturing in vigorous discussion, at the lustered rosewood bar next to the ballroom entrance.

7

MAY 7, 1915

NEAR THE POLO GROUNDS

MANHATTAN, N.Y.

GEORGE HERMAN RUTH ROLLED his legs over the dank, rumpled bed sheets and set his bare feet onto the coarse, slatted wood floor. He aimlessly watched the wheels of a milk wagon, just barely visible through the basement window, slowly crunching over the cinder alley-way, then disappearing from sight.

Despite his newly discovered nighttime debaucheries, rising before daybreak was still routine after those ten years at St. Mary's Industrial School back home in Baltimore.

He first arrived there as a running wild nine year-old, already practiced at thieving on that city's rugged docks. His exhausted parents delivered him to the St. Mary's priests hoping his absence would allow them to attend to their ramshackle saloon—its survival a lifelong struggle.

Now free, George had no interest in even a single moment of whatever quiet introspection Brother Mathias had insisted was part of a responsible adulthood. Everything in his life had changed since he left the stifling discipline of the Baltimore workhouse only fifteen months before. He was now in the American League; it was still hard for him to believe it.

After yesterday's game he had joined teammates at the Dugout, a saloon near the Polo Grounds. Taverns populated with gamblers, drunks, and prostitutes surrounded every major league ballpark. The patrons always spoke Ruth's language, although, even for them, he was a dose of uncontained energy that inevitably grew tiresome.

The night before was now little more than a swirl of colors and gestures. He had been plied with cheap beer and jostled by fans who had witnessed his one mighty swing of the bat that afternoon.

He was twenty years old and had just learned how to buy a train ticket, register at a hotel, and even how to order from a menu. He bought a bicycle with the first fifty bucks he pocketed as a professional baseball player. It was thrilling to mount it. It was his very own.

The veteran players determined immediately that this unschooled, gullible force of nature would leave his large handprints all over their game. His big, muscular body was the most imposing in the locker room. Ruth instinctively understood every nuance of the game, yet had no social graces. He was boorish. Babe was a nickname that described him perfectly. Big Babe might have even been better.

Still not fully awake, Babe looked around the room, recognizing nothing. He only knew that he had never been there before. He had by now found himself bewildered in many rooms in broken down hotels in every city on the circuit.

Usually without even a stub of introspection, he still couldn't help but replay the previous day's game. It was his Red Sox against their rivals, the New York Yankees. His teammates hated the Yankees and could be relied on to be in their best form against them. Babe really didn't give a damn about any of the teams in the league. He just loved to play baseball. Anyway, he couldn't remember the names of most of his own teammates. How could he ever get too upset about the other team if he didn't recognize them from one game to the next?

Since spring training, Babe had demonstrated his power in batting practices throughout the league. In every city he hit the ball farther than anyone thought possible. Even his body twisting into a knot when he missed the ball with one of his unbridled swings excited the fans. They arrived early just to watch him before the game. He enjoyed putting on a show for them.

Just the day before, finally, during a real game, he saw that pitch roll off the pitcher's fingers. It floated towards him, large, more like a basketball, slow as if thrown by one of the nuns at St. Mary's. Babe had sniffed a flash of burning wood as the bat connected with the ball. The solid crack rippled through the crowded stands. The ball landed deep in the right field seats. No one had ever before seen a ball hit that far in the Polo Grounds. Not ever. The buzz grew louder, exciting him as he rounded the bases for his first major league home run. It aroused something primal in him. He just wanted to it again—and again.

He wished that his seventeen-year-old bride, Helen, could have seen that one swing. She was in New Hampshire visiting her family, but surely she would have heard about it by now, he guessed.

Babe pulled up his pants and pulled a handful of bills out of his pocket. He laid them on the lavender pillow. The woman still curled on her side, tousled her almost waist length, stringy light brown hair. Her breasts hung over the bed sheet pulled around her waist. Great tits, Babe thought. He wondered if he had buried his face in them when they bounced around only hours before. I'm sure I gave her a great ride, didn't I? He asked himself.

"Jesus Christ, George, I thought you were going to break the bed. I may have to rest all day." She reached toward the pack of cigarettes on the nightstand. "Where're you going so early, honey?"

"There's a game this afternoon and I have to go to the hotel first," Babe said flatly. "I need some fresh air. It's kinda' stuffy in here."

"George, you are the *loudest* fucker I ever had in this bed," she proclaimed with amused certainty. "Come back anytime you're in town. But change your goddamn underwear soon, will you honey? Christ, are they filthy!"

8

BYRON MANEUVERED THE OLDSMOBILE over the rutted road bounded on one side by a rough stonewall marking the perimeter of the Van Hooten property. It had been a year since he last took this back road to Tufts College. It was a longer route, but he enjoyed the open farm country. Neither Helen nor Margaret seemed to notice the detour.

The two hundred fifty-foot high antenna in the distance towered over the radio station next to it. It had replaced an even bigger one, a three hundred foot antenna.

Helen had been a critic of the first antenna design. She and Harold Power disagreed about its stability. She was certain that it would not survive the first solid wind. It didn't. It collapsed onto the railroad tracks, and it took days to remove the mangled pieces. The town locals and railroad engineers enjoyed the demise of the college kids' tower. It seemed pointless to them to begin with—a rich boy's endeavor.

Miraculously, the college allowed him to build another antenna— but only to its present height of two hundred fifty-feet. He didn't think it would affect the range of transmissions they were planning anyway—so he agreed, mustering a feigned disappointment. Actually, he was elated that the trustees allowed him to build anything at all after the first antenna debacle.

"There are a few things I need for my story. You two can help me," Byron proposed. "I know Harold Power adores both of you. Lucky for you. Otherwise you might have to find another toy to play with."

"Is that a sexual allusion, dear brother? Perhaps something your wife would understand better than I do." Margaret tapped Helen on the shoulder. "Am I missing something?"

Helen cupped her hand over her mouth, leaned toward the back seat, feigning a secret with Margaret. "I think it might be some sort of locker room reference. I'm not quite sure."

Byron ignored them. "I'd like to hear what the trustees think about these audio transmissions. I mean they really can't have any idea what it's all about. Power should get an award for duping the university out of space for a laboratory and then letting him set up a private company to sell audio equipment. A very clever man."

"Yes, why don't you do an exposé on us, darling? Maybe if you succeed they'll get rid of our laboratory. We would love you for that." Helen turned to the back seat. "Margaret, what about that boor from Hearst you were talking to you last night? Byron told me about him."

"What was his name again, Byron? Vincent Chelios, isn't it?" Margaret asked. "Actually, he was fine. A bit pompous perhaps. All of those Hearst people say the same thing—'We should stay out of the war, but be prepared for it.' To his credit he's coming to see the laboratory today before he goes to New York—Byron, you did tell him how to get here, didn't you?"

"Yes, I had a pleasant conversation with him after you left," Byron said earnestly. "Actually, Vincent gave me two leads for getting over to

Europe to cover the war. The good news is that I already spoke to one of them earlier in the week and he's sure to hire me."

They ignored him as the car bumped along the dirt road. Margaret noticed her brother's red hair, just a shade darker than her own, and how it and Helen's blonde tresses radiated such color in the late morning sun.

"Byron, shouldn't you think about it a bit more?" Helen asked a few minutes later. "You will be a newspaper publisher one day. Not many other writers can say that. There is so much to write about here. That's not our war anyway."

"I don't want to be a sports writer for the rest of my life. Although I will cover the World Series this October, especially if the Red Sox are in it."

"So it's either the trenches and *poison gas* or the World Series." Helen tried to be light. She was nervous. She recalled her ambivalence when they first became lovers. Byron was her best friend Margaret's brother. How complicated need she make her life? She asked herself at the time. He was more of a boy than she wanted—too often he was oblivious to her. To art. To real adventure. She wondered what kind of a woman he would have been with if she hadn't come into his life? But now she had important news for him. She wasn't sure how he would react.

"Poison gas? What poison gas are you talking about, darling?" Byron asked. "Whose propaganda is that? That's just the British manipulating the news. They will say anything to get us into the war."

Byron turned onto a narrower road, through a canopy of maple trees. He inhaled the woody scent. A perfect day, he thought, watching the bright sunlight filter through the densely leafed branches. The Johansson farm had the biggest maple tree stand in that part of Massachusetts. At least that was what Mr. Johansson told him a few weeks ago when he stopped to buy a still warm jar of syrup. The tin buckets and sap spiles by now would have been cleaned off and stored away, awaiting next spring's sap running.

"Father thinks this is the best maple syrup in the state," Byron said. "I think the best comes from much farther west. Olsen's, isn't it?"

"Maple syrup?" Margaret leaned forward from the back seat, bringing the palm of her hand to her mouth to stifle a faux yawn. "Tell us more about your mad yearning to be in a trench with dead bodies, won't you, Byron? You've often let foolishness be your guiding light. Do you have a real surprise to tell us? "

"I have a surprise!" Helen did not wait for her husband's response. "I'm pregnant." She shrugged her shoulders and giggled. "I don't mean to upstage you, Byron—or to change the subject. After all, maple syrup is interesting, I suppose." She kissed Byron on his cheek. "Don't take your eyes off of the road, dear—I'm in a delicate way."

"Are you serious? I mean, why didn't you tell me before?"

"I just found out yesterday. Dr. Carlson gave me the news. I was just waiting for the right moment. It seems as if this might be the time to divulge all of our secrets."

"That's wonderful, dear. When are you due?" Byron patted her knee.

"In the middle of November. Or to put it in a way you will understand, after the World Series. I told your mother this morning. She is thrilled. By the way, it was Dr. Carlson who told me about the poison gas."

"Dr. Carlson? How would he know about poison gas?" Byron asked.

"He said his contacts in the military told him the Germans used it, probably chlorine gas, judging from the wounds, against the British and French a few weeks ago. They don't have too much information but it sounds frightful. It was even reported in the newspapers—I think."

"So Dr. Carlson told you, 'The Germans are using poison gas and oh, by the way, you're pregnant?'" Margaret asked lightly. "He used to have a much more refined bedside manner than that."

"Helen asked me a lot of questions about Dr. Carlson yesterday, Margaret." Byron turned partially towards his sister. "I told her that you and I have speculated about him for years. I'm surprised she hadn't asked me before."

"Oh, you mean whether he is one of those *artistic* types?" Margaret leaned in again between Byron and Helen. "Maybe Helen's curiosity was aroused when Dr. Carlson had his hand between her legs. Could that be it, darling?"

Helen reached into her bag for an apple and offered it to Byron. He bit off a piece. Helen flicked a small chuck off his lip. "They seem so guarded when they are together."

"They? You mean him and Dr. Welch together or your legs together?" Byron asked.

Margaret reached for the apple. "I'm guessing Helen is referring to the doctors. Well, they do have a curious relationship. Mother and Father would never discuss it. 'It's none of your business,' dear Mummy says."

"Dr. Carlson disappears whenever Dr. Welch comes to Boston. At least it seems that way to me." Byron slowed to accommodate four cows wandering across the road, the bells around their necks tinkling as they disappeared behind a hedge. "Even last night at Father's reception for George Creel. Usually Dr. Carlson would have enjoyed the evening, but he was nowhere to be seen."

"By the way Helen, a lot of people *do* consider Dr. Welch the most important figure in medicine today," Margaret said. "And just for the record, can we assume that we are talking about the possibility of the two doctors being homosexuals?"

"Actually, Father once told me, after he had a few drinks"—Byron tried to tell the story without laughing—"that before he courted Mother, Dr. Carlson had made some *bumbling*, that was Father's word for it, overtures to Mother."

Margaret giggled and covered her mouth. "They never told me *that* story. I don't know if I should be upset. Did they think I would be damaged forever by this passionate competition for my mother?"

"And then Father never saw Dr. Carlson in the company of another woman—nor did he ever discuss it with me again," Byron said, concluding with finality.

"Maybe dear Mummy is just a heartbreaker," Margaret suggested. "Who would have guessed?"

They emerged from the overhang of dense tree cover into hilly farmland. The radio station antenna was now close enough that it dominated the view through the windshield.

"Well, my dear," said Helen, putting her arm around Byron, "who would have thought we'd be sharing all of these delicious secrets on our way to the laboratory. How exciting this trip has become!"

Byron looked over his shoulder toward Margaret. "So, Sis, do we have any more secrets to share? Or have we exhausted the supply? My appetite is whetted."

Helen also turned toward Margaret. "You didn't know how full of surprises I could be, did you? Now it's your turn, Margaret—got a dark secret you're just dying to share?"

Margaret remembered Gaspar—*he* was her secret from Helen for the past few years. Her first taste of real sex, real seduction. Not like the awkward boys who groped at her in a darkened corner at a high school dance.

Gaspar posed in a life drawing class she and Helen attended at a small studio tucked into a narrow side street of Boston. He had reclined on a platform one overcast afternoon, dreamily looking out over the six students trying to capture his nude image. His sandy hair curled in a golden halo around his almost-pretty face, his cheeks pink as if bitten by a wintry gust. Margaret imagined those Adonisian figures peering up at the Ascension of Jesus in a Renaissance painting.

Whatever impelled her later that day up those stairs into Gaspar's tiny loft? She couldn't remember. She didn't know what to expect or how he would feel inside her—she did remember that. But she knew it was going to happen—and it was so exciting. The second and third time she went up the stairs she had a better idea of what awaited for her on the rickety bed with the musty sheets. The last time she found herself at his battered green door it was locked. Her knocks went un-answered.

The next day she had asked Gaspar why he was not waiting for her as they had planned. He forgot. That was all he said. Then he mount-ed the stage, dropped the towel from around his waist, and assumed his now familiar pose.

"It better be good if you are thinking this long, Sis," Byron said.

She could never tell Helen. Besides, she 'would absolutely die' if William ever learned about Gaspar.

Margaret paused a few seconds more then tapped the top of Byron's seat. "I had sex with William on the sink in the upstairs bathroom while you were outside at our birthday party last Sunday. Does that count as a secret?"

"It's not really much of a secret," Helen said. "You looked like that Cheshire Cat in that *Alice in Wonderland* book when you came back to the table. Even Suzette noticed. You are shameless sometimes, my dear."

Margaret laughed. "Thanks to your clever comments, I'm certain even our still innocent Sarah understood what kind of present William received from me."

"Innocent? She's sixteen, and I'm sure she has given at least a passing thought to the subject," Helen said. "I certainly did when I was her age, didn't you, Margaret? I still do if you need to know."

"Sex in that bathroom, Margaret?" Byron feigned shock. "That's unacceptable. That's where I brushed my teeth. Did you consider that before you did this deed? Anyway it's more than I want to know about you."

Helen consoled him with a pat on his shoulder. "You had better accept it as the *deed* is done already."

He glided to a stop at the side of the radio laboratory. No one had arrived yet. Margaret dug her hand deep into her shoulder bag for the door key.

"I'm excited about being a father, darling." Byron embraced Helen. "I really am."

"I am also very happy," Helen whispered into his ear.

They followed Margaret inside. Helen opened the windows to allow the dankness to evaporate into the spring freshness. The phone rang. Helen answered it.

"Hello? One moment—it's Vincent Chelios for either of you," Helen announced across the room. Margaret, sorting through scattered diagrams at a workbench, motioned Byron to the phone.

"Good morning, Vincent. Byron Townsend here." Byron listened, shaking his head slowly. "Oh, my God, no—"

Helen and Margaret stared at Byron.

"We had two of our family on the *Lusitania*—my God." He looked into the frozen faces of his wife and sister.

Margaret dropped the diagrams onto the table and rushed across the room, snatching the telephone from Byron. "This is Margaret Morrison. What happened, Vincent?"

"I was calling to apologize for my behavior last night, Margaret. Also to tell you that I had to cancel my visit to your laboratory today. The Germans torpedoed the *Lusitania* off the coast of Ireland. We are all covering the story. I didn't know you had family on it—I'm so sorry."

Margaret looked toward Helen; her face was buried in Byron's shoulder. He whispered reassurances in her ear.

"When did it happen?" Margaret asked. "What do you know about survivors? Did the ship sink? Dear Christ, I don't even know what to ask you, Vincent!"

"Regrettably it did sink, I'm afraid—ten miles off the coast of Ireland. It happened at one forty in the afternoon, British time. That would have been early this morning, our time. Nobody knows about survivors yet. It was close to the shore so there is a better chance for a rescue. It's night there now, and the scene is chaotic, as you can imagine. One of our best men, Pitney, is on his way to Lansdale where the Brits are coordinating the search. I will get your family members' names to him. I pray for them—I'm so sorry."

"Thank you, Vincent. I'm sure Father knows by now. Would you be so kind as to call him? This is horrible. I don't know what to say. I will call William, my husband. It is his sister and our niece who were on board. She is still only fifteen—thank you. Goodbye."

Margaret hit the receiver handle and gave the operator William's number. "Yes I know, Mary. Yes, it is terrible. Please put me through immediately—perhaps we can talk later. Thank you."

Helen and Byron intercepted Harold Power walking through the door. He listened intently to Helen's grim report. Margaret locked eyes with him for a moment; he could only nod vacantly.

"William Morrison—please—it doesn't matter if he is meeting

with Joe Finnerty. This is his wife, Margaret. It's an emergency. A serious one—thank you. I'll wait."

Helen came to Margaret's side. They embraced.

"William, I have terrible news. The Germans torpedoed the *Lusitania* this morning—the ship sank off the coast of Ireland. We don't know about any survivors yet—William, are you there?"

"Yes, dear. I'm here. This is horrible. Are Helen and Byron with you?"

"Yes, they are."

"Ask them to drive you to the inn. Aunt Agnes and Uncle Isaac will be devastated. They will need me there until we get more news—they couldn't bear it alone. Then tell Helen and Byron to go back to your parents. They shouldn't be alone either. I'll meet you at the inn."

"Good, I want to be with you right now," Margaret said.

"I'll leave right now. Wait a minute—Joe Finnerty is on the other phone line. He just heard the news." After a brief silence William came back on the line. "Margaret, Joe said to tell you and the whole family that he is praying that everything turns out well."

"Do hurry, William. Please."

9

MAY 7, 1915

GLENFIDDICH INN

NEW BEDFORD, MASS.

VIBRATIONS FROM THE ROUGH cobblestone reminded William of his first bicycle ride. Right there on Purchase Street. Uncle Isaac bought the bicycle from a man who had it buried under furniture on his delivery truck. It was a present for William's tenth birthday.

Uncle Isaac had stood alongside his friend Hans Stitler that day, outside Hans's butcher shop, judging William's shaky first ride past the pharmacy and the barbershop, ending with a pecan maple syrup roll celebration at McConnell's Candy & Sweets Shoppe.

Now William drove past familiar storefronts and faces that had always been part of his life. Shopkeepers waved at him. He smiled back with effort. The news had spread down Purchase Street and, by now, everyone heard about the sinking of the *Lusitania*. They understood that two of their own were on board, their fate unknown. Louella had been part of this community also. They had watched Gilbert Newell court her and had later applauded little Sarah's first steps when her doting parents visited the inn and walked these same streets.

William turned into a driveway framed on both sides by low stonewalls. He parked next to the sign GLENFIDDICH INN EST. 1890. It always had been a reminder that he and the inn were the same age.

The driveway's shingled awning, supported by a thick oak arched frame, had been built to shelter horse carriages from both the severe New England snows as well as the bright summer sun. Now eight Harley-Davidson motorcycles were parked close to each other—more than William had ever seen there before. Usually there were just one or two. Business must be getting better, he hoped. Uncle Isaac's motorcycle business. Not the inn business. That would always be a struggle for Aunt Agnes and Uncle Isaac.

MOTORCYCLES. THAT'S WHAT THEY were calling them now. No longer motor-bicycles. Isaac had started tinkering with the bicycle he bought for William's tenth birthday as soon as they returned from William's first ride. Isaac and Mr. Stitler spent many weekday evenings trying to entice a small four-stroke engine into powering the bicycle. It never worked. Neither of them could devote sufficient time to the project; the inn was always in need of Isaac's attention and Mr. Stitler's shop required the butcher.

William recalled the guest who had one day checked into the inn, the guest who brought the new world of motorcycles with him. *When did that happen?* Perhaps William was fourteen. The guest, a man with a stern, unsmiling face, stayed with them for several days. He had aroused a curiosity in William; the way he stared at Uncle Isaac when they talked, listening intently to every word. His nose seemed to be slightly flattened. William had wondered if the guest had once fallen off a motorcycle onto his face.

William, as he always did, had looked in the register when the man checked in. He saw 'Milwaukee' next to 'home address.' *Milwaukee*. It sounded so exotic, so foreign. The man carried a bulky leather-bound book of pencil drawings and, in the evenings, sat at the large front window, skimming through them.

One morning William watched, through the sitting room window, the man standing amidst the bicycles Isaac had accumulated on the side at the driveway. He picked up a discarded engine and fitted it snugly onto the shiny metal brace that Isaac had once welded onto the bicycle. He then attached a few cables hanging off the bicycle to the engine. He moved the bicycle around by its handlebars.

Isaac had, by then, come up the path and the two men talked while the guest absently held the bicycle, rolling it back and forth. After the guest departed, Isaac told William and Agnes that he would be a distributor for a new enterprise. The *Harley-Davidson Motor Company*, he called it. The company was starting to sell the motor-bicycles just like those he and Mr. Stitler tried to assemble a few years earlier.

The guest's name was William Harley. Mr. Harley even told Isaac that he was competing with a company from Massachusetts called *Indian Motorcycles*, but that Mr. Harley made a better product. He urged Isaac to look into it for himself.

William's first reaction to Isaac's plan had been fear. He thought they would have to move to Milwaukee. Isaac and Agnes must have seen his expression. They reassured young William that Isaac would be a distributor right there at the inn. Years later he understood that neither aunt nor uncle would ever consider leaving the inn.

WILLIAM CLOSED THE CAR door and walked over to the motorcycles. The newest one had a gearshift box he had never seen before. He rocked the machine back and forward.

"That's the new three-speed gear shift. It's the first one in these parts," Isaac said as he approached William. They hugged. Isaac kissed William on his cheek.

"This is awful, William. We can barely endure the wait. We probably have more information than you do. Donald Townsend called us a few minutes ago. He'll be at the newspaper until he gets word about Louella and Sarah. He won't leave—"

Isaac stopped and looked searchingly into William's eyes. "It's nighttime now where it went down. We will probably have to wait until their morning. That'll be in the middle of the night here. Aunt Agnes prepared your room."

They walked toward the house. Isaac put an arm around William's shoulder.

"Margaret's inside with Aunt Agnes. She arrived a while ago. Byron and Helen stayed for a few minutes, and then went to the Townsends'."

"How are Margaret and Aunt Agnes taking it?"

"Not well—about the same as me." Isaac picked up his canvas bag filled with produce for the weekend. William gently took it from him and carried it inside.

Margaret sat next to Agnes, holding her hand on the lavender couch dominating the sitting room. William embraced his aunt and sat on the other side of the round coffee table. The literature on the table had been one of William's earliest jobs at the inn. He always kept the guidebooks and newspapers in perfect order, especially when they had guests. He loved to help his aunt and uncle prepare for the tourists who, with each successive summer, began coming to New Bedford in larger numbers.

"Donald Townsend called," Agnes said, her voice wavering. She had been crying. "There are survivors. We can only hope and pray."

"Oh, dear Aunt Agnes." Margaret hooked her arm around Agnes's and moved even closer to her. "Thank God we have each other right now. William and I will be here with you as long as you need us."

"William, I just remembered something." Agnes managed a smile. "Mr. McCormick delivered that apple cider you love so much. He just made it this morning. I'll bring you a glass. Margaret? Isaac? Can I bring you anything?"

Margaret nodded. "The cider sounds divine. Thank you."

Isaac agreed.

"I'll help you," William said. He noticed how frail his aunt Agnes had become. Her hair, wrapped in a bun, was grayer than the last time he'd seen her. She never complained about her work but William knew, better than anyone, that the inn was a twenty-four hour job for both her and Isaac.

WILLIAM FOLLOWED AGNES PAST the wide staircase and down the hallway to the kitchen. He slowed to examine his high school graduation photograph, remembering each of the eight students posed with him.

He always believed that he knew the inn better than anyone else—that only a child could truly appreciate every nook in this rambling maze. Over the years he had explored every crevice from the stone walled basement up to every mildewed box in the attic.

The history of the inn had been told to its visitors in different voices. Sometimes William heard it as a tragic tale, a burden that had fallen upon Isaac. At other times the story was told with gratitude; the house allowed Agnes and Isaac to live the life they enjoyed. Every telling contained a nuance not previously revealed.

After the Civil War, Isaac Morrison's father, Amos, built a vast fleet of whaling ships. He quickly became one of the wealthiest men in New Bedford. First he built the family home, now this inn, with stone imported from Vermont, at least for the first floor of the house, and for the large servant house in the back. Later he added the second and third floor of the house with red cedar siding. Four witches' cap turrets protruded from the roof.

The result was a structure without the unified style of the other grand homes along the coast—not a single surface continued in a straight line for more than a few yards. It was a discordance of angles and oddly placed walls. The small balconies on the upper windows and the larger widow's walk added to the cluttered exterior. William had often seen people talking to each other, pointing up at one architectural detail or another. He had concluded at a young age that they had gone several streets out of their way just to see the house—it had always been the local curiosity.

In 1871 massive ice floes crushed much of the New Bedford whaling fleet in the Arctic Ocean. Many of the town's men drowned without a trace. The next years were difficult; the remaining ships had to go on farther, ever more perilous voyages to find their prey. To make the situation ever more dire, whale oil, which had fueled lamps everywhere, was being replaced by oil recently discovered in Pennsylvania. Whaling was in decline.

Some whalers moved into other industries. A few, those still with money, built textile factories. Amos Morrison continued on as a whaler. Insurance premiums were raised every year, and soon the few remaining whalers had to send their ships out uninsured. But whaling was in their blood. They could never be textile manufacturers.

In 1876, Arctic ice floes decimated the remaining whalers. This time Amos Morrison was left penniless. All his ships were gone. He died without ever reconciling his dramatic change of fortune.

One of Amos's sons, Henry Morrison, William and Louella's father, used his own meager savings to start a textile business. The other son, Isaac, struggled for survival in the family house.

Soon a new industry evolved in America—tourism. New wealth now meant taking the family on vacation. Massachusetts cleverly promoted its own historic sites. New Bedford, scenic and on the ocean, became a favorite destination for the wealthy from Boston.

Isaac reinvented the rambling stone and cedar mansion into a guesthouse. It took courage to move into the servants' quarters. Isaac never minded that the townsfolk evaluated it as the remaining Morrisons sliding down the social scale.

Isaac employed every advance in technology: Indoor plumbing, electricity, and separate bathrooms were installed as soon as he found competent contractors to do the job. There was never money left over. Dutifully, Agnes went along with every change.

When William was two years old, his parents died in a train crash outside Philadelphia. Agnes and Isaac gathered him up, along with Louella, who was already sixteen years old.

Their father, Henry, had established a trust for William and Louella. It allowed them to go to the best schools. William's young friends loved to explore the inn. William never thought of himself as anything but lucky to have new parents. Looking back, he understood how he and his sister Louella filled an otherwise lonely place in Agnes and Isaac's lives.

"THIS IS A NEW KIND of regulator." Agnes gripped a knob on the gas range set in the corner of the kitchen. "This regulates the gas so you can control the size of the flame." William read the dial. It had numbers one through eleven on it.

Agnes looked somberly around the kitchen, now cluttered with supposed 'time-saving gadgets' that Isaac endorsed and to which he applied his sometimes curious, often unnecessary 'refinements,' as he called them. "Sometime I wish Isaac would just stop tinkering—even if only for one week."

William laughed. "You're dreaming, Auntie."

"You're only too right," said Agnes, agreeing with a heavy sigh. "Well, since you were last in this kitchen we made some changes. One of those efficiency men stayed with us for a few nights. He was in town to go through a textile plant, I think. He came in here and started organizing it as if this was a restaurant. I told him we are not a restaurant nor a factory, so we didn't need to *save steps*. I told him that we didn't need to watch everything that our help does either. He said why not be efficient so you can have more time to do other things? It made sense, I suppose. We took some of his advice. Mostly, though, we ignored him." She smiled broadly.

"I would have expected that would be your response, auntie dear." William suddenly remembered Suzette, the Townsend family maid. He forgot she had transferred to the *Lusitania* at the last minute—more bad news to share with the Townsends.

Agnes stepped into a cold storage compartment—a crude metal case Isaac had constructed with parts he salvaged from an abandoned Anheuser-Busch refrigerated railroad car. She backed out with a bottle of apple juice and poured it into the glasses William had already positioned on the marble sideboard.

The telephone on the hallway table rang. William moved quickly to pick it up.

"Hello?"

"Hello, Mr. Isaac Morrison? This is Vincent Chelios. Donald Townsend asked me to bring you up to date on the information we have."

"This is William Morrison, Margaret's husband—Isaac is my uncle. I just arrived. Margaret is here as well. What news do you have, Mr. Chelios?"

"Call me Vincent, if you don't mind. I'm calling from the *American*. Our contacts in England tell us there is still confusion at the Cunard Line office in Liverpool. We know that some of the locals are on a rampage against German shops there. That's just adding to the confusion.

"A train has been chartered to take passengers' families to Queenstown, where the search and rescue effort is being mounted. The train is en route now. Ships are at the site looking for survivors. We should have more information fairly soon—I'm sorry I can't be more helpful."

"Vincent—did Donald Townsend tell you about Gilbert Newell?"

"Yes. That would be your brother-in-law. Your sister Louella's husband. Correct?"

"Yes, that is correct."

"Our man Pitney in Queenstown has been given his name and will try to find him. It is possible Mr. Newell is already on the train. I'm sure this must be very difficult for you. How old is your niece?"

"She's going to be sixteen in August. It's hard to imagine anything happening to them. I saw them off in New York just a few days ago."

"I'll stay here at the *American* until we get further news. Feel free to call me. I gave my telephone number to Margaret and Byron earlier in the day."

Agnes, Isaac, and Margaret surrounded William. "Thank you, Vincent. We will be here. Thank you so very much." He placed the phone on the cradle.

"What did he say, darling?" Margaret asked, almost in a whisper.

William shared the barren report.

He knew it would be hours before they would hear anything else. It was better for him to not ask the painful questions; why wouldn't they have returned with survivors already? The ship sank almost in view of the Irish coast a half-day ago—what was taking them so long?

Instead he turned to his wife. "Margaret, let's go into town. I need a few things. You probably do as well —we may have to stay here for a few days."

"A few days? Do you think it will take that long, William?" Margaret asked.

"I don't know what to think—let's walk into town."

"Yes, William, it might be good for both of you to go into town for a while," Isaac said. He glanced at Agnes, sitting on the sofa with her hands folded.

She nodded vacantly. "We have some preparation to do. We have two couples coming for the weekend. Marcel and Yvonne will be working with us so we can spend time with you. Terrible circumstances, I know. The guests should be here soon. You may even meet them in town."

Isaac managed a smile. "Stop by Hans's shop and ask him for a bigger order. He will be delivering it later—I know how you love the roast beef Marcel will cook for dinner."

THEIR STEPS ECHOED UNDER the covered wooden bridge spanning a rocky stream swelled by a distant mountain's spring runoff. They strolled in silence on the path not far from the old tannery.

"Those bastard Germans—torpedoing a ship carrying women and children. They are beasts." Margaret hugged William's arm tightly.

"I wish I could have seen this coming." William guided her around a thick tree crowding onto the gravel path. "I showed Louella the letter in the newspaper. I'm sure every passenger read it. It was right next to the shipping news that day."

"What letter?"

"The German ambassador published a letter in the newspapers that very morning warning passengers that all British sea traffic was subject to U-boat attacks. Of course it didn't seem like any passenger would change his mind. Alfred Vanderbilt was on the ship also."

"I don't care about him. I'm praying for your sister and our niece." She immediately regretted her shortness. "You know what I mean—I only have so much prayer in me."

William tried to laugh. "Neither of us has ever had too much of that."

He stopped, lit two cigarettes, and handed her one.

"Margaret, I forgot to tell you. When I was in the kitchen I remembered that Suzette transferred to the *Lusitania* at the last minute. They converted the other ship into a troop carrier that morning."

"Oh, no. That dear girl too! So many innocent people. Why didn't they attack the troop ship?"

"The Germans say that all of these big ocean liners are carrying ammunition, and so they are all targets."

"What nonsense. The Brits would never put innocent people in danger. Those Germans are despicable." She puffed hard once and then threw her cigarette onto the gravel.

"This is going to push us into the war. I don't trust the British or the French—or the Germans." William shook his head. "And certainly not those other countries."

"Do you mean Turkey and Russia? At least they have glorious art histories." Margaret shrugged. "Not very comforting, I know."

"Who gives a damn about art? A lot of people are dying because some old kings want just one more war before *they* die. That's Uncle Isaac's one-sentence history of all wars—now look at that! Almost ready to start a game."

They had wandered behind the home plate of a baseball diamond set on the bank of the river. The outfield footing, William knew from experience, was treacherous. Filled with gopher holes. By the end of June, the field would be rock-hard, causing a harvest of bloody knees and elbows until everyone went back to school in the fall. It had been part of William's childhood. Part of every New Bedford boy's childhood.

Two of the bigger boys faced each other, choosing teammates for an impromptu game. It was a speedy selection that started with the best players and wound its way down to the least competent; an early entry into a lifetime of peer evaluations. Every boy would always remember where he placed in that process.

The boys surrounding home plate watched them approach.

"Good afternoon, Mr. Morrison. We hope that everything's all right with your sister and your niece," the tallest boy said. "We heard about the *Lusitania*. Just so you know, we all feel bad."

"What's your name?" William looked closely at the friendly-faced teenager with the shock of curly brown hair. William dressed the same way when he was that age—wool cap, breeches billowing out around the knees, exposing long argyle stockings.

"I'm Samuel Palmer. You watched me at the inn a few times when my mother and your aunt—"

"Of course, Samuel. I'm sorry I didn't recognize you, but you have grown quite a bit. Thank you all for your kind words."

Margaret and William continued onto a street leading past the back entrance to the town library.

"It's such a beautiful day, William?" Margaret remembered saying that earlier in the day to Byron and Helen on their drive to the radio station. It now seemed so long ago.

William just nodded.

They stopped at the New Bedford Theater. A colorful poster promoted the current attraction, *The Birth of a Nation*.

"I'm surprised they are showing it here after the commotion it caused in Boston last month," William said. "I wonder if Jim Kelly knows what a tiger he has by the tail."

"It's beautiful artwork." Margaret moved closer to the display window. "The colors are so intense. Don't you think so?"

"Yes, they are," William replied indifferently, his attention not focused on a movie poster.

"Two tickets? The show starts in ten minutes," the young ticket seller announced from within a cramped booth next to the narrow entrance.

"No thank you, we're just passing by." William couldn't imagine sitting though a movie, any movie, right now. "Is Jim Kelly here?"

"No, sir, he'll be back in an hour."

"Well, just tell him that Will Morrison said hello. I had your job for two months when I was your age."

"Oh, Mr. Morrison! We all know what happened. Did you hear any news yet? I'm sorry, sir." The boy looked away, not knowing what other words were appropriate.

"Thank you, young man. We're waiting to find out—" William's voice trailed off.

Returning to New Bedford had always been a comfort to William, but today it was strained. Everyone wanted the latest news—and he didn't have anything to add to the few simple facts already in circulation.

The sign extending out over the storefront door read STITLER'S FINE MEATS, its black letters scripted onto a wooden plaque. Then, in lettering William always thought too small, EST.1894. William inspected the meat display in the window and then scanned the interior. It was just as he had left it five years earlier—still carefully scrubbed each day by whichever young helper Mr. Stitler had working for him. William did that job when he was twelve. It was his first job away from the inn. He understood years later that Hans Stitler reported on his efforts regularly to Aunt Agnes and Uncle Isaac.

"Well, if it isn't young William." Hans Stitler was not as big as William remembered, though he was still solid, with forearms corded from a lifetime of lifting bulky carcasses. William recalled how Mr. Stitler could hoist both him and his son Gunther, William's best friend back then, off the ground at the same time as if they were loaves of bread.

Scanty tufts of hair around Hans Stitler's temples accented his otherwise baldhead. *Like feathers on an egg,* William thought playfully. Hans moved around the chopping block and shook William by the shoulders with both hands.

"I can't tell you how sorry I am. I am praying for Louella and Sarah." He stopped and breathed heavily. "I'm praying for everyone else on that ship—for all of us. This is terrible, William."

William smiled. This dear family friend's manner was as kindly as ever, and his thick accent, still impervious to a clearer English. William knew there had been random acts of revenge against German shop owners whenever U-boat activities were reported—even though most of these men had been in America for decades. It was insane behavior, thought William, and just one more reason to hope for a quick end to the war in Europe.

"I know, Hans. It's terrible. How's Gunther these days?" William wanted to know about his childhood friend, but he also needed a respite from the day's terrible reality.

"Gunther still doesn't want to take over this shop when I give it up. He is in Chicago now. He has three trucks and is selling meat to the hotels and restaurants. He is doing very well. Gunther Stitler Meats, that's his company."

"Gunther couldn't wait for you to give up this shop because you never will, Mr. Stitler. He made a good choice moving to Chicago. Please give him my fondest regards."

Han Stitler tried to smile. "Maybe you are right, William—I'm sorry, Margaret. I didn't mean to ignore you. I just haven't seen this laddie in so long. I haven't felt this sad in many years."

Margaret touched his forearm. "I understand, Hans. I know how important you are to William as well."

William and Margaret recognized that Hans Stitler was offering a personal apology for Germany—unnecessary from this gentle soul who abhorred the savagery unfolding so faraway and so far beyond his control.

"I am going to the inn right now. I can give you a ride back. We can all squeeze into the front, yes?" Hans Stitler was happy with his suggestion. "I just have to make one stop before. At Luke Hooper's house. You remember him, don't you, William?"

"Of course I do. How is Mr. Hooper these days?"

"He broke a leg two weeks ago. He fell from his roof trying to fix a leak after that big rain. So we deliver food to his house today. He should be all right in a few more weeks."

William remembered. "Auntie wants you to add to the order for the inn. We may be staying for a few days."

"I already thought of that," Hans said. "I've been doing this for so long." He managed a smile.

THE PHONE RANG JUST AS William and Margaret entered the inn. Isaac got to it first. William and Margaret joined Agnes in another expectant semicircle. Hans Stitler unloaded his delivery in the kitchen.

"Hello, Donald," Isaac said. Then he grunted his understanding a few times. "Thank you, Donald. They will be with us at least until tomorrow."

"Uncle Isaac—please." Margaret stepped forward, reaching for the phone. "Father, how is mother taking this? I know it is difficult for the two of you. Are Byron and Helen with you? That's good. Father, William has other bad news. Suzette was transferred to the *Lusitania* at the last minute. They transformed the liner she was to leave on into a troop ship. Please ask your contacts to look after her as well—I know, Father. This is devastating."

She hung up the phone.

William noticed the couple sitting on the sofa. Agnes led him forward.

"William, do you remember the Gammons? They were guests with us when you were at Yale."

"No, I'm sorry, I don't, but very nice to meet you. This is my wife, Margaret."

"William and I were just walking through town," Margaret said, attempting pleasant conversation. "Everything looks like it did when I first came here a few years ago. The movie theater looks like it is doing a good business. They're showing *The Birth of a Nation*. William, we absolutely must make a point of seeing it—"

"We saw it in Boston a few weeks ago," Mrs. Gammons said, nodding toward her husband. "There was quite a stir in the audience. Several coloreds stood up and made a big show of their distaste for the movie. They ruined the movie for the rest of us. Police had to eject them. Can you imagine that?"

"Yes, the coloreds are all up in arms about that movie," her husband added, amused. "Some of them protested outside the theater. Do you know that in most places they wouldn't even be allowed in the theater?" He laughed. "Imagine that—niggers protesting on the streets of Boston."

"How dare you use—" Margaret decided not to continue; there were more urgent matters.

She faced William. "Father says that several survivors have been brought ashore—also many bodies. It's still too early to know the full story. But they have good people at the docks where the rescue ships are coming in. Nobody knows if Gilbert is still in Liverpool or on his way to Queenstown. We will just have to wait."

"Well, let's try to change the subject—at least until the next telephone call." William looked around the room for agreement.

Isaac came into the sitting room. "Good idea, William. By the by, I bet two dollars on Pebbles in the Kentucky Derby tomorrow. Who knows, I might get lucky."

William clapped him on the back. "That's the spirit, Uncle! Is Captain McMillan still taking bets at the fire station?"

"No, he retired last year. Moved to Boston to his daughter's house. Another fireman takes the bets now. Roger Reiss. A young fellow."

William smiled faintly. "It will be difficult to think about a horse race this weekend—but let's at least try."

II

"hundreds will hear the election night returns on the radio"

Four months later

10

SEPTEMBER 18,1915
HARVARD MEDICAL SCHOOL
CAMBRIDGE, MASS.

HELEN THOUGHT ABOUT THE exciting events she had attended since she arrived in Boston just a few years earlier—most had been initiated by the Townsends, especially Beatrice and Donald, now seated next to her, talking to Dr. Carlson. Their conversation melded into the excited undertone of the assembly hall.

Edward Carlson leaned over the Townsends to engage Helen. "Dr. Welch is the most important person in medical science today. There's no one else who even comes close to his stature—certainly not here in America."

She had never seen the doctor as animated as he was now, waiting for his colleague to arrive. Dr. Carlson's beanpole frame, draped in a rumpled suit, twisted toward her uncomfortably in his wooden classroom chair; she listened politely as he rattled off morsels of information meant to heighten her interest in the evening, but which were unnecessary as she thoroughly enjoyed being in attendance.

Helen felt the kick, more like a dull poke in her abdomen. A new life stretching out for space. It will be a great adventure, she thought.

Byron seemed to be excited about the baby. He had even offered a few names if it was a boy. Helen wondered if the names he had in mind were of current sports figures he was writing about. He would probably never suggest names for a girl, but Helen assumed that was natural for men like her husband—they seemed so oblivious to this kind of involvement. Byron would more likely accept enthusiastically any name she thought of for a girl. Nonetheless Helen was thrilled that she could bring new life into a family still so shattered by that horrific act only four and a half months earlier.

Helen felt a barrier between each member of the family since they finally learned the fate of Louella and Sarah. Nobody in the family seemed capable of discussing the facts Gilbert Newell and Vincent Chelios's contact, Pitney, provided in their many contacts.

Helen turned to the assembly hall behind her—terraced rows of desks and chairs inclining up toward entrances through which more attendees entered; every seat already occupied, the walls lining with the overflow of latecomers.

An unlatching of a wooden door at the side of the raised dais redirected Helen's attention. A stillness fell over the crowd as a short, bulky man emerged into the hall. He mounted the platform with a little hop that jiggled the paunch underneath his snug diamond-patterned vest. Smiling comfortably, he cast an approving eye over his standing-room-only audience.

Carlson responding to Dr. Welch's cue stepped up next to him. Dr. Welch whispered a confidence, and then Dr. Carlson turned toward the room.

"The man I am standing next to right now is, in the opinion of many, the most important figure in American science since Benjamin Franklin."

Dr. Carlson walked to a corner edge of the platform. "I had the good fortune to work for Dr. Welch during the Yellow Fever eradication program in Panama some fifteen years ago. Without his dedication, that early effort, as well as all of the public health measures since then, would probably have not been undertaken.

"Before Dr. Welch's forceful leadership there was no medical research in America. We all looked to Europe, to Germany especially, for leadership. There was not a single medical research facility in this country. That's why medical students had to learn German. And let me assure you it is not an easy language to learn—"

Dr. Carlson nodded, acknowledging the murmur of agreement.

"When I first entered medical school, there were no admission requirements. Student fees supported the faculty, and we never even performed a single autopsy, nor did we see a patient until we graduated. Only then could we hang out our shingle and try to bring sound medical treatments to poor souls addicted to patent medicines and snake oil."

The audience warmed to Dr. Carlson's earthy recollections. "We have come a long way since that time. Again all of the advances we have made are due to the persistence of Dr. William Henry Welch. Please welcome him once again to the Harvard Medical School."

Applause and the excited undertone increased as Dr. Carlson stretched out his hand in the guest's direction, then he stepped down and returned to his seat.

Round and playful, thought Helen. Dr. Welch—a cherub with a Buddha-like body. Just as she had seen in many of the Oriental paintings at the Boston Museum. A centuries old symbol of good fortune. *And probably Dr. Carlson's lover. How intriguing!*

Doctor Welch stepped forward. "Every time a comparison to Benjamin Franklin is made I pinch myself to make certain that I am not dead and just hearing an overly generous eulogy."

Helen laughed along with the Townsends and everyone else in the auditorium.

Traveling in the wake of the Townsend family provided many benefits. They knew everyone in Boston, and Boston certainly wasn't Denver—she had more adventures in Boston than she ever could imagine back in Denver. The image of President Wilson stepping out of his car for a Democratic Party dinner at the Parker House Hotel often came to her over the past two years. She just happened to have been leaving the hotel at that moment. It was so exciting to have been that close to a president. *He was so—regal. How he glided towards the hotel entrance without even acknowledging that whirl of activity around him.*

"—Similarly, I feel uncomfortable with the depiction of the last thirty years of medical research as a golden age of medicine." Doctor Welch chose his words deliberately. "Because so much has been learned about communicable diseases, it is even now suggested by some that in a short time we shall discover the causes—and even have a cure—for *every* disease. That is just wishful thinking.

"It is interesting to me that many advances in public health have been made by detective work, not by scientists. Cholera is just one example. Its symptoms are even noted in the Old Testament. There have been centuries of debate as to the cause of cholera but not a single scientist could ever prove his own theory.

"In the 1850s, during England's cholera epidemic, a young Dr. Snow drew a map of the most affected part of London and then set out to interview everyone he could. He asked about their diet. What did they eat? Where was their water taken from?

"He plotted the path of the epidemic on a map and finally focused on one public water well as the probable source of contamination. He convinced the city authorities to remove the handle on the well to prevent its further use, and immediately there was an end to the cholera epidemic. Now we know how crucial clean water is to public health. Still cholera is not eradicated—it is only contained."

Umbrellas still moist from the day's intermittent showers tinged the lecture hall with mugginess. Helen relived ascending the tight, winding wooden staircase to that model Gaspar's room somewhere in downtown Boston. His cramped bedroom had the same mustiness, as did the lecture hall. It had been so erotic when he greeted her with a towel wrapped loosely around his waist. When he closed the door behind her she knew that it would be an unforgettable adventure—and it was! It was certainly best to leave it unsaid to Margaret. *She would probably be absolutely aghast if she knew.*

"—And what I find most remarkable about Dr. Snow's investigation is that it could have been undertaken a hundred years before, or a thousand years before, for that matter. No laboratory work was necessary. Not a single microscope was used. Just interviews. Compiling rudimentary statistics. Plotting fatalities onto a map led him to the water pump. This could have been done by any dedicated newspaper reporter."

Dr. Welch glanced over towards the Townsends. Donald and Beatrice mimed their agreement.

So did Helen. *Plotting the path of a disease on a piece of paper! Simple common sense.* Yet nobody has thought of it until Dr. Snow. But then there are quack doctors also. *What was that doctor's name again?* She tried to recall it. Byron and Dr. Carlson ridiculed him many times. That doctor's experiments did receive a lot of publicity—even in the Townsend family newspaper.

MacDougall. Dr. MacDougall!

He had a practice somewhere in Massachusetts. He had known Dr. Carlson from somewhere or other. He believed that the human soul had weight, a "measurable mass" he called it. To prove it, he went about weighing terminally ill people just as they were dying so that he could quantify the weight of their soul as it left the body. Their bodies should weigh less right after they die, MacDougall reasoned.

Really dumb! Imagine putting all of that energy into something like that— and to think, men like Dr. MacDougall scoff at radio experiments, something certain to change the world. Not like a dumb attempt to weigh a dead person's soul.

That Dr. MacDougall must have been an idiot to waste his time that way, she concluded once again. To claim that he could detect a three-quarter of an ounce decrease in the dying person's weight in some of the six bodies he tested—what did he ever think he was doing? *Hardly scientific—a total of six bodies tested!*

Dr. MacDougall even weighed dogs as they died. He could find no weight loss and so concluded that dogs have no souls. *And to think newspapers write about this rubbish!*

"—Now we are at a crossroads of medical history," Helen heard Dr. Welch proclaim. "We stand once again before history's great crucible of communicable diseases—war. Tragically, this is a more devastating war than any previously known to mankind. Never before have we seen such mechanized destruction of human life as right now in Europe. Still there is every reason to assume that, just as in every war from the beginning of recorded history, diseases will exact the greatest human toll, not the evermore efficient methods devised to kill the adversary.

"Pneumonia has always been one of the great levelers of the military during all wars past, and so we now have several research teams around the country preparing for this possibility. Even though we are, thankfully, not involved we do intend to send medical units to the Western Front as well to assess conditions there. Surprising public health challenges will emerge from this conflict—of that we can be certain."

Helen's attention wavered. Doctor Welch's voice receded. Byron could be publicizing the work of American scientists as they track, and contain, the diseases coming out of those horrid trenches in France. That is the important work that must be written about, not the romantic nonsense of describing battles. *American arts and sciences are—right here in Boston— not on the Western Front—and Byron doesn't appreciate that he was born into it—at the center of this exciting age.*

11

SEPTEMBER 20, 1915

FENWAY PARK

BOSTON, MASS.

RUSTY ORANGES AND REDS seeping through the green autumn New England foliage signaled an end to another baseball season. William, and probably everyone in Boston, knew that this would not be just another baseball game in Fenway Park. It would be fiercely played. The visiting team was the Detroit Tigers, Boston's despised rivals. The Red Sox had beaten them two of their three games the month before in Detroit, where Ty Cobb, the Tigers' hateful superstar, showcased his vicious play for the hometown crowd.

Those games had been ugly, the tough Boston pitchers using the Detroit batters' heads for target practice, and the Tigers slashing at the Red Sox players with their sharpened spikes as they slid hard into the bases. Now the rivalry was back in Boston. The Red Sox had won the first three games, crushing the fight out of the Tigers and insuring themselves the pennant.

Babe Ruth led the league with four home runs. Fans were filling the stadiums in every city just to watch him attack the ball with that muscular swing of his heavy bat. With just a few more games left in the season, William was glad to finally get out to Fenway. And today, Ruth would be pitching—and batting.

Byron had parked his car a few trolley stops from Fenway Park. Going the rest of the way on the trolley was easier than driving into those cramped streets, especially on game day. Six of the Royal Rooters, the self-proclaimed official fan club of the Red Sox, already drunk, bounced off each other as the trolley swayed around the curves of the track cutting through the city.

Their destination was one of the saloons on the fringe of Fenway Park where they gathered before each game to make a boisterous entrance onto the field. The blue rosettes on the lapels of their black suits easily identified them. A vulgar lot William would rather have at a distance than hanging all over him as they were now. A few improvised a dissonant chorus of "I Didn't Raise My Boy to Be a Soldier," oblivious to the melody. Mercifully, their voices melded with the chatter of the out-of-round metal wheels on the tracks.

The trolley lurched to an abrupt stop at the platform. The momentary calm as the doors snapped opened lent clarity to the last lines of the song:

There'd be no war today,
 If mothers all would say,
 I didn't raise my boy to be a soldier.

The Royal Rooters stumbled down the few steps and rushed out of sight.

William and Byron descended into a stream of bobbing black derbies and a smattering of late season straw hats. The crowd maneuvered through the narrow sidewalk alongside Fenway's red brick walls. William could see the reason for the ballpark's sharp angles. It was tucked tightly between railroad tracks and busy streets, almost as if it had been dropped there as an afterthought. The red brick walls melded the ballpark into the nearby warehouses and factories. Despite its already well-worn appearance, the ballpark had been there for just three years.

Vendors waved scorecards and hawked their peanuts and cracker jacks. Carts with colorful umbrellas advertising their hotdogs and sausages added to the congestion. William remembered at Yale the students called them 'dog carts,' an allusion to the suspected meat in the sausages.

"There's Patrick," Byron said, pointing into the passing crowd.

William surveyed the buoyant throng of men elbowing their way past him. "Who's Patrick?"

"Patrick O'Reilly—Anne's brother. The girl working for my mother. You remember, at our birthday party. He works in the Red Sox locker room."

"Oh, yes."

"You probably don't remember him but I see him at home games," Byron said. "He fills in some of the blanks. You know, what the players won't tell us. Even if we can't print most of it, it's still great to hear." He nodded toward the man who abruptly stopped in front of them.

"Patrick, how are you doing?" William asked as he moved alongside the black-haired boy with the shiny white skin.

Patrick waited for the peanut vendor to retrieve a mound of bags from his bulging burlap sack. Both were oblivious to the crush of men streaming past them.

"Oh, sorry Mr. Morrison. How are you? Hello, Byron."

"That's a lot of peanuts. You must be hungry," William said lightly. Patrick looked confused.

"They're not for him, William." Byron answered for Patrick. "He sometimes sneaks out of the locker room to get food for the players."

"That's right, sir. Our locker room is just past that entrance." Patrick gestured over his shoulder. "So I come out here. I always buy them from Tony." He motioned toward the peanut seller. "Tony's been here since the park opened. Same as me."

Tony tipped his cap smartly at them.

"Byron tells me the game the other day was brutal. The cops had to take Cobb off the field," William said, jostled by a passer-by.

"They did indeed, Mr. Morrison." As Patrick dumped the peanut bags into a canvas baseball bat duffel bag, his politeness segued into an agitated recitation. "Even the fans wanted a piece of Cobb. Mays threw a few pitches at his head. When that son-of-a-bitch slid home he spiked Corrigan. Corrigan tagged him real hard on the mouth. Slapped him in the mouth with the ball. Cobb just got up like nothing happened. When he took off his pants Corrigan had a bloody slice across his thigh from that prick. I got to get back now, sir."

Tony, having filled Byron's peanut request moved on, crying out his simple message in a strong tenor, "Peanuts! Get your peanuts!"

William absently watched Tony disappear. "Oh yes, good to see you, Patrick. I'll tell your sister that I saw you."

"Nice to see you again too, Mr. Morrison." Patrick said, turning toward a crowd funneling into an entrance.

William and Byron kept pace with the flow around them, finally handing their tickets to an old hunched over attendant, and then each timed his quick move through the turnstile so that it didn't waver in its rotation.

William and Byron worked their way up the ramp, William's anticipation growing as each step revealed more of the crowded stands and the manicured field. When he was younger every boy dreamed of batting against Cy Young or Christy Matheson. Pitching against Ty Cobb or Napoleon Lajoie. Now, every boy dreamed of being Babe

Ruth—or just watching him at bat. Even William could hardly wait to see Ruth in action.

They stepped down the short metal ladder into the press box; Byron greeted some of the bored Detroit writers waiting to get through another game. At least this game might provide exciting copy. Baseball writers welcomed any ugliness on the field—the more action, the more embellished account they could write. If they had their way, batters would be avoiding balls thrown at their heads all day. Most of the writers didn't give a damn which team won anyway, as long as there was free food and drink at the hotel and at the ballpark.

Byron tapped Nick Flatley on his shoulder to get his attention. "Nick, this is my brother-in-law, William Morrison." William reached over a typewriter to shake Nick's hand.

"Nick Flatley writes for the *American*," Byron continued. "And this bald-headed bastard is my buddy, Ralph McMillan. He *tries* to write for the *Journal*."

"I read both of you all the time." William stretched out far enough to grasp Ralph's hand. "It's great to meet you."

"You missed the excitement the other day with that fucking maniac Cobb," Ralph McMillan said, pawing at his shirt collar, already drenched with sweat. "If you read us, you know about it. At least you'll get a chance to see Ruth today."

Red Sox players surrounded home plate. Babe Ruth stepped up to take his practice swings. A sizzle sparked through the stands. William tried to imagine swinging against big league pitching with a heavy piece of wood like the one Ruth used. *I'd never get it around fast enough to hit a ball. Not even once. Not now, and not even when I was eighteen.*

William noticed Joe Finnerty moving into a row of seats behind the press box. Joe greeted two men William had never seen before. He assumed that another deal was in the works and that he would hear the con sooner or later. After all, Finnerty would never sit through a baseball game just to watch it.

A sharp crack directed William's attention back toward home plate.

Everyone in the press box followed the trajectory of the ball. Ruth had sent it on a high arc deep into the center field stands. The ball landed amongst a tight circle of men standing in the gambler's section created by the team's owner to keep this rabble away from the ladies and families they wanted to attract to the higher priced seats near the infield.

William turned to Ralph. "What's the line for the World Series? Are the Red Sox favorites?"

"Last I heard we were 9-5 favorites. Are you a betting man, William?" Ralph asked. "Today's game doesn't mean shit. Most of the action they are taking out there is for the World Series."

William hoisted the binoculars hanging from Byron's neck and focused on the distant seats. He thought that it might be Devin Keane surrounded by gesturing men. And it was! *That oily little bastard. Now he takes baseball action.* William had only seen Devin once since they tested that monstrous molasses tank in the spring.

"My brother-in-law gives me the binoculars for a birthday present and now his eyes are glued on them." Byron faked an attempt to pull the binoculars out of William's hands. "Those Royal Rooters are all over the bookies out there."

Ralph again pulled his wet collar away from his neck. "They're a bunch of loud drunks but they're good for a story every once in a while."

William handed the binoculars back to Byron and turned toward Joe Finnerty, engrossed in conversation with the two men who were now leaning in toward him, listening to his every word. Joe looked every bit the stylish sportsman in his sharply pressed blue serge suit, with a blue and red tie decorating his starched white shirt—a straw hat tilted slightly left. His face shined as red as any Irishman's in the ballpark, but William would bet that Joe didn't have a drink all day. He was too much of a shark to ever give up his edge for a shot of whiskey. His joviality, accented by that toothy smile, was calculated to disarm the unwary.

Finnerty caught William's attention. He motioned William towards the seat next to him. It was on the aisle, fortunately. William would be able to stretch his legs out. The rows were so close; he knew his right leg would cramp after a few minutes—and he would never want to show discomfort to the always-alert Finnerty.

William hopped up the few steps on the press box ladder and slid into the seat. Finnerty introduced him to the two men on his other side. William couldn't hear their names but it didn't matter; he'd catch up on that later. Finnerty turned halfway toward the men and continued his story.

"So du Pont has the goddamn Brits by the balls." Finnerty positioned himself to include William. "They ran out of high grade explosives almost as soon as the fighting started. You see, you need twenty tons of nitrates to make one ton of smokeless powder. That's a hell of a lot of nitrate to get across the ocean and with all those German submarines—it's impossible. The British don't even have the shipping for it anymore so they go to Pierre du Pont. But he doesn't want to build a new plant and then get stuck with it if the war ends quickly. So he tells the Brits they have to pay him enough in the first contract to pay for the plant—he also makes them put the money in a United States bank to guarantee it."

The men nodded, intently following the tale.

"The Morgan Bank gets the best deal of all," Finnerty said with gleeful admiration. "The British makes them their exclusive purchasers for everything in America. Now that's something. Morgan has a fucking license to steal."

William knew that nothing could make Finnerty more excited than the possibility of controlling an entire country's purchase orders, especially when they were buying everything and didn't care about cost. Never mind the wills and trusts at the bank that named Finnerty as executor. Taking pocket money from those widows was just fine, but Morgan's deal—billing an entire nation distracted by war —now *that* would be fabulous. Especially when the country is Britain, which the Irish soul of Finnerty despised, a weakness that even he could not avoid.

"So now du Pont is on his third or fourth contract." Finnerty approached the tale's glorious conclusion—one he could savor once again. "He's still charging the Brits a buck a pound, instead of the going rate of fifty cents. How would you like a piece of that deal?"

Finnerty leaned over to William, lowering his voice. "I'm trying to buy the Red Sox from Joe Lannin." He leaned closer still, now practically on William's chest. "Lannin is getting his balls broken by the commissioner. He's never been part of that crowd. I think he would sell for the right price. Lannin hates the commissioner. The commissioner and a lot of the team owners hate Lannin. The only problem is that Lannin hates my guts too." Finnerty laughed. "The hell with them! I think we'll get it. Imagine that? Owning the Boston Red Sox."

"Well then, Keane shouldn't be taking gambling action out there," William said, looking out toward center field, then turned to Finnerty. "Not if he's going to work for the owner of the team." He shrugged an unspoken 'isn't it obvious?'

Finnerty put his hand on William's shoulder. "Never mind Keane. He's just taking the heavy action the bookies can't cover themselves. They lay it off to Devin, and we cover it—for a fee of course. We are bankers after all."

He looked at William to see if his joke was appreciated. Finnerty rotated his finger, signaling for four beers to the pimply-faced sweating boy carrying a heavy metal case up the steps.

He leaned back to include the other two men. "William, our bank is buying a copper parts company out in Pennsylvania. I don't know how to structure the deal yet. We're still looking over the books."

"Copper? What the hell do you know about copper?" William lowered his voice to exclude the other two men.

"Not too much. But I do know about undervalued assets." Finnerty raised his voice so the others could hear. "The owner, a kid in Albany, inherited the company from his parents. He doesn't give a damn about the business. He doesn't even know what the damn thing is worth. I think we have a more realistic idea of what it's worth than he does."

"Doesn't he have advisers to tell him what it's worth?"

"Sure he does. Very good advisers. Here they are." Finnerty waved his hand triumphantly toward the two men next to him. All three smiled at William.

"If we make this arrangement they will be working with us, of course," Finnerty explained. "If we get the company maybe we'll move some of the inventory to the docks near Purity Distilling. You remember Jell, don't you William? That storage tank we bought? He works for us now. He'll oversee the warehouse."

Jesus Christ, thought William. Du Pont. Taking World Series action. Buying the Red Sox. A copper company. *And the game hasn't even started yet.*

"COPPER?" BYRON GUIDED HIS car over the trolley tracks too fast—William bounced.

"William, you know Finnerty will make a buck from it. But what's in it for you? I've wanted to talk to you about him for a while. But it never seems like the right time. With Helen pregnant, and everything else happening these days."

Byron didn't want to mention the *Lusitania*. Margaret told him William would jump up in the middle of the night and then just as quickly fall back to sleep; frightening episodes that only started since the ship was lost.

"I know, Byron. Your family doesn't trust Finnerty. I've heard it from Margaret. Does this have anything to do with maintaining the Townsends' good name in Boston?"

"I don't think anything you do will hurt the family's *good name*— whatever that is, William. We don't have to trust Finnerty," Byron said. He braked, allowing two mounted policemen to cross in front of the car. One acknowledged his courtesy. "It is you who have to trust him. I'll tell you what you already know. There are a lot of opportunities for you besides Finnerty. A lot of bankers would want to have you on their team. You do know that, don't you?"

"Yes I do, Byron. I don't plan to be with Finnerty forever. Don't forget this is a legitimate bank I work for. Don't you think other banks are doing the same thing?"

"That's bullshit William. Joe is unique, and not always in a good way. He has no loyalty to you. Remember that character Icarus, the one in Greek mythology—despite his father telling him that he had wax wings and shouldn't fly too close to the sun, he did it anyway. The wax melted and he fell back to the earth —"

"—I must have missed that class." But William did admit to himself that he often wondered what attracted him to Joe Finnerty. The word that often came to mind was *primal*. Joe could attack his prey and shake loose the dollars. William was certain that as long as he remained aware of Joe's amorality, he could keep myself outside of Finnerty's smothering grasp.

The game had lasted thirteen innings. William was tired—his right leg throbbing. Luckily, Finnerty left in the eighth inning with the other men. William could then stretch his long legs out in the empty aisle. But thirteen innings? Christ. He would have left earlier but Byron had to stay to the very end to get his story to the sports desk.

Byron wanted to put Finnerty aside. "William, I forgot," he said. "Helen has a few copies of a radio magazine for Margaret. I forget what the damn thing is called. You probably have some issues at your place. Let's stop at my house and get them before I take you home."

"Good idea. Listen, Byron, now I want *you* to hear what I'm saying. Everybody is using this war for his own purposes. Even you." He looked over at Byron, who gestured for William to continue.

"You want to go to Europe to be a war correspondent. What's the difference between you doing that and me working some deals for the bank? We're both trying to do something for ourselves."

"I'm glad you said that, William. I know Helen hates the idea of me leaving, with the baby due soon. She has been giving me a difficult time about it—"

"And she should. I agree with her. Helen thinks you're abandoning her for a dumb adventure. She wants you to write about medical advances, instead of mutilated bodies. I know that because she tells Margaret."

Byron nodded. "I know, but this would be an opportunity to get away from the sports desk. It would be great for Helen and me. And she does have the family around her. She won't be alone—"

"That's nonsense. It has nothing to do with a *better life* for Helen."

"It's something I need to do. War correspondents are sitting in London and Paris, being fed lies by the British and French. The military

117

won't let them get close to the fighting. They have to watch what they say or they get shipped home. It's the story of our lifetime—but there is another way of getting the story."

"And that is what?"

"To go over as an ambulance driver. They have been recruiting volunteer drivers from Harvard since the war started. Not just Harvard, but all of the universities."

"I know, Byron. They've been raising funds for ambulances and uniforms for a while. I gave them money. Why don't you just make a contribution and call it a day? Stay home with your wife."

William absently watched a junk cart driver inspect his scraggly horse's shoe. "Most of those volunteers think England and France are still the mother countries. But your wife is going to be the mother—not exactly the same thing, is it?"

"I know what you mean. For me it's a way to get to the Front. Last April, for the first time, the Home Office gave the drivers permission to pick up the wounded at the front lines. Things must be getting worse for the French to allow that. A lot worse probably. So I could get to the Front as a driver and get the story back home."

"Byron, you didn't hear a word I said. Did you?"

WILLIAM DIDN'T EXPECT MARGARET to be visiting Helen, but that was unmistakably her Model T parked close to the open front door. It was one of the last cars to be painted a midnight blue with black fenders. Margaret had added a thin red trim around the running boards. This was thought to be scandalous by other drivers, who, according to Margaret, would never have the imagination to embellish their cars with anything original.

The other two cars in the tight semi-circle driveway surprised William even more.

Byron was also curious. "That's my parents' car and the other one looks like Doc Carlson's Packard. What are they all doing here?"

Beatrice Townsend rushed out to meet them.

"Mother, what are you doing here?" Byron asked—Beatrice Townsend was not likely to arrive anywhere unannounced. "Is that Doc Carlson's car?"

"Yes, I'm afraid it is—it's Helen. Luckily, Margaret was here. She called us. Helen had a miscarriage. Edward is examining her. Your father is here too."

Donald Townsend appeared at the open door. "Byron—" he faltered. He motioned them inside, as if receiving guests at his own home.

Margaret rose from the sitting room sofa. "Oh, William. This is dreadful."

Beatrice followed William. "We brought Anne with us. She can stay overnight with Byron and attend to the house."

Dr. Carlson jogged down the steps; everyone turned toward him.

"We don't have time to lose. We need to get her to the hospital immediately. This is very late in her pregnancy to miscarry," he said. "The ambulance is on the way."

A FRIGID NIP IN THE autumn night hinted at the New England winter still to come. Margaret and Beatrice receded into the billowy couch in the sitting room, consoling each other in gentle tones. William remembered that he and Margaret had bought the couch for Helen and Byron as a wedding present. It had been delivered to their house by mistake. Margaret had insisted that they make love on it before she called the company to take it away. An inspired suggestion, as it turned out. At least, he thought it was the same couch. It looked a little different. Maybe Helen had it recovered—*Aunt Agnes would do that at the inn every few years.*

Donald poured whiskeys for Edward Carlson, William, and himself.

He tipped his glass toward Dr. Carlson. "Edward, I don't know what we would have done without you today. I'm sure Helen would have died if you didn't respond so quickly."

Edward nodded vacantly. He shook his drink, swallowing half of it in a gulp. "I made arrangements for Byron to spend the night at the hospital if he wishes. We can call over later and see how he's doing there—or we can go. When I left the hospital, Helen was resting comfortably. She will need time to recuperate. The good news is that she has all of you to care for her."

"And she has you too, Edward. We can't thank you enough," Beatrice said. "On second thought, Donald, I will have a small drink."

"I know this may not be the right time." Margaret spoke loud enough to capture everyone's attention. "I don't know if there is ever a right time for this —"

"Read the letter, dear." Beatrice urged Margaret. "We should all hear it."

"It's from our darling Sarah." Margaret said softly, removing a letter from the sofa cushion. William stiffened. "We received it today, William. While you and Byron were at the baseball game. Luckily I went over to Helen's to read it to her first and arrived just as she started to bleed."

Margaret fanned out the many pages of tightly formed script. "It's quite a long letter, as you can see. It must have taken her ages to write," she said, trying to lighten the somber mood around her.

"Do read the letter, Margaret." Donald commanded impatiently. He sat down next to his wife. He took Beatrice's hand in his. It had been the family's hope to find out exactly what had happened to Sarah and Louella. It seemed that nothing but Sarah's own account and re-assurances of her recovery from that frightful day would satisfy any of them—and now finally they could hear her own words.

"It's dated August 15. Sarah wrote it in Glasgow."

My Dearest Aunt Margaret and Uncle William,

It seems years have passed since we spent that afternoon together at the birthday party. I took many pictures on board the Lusitania but, of course, the camera was lost. Thank you for it but I don't really need one here as there is so little film to buy anywhere in Scotland now. Actually, everything is hard to find in any store. The talk everywhere is only about the war in France. It seemed far away when I was with you a few months ago. The adult discussions we used to have with the family about art and culture are of no interest to people here. I am certain that it is because everybody here has lost someone they know.

I had my sixteenth birthday party at the hospital. I know that Father wrote to you about it. My leg was broken badly and I still need crutches to walk around with. I also broke two ribs. I am lucky to have survived.

Across the street is a military hospital that is filled with soldiers with horrible injuries. I go over there almost daily to volunteer. It takes me awhile just to cross the street but at least I can walk. There is so much to be done. It makes me feel good that I am helping peo-ple. Every day more men come into the hospital. All of the hospitals in Scotland are filled with the wounded.

Father told me that when I am ready I should write to you about the Lusitania. He said I should only do it when I wanted to. I want to tell you about it now.

As soon we left New York the talk was all about the war and the German submarines. Maybe because it was a British ship and most of the people were British, the talk was about Europe. The Americans did not talk too much about the war. Sometimes I heard them say that America should not get involved in a European war. Mostly they talked about movies, and the theater. You could tell by their accents they were the Americans.

There was more talk about submarines as we came close to the British Islands. The last night we entered what some of the men called 'the war zone.' People wondered why the ship was traveling so slowly. Captain Turner told us at the concert the last night that there were submarines in the area but that the Royal Navy would meet us the next day. I think he intended to make everybody feel better, but we were even more fearful after that.

When I awoke there was thick fog and the ship's foghorn was sounding. I went outside and people were frightened because they thought the foghorn would call attention to us.

By lunchtime Ireland came into view. The fog had lifted and the bright sun warmed us. The water was very smooth and people were in a better mood. It was so exciting that Great Britain was finally in front of us and the wonderful adventures I had dreamed about were now in our reach.

Mother and I had lunch with two new friends at my favorite place on the ship. It was called the Verandah Cafe. It had plants and outdoor tables just like I imagine restaurants in Europe would be like. Mother liked it also. After lunch we walked along the boat deck. That is where many of the lifeboats were kept.

Mother was walking far ahead of me with a new friend that we had made. Her name was Hilda Epps and she was Canadian. She was going to London to wait for her husband, who was an officer in

France with the Canadian Army.

I heard somebody say, "It looks like a porpoise." Somebody else said, "No, it is a torpedo." I walked to the rail but before I got there I felt a tremendous thud and the ship shook. I saw Mother turn and from far away she looked in my direction. Then I felt a much bigger explosion from inside the ship. Things flew all over the deck and the ship shook even more. Something hit me on my head and I fell down and was thrown into a railing. I remember looking down and seeing the cash register from the Verandah Cafe land with a crash at my feet. Its drawer opened and I could hear the change ringing as it spilled on the deck. I don't know if that is what hit me in my leg or not. The rest seems as if it came from a terrible dream. I am still not certain what happened, even though I remember new things about it every day.

Passengers and some of the crew ran past me in every direction. Hot steam came out from below the deck. It was burning people. They were screaming. The bow of the ship was pointed down into the water. The deck was slippery with water and pieces of coal that came from someplace.

Crowds of people gathered around the lifeboats. They looked so nervous. The sailors were having trouble getting the boats down into the water because the ship was tipping over. I saw Mother waving towards me. She was surrounded by people and was pushed onto a lifeboat. The lifeboat swung like an upside-down metronome, like in my music class. It was lowered towards the water and was still swinging back and forth. I heard it crash into the ship.

I saw a woman fall backwards with her hands and feet stretched out. She fell all the way down into the water. I could hear the splash even over the screaming on deck. Then the lifeboat hit hard into the ship again. Everybody on it tumbled out and the lifeboat crashed down on top of some of them. The screams were horrible to hear.

The ship started to sink even more. There was a lot of pushing and shoving. I think I already had broken my leg but I can't remember that too well.

I saw Mr. Alfred Vanderbilt, with his valet standing alongside him. I knew who he was of course. We had watched him everyday whenever he passed us. He was always dressed so elegantly. He was very friendly to everyone for a man in his position. A lot of the passengers talked about him. He was standing next to a lifeboat, beckoning towards people with children. He was tightening the children's life vests and putting them into the lifeboats. He was very calm. I saw him give his life vest to an older lady. I think her name was Mrs. Winters. They put her into a lifeboat.

Soon a great wave of cold water surged over the deck, carrying dead people and broken parts of lifeboats into the ocean. I held on tightly to the railing. It was very scary. My hands let go and I was in the water. Thank goodness for Aunt Helen's swimming lessons. I don't remember swimming, but at least I wasn't afraid to be in the water. I saw the ship's propellers come out of the water. Someone was caught in a lifeline and I thought he was going to get chopped up by the propellers. They were really big.

I was sucked into the smokestack that was in the water and everything went dark. I thought I was dead for a moment. Then a burst of warm air and dirty water shot me back into the ocean.

Later I awoke and I was in a wooden box. I must have fainted. There were white or blue bodies, some of them nude, floating around me. The sun was going down. I thought I was dead and in a coffin. I remember now there were wooden boxes on the ship that stored things near the lifeboats. I think I was in one of them. I don't know how I got into it.

That night was very cold and silent. I saw the stars. I was afraid to move. I didn't want to look out. I remember being taken onto a ship. I heard someone say, 'She's alive. I thought she was burned to death.'

I saw the words Indian Empire on the side of the ship. I looked at my body and it was covered with soot. A towel, more black than white, lay crumpled alongside me. I remember thinking someone must have wiped the coal dust off my face with it.

I am not sure if it was a dream but Suzette was sitting at my bedside. She said that she would be with me as long as I needed her. I asked her about Mother. She didn't know. She said that they were still trying to find everybody. I fell asleep.

Father came. I think it was the next day. I awoke and he was standing over me. He looked so frightened, with his hat in his hand. It was then that he told me about Mother. He had searched everywhere and looked in every morgue but he couldn't find her. We both cried.

I also remember being in a car after I left the hospital, seeing many handbills on the sides of buildings. They were from people searching for their loved ones. A few even had photographs. I remember one about an eight-year-old girl with curry hair. It was too far away for me to read the details. I heard someone say that people were hoping the lost passengers would still be alive, maybe with fishermen along the coast.

Mother talked to me on the ship like a friend. It made me feel very grownup. She told me some of her problems with Father. But I know they loved each other very much. He has been an absolute prince since he took me on the train to Glasgow. He is always at the hospital. I love him very much. I miss Mother with all my heart.

With my undying love,
Sarah

P.S. I will begin another letter to Aunt Helen and Uncle Byron immediately. I just have to stop for now. It has taken me many hours to write this letter and I feel very sad. I love and miss you very much.

Margaret put the letter on the table and looked around the room. "That poor angel. What she has been through. What we all have been through."

"What a story." Donald said quietly. "Maybe we should print that letter—"

"That is a terrible idea, Donald," Beatrice snapped. "This is a personal letter to her family, not a foreign dispatch."

"Well, it says so much more than most foreign dispatches I've read," Donald said stammering, surprised at his wife's sharp tone. "It is such a straightforward eyewitness account. I wish all of our—"

"Nonetheless, perhaps we should ask her first," said Beatrice, softening. "She is such a brave young lady."

"—And very lucky to be alive." Byron stood in the doorframe to the sitting room. "And so is Helen."

"How is she?" Dr. Carlson asked. "Is anybody with her right now?"

"Yes, we have a nurse with her—and Dr. Hastings is also there. I came back to pick up a few more things. We can all go there together. I heard the end of Sarah's letter." Byron pointed upstairs. "I saw a letter on the table next to the bed when we went in to take Helen to the hospital. It might be the other one Sarah mentioned. I'll get it." He turned and started up the staircase.

"That second explosion that Sarah heard must have been munitions aboard the *Lusitania*," Donald said. "There is nothing else that could explain it."

"There is still no proof of that." Dr. Carlson lifted the decanter on the coffee table and refilled his glass. "It's hard to believe that the British would put civilians in harm's way—to say the least in this instance."

Byron returned with the unopened letter. He handed it to Margaret. She declined. "It's your letter, Byron. It is addressed to you and Helen. Please read it—thank you."

Byron sat on the leather ottoman next to his father and opened the envelope. He removed the letter and turned it right side up.

August 17, 1915 Glasgow

My Dearest Aunt Helen and Uncle Byron,

I don't know how the postal system is working but Father said that he will find a way to get the letters to you if I write them. I wrote to Aunt Margaret and Uncle William about the last day on the Lusitania. It was very hard for me to do but I know that you wanted to know what happened.

One night, Mother and I were talking about our family with a woman. When I called you my Aunt Helen, this lady, I think her name was Laura Casson, said that we were not really related to each other. You are married to Byron, who is the brother of my Uncle William's wife. So she told me that you are not really an aunt. It was confusing. I told her that you would always be my aunt and uncle, no matter what anyone says. Mother was upset because she thought that I spoke rudely. I didn't mean to of course, but it did bother me that someone would say this about us.

Thank you for sending me the story Uncle Byron wrote about the audio laboratory at Tufts College. I know how Aunt Margaret and you were so looking forward to that wireless transmission of music in June. I am glad it was successful. There is a man here who also does those experiments with wireless transmissions. I forget his name, but you had asked Mother to try to find him. She was looking forward to taking me along, even though she laughed about these experiments. Mother had no idea what they are about. It seems so trivial now; there are so many more important things to do. At least that is the way I feel. I hope you understand.

The doctors and nurses at the hospital across the street work all day and night and there will never be enough of them to take care of all the wounded, of which there is an endless number. The doctors say that they have never seen these kinds of wounds before. The artillery and machine guns are ripping men apart. They say that the new medicines at the Front are keeping more soldiers alive, so many are living in great pain and have lost limbs or their sight. It is really hard to believe their wounds until you see them. It is so difficult to describe. It would make me cry just writing about them. Most are so awful and these young men will have to live with them for the rest of their lives.

The soldiers all thought the war would be exciting and patriotic. Once they arrived at the Front they saw terrible things. Many cry when they talk about it. They all hate the generals who are making the plans. They say that the generals have no idea about what the trenches are like because they never go within miles of them. Some of the generals even say that if they went close to the Front their plans would be affected by seeing their dead and wounded soldiers.

The one they hate the most is a Scottish general, Douglas Haig. His father is the founder of Haig Whiskey, a distillery here in Scotland. Father told me that General Haig went to military schools, as most rich boys do over here. The soldiers in the hospital hate him and the other generals because of the unnecessary loss of life.

Some even say that General Haig ordered his own soldiers to be executed for desertion or treason. He doesn't know how frightened the boys are, being bombarded all day and night in those trenches.

"—And most of those executed soldiers are Irish. The British will find any reason to kill the Irish." Anne O'Reilly stood just outside the sitting room. She looked around the room, settling on Beatrice. "I'm sorry for interrupting, ma'am."

"That's all right, Anne. How do you know about this? Is this common knowledge? Military executions in this day and age. I haven't heard of that!"

"Everyone knows about it, ma'am. At least the Irish know about it. The British are much harder on the Irish than on their own kind. Even when the military doctors say the soldiers are suffering from the shock of the war, the generals have the poor lads executed anyway."

"That's horrible," Margaret said, her voice rising. "Then the British are as indecent as the Germans."

"Indecent? The British? Yes ma'am. They are far worse than indecent—" Anne stopped herself. She knew she could easily overstep the bounds that were very generously set by Mrs. Townsend.

Margaret looked away, stung by the sharp despair in Anne's life. She glanced over to the photograph on the maple armoire of her and Helen, William, and Byron: four faces sticking through holes into the pilgrim jail scene painted onto a pine board. It was just a silly afternoon at the Massachusetts State Fair, she recalled fondly. Now their Sarah was in the midst of a ghastly war fought by young boys the age Byron and William were in the photograph. "Why are we not printing these stories?" She asked her father.

"There is military censorship at the Front. It is difficult to confirm these executions are happening. If it is true—"

"It is true," Dr. Carlson said with his usual authority. "Many British doctors tell the generals that these men suffer from battle fatigue, but the generals do not recognize that as an illness. So the desertion charges stand and the men are executed. They are fighting a modern war with old military theories. These generals are just sons of the rich who had nothing else to do but to become generals."

"And one of the generals is the heir to Haig Whiskey. The whiskey that Joe Finnerty passes around town to get whatever he wants," Margaret said, turning to William. "Do tell Joe Finnerty about General Haig, will you please, William?"

Donald ignored his daughter's indignation. "Please continue reading, Byron." William, relieved to hear the request, turned toward Byron.

Byron found his place in the letter.

These soldiers in the hospital are only a few years older than me. One of them has become a friend of mine. I talk to him every day. His name is Samuel Fredericks, a charming young man of nineteen, from Edinburgh. Tragically he lost his right eye and has trouble breathing owing to inhaling poison gas. There are many soldiers here who can hardly breath anymore. They gasp for air all the time.

The patients are very courageous and they give each other such caring support. It is so very touching to see. Some serve as guides for the blind. Others carry patients who can't walk. It makes me feel very good to be near them. There are many women and girls who help at the hospital and I am making new friends. They tell me a lot about Scotland and ask questions about America.

I regret I must close now. I miss you both and Grandmother Beatrice and Agnes, and Grandfathers Donald and Isaac. I don't know what that lady on the Lusitania would say about who is my grandmother and who isn't. I do know you are my family and I wish I could be with you right now.

So I end this letter with the best of love to both of you and the rest of my beloved family,

Sarah

P.S. I wrote about Suzette. I know that Grandmother Beatrice must be happy to know that she was at my side until Father came. She is living here in Glasgow. Father said he would help me find her.

THE TORPEDO HAD STRUCK between the third and fourth funnels—just one of the hundreds of indelible details of the sinking William had read and reread over the past five months. How deep inside did the torpedo penetrate? Was there really a second explosion? The entire hull must have shook. He often tried to imagine the terror on board. *Damn Teutonic efficiency.*

He sat on the edge of the bed and removed his shoes. He had cradled a cigarette in a notch in the glass ashtray at the side of the bed. He gazed at Margaret at her vanity, brushing out her deep red hair. *So sexy.* Her long legs crossed at the ankles, curled around the backless upholstered seat. Her white fluffy nightgown had ridden up her thigh.

"Something I can do for you, Mr. Morrison?" Margaret asked, looking flirtatiously at him in the mirror. She nodded toward the cigarette. William picked up the ashtray and carried it to her. He handed the cigarette to her over her shoulder, pressing his groin into her back.

"Wouldn't you imagine that your belt is a bit harsh on my back? Please do me the favor of removing it before proceeding."

He leaned down, embracing her from behind. She smiled. "What exactly do you have in mind? Spell it out, big boy. I'm game, as they say."

"I'm sure we can invent something interesting to end this strenuous day."

Margaret murmured her agreement, dragged on the cigarette and handed it back to William. "I thought Helen would bleed to death before she got to the hospital. And those letters! What Sarah has endured in these few months. Those bastard British loaded that ship with munitions. They knew about it all the time. They don't care about civilians any more than the Germans do. And those generals at the Front. They all still rich boys from private schools sending young men off to—to what?"

"I thought you believed in the British? Like your father," William asked, but hoping not to hear more. "They are the good guys against the bad Huns. Isn't that the way it is?"

"They're all bastards." She swept her hair back over her shoulder. "What were we talking about before, dear?"

"Wanton sex at the end of an exhausting day?" William moved his hand inside the frilly trim of her nightgown, sliding a finger over an erect nipple on route to the moistened center of the V formed by her legs, now separated ever so slightly.

"I thought we were talking about getting that troublesome belt out of the way and you out of your clothes."

12

MARCH 30, 1916

THE SALISBURY HOTEL

NEW YORK. N.Y.

"PANCHO VILLA? BYRON IS in Mexico? Who is he working for? Donald, I know you can't afford to send a correspondent for a chase through the desert!" an incredulous George Creel asked while motioning to the waiter. Donald Townsend acknowledged Creel's questions with a resigned nod.

"I introduced him to the wire service people a few months ago," Vincent Chelios said. "He was determined to go to France. I didn't know he went to Mexico."

Vincent watched a couple, arms locked, their bodies tilting into the wind, hurrying past the restaurant's large, scalloped window opening onto 45th Street. They lurched through the late winter dump of snow, and then disappeared past the window frame.

Donald Townsend swirled the drink in his hand. "My son is a damn fool. Why the hell does he need to be looking under rocks, or who knows where, for a small-time bandit like Villa? His lovely wife had a miscarriage six months ago and he leaves town. She almost died. Thank God she recovered well."

"Have you heard from Byron yet?" Creel inquired. "There are dozens of correspondents down there already. Probably more reporters than soldiers in Pershing's army."

Vincent laughed. "Or in Villa's army. Or whatever it is called."

"*Villistas*—that's what his men and supporters are called." Donald said, shaking his head in disbelief that they were even discussing Pancho Villa. "Byron used the term in a letter he sent from Columbus, New Mexico—that's the town Villa torched." He leaned back to repeat his order to the waiter, and then continued. "We haven't heard from Byron since Pershing crossed the border into Mexico. Frankly, Vincent, it's just a wild goose chase you Hearst people are inciting."

Donald had published his opinion the week before—the search for Pancho Villa only predisposes the public for grander wars. Unfortunately, the Brits had already generated enough propaganda intended to eventually entice American boys to the Western Front.

"Mr. Hearst thinks it's a matter of honor that we retaliate for Villa's border attacks," Vincent said, embracing the company line.

"What kind of honor is it chasing bandits through a countryside they know like the back of their hand?" Donald stirred his drink and looked away. He had often thought that the younger reporters, including his own son, had to test their own bravado with other men's asses—they weren't going to be getting shot at, they would be writing the stories somewhere else. Even those correspondents in Cuba fifteen years ago wrote as if that war was swell. *It wasn't. It was dirty—vile. Created by an earlier generation of newspapermen.*

Vincent did not respond.

Donald smiled, entertaining another thought. "Why doesn't *Hearst* himself put on a uniform if he wants to defend his honor? And tell him to get a uniform for Byron as well? Let both of them knock on doors in a shit-box Mexican town, asking, 'Which way did Pancho go?'"

Creel slapped his hands together and laughed. "Donald, I would pay good money to witness that exhibition."

Donald Townsend had traveled to New York to meet George Creel. Creel had just been appointed public relations advisor to President Woodrow Wilson. Creel came to New York to confer with friendly newspaper publishers and editors from the East Coast—people he could count on, like Donald Townsend. The 1916 presidential campaign would start very soon, and Creel was already building his publicity machine. Nobody in the Democratic Party could help shape public opinion as cleverly as George Creel—Donald Townsend was certain of that. He had seen Creel in action enough times—and there was certainly nothing wrong with having a reliable source this close to the president of the United States.

Donald always admired Creel's steadfast determination, regardless of its focus; only one year before Creel had mesmerized Donald's sophisticated audience, recounting the horrors of child labor in America. Today Creel was just as assuredly building support for Wilson's successful non-intervention policy in Europe. Donald had already detected the emerging campaign theme: *Vote for Wilson: He kept us out of war.* A simple message for America to absorb when they go to vote next November, thought Donald: *Wilson kept us out of war.*

"How is she now?" Vincent asked Donald.

"Who?"

"Helen, Byron's wife. I know it takes time to fully recover. I lost my wife two years ago during childbirth. I know how difficult it must be for Helen."

"I'm sorry, Vincent. I didn't know—Helen is much better these days. Thanks for your concern," Donald said, glad to give an upbeat report about Helen's wellbeing. "Actually, she and Margaret are here in town. They'll be joining us in a few minutes. I am, in a manner, chaperoning them on this trip to New York. They came down to meet a man named Lee DeForest. He invented some of that radio equipment they are using these days. Bulbs or something."

"I remember very well—I intended to meet them at the audio laboratory at Tufts College the day the Lusitania sank." Vincent looked out the window again; a street barren of pedestrians; the only motion, a few swirls of snow stirred by the frosted March wind. "It will always be difficult to forget that day. It would have been anyway, but trying to find out about Louella and Sarah made it an absolute nightmare. I'm sure it was far worse for your family, Donald."

Donald nodded slowly. He had often recounted that long wait for news of Sarah and Louella's fate. It took months before the family could finally accept that Louella had been lost at sea.

Vincent and George Creel looked past Donald.

Donald turned, following their gaze. Margaret and Helen glided over the thick Persian rug toward them. Two waiters chatting at the empty bar casually tracked the women's progress. Donald noticed the man entering the restaurant behind them, ogling the duo from head to toe.

They stood up as the women reached their table. "You remember George Creel and Vincent Chelios, don't you, Margaret?" Donald asked. "And this is my daughter-in-law, Helen Townsend." He slid the chairs under Margaret and Helen as they sat down.

The waiter moved toward them. The men sat down.

Margaret indicated to the waiter that she didn't want a drink. "I never had the chance to thank you, Vincent, for your help during that frightful weekend," she said. "You could imagine how desperate we were to find out about Louella and Sarah. Every second seemed like an hour."

"Oh, you are the gentleman from Hearst that Byron and Margaret met at Mr. Townsend's reception for Mr. Creel. That was the night before—" said Helen with sudden recognition; it was still so difficult to speak about the day they learned of the *Lusitania's* sinking. "I also want to thank you for your help."

"I only wish I could have altered the results," Vincent said wistfully.

"Unfortunately, or perhaps fortunately, we are not given that power, Mr. Chelios. It is not ours to have," Helen said with certainty. "And Mr. Creel, by the way"—she turned toward him—"my parents were very excited when I mentioned that you are an associate of my in-laws. I'm from Denver, and they have read your columns in the *Rocky Mountain News* for years. They will be thrilled to know that I met you in person. My mother particularly."

Creel nodded graciously, acknowledging the compliment. "Well, at least I hope she will vote for Wilson in November. And if she votes against him, I hope she only votes once."

Helen smiled. "I'll be certain to tell her. Both of my parents are Wilson Democrats—and they will be, as long as he keeps us out of war. I think everyone out West wants us to stay out of Europe. I'm glad that my mother can vote. It's hard to believe these Eastern states still do not allow women to vote."

"You're right, Helen," Vincent said quickly. "The further from the East Coast one goes, the less eagerness there is for intervention. In San Francisco, all the talk now is of an invasion by the Japanese—they have no interest in Europe at all."

"Margaret, your father tells me you are convinced that radio will be the newspaper of the future," Creel said, ever the journalist seeking the heart of a story. "I understand your enthusiasm. I suppose it's a valid idea, in theory, but it strikes me as something out of one of those futuristic novels by Mr. Wells or Mr. Verne. But how it actually gets heard is something that is, perhaps, beyond me."

"Every month more groups just like ours are sending out wireless audio transmission—a little stronger signal each time," Margaret said, proud of the progress that had been made. "I am speaking about the human voice, not Morse code—and this is only the beginning. "

Helen's ardor for the subject was no less than her friend's. "Mr. Creel, can you imagine someone sitting at a microphone, sending out the president's ideas to people listening in their living rooms? Wouldn't that be dramatic? News would arrive instantly—without cables."

Margaret continued. "Most people don't understand that this is *not* a wireless telephone; a telephone call is from me to you. With radio, hundreds of people, maybe more, can hear it. Anyone with a receiver. Just a box with a speaker and a vacuum tube that allows for the signal to be received."

Margaret had never seen Creel in daylight before. A white curtain strung across the bottom half of the window bisected him with a softer light. A softer light that did not diminish the ruggedness etched across his face. Ruggedness honed, she was certain, by years of battles with government officials in whatever city he prowled for news. There was something athletic about him. More like a boxer than the Gypsy violinist he reminded her of when she last saw him at her father's reception—when she first met this Vincent Chelios.

"But Margaret, what if everybody was sending out messages on these transmitters? Wouldn't you hear all of them at the same time?" Creel asked.

"No, Mr. Creel, you wouldn't. There are assigned frequencies. The government calls us 1XE for example—that's our station designation. Every station sends out a signal in one range, we call it frequency, so that it doesn't interfere with anyone else. The listener can turn a knob and hear another station. Another frequency. We call that tuning. It's simple."

"Not that simple if you are used to the printed word for your whole life," Creel said. "I've heard about you radio enthusiasts before. You're a single-minded bunch. Driven." He smiled and added good-naturedly, "Hell-bent on foisting this new technology on an unwitting, and maybe unwilling, public."

"—You're darn right!" Helen interrupted, unable to hide her passion despite her light tone. "Lee DeForest invited us to visit the radio laboratory he's building in Highbridge, wherever that is."

"It's in the Bronx," Vincent said. "I covered a grisly crime there several months ago—I'll spare everyone the details."

Margaret filled in the next day's schedule. "We're going to meet him tomorrow morning if the weather allows. His ex-wife, Nora Blatch, told us about wireless audio a few years ago. We became involved because of her."

"Nora Stanton Blatch? Isn't she part of the suffragette movement?" Vincent asked. "We did a story on her a while ago. Her grandmother spoke to Congress around the time of the Civil War. There are a few generations of Stanton suffragettes."

Margaret would not have recognized Vincent if her father didn't just reintroduce them to each other. He was different than the contentious man she had met at George Creel's reception in Boston. Now he was a delightful luncheon companion. But then again, so much had happened since then. We have all changed since then, she thought.

She noticed his pad and pen sitting neatly on the table; no stray pages poking out, like her brother or the other reporters she knew at the *Boston Examiner*. A deliberate man. And handsome. *A very strong profile. It would be interesting to draw his face. Perhaps with charcoal.*

"Would Mr. DeForest mind if I joined you tomorrow?" Vincent asked, glancing from Margaret to Helen and then back again to Margaret. "I did plan to go to your laboratory that day. I would very much like to see how radio works—"

"Actually, I would appreciate it if you did go, Vincent—if you don't mind me sticking my nose in your business," Creel interrupted. "I don't feel comfortable with these two young ladies being by themselves in this city. And Highbridge is well off the beaten path."

"The Bronx is quite off the beaten path—but I'll be happy to brave the trip once again." Vincent raised his wine glass and raised it toward Margaret and Helen.

"There is a subway line that goes almost to Mr. DeForest's door," Margaret said. "We thought that might be an adventure for us."

"Although, like George, I'm also not thrilled about two young ladies going unaccompanied, even if it does seem to be a straight forward trip nowadays—if the weather permits. There's a very efficient subway system in this city now." Donald had done a hurried investigation. "From what I understand there is a station close to this DeForest fellow. At 149th Street and the Grand Concourse. Wherever that is?"

"It's called the Mott Avenue Station, and it's supposed to have beautiful tile mosaics on the walls," Helen said enthusiastically. "They say a lot of the stations have these mosaics. Mr. DeForest will have someone meet us there who will drive us directly to his radio laboratory."

"A modern underground mass transit system. It's very impressive," Vincent added. "I know it's there—right beneath us. I just haven't used it yet."

Margaret feigned a stern reprimand. "Vincent, shall I remind you that Boston had a subway system before New York?"

"Margaret, I don't plan to challenge you ever again." Vincent shrugged his surrender to that intention. "I do hope it's all right if I join you tomorrow."

"I'm certain Mr. DeForest wouldn't mind, especially since you're a newspaperman," Helen said. "He seems to be quite publicity minded.

I'll give him a ring."

"That would be excellent," Creel said lightly, bringing the arrangements to a close. "Then Donald and I—we *old folk*, as it were—can have breakfast tomorrow, and maybe lunch, and I can fill him in on the latest White House gossip."

13

MARCH 21, 1916

DEFOREST EXPERIMENTAL LABORATORY

BRONX, N.Y.

MARGARET AND HELEN SCRUTINIZED the MOTT AVENUE sign with the same deliberation they often examined a newly acquired work in the Boston Museum. Passengers hurrying along the platform glanced curiously at them without breaking stride. How peculiar such concentrated interest in a subway station sign must have seemed to them.

The signs were just above eye level so even the shortest person on a crowded train could easily read them as it pulled into the station. To Margaret and Helen these signs, equally spaced throughout the station, were artistic gems. In each one, the name of the station was spelled out in white tiles set into a rectangular box of green tiles. Ochre and beige tiles framed the border of that box. All of the tiles were so small, each one only slightly larger than a thumbnail—thousands glittering on each wall of the station.

"Incredible workmanship," Helen said, stepping back from the sign and taking in the bursts of mosaic curlicues and precise brick covering the platform walls on both sides of the tracks that emerged from one darkened tunnel and then disappeared into the black at the other end of the station.

Vincent Chelios gazed around the station, now empty of passengers. "I wonder when they built this. It's so bright and shiny."

Helen stepped closer to the track and peered into the darkness toward the next station, its lights just barely visible at the far end of the tunnel. "I think this was opened in 1904 about when Mr. DeForest invented the first Audion tube. I remember reading about both the subway and Mr. DeForest in one of those scientific magazines. Eight thousand men cut through the rock beneath this city to build all of these train lines."

"It's so exciting to see such artistic craftsmanship in a subway station," Margaret said, stepping forward toward the wall and then backing up again in careful appraisal.

It was the last exciting diversion they would experience on the way to DeForest's radio laboratory.

THE BRONX'S DRABNESS WAS in sharp counterpoint to the gentility of the mid-town Manhattan of the previous afternoon. The two boroughs could have been oceans apart instead of just a sliver of separation enforced by the Harlem River.

Tangles of electric and telephone cables held aloft by often less than fully erect wooden poles coursed through the Bronx streets in every direction. Tenements, some crowded together and others isolated by vacant lots, appeared hastily constructed with little attention to the comfort of the families crammed inside.

Narrow loading docks, designed decades earlier for horse drawn lorries, opened into dimly lit factories. Rolled-down awnings protected the practical offerings of dry goods, produce, and tools in front of the small shops lining the streets. Margaret and Helen were now a world away from the elegant storefronts they had hurried past the day before.

A thin layer of ice and snow, and the frigid March wind, accented the blandness of these surroundings as they drove toward DeForest's laboratory. But even on a pleasant spring afternoon this would not be a neighborhood that either Helen or Margaret would find conducive to a leisurely window-shopping stroll.

LEE DEFOREST GESTURED THEM up the narrow wooden staircase of a bleak three-story brownstone building, set on a street lined with similarly characterless structures. He followed behind Vincent. "I'm glad these two lovely ladies have you to protect them in this rat-infested city—the four-legged and the two-legged kind," he said.

"Thanks for your vote of confidence, and for letting me tag along, Mr. DeForest—although I'm not sure how much good of a bodyguard I'd be in a pinch," Vincent replied congenially. "As a newspaperman, I'm curious about this new technology, but I'm not sure I understand even the basic principles."

"Most of us don't understand the *principles*, Vincent," Lee said evenly as if it was an obvious truth. He pulled open a door at the top of the staircase leading into a high ceiling room with rough brick walls and three windows facing into apartments in the building across a narrow alleyway. "We make up *the principles* as we go along—that's why we sue each other so much."

Helen judged that Lee Deforest was used to, or maybe he demanded, being central to every conversation. His presence was the opposite of Harold Power, the other giant figure to Helen in the world of wireless audio. Power spoke quietly to his colleagues—even deferentially. He never gave a hint of sexuality and kept carefully wrapped his life away from the audio laboratory, if he even had one.

Lee DeForest's life, however, had long been open to rumor and speculation. Everyone in the radio community followed with fascination his turbulent relationships with women. His firm handshake was that of a solid workingman rather than of a scientist. He likes women and he could be a dandy, thought Helen. *Yes, his manliness and sharp intellect would be attractive to women. His reputation as a womanizer is probably justified.*

DeForest led them into a conference area partitioned from the loft by low, roughly fashioned bookshelves. "Sometimes, Vincent, our task is made even more difficult by the quacks out there. I just read a story, claiming that mine blasts and ships sinking in the Atlantic can be traced to radio waves. It's complete nonsense of course, but the public believes these stories—and that one was in a technical magazine, no less."

He motioned for Helen and Margaret to sit on one of the two identically faded floral print sofas facing each other.

Pyramids of boxes against the walls and rolls of wires on the unfinished wooden floor suggested to Helen that DeForest was focusing on still another leap forward in his life's work. Nora Blatch had described her years with DeForest, as "an unglamorous subsistence in a sea of boxes and crates." That much had not changed. Nor had his brilliance and personal daring diminished. Mail fraud charges, patent wars, and shabby stock promotions still swirled around him. He fled California, leaving a trail of bitter lovers and business partners, yet he still maintained a loyal following in the ever-quarreling world of radio.

"Helen, what is your view of the future of radio?" Lee asked. A simple question that took Helen by surprise.

She wondered if he was really interested in her opinion, or whether he was going to switch to a more flirtatious tone. It had happened before, an earnest interchange with a man eventually becoming uncomfortable for her.

"Mr. DeForest, as you know better than we do, radiography is changing everyday," Helen replied, her tone carefully calibrated. "Just a year ago Margaret and I saw one of the new vacuum tubes for the first time—" she paused recalling the excitement of that moment "—and that one is now no longer *new*." She pointed at half-opened boxes on the floor. "These tubes are far more evolved—I heard. Soon anyone can set up a transmitter or build a receiver. That's what we have been doing at Tufts. Do I sound like I am making a speech?"

"Too bad I missed your station's broadcast, Helen," DeForest said earnestly. "Three hours of music. That's terrific. I hear that it was as clear as a bell. Well done."

"Thank you. We are very happy with the results," Helen said. Margaret agreed.

Vincent picked up the tube that DeForest had put down on the table in front of him. There was little inside the glass that would ever make sense to him at anytime—but now his thoughts had wandered elsewhere.

He had always been told that giving the speaker one's undivided attention was just plain courtesy. Now it also gave him an opportunity to examine Helen's features—her cheeks looked still flushed from the Harlem River winds. He urged himself not to stare too long into those aqua eyes.

Vincent had noticed Helen immediately when she entered the restaurant with Margaret the day before. She had a simplicity still untarnished by East Coast society—more like San Francisco than Boston.

Lee interrupted Vincent's contemplation. "We hope, within a few months, to broadcast from this studio every night. We'll read the news and play music. The number of people buying receivers is increasing every month. It's quite an affirmation of our work. All of our efforts." He scrutinized two workers at the other end of the room, kneeling over a low bench, soldering components together. "It's going to be exciting around here soon."

"Mr. DeForest, I have no idea what you are talking about." Vincent shrugged his shoulders and smiled. "Could you explain it perhaps in layman's terms—please?"

Lee nodded, removing another bulb from a layer of tissue paper. "I'll give you my two minute lecture." Vincent waved his hand slightly, motioning DeForest to continue.

"This vacuum tube fulfills several functions that are necessary for voice or music, *any audio*, to be carried in the air without wires. And then to be heard clearly on the receiving end.

"We need to make the faint voice signals from a microphone strong enough to be transmitted through an antenna. This tube has these wires and a filament and this little metal grid. You can see it here."

He moved closer to Vincent, pointing to the center of the tube with a pencil.

"The way it is constructed, the faint signal can feed back onto itself until it becomes a strong signal. And so, this tube has the ability to amplify the signal. That is necessary for it to be sent great distances. It can also receive a strong signal and reduce it back to a faint signal so that it can be heard in your home. The same tube, the one trans-mitting, and the other on the receiving end, can now accomplish the most difficult part—managing the strength of the signal on both ends of the transmission. *Extraordinary* when you think about it."

"And it's all in that bottle, so to speak," Vincent said, nodding with appreciation for this deceptively simple principle.

"Exactly—it's all in the bottle," Lee repeated, savoring the clever metaphor.

"How difficult is it to raise money for this?" Vincent asked.

Lee rolled his eyes—so much of his life had been spent in never-ending efforts to finance his work. "In the earlier days, the only way to raise money was to talk about wireless telephone. Point A to Point B. Someone talking to someone else. You can charge a fee to the caller or to the receiver. Investors could understand that. However, the idea of a transmission that could be received by a lot of people has always been, and still is, hard to sell to investors. Why would anyone pay to speak to people they don't even know? Where's the revenue to come from if just anyone with a receiver can listen for free? That's all the money people want to know."

"That I understand easier than the technology—they always want to know that. Where will the revenue come from?" It wasn't Vincent's intention to glance at Helen, but he did. She smiled and looked away.

Lee placed the bulb back into its protective paper wrapping. "Things change every day—just as Helen was saying. It's possible that one day there just may be a receiver in everyone's sitting room. With enough people listening someone may want to pay for publicity. I can see a company like A&P may one day want to announce a sale in all of their stores. They have over six hundred already. Or maybe they would want to announce the location of a new store opening. And Woolworth's? They built that skyscraper a few years ago in New York, and they open new stores all the time. Instead of just newspapers, maybe one day they might want to use radio for advertisements too?"

"Perhaps," Vincent said thoughtfully. "But there also seems to be a potential for someone to send out wrong information to a lot of people."

DeForest smiled—he had heard that cautionary note before. "That's the same problem you newspaper people have, isn't it, Vincent? I can tell you firsthand how many stories you reporters get wrong about me and what we are doing—"

A worker called from the next room. DeForest excused himself.

Vincent turned to Margaret and Helen. "I don't mean to change the subject, radio transmissions are very interesting—but we are also, after all, speaking about publicity. I want you to know that I'll be working on the Wilson campaign. I finalized my role with George Creel just last week. There'll be a need for many creative services—photography, illustrators, and designers. You are both enormously talented people. Creel and I talked yesterday about the possibility of both of you working with us."

"Thank you, Vincent, but I have too many commitments at the newspaper—and the radio station." Margaret responded first. "Is the work in Boston?"

"Yes. We are opening a bigger office there—even though the newspapers say that Wilson can't win in the Northeast. Maybe, Margaret, that's just an example of the erroneous newspaper information Mr. DeForest was talking about. By the way, we are not asking you to join us as volunteers, but rather as staff."

"It sounds exciting, Vincent, but our newspaper has always had a larger circulation and more advertisement work in presidential election years. I couldn't even consider leaving right now."

Vincent nodded his understanding, and looked at Helen for her response.

"I'll ask my husband whenever he returns from Mexico."

14

JUNE 13, 1916

GLENFIDDICH INN

NEW BEDFORD, MASS.

"CAN'T YOU LIFT IT, you candy ass?" William taunted Gunther Stitler.

Many years before, Isaac had gone to visit his friend Hans Stitler at his butcher shop. Young William went along with him. Gunther had been on the street with a bucket of soapy water cleaning the front window. He asked William who would be pitching for the Red Sox that afternoon. They became close friends that same day.

The two young boys shared great adventures exploring the inn—its quiet, dark corners that sometimes sheltered William from the loss of his parents when that understanding became too powerful. His older sister Louella had mothered and protected him but it was Gunther, his own age, who gave him a confidant every child, especially one lost in tragedy, needed.

"Me a candy ass, William? You're the one who has become soft, sitting in a bank all day!" Gunther said, shaking his head, pretending disappointment. "I'd be better off picking these motors up by myself. But I don't want to embarrass you in front of your family."

William dismissed Gunther with a slight wave of his hand.

They synchronized their movements, together lifting the largest rusted motor onto Gunther's empty meat truck and coaxed it forward toward the back of the cab. Gunther jumped into the truck, securing the motor with a frayed rope to the metal rings embedded on the truck's inner walls. Then they turned towards the inn to collect the rest of the cargo.

Isaac stood to the side of the truck, watching. "Lucky for me you are here, William. Otherwise young Gunther would have me lifting with him."

"No, Mr. Morrison," Gunther said, a smile rippling across his face. "Not you or my father. Those days are over. I knew William would be here. Besides wanting to see this goon, I thought that he might still have a strong back. I think I may have been wrong."

Isaac laughed, appreciative of Gunther's joking. He had worried about William's solitude when he and Louella first came to live at the inn. Isaac was relieved and grateful when Gunther came into his dear William's life.

William looked past the rose garden, now thriving in the New England summer. It was Aunt Agnes's private domain. Each summer she finessed perfect roses out of each bush. The younger William found it curious that his aunt had a name for each variety of rose. He once asked her why they all needed distinct names. She had an explanation of some sort. It just didn't make sense at the time.

The rose bushes partially concealed the three women on the porch. Margaret, Helen, and Agnes chatted, positioned around a small table shaded from the sunny summer afternoon. William recalled painting the white latticework above the porch many times—with varying success.

Luckily for Helen, she has us as family while Byron stumbles around in Mexico, thought William. Six months and still gone. At least Margaret knew he wouldn't do such a foolish thing. *But she could still break my balls about Joe Finnerty*—he caught her glance and smiled.

"Now don't work yourself into a horrid sweat, William," Margaret called out. He started walking alongside the porch, the carpet of wooden chips on the narrow path faintly grinding with each step. He wiped at his brow, feigning exhaustion.

Agnes touched her hand to Helen's forearm. "I'm glad you could join us today, Helen. It is such a beautiful afternoon. I just love these summer days. Perhaps we can put this tea to the side, and instead, I find a nice bottle of wine in the restaurant?"

"Yes, thank you, wine would be perfect," Helen responded quickly.

"A wonderful idea, Aunt Agnes," Margaret agreed. "Whatever you select will be delightful."

Agnes took Helen's hand in hers. "I do want you to know that you are welcome to stay here as long as you like, Helen—with Byron gone, you must be lonely at times."

"Thank you, Aunt Agnes, having everyone near me has been a wonderful comfort. Byron thinks this assignment will help his career. I'm just glad he will be coming home next month. From what I've read, we're not coming close to getting Pancho Villa anyway." Helen covered her mouth to hide a small laugh. "It seems so comical, doesn't it?"

Margaret, not as amused as Helen, grumbled with frustration. "All this attention over Mexico—and a small-time bandit. They haven't even seen this Villa bastard—not even once."

Agnes gasped. "Margaret, your language!"

"Sorry, Auntie. All they're doing is testing new weapons in that desert. Every saloon in Mexico is making money and the Army even brought along its own brothel to service the soldiers while they are out looking for these bandits."

"What? A *brothel*? And the army pays for it? " Agnes shook her head, shocked by the image of a brothel traveling through the Mexican desert—although the bawdy notion also amused her.

Margaret gazed at Isaac standing beside the truck. "All this Expedition, as they call it, does is to make war look like an adventure," she declared. "I hope people are reading the news from France. The British and French are still getting killed by the thousands every day. The Germans too, probably. What's the point?"

"Well, maybe this will quell Byron's burning desire to be a war correspondent in Europe," Helen said, leaning over to smell one of the roses cascading over the porch rail. "Maybe he can work it out of his system. At least if he won't come back for me, there is always the Red Sox." She managed another small laugh. "William says it's a certainty they'll be in the World Series again."

"Who gives a damn about a World Series? He should be with *you!*" Agnes said, more assertively than the two younger women would have expected. She saw their surprise and giggled. " Helen, why don't you read Byron's letter? Only the parts that won't embarrass you."

Helen smiled. "It's really not that steamy, Aunt Agnes."

Agnes had another thought. "I think I should get the wine before you start, darling." She rose, following the path curving to the back entrance of the inn. She stopped to tend to a rose bush, removing whatever detritus could be whisked off with bare hands. Then she continued on her mission.

"Honestly, Helen, I'm glad that you will be working with Creel and Vincent," Margaret said. "It will give you something to be involved in, besides waiting for another letter from Byron or wondering how his career will proceed. It sounds so exciting. I hope Wilson can keep us out of Europe—I know he wants to. If you're going to work for him please be so kind as to make certain he doesn't change his mind."

"I don't know how convincing I am these days," Helen said with a sigh. "I can't even keep my husband in town. By the way, I spoke to Vincent a few times. There are other women working for the campaign. So it won't be one of those horrible situations being the only woman. The men even support the suffragettes. Creel, Vincent, the others. So very enlightened isn't it?"

"Perhaps we should toast them—these *modern* men," Margaret suggested as Agnes stepped onto the porch with a bottle and three wine glasses.

"Well done, Aunt Agnes." Helen reached out for a glass. "Where are William and Gunther taking those—what are they exactly?"

"Motors—I think," Margaret guessed.

"No. Not just motors, dear. Old, rusted, *useless* motors. Of all sizes." Agnes pulled a shiny corkscrew from her apron pouch. "That's what they are. Junk, if you ask me."

She twisted into the cork. "This is a bottle we wanted to open for our only two guests coming this week. They cancelled. I wonder if visitors are going to be afraid to come to the ocean this summer because of all the talk about preparing for a German invasion."

"I don't think an invasion is likely." Margaret had discussed this at the newspaper many times. "But there are a lot of people campaigning for us to build up the military and guard the beaches. It's foolish and just puts us in a war mentality."

"Aunt Agnes, what were you saying about William and Isaac and those rusted motors?" Helen asked.

Agnes, focused on filling the glasses to their brims, didn't answer. She looked at the now almost drained bottle. "Well, I can always get another one if we want."

Helen and Margaret picked up their glasses to toast their hostess.

"Oh yes, Helen, sorry, you asked about those motors. Isaac had—who knows how many motors stored away for years. Some since William was a young boy. They're taking them to Hans's shop. Hans and

Gunther are building some kind of refrigeration units, perhaps for trucks. I'm not sure. Good riddance, if you ask me. Did you have a letter to read, dear?"

Helen had already taken the letter out of her shoulder bag and began reading it to the two attentive women:

May 20, 1916

My dearest Helen,

You know how much I miss you. I think of you every day and hope that this letter finds you in good spirits.

It is very exciting to see my bylines as a war correspondent and not just as a sports writer. Many of the soldiers and other writers here are avid baseball fans and are impressed that I write about the Boston Red Sox, and that I was at the World Series last year.

As you know, I will be back in July, regardless of the outcome of this so-called Expedition. I am sure that you read some of my dispatches, as Mother promised to collect them when they appear in other newspapers. Even at a baseball game I endeavor to embrace the ideals of the fourth estate, hence I refrain from editorializing in those stories. I have the good fortune to not be so constrained now, and so I can tell you about the real situation, at least as I see it.

When I arrived in Columbus, New Mexico, there were still a few buildings smoldering. Pancho Villa and his men did a thorough job of destroying the small town that morning in March. The people I talked to the day I arrived there told me they are still disgusted by the U.S. military.

The night before the attack on the town, Pancho Villa surprised the nearby Army barracks. The townspeople are livid because many of the soldiers in the barracks were drunk when Villa attacked and they couldn't even fight back, let alone offer a defense of this town the next morning when Villa rampaged through it.

They also discovered that Villa buys his weapons in the United States with money he gets from the American mining companies in the northern part of Mexico. The owners pay him good old Yankee greenbacks to leave their mines alone.

I'm sure that you read that Villa attacked these border towns because he is angry with the U.S. government for betraying him. However, so little seems to be written about how popular Villa is here in Mexico. You would never believe it!

The Mexicans tell Villa everything he needs to know about us. I'm sure he even knows what we eat for breakfast every morning. There is not a single Mexican who would not betray us to him. That is not the most comfortable thought. I'm sure I would do the same in Boston if foreigners invaded us.

Some of the correspondents laugh openly at the folly of this Expedition. These mountains and deserts are perfect for this cunning Villa to hide in. We have no idea where he has gone, and you can be sure that the Mexicans would be lying to us if we ask them to even point us in his direction.

The American soldiers are justifiably frustrated because of a rule that they cannot defend themselves against the Mexican soldiers who sometimes shoot at them. That is the only way the government down here would let our troops into the country, even though we are supposed to be looking for their enemy also. We have more to fear from the Mexican soldiers than we do from Villa.

On a more humorous note, last week I lost my footing and tumbled down a rocky hill. I couldn't stop my fall. The binoculars around my neck, the ones William gave me, bounced off the ground a few times and hit my face. I think my cuts and bruises are probably worse than any of our soldiers have received since we arrived in Mexico. I wonder with some amusement if I might even emerge from this trip as the only decorated member of this Expedition.

I wanted to see if the binoculars were damaged so I focused them on a nearby ridge. Two of Villa's men pointed at me and laughed. They must have seen me roll down the hill. One of them turned around and lowered his pants. Then he bent over and shook his bare buttocks at me.

Everybody here believes that the only reason for this Expedition is to make our president look good. Wilson is trying to appear to be strong by invading Mexico. If he doesn't do something, Congress will declare war on Mexico—then he would be in a bad spot if he had to join the war in Europe. That would be two wars more than he, or any of us, needs, in my humble opinion.

I will tell you more when I see you soon. I love you very much.

Your loving husband,

Byron

On the trail of Pancho Villa with General Pershing's Expedition

"He went all the way to Mexico to see a few Mexican asses—and men's asses, no less," Agnes said, holding her hand to her mouth, giggling.

"I think the old gal had one too many," Helen suggested wryly.

"That does appear to be the case," Margaret said, delighted to see both Helen and Aunt Agnes enjoying themselves, despite the burdens of the past too many months.

15

JUNE 29, 1916

THE COLUMBIA TRUST BANK OF MASSACHUSETTS

BOSTON, MASS.

"THERE IS A GOD AFTER all, William. My sainted mother was right." Joe Finnerty's long fingers curled around the cigar he had just lit. "Sometimes when you think a golden opportunity has wiggled out of your hands, you find it right back in your lap—and even more seductive than before."

He motioned William towards the chair next to his oval walnut desk, its thick beveled glass top covered with neatly stacked documents.

Yes, there is a God, thought William. *And yes, Joe Finnerty, you are an asshole. Pompous at times. Gloating at other times. But most often an asshole.*

William settled into the designated seat. He looked at the family portrait on the mantel over Finnerty's shoulder. Joe, his wife Rose, and their little daughter Clarisse. William guessed she must now be three and a half years old. She was smiling shyly into the camera, her thick dark hair pulled into a neat bun. William had witnessed how much effort Joe put into being the respectable family man, and he did really adore that little girl. Nonetheless, he would also have sex with anyone he considered a worthy conquest. *And that would include almost any woman.*

Nothing thrilled Joe more than the action from his deals and double deals. William had long ago observed that Finnerty would rather make a buck under the table than ten dollars legitimately—a difficult affliction for William to understand, but he did allow that it might be more prevalent in the business world than he had once thought possible.

"You remember at Fenway Park last September, we talked about a copper company?" Finnerty looked at William triumphantly.

William had seen this glow before.

"Listen to this yarn, William. There's a moral to this story—a delightful moral. A profitable one." Finnerty tilted his head towards the ceiling, exhaling a trail of white smoke.

"Last year Samuel Harris, his wife, and son Hiram are on a train returning home to Springfield from out West somewhere, I forget where. Anyway they meet an old friend of mine, Benjamin Wilkinson, on the same train. Benjamin and old Sam Harris start talking. Harris tells Benjamin that he's interested in selling his company. He manufactures industrial copper fixtures —whatever the hell they are.

"Benjamin listens to old man Harris's whole life story. They have drinks for the rest of the trip. They become friendly. It seems Harris also has a craving for speculating in the stock market. He confides to Benjamin that he doesn't want his wife to know he has run into a little financial trouble. He has a great business, just a cash flow problem. He thinks it might be a good time to sell if the price is right.

"Benjamin tells the old man that he works with some big investors, and maybe he can arrange for them to buy the company. Benjamin would get himself a finder's fee from the investors. Harris is fine with that. So Benjamin invites Sam Harris to come down to New York to talk to the investors.

"Sure enough, Harris goes to New York. He's having lunch with Benjamin when another man comes into the restaurant. He sits down near them, orders lunch, and starts to look through a pile of telegrams. Benjamin recognizes him. His name is Andrew Smithers, a retired judge from Youngstown, Ohio, Benjamin's hometown. Benjamin goes over and introduces himself. Judge Smithers vaguely remembers Benjamin's late father, a lawyer, who appeared in his courtroom a few times. Benjamin invites the judge to join him and Harris for lunch.

"Judge Smithers tells them that he's now working for a group of big stock brokerage companies. They want to bury some of the smaller shops around town by manipulating stock trades. If they can bust the prices of the stocks the small brokers are holding, the judge says, they could ruin them and get them out of the business.

"So Benjamin asks Judge Smithers for a stock tip, let's say for old time's sake. Judge Smithers takes a hundred smackers from Benjamin, but old Harris isn't interested. So the judge leaves with just Benjamin's money. Benjamin and Harris have to wait a day or two anyway because one of the investors Benjamin lined up to buy the copper business was sick and the other had a family problem somewhere.

"Anyway, the judge meets them in the hotel the next day and gives Benjamin two hundred and twenty five dollars, a nice piece of change for his hundred bucks. Harris sees the quick money and now he wants in, so he and Benjamin give Judge Smithers a few hundred bucks. The next day the judge lays out a nice profit for both of them.

"Harris forgets about the sale of his copper company and arranges to stay in New York for a few days more." Finnerty paused, then rocked back comfortably in his chair, his fingers entwined behind his neck. "Well, you know where this tale is going, don't you, William?"

"As you're the one telling the story, Joe, I assume someone is going to get robbed."

Finnerty laughed. "I know there's a compliment somewhere in your crude deduction. Anyway, so Judge Smithers suddenly has to go out of town. But Benjamin and Harris like the payoffs. So the judge takes them over to the brokerage office and introduces them so the office people will know them. Then he can call Benjamin and this Harris fellow with the tips and they will give him a piece of the action when he gets back to New York. But they can't tell anyone—not even a word. He will only let them in on the deal because he knew Benjamin's late father. Both Benjamin and Harris love the arrangement."

William interrupted. "I have a question, Joe—can I assume the old judge and your friend Benjamin are not who they appear to be?"

"Indeed, William. Benjamin Wilkinson is really Two Ton Ben, a name he couldn't shake as easy as the baby fat he once had. He is without doubt one of the greatest con men I know. The judge is a great thief himself. The two of them have been working this con for a couple of years."

William motioned, urging Finnerty to continue. *Any scam would delight Joe.*

"The brokerage office was all a setup, of course—the young guy on a scaffold writing price quotes on a blackboard—the men on phones— and a lot of cash changing hands. I must tell you, William, with some pride, that I was part of the theater that day. I was in town visiting my infirmed sister Kathleen and Benjamin told me what was going on. So I stopped by and played the part of a prosperous trader. They had this Harris fellow by the balls. In fact, I even got the going rate of fifty dollars for my stellar performance from Christopher 'Big Red' Johnson, the guy playing the office manager. I put the money in the poor box in the church down the street. No matter what anyone tells you William, it is indeed more blessed to give than to receive. Believe me."

William glanced again at the Finnerty family portrait on the mantel. "How do you even know these grifters?" *What a fraud. Churchgoing. Holding his daughter's hand.*

"It takes all kinds to make this world go 'round, William," Finnerty said, philosophical once again. "Anyway, so old man Harris gets so caught up in this bullshit that he wires back to Scranton for $67,000 to cover a check Big Red, the office manager, said he needed for collateral. Benjamin tells him that he was also putting in $25,000 on deposit. Of course they lose the money because the judge fucked up the trade when he called them from out of town. Or whatever the story was, I don't remember. Anyway, Harris and Benjamin are outraged. Benjamin even tells Harris that if he ever gets his hands on that Judge Smithers, he'll kill him."

Finnerty looked at William to see if he appreciated the con man's indignation.

"But here's where you come in, William—"

"Not in this story, Joe."

"Just listen for a minute. Harris is so sick from his loss that he dies of a heart attack on the train going home. That should be the end of it—but it's not. His wife waiting on the platform sees Harris coming off the train as a corpse. She gets a stroke and dies two days later."

"And I fit in—exactly how?" William couldn't finish this rather plain inquiry without laughing.

Finnerty ignored William's amused intrusion into his tale. "Their son, Hiram, takes over the business and very soon he's looking to sell the copper company. But he doesn't know how to do it. He remembers Benjamin Wilkinson, the man he met on the train. The man his father talked so glowingly about. The same Two Ton Ben who really just swindled his father. Hiram finds Benjamin's number and calls him to see if Ben can help him arrange a sale of the company. Benjamin can't believe his good fortune. All he knows for sure is that the son, Hiram, is as dumb as a tree stump.

"So Two Ton Ben goes to Scranton and talks to Hiram. Hiram wants him to talk to the family lawyer. At this point Benjamin is sure he's out of luck and out of the copper business. He could never bullshit the lawyer, he thinks. But he's up to the challenge. What the hell, he has a reputation to uphold.

"Benjamin goes to see the lawyer. Two minutes into the conversation he sees that all the lawyer is interested in is a piece of the action. The lawyer doesn't give a damn about Hiram. That's when Benjamin calls me into the deal—me being a respectable banker and all that.

"So I meet Benjamin and the lawyer last year. Both of them were at the game at Fenway last year, remember? You met them. The lawyer is the one with the spaces between his teeth. Looks like the goddamn hack saw I have in my woodshed."

"When was the last time you were in a woodshed, Joe?" William was certain that Joe Finnerty never did a real day's work in his life. Unless one was to consider using his father's political influence and limitless bottles of Haig Pinch to worm his way into the bank presidency as honest work. He was nonetheless the youngest bank president in Boston. Twenty-eight—only three years older than Byron and William. *That was some kind of an accomplishment, wasn't it?* William often conceded that it was.

Finnerty relit his cigar. "So then Benjamin and I go with the lawyer to Springfield to meet Hiram. Hiram is sure that his father invested a lot of money in warehouses loaded with copper out west. But the lawyer tells him that old Harris really lost it all in worthless mining stocks. That's believable to Hiram because he knew dear old dad was a degenerate stock speculator. I tell him that I will do a full accounting of the assets. We finally made a deal with Hiram just last week."

Finnerty stopped, and then remembered another facet of the story.

"We still have to do another inventory and make certain we don't get robbed. That would be ironic, wouldn't it? If we get robbed by this Hiram dumb-as-a-tree-stump fellow. I suggested that you would run the company. I can't myself because I need to be at arm's length from this deal. There are regulations we are supposed to adhere to, you understand."

Finnerty paused, self-satisfied once again with his skill as a storyteller. "That's the short version. Grand, isn't it?"

"I don't like it. I like what I'm doing now. The bank is doing great, isn't it?" William had already determined to leave Finnerty—Ralph Ennis had told him that it would take six months at least more to have his new brokerage operational. William was flattered that Ralph had come after him, enticing him with a grand vision of future prospects. Ralph's inclusion of three others from William's Yale baseball team made the offer even more attractive.

"William, I'm really counting on you to handle this operation. I need you in on this one. You could be the head of a big metals corporation if it all goes well. And therein is the moral to this tale."

William opened his hands wide, beckoning Finnerty to elaborate.

"Out of the ashes of an old man's greed and folly arises opportunity for a young man unfettered by such character defects."

"And the process is helped along by a theater of con men." William still couldn't stifle his amusement with Joe's tale.

"Every great change has its own, very unique catalysts." Finnerty swiveled in his chair toward the window, a wordless declaration that the meeting was over.

16

JULY 4, 1916
RADIO STATION 1XE
TUFTS COLLEGE
MEDFORD HILLSIDE, MASS.

JUST THE WEEK BEFORE two ocean steamers had picked up the station's music broadcast at one hundred nautical miles out at sea. Every crewmember on one of the ships stood in line to listen. Harold Power heard about it a few days earlier.

"One hundred miles out at sea! That's certainly enough reason for a Fourth of July party," Power had announced.

A blond-haired boy lifted his friend unto his shoulders, supporting him until he could claw onto the limb of the maple tree next to the entrance to the laboratory. Then the boy on the ground jumped, his fingers and toes no match for the smooth bark, trying to get up onto the limb with his friend. Instead he just slid back to the ground. William concluded that it would be a futile effort.

Margaret sat on the wooden bench next to him, and fussed with William's open shirt collar. "A penny for your thoughts, Mr. Morrison."

"Look at those two boys—one lifts the other onto the limb, never thinking that there wouldn't be anyone around to lift him up."

"Rather profound, William—especially for a Fourth of July celebration."

"Maybe it is a mundane observation. Let me offer you this glass instead." He handed her the draught of beer resting at his side on the weathered oak bench.

"Harold Power thinks we can improve the broadcast range of the antenna," Margaret said, looking straight up to the top of the steel structure.

William didn't follow her gaze. "Actually, I've been thinking about Sarah over there in Scotland. And just having only her father with her. I'd like to be more to her than just a distant uncle. It would be wonderful to get her back here, wouldn't it?"

"I wouldn't say that Gilbert is *all* she has." Margaret leaned her arm over William's knee propped up on the bench. "Sarah seems to be occupied with other people, thank goodness for that. As a husband to Louella, Gilbert may have been a rotten choice, but as a father to Sarah he is admirable."

"I know it's time for me to leave Finnerty."

"That's rather out of the blue, isn't it? Have you thought about it before?"

"The simple answer is that I am more inclined to eventually having my own business. Maybe one that Gilbert can be involved with. Then we could have Sarah close by. I might even throw in soon with Ralph Ennis for starters."

"So you're serious about leaving Finnerty?"

"Of course. Some of his activities approach intolerable—even for me."

"Anything you want to tell me?" Margaret handed him the glass.

"No—nothing particular. The details aren't important." He paused for a moment. "It would take a lot to coax Sarah back here—don't you think?"

Margaret shrugged. "I wouldn't blame her for not wanting to return to the United States. If I had been on the *Lusitania* I probably would never travel on another ocean liner—*not ever again*. Especially with German submarines still in the same ocean. I—"

"—German submarines on a beautiful afternoon. How uplifting." Helen came up behind them. She had let down her hair; the wavy locks swayed off her shoulders with each bouncy step.

Margaret clapped her hands together. "A charmingly theatrical entrance, Helen. We're glad you came. Tell us more about the Wilson campaign."

"Perhaps with a glass of wine I can be coaxed into giving you the inside story of a presidential campaign—the beginnings of one anyway."

"Only beer is being served at this station." William said, handing her the glass.

Helen raised it to her mouth. "I've met wonderful people at headquarters. We're just setting up now. Some of them worked in Wilson's last campaign. They're quite fond of him."

"That, I suppose, is always a plus for the candidate," William said dryly.

"I told one of them that I wasn't sure of my role. He said that is the office joke—the campaign will be over by the time anyone determines what he is supposed to be doing. Actually, everyone is quite competent. They say this will be one of the closest elections in history—regardless of who runs against Wilson. It's exciting. It reminds me of this radio laboratory—everybody moving in the same direction."

Helen motioned for William to refill the glass from the barrel at the side of the bench, mouthing the word 'please.'

"Helen." He motioned her to sit down. "Margaret says you received another letter from Byron. What's the news from the *Mexican Front?*"

Helen and Margaret looked at each other acknowledging the joke—the search for Villa had disintegrated into easy fodder for political cartoonists. Hardly a front, not even an army to engage. Only amused locals.

Helen glanced at the boys around the maple tree. "I didn't bring the letter with me, but I can tell you that it was succinct. 'Helen, I miss you. I will be home soon after you receive this. Everything is wonderful.'" Her eyes glistened.

Margaret leaned across William and ran her fingers gently through Helen's hair. "So, Helen, may I provide a more thorough summary for William's benefit?" Margaret proceeded without waiting for approval. "William, as of right now, the U.S. military is shooting, not at Villa's men, but at the regular Mexican soldiers. They probably can't even tell the difference. Nobody wants us there anyway. Byron said that he witnessed a shootout on a street, who knows where? Between an American soldier and a Mexican soldier. Byron has been spending a lot of time with a very interesting character—what's his name, Helen?"

"Henry Mendes. From El Paso, Texas. According to Byron, he traveled with Pancho Villa for a year or two. Byron said Henry is coming to Boston in the fall to either attend or lecture at Harvard. I don't remember which. Let's show William the new equipment inside."

17

BYRON SIDESTEPPED THE CROWDED bar, his destination was the round table stuck in the far corner of the saloon. He distinguished the silhouettes of his sportswriters' fraternity through the smoky haze.

Henry Mendes followed him.

"Who the hell did you bring back with you, Pancho Villa himself?" Nick Flatley asked, taking a harsh look at Byron's companion.

Henry Mendes's ill-fitting, coarse gray suit marked him as not a Bostonian, nor probably from any big city. His goatee and curled moustache characterized him as perhaps a European, or even worse to these men, an eccentric intellectual.

"So, *you're* Henry? Have a seat. Byron wrote us about you." Nick offered Henry a space at the bench. Then he looked over at Byron. "I know what you're going to ask. What did you miss? How is Ruth doing? Right?"

He held up his hand, stopping Byron from answering. "It doesn't matter what you were going to ask—I have the best baseball story of the year for you, Byron. Listen to this. Last month the Cubs played

Cincinnati and they only used one ball in the whole game. Can you imagine that? One fucking ball. Half of the owners in the league would love to do that every game. Those cheap bastards."

"Who cares about one ball?" Ralph McMillan laughed, thinking of another story to tell Byron. "Byron, you should have been on the last road trip. In Philadelphia some of their players are getting on Ruth." He stopped to pick up the remnants of a roast beef sandwich, biting off a hunk.

"Oh, yeah. I forgot about that," Nick said. "Tell him about that, Ralph. It's a knee-slapper, Byron."

"What the hell do you think I'm doing?" Ralph swallowed quickly so that he could continue the story. "They're calling Ruth that *Tarzan of the Apes* shit they started last year. Some of them are calling him a 'half a nigger.' You know they think his mother's colored. He's getting really angry. So when the game is over, he runs across the field and bursts into the Philadelphia locker room. He grabs one of the guys, the smallest one on the team of course, and starts throwing some of those girlie punches of his. Connie Mack breaks up the fight and Ruth sees all of us standing there, watching. He gets embarrassed and says to the Philly guys, 'I don't mind you calling me names, but leave that nigger crap and my mother out of it.' He sulked out like a big awkward kid. We all laughed like hell."

Ralph pointed to the waiter and motioned for a beer for Henry. "Henry, wait until you see this guy. He hits even better than he pitches."

"Oh yeah, Byron, I think that Lannin wants to sell the Red Sox," Nick said. "After he fought so hard to get control of the team from his partners last winter—now he doesn't know what the hell to do. I think it's too much for him. I bet he gets rid of the team whether they get into the World Series or not."

"So how did Timothy Stevens do covering the games for me?" Byron asked.

"Anyone can do your writing. That evergreen bullshit you turn in. Only a doting father could love it."

Byron waved off Nick's teasing evaluation. "Well, sorry to disappoint you gentlemen. I'll be covering the World Series if we get into it. I also have some feature stories I'm doing. Helen is working for Wilson. I don't see too much of her since I got back. I may write something about Wilson."

"Henry, how did you run into this character? I mean there's a whole desert out there and you find this hack?" Ralph asked.

"A few journalists were in a cantina," Henry responded, though an explanation wasn't really expected. "Byron was telling them about last year's World Series. When I heard he was from Boston I started talking to him. I knew I was coming up here for the year."

"So, Henry, what's it like traveling with Villa?" Nick, as had the other writers, already concluded that the Expedition was nonsense. "Do you think the Germans put him up to the whole thing? I mean it makes sense for them to want him to raid around on our border and keep our minds off Europe."

"The Germans had nothing to do with it. I think Villa is fighting for the people. He wants land for the peasants. Just like they are doing in Russia."

"Now Henry, that's a crock of Bolshevik lies." Nick responded quickly. Everyone laughed, none more heartily than Nick himself. "They're all bandits. And he killed a bunch of Americans. So I hope they string that little Mexican up by his balls. No offense, Henry."

Nick turned to Byron. "So—what now? Are you off to the war in France? In case you haven't heard while you were poking those Mexican girls, Europe is more brutal now than even a year ago."

"I'm thinking of joining the ambulance corps. I know you'll never understand, gentlemen, but what the hell. That's a way to get to the Front and maybe do some good."

"Do some good?" Nick asked, astonished. "What, are you crazy? There is serious killing going on over there. A couple of months ago the Brits lost forty thousand, maybe fifty thousand soldiers in one goddamn day. An American shouldn't be within a hundred miles of the front. And now you want to drive an ambulance. *To do exactly what?* Take a few corpses somewhere for burial?"

"What about your wife?" Ralph asked. "She thought you were a moron for going to Mexico. Now you're leaving her again."

Byron wasn't prepared for the edge to their usual banter. "Listen, guys, Helen just has to understand. With her involvement in the Wilson campaign and all, she'll be busier than Babe Ruth in a whorehouse."

18

HELEN STEPPED OFF THE trolley, avoiding the small puddles of early morning rain as she carefully made her way to the hotel's entrance. A banner straddled the arched lobby windows, **WILSON AGAIN, 1916.**

She greeted Milton, an immense block of a doorman, whose red and black livery, replete with top hat, accentuated his bulk. Even after one month, Helen still felt proud when Milton greeted her each morning by name, opened the glass door, and waved her through with a wide sweep of his white-gloved hand.

She had become a moving component of a presidential campaign. She would have never considered it possible several months ago, but here she was, enmeshed in the frenetic activity.

That morning Helen awoke excited with a yearning unconnected to Byron, snoring softly next to her. There had been no connection between them since his return from Mexico the month before. She knew it as soon as they began to make love the first night he returned. Her arms did not pull him deeper inside her. They were just wrapped around a man's torso. Instead of coaxing out every bit of pleasure, she welcomed Byron's release—the sooner the better. *He didn't even seem to notice. Maybe he never did.*

Helen understood the source of her excitement that morning. It had crept up upon her quietly over the past few weeks. It was Vincent Chelios. He would be coming up from the national campaign head-quarters in New York that afternoon. She couldn't explain why but she could hardly wait to be near him.

She hadn't seen Vincent since his last visit more than a month before. She remembered waiting patiently that first day she joined the campaign for him to look in her direction. She had rehearsed a casual smile while he busied himself across the room. She never did get an opportunity that afternoon to deliver what she hoped would be a sim-ple acknowledgement of a colleague; he had left hurriedly, passing her desk, saying, "Keep up the excellent work, Helen." She wasn't certain if Vincent looked at her when he said it—she had turned away.

Now Helen started up the carpeted staircase connecting the chan-deliered lobby to the hotel's mezzanine. With each step, the staccato chatter of ticker tape spatting from two telegraphic machines grew louder. Staffers streamed past the top of the staircase, carrying papers and folders. She surveyed the large open space, a room already teeming with eager colleagues.

Isn't this an enormous expense just to maintain the appearance of a possible victory? Helen wondered. After all, newspaper editorials claimed that Wilson already conceded everything east of the Missis-sippi and north of Ohio to his Republican challenger, Charles Evans Hughes. Wilson's only hope was a huge turnout in the Midwest and West where his neutrality message resonated. The big Eastern cities were a morass of Irish and German political crosscurrents that seemed to grow more anti-Wilson each week.

"Good morning, Helen." Mrs. Fiona Donnelly pointed towards the far wall. "Your design is beautiful. It will be a pleasure to see it all over the city."

Helen turned toward the poster she had just finished the week before. Hanson's Printing delivered it that morning. She determined that the bold colors still needed just a little more work. She would stop by Mr. Hanson's after she left the hotel. She always looked forward to his printing room disaster stories. It would be, she was certain, an amusing end to the day.

"Good morning, Mrs. Donnelly, and thanks. It does look striking, if I do say so," Helen said, thrilled that her layout idea was now concrete and monopolizing a wall of the mezzanine.

Nobody assigned Mrs. Donnelly the office manager job. It was a perfect fit—she gravitated toward it. Nobody objected. Short yet stout as a fireplug, she surveyed her dominion over reading glasses perched on the end of her red nose.

Mrs. Donnelly had worked tirelessly for Wilson's 1912 campaign and was now a favorite of George Creel's. Her husband, a longtime Boston Democrat precinct captain, froze to death one night in a drunken stupor behind the River Liffey Tavern during a blizzard two years before. That was the account Helen heard around the office.

HELEN RETURNED TO THE mezzanine after a tea and carrot soup lunch in the hotel restaurant. She turned to her left, as always, toward her desk. Her stride slackened. Vincent Chelios sat next to Mrs. Donnelly. He wore a finely tailored brown suit and brown and white shoes; his right leg crossed high over his left. He balanced his straw hat on his raised knee—his black hair, combed straight back, as glossy as the surface of her polished ebony nightstand. *Beautiful, thick hair!*

Vincent smiled, hanging onto Mrs. Donnelly's every word. No doubt a behind-the-scene political story she overheard her husband tell years ago, thought Helen. As Mrs. Donnelly reached the end of the tale, Helen circled into her seat at the adjacent desk.

"That's rich, Mrs. Donnelly." Vincent said, looking half over his shoulder in Helen's direction. "Hello, Helen."

"Hello, Vincent." She nodded politely.

Vincent turned back to Mrs. Donnelly. "What a story. Finnerty is making quite a name for himself. He's a scoundrel, but at least a Boston bred one. It should give you a sense of civic pride."

"Strangely enough, Vincent, I'm not too proud of him." Mrs. Donnelly looked at Helen. "Helen knows Joe Finnerty as well, don't you dear?"

"Yes, I do." Helen rolled her eyes, exhaling deeply. She gauged it to be an appropriate response to a mention of Finnerty—and conveniently, a release of her nervousness.

George Creel opened the conference room door and stepped forward. He then stood motionless, his hands on his waist. A heroic, theatrical pose thought Helen. *Margaret did say he takes himself too seriously at times.*

"Ladies and gentlemen, may I have everyone's attention please? Thank you. Kindly come into this conference room. Gentlemen, please bring in a few extra chairs." Creel spun around and went back into the room.

"How have you been, Helen?" Vincent stood up, tapping the brim of his hat in his hand.

She fussed with papers on her desk. "Vincent, so nice to see you again. I hope all is going well for the campaign in New York."

"I suspect that we'll be hearing a state of the campaign speech from George right now." Vincent lowered his voice. "He's been touring the regional offices refining his message to the troops. Let's see what he comes up with today."

He smiled, gesturing for the women to proceed in front of him through the tight space between the desks. He detoured toward a chair and picked it up.

Helen moved ahead of the others into the conference room, hoping for a place at the table from where she could avoid casual glances at Vincent. She found a vantage point allowing an unimpeded view of George Creel, now standing at the head of the long table, next to a chalkboard on an easel. He examined the polished wood floor, waiting for everyone to be seated. As the shuffling of chairs diminished, he looked up.

"Good morning. I want to say that you are all doing an excellent job for the president. He has asked me to give each and every one of you his thanks and congratulations on a job well done."

He paused and moved towards a corner of the room.

"I read the newspapers' speculation about the strategies of both campaigns, the same as all of you do. However, I can assure you, as an old newspaperman myself, much of it is nonsense. I've been known to write a few whimsical stories in my own career." He knew this was a hometown audience, and waited for the subdued laughter that followed.

"So let me not, as we say in the newspaper business, bury the headline—and that would be 'this will be the closest presidential election in our nation's history.' Of that I am certain. That means it's even more crucial that we get the word out in every way possible. Yes, it is true that we view, unofficially of course, the Northeast as a loss. And yes, we see the Irish and German vote lost to us. We're just too pro-British for them. We will never change that."

He looked around the table, making eye contact with two copywriters seated in front of him—they both nodded their expected agreement.

"We have to constantly remind voters that it was President Wilson who convinced the Germans to stop their submarine attacks on neutral ships. And that means no more loss of American lives which makes neutrality an easier sell to the public."

Creel breathed deeply. Also a bit theatrical, thought Helen. Then he walked around the table and stationed himself behind Vincent.

"There is little for us to do now but to target voters in the still undecided states. If only we knew for certain how to reach them. But luckily for us, President Wilson can do what Hughes never could. He can put lightning and fire in his speeches. Hughes's dignity works for us—he's very much a dullard in person."

Creel put his hand on Vincent's shoulder. Vincent looked up, directly into Helen's eyes. She didn't know whether to smile or to casually look away. She looked away, but not as casually as she hoped. Vincent half turned toward Creel, who continued.

"We'll be lucky if the Republicans stay on their present course— they are attacking Wilson's record, but they can't say what they would have done differently in the past, nor what they would do now. Hughes has been a Supreme Court justice since 1910, so he hasn't made a political statement in six years. If he had, it would be so dull nobody would remember it anyway. Sometimes I feel sorry for him—but not too often." He smiled and paused again.

Helen imagined Vincent's arms around her, holding her close. He had had such a light scent of witch hazel when he brushed against her as he carried the chair into the conference room. Was she being too obvious? That was her concern, not George Creel's views of an upcoming election. She hoped Creel would move away from Vincent.

Creel's voice punctured Helen's daydream. "There is an important aspect to the campaign that will set Wilson apart from Hughes. It came to me recently after we worked on getting a quote of support from Thomas Alva Edison. Of course it was a miracle considering Mr. Edison is a Republican, and he is about as quotable as is this pock-marked conference table."

He waited for the predictably amused reaction to subside and then he continued. "Edison said, 'they say Wilson has blundered. Perhaps he has, but I notice that he usually blunders forward.' That gives us another facet of the president to work into the campaign—a man who looks into the future, unafraid of taking chances. One way we can use that is having the president interested in new inventions and ideas. I was just thinking this morning—as I do every morning let me assure you."

Vincent smiled, acknowledging Creel's light tone, then glanced into Helen's eyes. Creel moved further down the table, allowing her focus to avert contact with Vincent.

"I think we should give thought to the president making a speech on the radio. Even though only a few people will hear it, it will make Wilson *blunder forward*, as Edison says."

Creel paused and then gestured toward Helen. "Actually, Helen Townsend made this suggestions sometime ago. She has been working at the radio station at Tufts College and can coordinate our efforts. Will that be acceptable to you, Helen? Don't mistake my motives. Your artwork is exceptional. In fact I would like to use some of it in our national campaign."

A few people in the room murmured their approval. Others applauded lightly. Mrs. Donnelly touched Helen's forearm. She had become very fond of Helen and encouraged her growing visibility in the campaign office. Helen, in turn, appreciated Mrs. Donnelly's ability to gently resolve personal disputes and grievances, as they were certain to emerge in such a tense, high stakes operation. Her experience in the political trenches also gave Mrs. Donnelly the credibility to urge the staff past the setbacks that arose everyday.

"I'd be delighted to be part of your radio campaign, Mr. Creel," Helen said as calmly as she could.

"Mr. Chelios is handling some of the communications issues for us so you will be working with him," Creel said, nodding in Vincent's direction.. "If that is all right with you, Helen?"

"Yes, of course it is." She allowed herself a glance towards Vincent; they nodded politely to each other.

It was a professional acknowledgement. Helen was pleased. "Actually, I'll be going to the printer this afternoon with Mrs. Donnelly—Vincent, would you care to join us?"

"Thank you Helen, I would like to very much," Vincent said graciously. "I'll be leaving for Buffalo tomorrow morning and this will give us a chance to talk a bit more about the radio transmissions. I'm particularly happy that Mrs. Donnelly will be part of our Wilson's *forward blunders* project."

Helen smiled as effortlessly as she could muster and then looked over to Mrs. Donnelly, gathering documents into a folder. She waited for Mrs. Donnelly to waddle toward the door. She and Vincent followed.

"I hope this is not your evening's entertainment, Mrs. Donnelly," Vincent said, pointing at the folder with mock disappointment. She shook her head, hinting that perhaps she had better plans—perhaps even with a gentleman caller. Then she giggled.

Helen accepted as an unexpected turn of good fortune that she would be with Vincent for even a while longer, even if only confined to a crammed print shop with Mr. Hanson and Mrs. Donnelly. Mrs. Donnelly's presence would at least make her awkwardness less noticeable—or so she hoped.

Helen moved the conversation to firmer ground—to a subject she could engage with a lighter touch. "Mrs. Donnelly, you and Vincent were sharing a laugh at Joseph Finnerty's expense. My sister-in-law Margaret and I have our own stories. I didn't know that you knew him."

Mrs. Donnelly shook her head slightly. "I never met him. My late husband, Thomas, told me about this young Irishman who once came to him with a proposal. That was a number of years ago, it seems. The captain of the Harvard baseball team needed some sort of license to open a movie theater—on Essex Street, if I remember well. Mr. Finnerty was determined to get it for him."

"And no money would have changed hands between Joe Finnerty and your husband, now would it have, Mrs. Donnelly?" Vincent asked in an admirable Irish brogue.

Mrs. Donnelly amused, shrugged her shoulders. "It's never been my place to inquire about men's business. It seems that Mr. Finnerty wanted a varsity letter to wear around Harvard. He was on the baseball team but always sat on the bench. The only way he could get the letter was to appear in a ballgame. He craved that letter because the Protestants wouldn't let him into their clubs—or something like that.

"So he finds out that the captain of the team, I never knew his name, is having trouble getting a license for a movie theater he wants to open. Joe finds my dear husband Thomas, and, how shall we say? They make an arrangement for the license."

"Oh yes, I actually heard that story from Byron; he was on the team a few years later," Helen added. "It seems that even with the deal they made, the captain couldn't bear putting Joe into the game. He was that bad a player. So finally, on the last game of the season, in the last inning with Harvard six runs ahead, Joe gets his chance—the captain puts him in. Joe didn't care of course. All he wanted was the letter to wear around Harvard. Wouldn't you know that on the last out of the game the ball goes to Joe playing first base. He picks up the ball, steps on the base, and the game is over. The pitcher comes over for the game ball. Joe sticks it in his pocket and walks away. To this day he's still telling everyone he won the game for Harvard."

Vincent laughed. Mrs. Donnelly smiled. "I never heard that part of it. Quite a character, wouldn't you say, Helen?"

"Oh definitely, *quite* a cad."

Helen waited a moment and then looked at Vincent. "Vincent, what are your expectations for the rest of the campaign?"

"It's really difficult to predict, Helen. As long as the Germans don't renew their submarine warfare and Americans don't get killed, we have a good chance of staying out of the war. And then Wilson has a good chance to win the election. Maybe this war will burn out on its own accord. Who knows what will happen?"

Helen nodded thoughtfully. *Yes, Vincent, who knows what will happen?*

19

AUGUST 13, 1916

CRYSTAL LAKE

NEWTON CENTRE, MASS.

MARGARET REMOVED THE NEATLY folded letter, smoothed it out carefully on her lap, and started to read it aloud.

> July 15, 1916
> Glasgow, Scotland

Dear Aunt Margaret and Uncle William,

I had my seventeenth birthday in our little home. Actually we are lucky to have a home this comfortable. Father has more time available because he lost his manager's job. His company will give it back to him when this absolute nightmare ends for all of us. Now Father has a part-time job and does volunteer work with the fire department. Everybody is doing something to help.

The morning of my birthday party, I was at the military hospital. I wrote to you before about being a tutor to some of the boys who do not read or write very well. Sometimes I wonder why I am doing this. If their medical condition improves, they will only want to return to their mates at the Front, even though they know that death awaits them. Others die only minutes after I have been talking or joking with them. I know now that I would very much like to be a nurse. Nurses will be needed for the rest of my lifetime to care for the wounds that I see on these boys every day.

The most frightening wounds for the men are the ones to their faces. Some of them have no features at all, and small pieces of metal are still in their facial bones. For this reason there are no mirrors in any of the wards. Many of the men even lose control of themselves after seeing their reflections in the window glass. All of the nurses, and everyone else, are instructed to look the patient straight in the eye, and to never look away from them. This is because the men are very sensitive to reactions to their faces.

The doctors are now beginning to make facial masks to cover these terrible wounds. They are molding and painting the masks from photographs of the patient before the war. The results are terrible and all they do is cover the wounds.

I have seen people in the street hurry away from these horribly disfigured men and I know they will have a difficult time for the rest of their lives. They may never find comfort in the very society that sent them to the war.

I have already told you how everything has disappeared because of the war effort. There is so little for the people now. Last winter everyone went cold for lack of coal. Medicines for older people, and even writing paper and pencils, are getting hard to come by in this city, even though whole forests are being cleared in the Highlands for wood for the war. One of the Scottish soldiers said that it was as if everything that his country had was being "sucked down a giant toilet in France." It was really awful to think of it like that, but it is true. If you were here you would certainly agree.

But what has been absolutely frightful on my rides through the city is the absence of young men. Men who I could imagine being my older brothers, or my sweethearts. I don't have one yet, Aunt Margaret, but I will tell you all about it if that ever happens. I feel bad for the girls my age who have lost their brothers and sweethearts. They talk about it all the time. There is little else to talk about here.

I wrote about the battle at the Somme. That is what everybody is calling it. It was terrible. We already have many casualties just from that one battle.

None of the soldiers were prepared for the battle or how horrible it was. Many of them were new recruits, hardly ready for the Front. Not that anyone could ever be ready for that! There are always new soldiers because so many are dying every day. General Haig, who is despised by all of the Scottish soldiers, is now the commander of the British forces in France. I think I wrote to you about him before.

They say that he bombed the German front lines at the Somme River for days. He thought the Germans would be so weak they could not resist an infantry attack. So he ordered the infantry to advance. Gen. Haig didn't know that the Germans had dug deeply into their trenches. All they had to do was wait for the British artillery to stop. Then they would know that the infantry would be coming towards them. The Germans went back to their machine guns and shot down row after row of Brits.

General Haig and the other despised generals just kept ordering their men forward, even though they knew the Germans were picking them off like toy ducks in an arcade. By the end of the first day, some of the soldiers heard that sixty thousand British soldiers were dead or wounded. It makes me cry, like everyone else here.

I love these men in the hospital as I love the women in the streets

and shops, and the nurses who allow me to work alongside them. I
am sometimes shamed by their bravery.

I must end now.

With love from your adoring niece,

Sarah

"Margaret, thank you for letting me share this very private moment with you and your family," Henry Mendes said quietly. Nobody in the room responded. There was only silence for a few moments.

Dr. Carlson reached over to pick up the whiskey Donald Townsend had poured. "So, Mr. Mendes, Byron tells us that you are attending Harvard this fall? Perhaps lecturing to undergraduates? Byron said literature—the Classics."

"That's correct, Dr. Carlson, I plan to start my advanced studies this fall as well."

"Henry traveled with Villa for two years," Byron said excitedly. "He speaks Spanish fluently and really understood what was going on. He said right from the moment I met him that Pershing would never find Villa. It was impossible with all of those mountains and desert."

"Imagine that darling girl writing how she was shamed by everyone's bravery over there," Beatrice said aloud, but more to herself than to anyone in the room. "After all she has been through she should never think herself less brave than the others. She is a very sensible young lady and will learn her own strengths quickly. *'Courage is knowing what not to fear.'*"

"Plato," Henry Mendes said, nodding his appreciation. "We will all be called upon to show great strengths very soon, Mrs. Townsend. Although I must confess my favorite Plato observation is: *'It was a wise man who invented beer.'*"

"An insightful quotation, Mr. Mendes," Dr. Carlson said, holding his glass out to toast Henry. "Although I prefer wine. Perhaps Plato was referring to all fermented beverages."

"I don't suppose we will ever find out," Beatrice concluded, enjoying the references to Plato.

Is this Mendes a con man? William wondered. Leave it to Byron to be impressed by him. And Margaret is so fascinated, agreeing with everything he says. Sure, the "workingmen are fighting the war for kings and profiteers" is true—even Uncle Isaac says that. It was just the way he said it that William couldn't quite trust.

Henry habitually stroked his graying mustache and goatee as if to signal a weighty insight, or perhaps he thought he was expected to validate everyone's comments. An academic, a bit too filled with his own presumed intellectual superiority, William decided.

"It is absolutely inhuman that both the Brits and the Germans are developing all of these gases," Margaret said, without the indignation that William would have expected along with such a declaration. "Sarah has written to us about the devastating effects they are having on the infantry. I'm surprised her letters even get through. It would be horrific to think that we too would use gas. That is enough of a reason for us to stay out of this war."

"We are already developing gas warfare." Henry's shrugged shoulders suggested it was common knowledge. "Right here at Harvard, the government is sponsoring a chemical warfare program. Also down the street at MIT. I understand that they're experimenting with phosgene. The French just developed it. It chokes whoever breathes it. It's a slow, painful death. They are mixing it with chlorine. It seems to be known to many—even I know about it."

William listened absently. *This Mendes guy's suit just hangs off his body. Maybe he had a nap in it earlier. No muscle tone at all. No shoulders. God, look how his body flares at the waist—he looks like a pear in a cheap suit.*

"That's impossible," Margaret said. "I mean, how could a university allow themselves—"

"It is true, Margaret," Dr. Carlson's said in his usual easy manner. "It is, as Mr. Mendes says, not what one would consider a well-guarded secret. Universities all over the country are letting the government support these kinds of programs. It's part of their preparedness mentality. I personally think it's a terrible idea."

"Terrible? *No country* should be developing gas. We should be an example to Europe," Margaret said, looking around the room for agreement.

"No, Margaret." Henry's tone was professorial, as if correcting a student. "As long as this country is run by industrialists we will play our part in the world madness. Nothing will change until the workers take over."

Those manicured fingers. The smooth hands. Maybe he did spend two years with Villa but he is not a soldier of fortune. William would bet the Henry would never get his hands dirty—he would have others do the fighting.

"That's nonsense as far as I'm concerned. It would be much appreciated if you do not mention that again in this house." William regretted his sharp tone instantly.

"How dare you, William?" Margaret asked in a seething half-whisper. "We do have free speech in this country. Some people even fight for free speech, while others just make money—"

"William, please do feel free to call this your house," Donald said, offering a milder tone. "However, remember that we do encourage free speech here. Even if it is ridiculous—as it is in this case. I believe a drink is called for."

"I'm sorry, Henry," William said, stung by Donald's reprimand, despite its gentle delivery. He knew better than to make known his disposition toward someone he didn't trust—especially a stranger. After all, Henry's intellectual babble was just that, nothing more.

"Margaret and Helen are working with me on a story about Wilson and radio." Byron addressed William, eager to moderate the tension. "Helen says it will be good for the president's campaign. He will look like a man of action—the president of the United States making a speech on the radio. A historic moment, wouldn't you say?"

"Yes, the potential for these radio broadcasts is greater than we realized." Donald Townsend looked over to Beatrice for acknowledgment.

Beatrice ignored her husband's assessment of audio transmissions. "Sarah's description of the war, and life around her, is absolutely chilling. *There is truth in wine and children*—Plato said, and he probably meant beer as well."

Mendes' wink showed that he heartily agreed.

20

"I'M SURE EVERYONE KNOWS Margaret Morrison," Vincent Chelios said, standing at the front of the crowded conference room. Helen had noticed more desks added to the mezzanine with each passing week, lending an even greater sense of purpose to the headquarters. "We're looking forward to associating the president with the developing technology of radio. Both Margaret and Helen Townsend have considerable experience in this field. They deserve credit for their efforts."

Helen responded to his acknowledgement with a gracious smile. *A very dapper suit—gray with white pin stripes. And a matching silk tie. Yet he isn't a dandy. There is certainly nothing prissy about him. Nothing at all.*

Vincent bowed slightly in Helen's direction. "I don't know how many of you have read the story published this week. Helen's very talented husband, Byron Townsend, wrote it for *The Electrical Experimenter.*"

He surveyed the room. There was no response. He smiled.

"I didn't expect that many of you actually read this magazine with any regularity—and it appears that I was right. Neither do I. So we are printing copies of the article for everyone. Mr. Creel is also sending it to friendly newspaper publishers around the country. 'The president as a visionary' will be comforting to everyone these days."

Helen knew that Margaret shared her excitement. She didn't have to look over to her for confirmation—they were developing publicity for the president of the United States!

Vincent continued, "I would like to read parts of the article." He picked up the magazine.

> All ye, people of the United States; His Excellency the PRESIDENT! This greeting may be heard all over the country, in the not-too-distant future, and not on a phonograph either, at least if radio enthusiasts have their way. Their idea is to link the larger cities and towns by radio to the powerful transcontinental government wireless station at Arlington, near Washington, D.C.
>
> Then, when the President speaks before Congress or even his inaugural address, anyone with an inexpensive receiver can hear it, instead of just the select few within hearing distance of the speaker, as has always been the case in the past.

"I won't read the details of the recent test broadcasts but they are outlined in the story." Vincent motioned toward Helen. "Of course you can just ask Helen. She knows a great deal about this. Certainly more than I do." He smiled at her. She glanced away, managing a barely audible "thank you."

A modest woman, Vincent thought—even eye contact seemed difficult for her. He had to stop himself from staring at her when he met her and Margaret that morning in the hotel lobby. He wondered if it was obvious to either of them—he hoped not.

"Let me pick up this story a little further." Vincent said.

> It is now possible for the President to make his speech at the Capitol in Washington, and have his voice picked up by a battery of sensitive microphones, located in front of him. The microphones would transform the voice into electric currents, passing over a wire circuit to the radio station at Arlington. Here, by means of a sensitive vacuum tube, the voice waves would be amplified in power and propagated from the great Arlington antenna with the power of several hundred horses. These oscillations would fly through space at great speed, and take but a fraction of a second to traverse the space between Washington and San Francisco, or between the Capitol and Honolulu, for that matter.

Vincent looked for a response from Mrs. Donnelly. With a wave of her hand, she encouraged him to continue.

> The President's speech as received by radio in all the large cities throughout the country would be amplified if necessary through an apparatus equipped with large speakers, so that an entire theater could hear the words distinctly. The receiving apparatus could be placed outside of public buildings, too, when desired. Not only would just privileged locations hear the President's words, but all amateur stations, of which there are now many throughout the country, could receive the message as well.

Vincent placed the magazine on the conference table next to Helen. He leaned over her. She knew there was a flushing of her face.

Vincent moved to the other side of the room. He turned and looked at Helen. "Thank your husband for this wonderful article. We know he was busy with his World Series features. Of course we're especially happy that the Boston Red Sox won—but don't publicize that, as we are supposed to be impartial." Vincent winked, acknowledging the expected conspiratorial undertone of appreciation from his audience.

"Which brings us to another matter," he said, his tone turning somber. "We really shouldn't be too concerned about impartiality—especially in this part of the country. The recent Maine local elections went against us fairly decisively. Maine has always been a predictor of national elections. Needless to say, the results do not make us too happy. We'll be fighting on anyway, of course."

Vincent sighed, smiling grimly. "Even the liquor interests are against Wilson for making the Navy dry. This will be a very difficult election indeed."

Moved by unseen inspiration, Mrs. Donnelly clambered noisily to her feet, ignoring the flatulent sound her chair made, and the ensuing titters, and declared passionately, "I know we're going to win! I don't care what we Irish or anybody else has to say about Wilson. I don't believe that the president will lose just when we need him the most."

Then she added in a still robust tone, "Vincent, some of us are planning to go to New York for election night. Hopefully you have room at the national headquarters celebration for your Boston party faithful."

Vincent nodded graciously. "Of course, Mrs. Donnelly. It would be my pleasure to be your host in New York—we'll have a wonderful celebration. Is anyone else interested?"

"A dubious benefit of not having the right to vote is that some of us can go down to New York to watch the election results on chalkboards if we want to," Margaret said, not certain if her sarcasm eluded Vincent.

It didn't.

"I do want you to know that women's right to vote is an important issue to the Democrats," Vincent said, reassuring the staff. "I honestly don't know when Wilson will address it. Right now he's walking a tightrope to keep this country out of war—thank goodness women already have the right to vote in many of those Western states. That is in good part why we will win those states."

The female contingent clapped their approval.

Margaret felt emboldened. "Vincent, ask Mr. Creel if he finds it as odd as we do that women in Massachusetts, Rhode Island, New York and the rest of the Eastern seaboard where the signers of the Constitution came from cannot vote for the president—while those supposedly less sophisticated states like Utah, Colorado, and Wyoming have no opposition to women voting."

"I'll be sure to make your views known."

Then Vincent turned to a lighter theme. "The only thing I can assure you about election night is that the president will not be in New York. It's no secret that Wilson loathes New York City. I know that this sentiment has been printed many times so I don't mind saying it publicly. He hates the idea that the national campaign headquarters is in New York. In fact, Wilson says that New York is 'rotten to the core and should be wiped off the map.' A strong statement if you ask me. Sometimes I wish he would make that kind of a statement about more important matters—especially women's right to vote."

Vincent waited for the swell of agreement to crest. "Margaret, I understand that Mr. DeForest has been transmitting music programs several times a week. I hear that he'll be broadcasting the results as they become known on election night. That should be very exciting."

"Yes, I spoke to him last week," Margaret said. "He is planning to do just that. Helen and I may go down to New York and be with him for that broadcast. I don't know how my parents will feel about that. Not to mention William or Byron. Whatever shall we do?" She smiled.

Mrs. Donnelly did not waste a moment. "I'll be happy to share a room with the both of you if it will make Mr. and Mrs. Townsend, and of course your husbands, more comfortable."

Yes, it would be exciting to be at national headquarters on election night, thought Helen. *Not in Boston—but in New York. It promised to be very exciting indeed.*

21

WILLIAM TRACKED THE SHARP winding road cut into the canyon walls, threading his Dodge along the rutted barely two lanes of compacted dirt. His descent from the lodge in the rain on his last visit had tested his nerves—a short slide, and the uncertain grasping of the tires that could have taken him over the edge, straight down into a soaked bed of brown pine needles. He couldn't measure how far down the fall would have been but it would have included a few bounces off jagged rocks protruding from the side of the cliff.

He remembered exhaling deeply when he reached the flat straight road back to Boston.

Now the setting sun filtered through the branches of the still shedding trees as he made the trip back up the hill. The muted yellow lights streaming from the lodge above him reminded William that hollowed-out pumpkins would be poised in windows all over Massachusetts in just another week. He had always looked forward to helping Uncle Isaac carve the jack-o'-lanterns—which they would then set down on the porch floor with the candlelit faces peering through the railings of the inn.

Finnerty's announcement of a 'country business meeting' always meant a sex party at the lodge hidden away in these wooded hills. William wasn't invited to many of them—they were mostly for Finnerty's out-of-town clients. Finnerty probably knew these frolics weren't William's style, so he didn't often mention them. But he was insistent on William's presence this evening.

William never understood Solomon McFurness's relationship to Finnerty. Did he rent the lodge to Finnerty for his parties? Or was he another character in Finnerty's schemes? Just like I am, thought William. MacFurness probably never came near this place except when Finnerty was in action. Maybe he did take his family up here at Easter or Christmas. Maybe he enjoyed watching his daughter sleeping in a bed Finnerty had sex in with one of his whores the night before. *Who knows?*

William stepped inside the lodge, welcoming the rush of warmth from the roughly assembled stone and brick fireplace. He removed the heavy fur coat he had just that morning retrieved from its summer hibernation in a garment bag stuffed into a closet in his basement. He threw it over the purple upholstered chair at the entrance to the sitting room.

Movement along the floor, past the chest of drawers supporting a MacFurness family photograph, caught his attention; two silk stocking-covered legs protruded out from behind the oversized Victorian pink and white patterned sofa. William stepped closer, a pale naked ass pointed up at him in a surprising welcome. The owner of the legs and ass had positioned herself over MacFurness's groin, her head bobbing up and down. MacFurness, propped up against the wall, greeted William with his eyes half opened, seemingly confused, as if struggling to follow a discordant symphony.

William turned towards the footsteps on the creaking staircase.

"You must be William Morrison. I heard you were coming to the party." A deep voice addressed him.

The speaker reached the bottom step. A woman straddled his back, her legs gripping his waist, her arms locked around his neck. She wore only white bloomers. She released her tight hold to wave a greeting, her breasts flopping in unison with the back and forth sweep of her hand.

"Joining the party?" She was drunk.

The man twisted and shook his torso a few times, peeling her off. She snorted at some boozy private joke and tottered towards the chair William had just thrown his coat over. She rested her head in the coat's thick fur and fell asleep, snoring gracelessly.

The man approached William with his right hand out, his wrinkled white shirt stuffed into unbuttoned pants supported by blue suspenders.

"And you are?" William asked, shaking his hand.

"Hiram Harris."

"I'm William Morrison—how do you do, Hiram? And you are a friend of Mr. MacFurness?" William glanced toward the still stunned MacFurness sprawled behind the sofa.

"No, I'm with Joe Finnerty. He said you're going to run my copper fixture company after he arranges the sale," Hiram said, expecting William could now place him.

"Oh yes, that's right—the copper company." William scrambled for the right tone; after all it was, at its core, just another con game that Finnerty had improvised—and this Hiram was the mark.

Hiram nodded his head more vigorously than William thought their interchange warranted.

"I didn't know you were coming to town. I hope you'll be staying a

203

few days," William said, not certain why this was a hope of his. "Is Joe Finnerty around? I didn't see his car outside."

"Yes, he's upstairs in the back bedroom." Hiram gestured upward toward the second floor, a leer across his face. "I drove him here in my car." He seemed proud to have provided this service.

William started toward the staircase; Hiram's too firm grasp on his elbow stopped him. William studied the hold on his arm and then stared into Hiram's eyes. He felt an instant loosening of the grip.

"I'm sorry." Hiram stepped back, giving William space. "I need to talk to you. It's important."

He glanced around for a discreet place—although it was unlikely the others in the room would be interested. William glanced at the legs still protruding from the side of the couch, short irregular quivers marking whatever progress was being made.

Hiram guided William to the vestibule and looked up the staircase, assuring himself they were alone. "I know my father's company is worth more than Mr. Finnerty is telling me—I just know it. I think that Benjamin fellow who we met on the train is telling me a story." A curt nod added a grace note to his theory.

Their eyes locked a few inches apart.

Why would he trust me? William asked himself. Dumb as a tree stump, isn't that how Finnerty described him? *Or was that Two Ton Ben's appraisal? What difference did it make anyway?*

Hiram firmed his shirt inside his opened pants as if readying himself for inspection. His bare-breasted lady jockey released a burst of gas onto William's fur coat. She punctuated it with a lazy, semi-conscious 'excuse me' and then furrowed back into the coat.

William's nose wrinkled in disgust. "Want to buy a good fur coat, cheap? Although I'm not sure it will ever be wearable again."

Hiram, preoccupied, ignored the jest. "This is the way I see it," he said slowly, attaching the same gravity to each word. "Mr. Finnerty knows that my father bought a lot of copper fixtures out West. Maybe $150,000 worth. My father knew they would be worth a lot of money— they need copper for everything now, don't they? Mr. Finnerty is saying my father lost it all on Wall Street. I don't believe that. I just can't find the records. My lawyer hired a private detective out West to determine my father's rightful ownership. I know the company is worth more. A lot more. If I get proof, I'll go to the police."

"Those are serious charges, Hiram. I'm sure Joe Finnerty is working hard to determine the right valuation." *It sounded like the right thing to say.* William reassured himself that it was. "Listen Hiram, I have to talk to Finnerty. Wait down here for a few minutes. Watch MacFurness over there for some tips."

William gestured towards the corner from which emerged no sign of life; even the stocking feet were stilled.

Hiram shook his head. "I don't need any tips. I know exactly what to do."

"Excellent," William said, turning quickly and starting up the carpeted staircase.

RUSTED BED SPRINGS THUDDED with the steady, rhythmic movements of the activity it supported. William followed the distinctive sounds to a room at the end of a narrow wood paneled corridor and knocked on the door. *Fuck Finnerty if I interrupt him.*

"I hope that's you, William. What the hell took you so long? Come in."

William could hear movement on the mattress as he opened the door. A woman swung her leg over Finnerty's bare chest, hastily pulling a thin blanket around her body. Finnerty lay nude on his back, a blanket covering his midsection, barely concealing his still erect member.

William recognized Hazel, the waitress from Paine's, the restaurant next to the bank. Both Finnerty and Keane leered at her a little too often whenever William met them there for a morning coffee. But then Finnerty eyeballed every woman, even Margaret and Helen. Hazel was a big girl, the kind that always attracted Finnerty, even though his own wife was petite and not unattractive, just plain.

"Hazel darling, why don't you leave us alone for a few minutes?" Finnerty suggested, tweaking her breast through the blanket.

"Just when we were getting started," Hazel said, pouting her disappointment. "You were getting good, Joey. Nobody ever stopped with me like this before."

"I told you I was unique, dear." Finnerty bared his toothy smile. "Now why don't you take that nasty smelling little fur pot of yours into the other room? We'll indulge again later. Be sure of that."

"How do you know it smells nasty, Joey? You didn't even get your nose near it," Hazel shot back with a teasing sneer.

She smiled at William, arose from the bed, and dropped her meager share of the blanket onto Finnerty. Finnerty watched her as she left the room. "Close the door, darling. It's a great ass by the way. I always knew it would be."

He waved towards the frayed wicker chair wedged into the corner behind the door. William sat down. He felt it squirm beneath him.

"You see, William, *coitus interruptus*—proof positive there is nobody more important to me than you." Finnerty made no effort to cover his now flaccid cock. Flabby and listing, it lolled against his pale white thigh, much to William's discomfort. "We may have a problem with this Hiram moron downstairs. I wanted you to come up to the lodge to meet him."

William looked toward the door.

"Don't worry, William. Hiram is incapable of anything subtle. That includes sneaking down the hallway to listen to us. Trust me—"

"Joe, he told me that he doesn't believe you or his attorney. He thinks you undervalued his assets."

"*We undervalued his assets?* You really sound like a banker now, William," Finnerty said, his tone a bit too mocking for William's comfort. "What else did he tell you?"

"He's hiring a private detective out West to check into his father's holdings. Then he intends to go to the police."

Finnerty stretched his bare legs out, resting his ankles on the wooden footboard. He ran his hand through his thin, sandy brown hair, coming to rest at the back of his neck. William looked away. *For Chrissake, cover yourself, you immodest bastard. Who needs to see your dick?*

"We should be able to fix this quickly, William." Finnerty nodded towards the door, motioning for William to insure that Hiram, indeed, was not lurking outside. William peered out and then returned to the chair.

"What you don't know William is that the detective Hiram is hiring was recommended to him by his attorney—who, if you remember, is my partner in this venture. Herman Oliver is the detective's name, and I'm happy to tell you, he's a fine investigator. A former federal agent. He's worked for me several times on other *sensitive* matters in the past. I'm confident that his search for assets will correspond to our meager inventory."

"I came to tell you that I didn't want any part of this deal," William said bluntly. "You know that already. I told you a couple of times."

Finnerty breathed deeply. "I don't think we should be discussing this right now. But I do think you should know there is a lot of money on the table on this deal. Maybe we can rethink your *participation*."

"Money is not an issue, Joe, " William said firmly.

Finnerty evaluated William's response. Usually a few more bucks in the pot would seal a deal with anyone. "Why don't you rethink your position, and we'll talk about it in a few weeks."

"I don't think I'll feel any different then," said William, "but it's worth a wait."

Why wait? Nothing will change. William was certain of that. He felt no impulse to tell Finnerty about Ennis' offer for him to join the new brokerage. He could tell Finnerty later, when he was ready to make the change. *Don't give Finnerty any more information than he needs—nothing good will ever come of it.*

"By the way, William, what is going on with your brother-in-law? Is Byron still spouting off about Europe? What the hell does he expect to find in the trenches? Something besides bodies? Lice?" Finnerty cackled at his own wit. "I read his story about Wilson making a speech on the radio. Great idea. Let me know if Margaret or Helen figure out how to make a buck out of that contraption."

"Sure, Joe, I'll be sure to discuss it with them."

"I heard his lovely wife is working for the Wilson campaign. I'd never let a little darling like her alone amongst politicians. Warn her about them. A sordid bunch they are. Trust me—we've bribed enough of them." Finnerty laughed again.

"I'll be sure to give Helen your warning." William moved toward the door.

Finnerty raised his voice, "Hazel, my dear. I hope you haven't strayed too far. We have some unfinished business." Then he spoke lower, "Do send her in, William, if you see her idling about."

22

OCTOBER 29, 1916

MEETING HALL

BOSTON, MASS.

"BYRON, I DON'T KNOW why *you* are here. There isn't a baseball player in sight. Isn't there a ship leaving for France that you can get on today?" Margaret didn't bother looking at Byron; instead she concentrated on the table at the front of the stage. Dense cigar smoke wove a thick, gauzy curtain in front of her, but she could still identify some of the men arranging papers and chatting to each other.

"You and Henry Mendes did not invent the opposition to this war," Byron said, staring straight toward the stage. "A lot of us feel the same way."

Margaret ignored him.

Henry Mendes hunched over the table, talking to a wiry, balding, bearded man: Sean Hanratty, feverishly fundraising along the East Coast for the Irish Rebellion. The Rebellion—ignited by the Easter Rising massacre of Irish protesters by British soldiers only a few months earlier. Now the Irish in American cities agitated against any American alliance with the British. The British censored all reporting of the

Easter Rising, fearing that the details would likely diminish whatever appetite America might have to support them.

Billy O'Reilly, his baseball duties now dormant for the winter, and Anne stood next to Margaret and Byron. Their passion for the Irish Rebellion had been held too close for Margaret not to avoid its sting and pain.

John Reed, the man they had come to hear, stood at the table, sorting through a tattered folder. He looked up, engrossed in his own thoughts; then he refocused on the papers he removed from the folder. Margaret recognized him immediately from the newspaper's file photographs. She had heard someone once describe Reed as a 'towering high-pockets of a man with a forehead wide enough to use as a classroom chalk board.' He was handsome in his photographs, and even more so in person, she decided. Henry had given her a loosely tied stack of his articles. She thought they were brilliant with a simple, consistent theme; the workingman always fought the rich man's war. Helen had told her recently that Reed lived with bohemians in Providence—and they had sex with each other's wives and girlfriends.

"Byron, you've talked about going to Europe for over a year now. Whatever you do there will be the same as you did in Mexico—glorifying foreign wars. And Mexico is a foreign country, not to be invaded by us whenever we want to—"

"You have become quite the agitator, haven't you, Sis?" Byron turned to face her. "Do you think all of these panel discussions mean a damn thing? Who the hell appointed Henry to tell us about the universe—"

"I thought Henry was your friend—your *comrade* from some far off adventure. You appear to be enthralled with his every word. Am I mistaken, Byron?"

Anne and Billy stared at the stage. Margaret scrutinized them—

cannon fodder. Sarah's letters described boys like Billy—docilely obeying orders, never questioning anything. Every country has millions of them to throw at each other. *Criminal.*

"Henry's a blowhard," Byron said, his attention again on the men at the table. "An academic. He's against the war but will watch it from the safety of a lectern at Harvard. I think he'd rather meet people and discuss politics than to live anything real."

"Oh, I see, and you live reality by writing about it," Margaret countered, her hand waving dismissively. "Don't you wish sometimes the world would wait so that you can spend a few days at Fenway every October and then drift off to another war? I have yet to read anything original in your *Mexican war correspondence.*"

"Well, I'm leaving in two days for Europe—finally. I know you're angry because I'm leaving Helen for a prize assignment."

Margaret snorted. "Prize assignment? The most horrific event in the history of mankind, but for you it's just a career opportunity."

"I see—" Byron said, then stopped as the crowd pressed in on them.

The hall had a rough grace to it. Just like the audience, Margaret thought. Now fifty years old, it was built by Irish workers, with help from the Catholic Church, as their own meeting place. Ornately carved horses supported the railings and banisters throughout the room.

"Do you think by attaching yourself to the ambulance service you're making it better for Helen?" Margaret said, renewing the argument. "If you're doing this to demonstrate your independence to Father you could have chosen a more sensible way, don't you—"

"My name is John Reed, and I have a magazine called *The Masses.*"

Reed was now at the front of the stage. He paused for the scattered applause to fade. "You can pick up copies of *The Masses* at the doors when you leave. They're free for the taking." He surveyed the audience.

"A year and a half ago I was on my first voyage to Europe. The rich talked only about the war. Yet not one amongst them would ever be called upon to get his hands soiled. Far below our deck, in steerage, thousands of poor Italians crammed together in the most frightful conditions, yearning to return home so they could fight whoever they were told their country's enemies were. From where did they get this obscene patriotism? From where came this need to leave America—a country that held promise for them, in order to find nothing more than a probable death? Why did my companions in first class not feel a similar call to arms?

"Nobody in this country can yet imagine how extreme are the casualties suffered on those battlefields. Yet the rich tell us that we here in America should prepare for the enemy on foreign battlefields. I say that they are the three percent of the population who controls sixty-five percent of the wealth and that they are the enemy we should prepare to fight against. Right here on these streets. Not against another worker in a foreign uniform—"

"Isn't he a brilliant speaker?" Henry Mendes had moved close to Margaret. "I was with him in Mexico, with Villa. He barely remembers me. I joined the correspondents just before he left—I'm glad you're here, Margaret."

She appraised Henry, not certain if his words carried other meanings. Despite his breezy air of sophistication, he sometimes wanted to be flirtatious—it was obvious. She had decided that he had no understanding of how to proceed, or lacked the courage to do so. Despite Henry's condemnations of the corporate rulers, he lacked their ability to make their sexual intentions clear, as Margaret knew all to well. William had once derisively suggested that Henry's asexuality alone fueled his ambition to bring down the ruling class—he was, simply, a frustrated man. Margaret had lost track of John Reed's speech.

"—It is almost as if the rich and the kings would allow their entire working classes to be consumed by this insanity." Reed gazed along the dark wood railing above the main floor; roughly dressed workers leaned their elbows on it, staring down at him, silently.

"Just a few minutes ago, I asked the host of this meeting what is the capacity of this assembly hall. He said 'nine hundred.' It saddened me greatly and I will tell you why.

"This room is filled right now, is it not, ladies and gentlemen?" Reed asked, looking deep into the audience. "You have all come here for a reason." Whistles and clapping of calloused hands filled the hall. Reed motioned his audience to quiet down. "Look carefully around you. Look at the capacity of this room. Nine hundred people."

He paused again. "In France I asked doctors how many soldiers had been killed. Nobody would answer. It's the last thing they want us to know. But I did manage to come to some conclusions with the help of French comrades working to bring this nightmare to an end. The French believe that nine hundred of their soldiers die each day. *Nine hundred every day.* For the entire two years and two months since the war started."

Reed stopped and looked down at his notes, allowing his audience to absorb that understanding. "And that is just the French. The same numbers of British and German soldiers die every day. Nine hundred British and nine hundred Germans every day. And the Russians. Never to return home again. Hospitals will be filled all over Europe for the rest of our lives with the injured, many of them will never see a tree again, or walk across a street."

Reed looked down, overcome with his own words. "So look around you. A roomful this size, of soldiers from each combatant country, dies every day—and that doesn't include civilians caught in the fighting."

Margaret stood amongst the hushed crowd, feeling Reed's words rekindle her outrage. *This is the message that should be heard on radio.*

Margaret, now conciliatory, turned to her brother. "Byron, you should work with groups like this—here in Boston. Your story urging Wilson to speak on the radio was wonderful. *You* should be broadcasting on the radio. I know you agree with Reed's message, even if you are an idiot. We can tell the truth to everybody immediately. Soon we'll be able to broadcast to maybe hundreds of people at a time—maybe more."

Byron listened intently to Margaret's calmly stated vision. He thought for a moment, measuring his words. "Margaret, there is little that will change the course of this nightmare. Neither radio nor John Reed—certainly not Henry Mendes. There is only senseless flag waving in every country. I don't need John Reed to tell me that. But I know my place is there, at the Front. One day I may wish I had listened to you. It will probably be too late then. But do know that I love you and Helen very much."

23

MONDAY, NOVEMBER 6, 1916

MANHATTAN, N.Y.

THE TRAIN RATTLED ALONG the elevated track toward Grand Central Terminal, its last stop. Helen stared down at the intensifying activity on the streets as they rolled through Upper Manhattan. Maybe it was just a shared, unseen pulse amongst the people below her; somehow they moved faster here than in Boston. The buildings seemed larger and stacked closer together. She followed this same route to New York with Margaret and Donald Townsend only a few months before when she first met Vincent but there had been none of the anticipation that overcame her as she now sat pressed against the window.

New York had been cold and snowing, but so very exciting that last trip. Men whistling at them. Lee DeForest grander than she imagined. George Creel. Donald ordering his favorite dishes in that restaurant. And then there was Vincent.

Lee DeForest would be broadcasting the election results the next evening as soon as he received them from the *New American*. He thought that as many as a few thousand people might be listening to the broadcast. They would know as much about the elections as would anyone else in the country.

Flivvers and horse-drawn carriages nimbly avoided each other below her. One engaging street vignette would disappear out of view, to be replaced by still another.

Then the train boomed into the tunnel. Sudden darkness. Life and movement overtaken by screeching metal wheels on metal tracks.

"I'm sorry Margaret was unable to come down with us. I never knew how much work there is to get a newspaper out every day." Mrs. Donnelly leaned forward and raised her voice to gather Helen's attention. "It would have been wonderful to have her with us tomorrow. Imagine, Election Day at the president's campaign headquarters! My husband would never have believed it. As hard as he worked for these men, they never invited him to such a thing."

Helen had heard the gossip many times—Mr. Donnelly was not a kind man to his wife. She had to suffer his drunken, often violent, rages. Yet she spoke proudly of him, never a hint of anger. It's not a simple role, being an Irish wife, Helen thought. She knew that she couldn't do it. She could never waste her life with such a drunken brute.

Helen, realizing that a response was appropriate, collected herself from her musing. "Yes, Mrs. Donnelly, tomorrow should be memorable for all of us. I'm glad someone from headquarters will meet us. It would've been difficult pushing our way through the crowds at the station. I hope you have time to see your relatives while we are in New York."

"Oh yes, I will see my sisters indeed. I even invited them to headquarters. They are thrilled. It will be the biggest event of their lives." Mrs. Donnelly seemed in a surprisingly giddy mood, which Helen found refreshing. "I'm so glad the campaign people were able to find a room at the hotel for us, Helen. Very convenient."

Helen closed her eyes and breathed deeply. She imagined that tomorrow would be a long day and evening. Thoughts crowded each other—from the mundane tracing of the route from the Grand Central Terminal to the campaign headquarters to the more complicated question—with what attitude should she greet Vincent? Or—how should she *try* to greet him?

Whatever happens with Vincent shouldn't really matter, she insisted; after all, the next day a president will be elected and the future would be changed, regardless of the outcome. Being part of this election would be special enough—at least that was her belief when she started working for Wilson. Now she found herself in a maze of intrigue with someone who was probably unaware it even existed.

THEY SAW VINCENT AT the same moment; just as the train stopped, there he was, standing on the platform, looking directly at them—he smiled broadly and touched his hat lightly. *A coincidence that he was right in front of her?* Helen decided that it was best to not give it too much thought. She picked up her purse lying on the empty seat. She raised herself up onto her toes to lower her hatbox from the overhead rack.

"Let me help you with that, Helen." Vincent had entered their compartment. *How much time had elapsed? How did he get to the compartment so quickly?* She moved out of Vincent's way, giving herself a chance to say to his back, "How nice of you to come and see us to the hotel, Vincent."

"My pleasure Helen. Hello, Mrs. Donnelly." Vincent said. He embraced her as if she was an older sister. "Do you ladies have anything else in the overheads?"

Mrs. Donnelly pointed toward two bulky leather bags propped onto the seat. "No, just these. Besides our luggage of course."

Political gossip bound Vincent and Mrs. Donnelly together, thought Helen. She probably never had a single light conversation with her husband. He must have been a real bastard, even though Mrs. Donnelly would likely defend him to her dying breath.

"Here, let me take these bags and your hatbox," Vincent said, turning to Helen. "I have a porter ready to pick up your luggage. And a car to take us to the hotel."

So assured. An experienced campaign organizer, Helen had already established that at the Boston headquarters.

"We must thank you, Vincent," Helen said, looking past him toward Mrs. Donnelly. "We were just talking about how difficult it would be to find our way through this station. I've never seen so many people."

"The streets are absolutely filled today," Vincent said over his shoulder as he stepped down to the station platform. "You can feel the excitement. Everyone is talking about the election. I have never seen New York City this alive."

Helen thought he should have allowed them to step down first. Then she understood when he turned, offering Mrs. Donnelly his hand. He grasped both of Mrs. Donnelly's elbows as she made a surprisingly spry hop to the platform, wobbling like a bowl of jelly when her feet landed with a solid thud. Vincent then held his hand out to Helen. *So courtly.* He must have a hundred last minute details to be concerned about, Helen told herself.

"Thank you," Helen said, careful to keep her eyes on the platform as she stepped down gracefully.

"MANY THOUSANDS OF PEOPLE are expected in Times Square tomorrow night," Vincent said, turning to the two women in the back seat of the taxi, surrounded by bags and hatboxes. "Too bad we don't have a chance of winning New York state, or even New York City for that matter. What on earth do these people see in someone like Hughes? He can put anyone to sleep, and yet here are the most sophisticated people in the country voting for him."

"Perhaps sophistication and intelligence are two different qualities," Helen suggested. "I hardly find people here on the East Coast more intelligent than my neighbors in Denver—one is more likely to hear in Boston or New York how we should send our own men to Europe. I don't think you will find a soul in Colorado who would want to send their sons to France. In my view that is intelligence."

"I agree," Vincent said, gesturing for the driver to make a turn to avoid a crowded side street. "Sometimes when you spend time in this city, you begin to think of it as the center of the universe. It does have that effect on some people."

"I'm sure it wouldn't have that effect upon a man like you, Vincent," Helen said, hoping it did not sound as flirtatious to him, or to Mrs. Donnelly, as it did to her as soon as the words escaped.

"WE ARRIVED YESTERDAY, LEE."

"So nice of you to call, Helen. You can imagine how busy I am right now. Our broadcast will begin in five hours." Lee DeForest said. "Too bad you and Margaret could not come up here to the studio and take part in tonight's program."

"Margaret couldn't come down with us. This is a busy week for the newspaper business, as you can appreciate. But we'll be listening right here at campaign headquarters. There may be two hundred people in the room they set up for your transmission. It looks very impressive. The audio speakers are as big as I have ever seen."

"It's nice to know you'll be listening. Imagine if the president had actually made a speech on radio. We could have transmitted it all over the city. Too bad he didn't have time to do it."

Helen focused on the huge chandelier directly above her. Its gilded brass arms splayed out in every direction, each holding dozens of bright bulbs. The domed room was once an elegant banquet hall, now in disarray after months of serving as the epicenter for a presidential campaign. Men still hunched over, deciphering messages from all over the country.

What did Lee say? "—Oh, yes, that's right, it would have brought enormous attention to radio broadcasting if Wilson had made that speech."

"I understand Byron joined the American Ambulance Corps and is somewhere in France. The last time you and Margaret visited me here at the studio he was in Mexico chasing after Villa. The newspapers are flooded with stories written by the ambulance drivers. I'm sure most men would have stayed behind with you."

Helen's cheeks flushed. DeForest flirted, but she also knew he was right; throughout the day she noticed the admiring glances of the New York campaign workers. She suspected that she had ignited more than one fantasy amongst these tired, but thoroughly focused, men. "That is very kind—there is nothing to do now but await the vote count. Yet everyone is still rushing about as if they have a purpose. As if they can still squeeze out one more vote for Wilson."

"We've also been fiddling with every tube and wire all day. We know everything is ready, but we just can't seem to sit down and calmly await air time—"

Helen's attention diverted to the workers and waiters hauling linens and food trays, still more audio speakers and rolling large spools of wire across the immense oval carpet. In just a few hours the room would start to fill as the Wilson team and friends gathered for the food and live radio broadcast. Amused, she recalled Byron's description of hungry baseball writers, forever trolling hotels around the country for a cheap buffet or even better, a free lunch with free booze. Tonight there would be more interest in a radio broadcast than in food: a wireless audio transmission from a few miles away will be heard in this very banquet room. Most of the celebrants had never heard a radio broadcast before. *They will tonight.*

"Helen, are you still there?"

"Oh, sorry, Lee, I lost you for a moment. The station's sales of receivers over the past year almost doubled. We even have a contract with the Navy—even they are interested in wireless audio now."

"They have been for years. They claim control over wireless everything. I'm sure as radio grows all of those government agencies will want to control it. But I must give a lot of credit to Harold Power. He managed to set up a radio equipment business at Tufts. Receivers, amplifiers. He probably still gets funds from the university as well. What a scoundrel."

"Oh no, Harold is not like that at all. He's devoted to wireless audio the same as we all are—"

"I'm just teasing, Helen. Harold is a wonderful man. Believe me, I know scoundrels in this business and Harold's not one of them. In fact, many people put me in that category. No matter, now I have to get back to my preparations. Call me tomorrow, and let me know how it sounded in that room."

"I certainly will. Good luck, and I hope to hear you say that Wilson won the election."

"I hope that's the case even though I'm supposed to be neutral. You understand—just a radio reporter," DeForest said, clearly amused by the vision of himself without the ability to voice a strong opinion.

"We'll talk again."

Helen returned to her room, to change into a dress she hoped would stand out that evening.

SHE HAD NOT SEEN Vincent since the day before—when he waited patiently as they checked into the hotel, and then he had tipped the bellboy and quickly disappeared. Later, Helen convinced Mrs. Donnelly to join her at the hotel bar for a drink. Actually, it didn't take a lot of convincing; Mrs. Donnelly was known to like a nip of Jameson. Wilson campaign workers crowded around the bar relieved the long hours of the past few months were now over. Helen had looked around several times, hoping to see him.

"I don't think Vincent is here, dear," Mrs. Donnelly said, barely audible above the chatter. Helen pretended she didn't hear it.

"IT APPEARS THAT PRESIDENT Wilson will not be elected for a second term." Lee DeForest's voice carried through the room too clearly.

Helen was numb.

"The *New York American* is already forecasting victory for Justice Charles Evans Hughes," Vincent said, leaning over her shoulder, startling her. "According to the results from New York, New Jersey and Connecticut Mr. Hughes won by a bigger margin in these states than expected."

"I know how hard you've worked on this campaign, Vincent. I'm sorry," Helen said, saddened that so many people had committed so much of themselves to what they believed such an important cause, and now all was lost.

"Everyone worked hard, Helen. I just know we would've had a bet-

222

ter chance to stay out of the war with Wilson."

"I never thought that I would be so unexcited to hear something over the radio. I will have to tell Mr. DeForest to broadcast more pleasant news in the future." She tried to sidestep the grim reality if only for just one more moment.

"Do use whatever influence you have on him." Vincent guided Helen towards the still crowded bar and gestured to the bartender. He pointed toward the champagne bottles and held two fingers in the air.

"Our forecast is still not as certain as Lee's," Helen said, not yet accepting the news as established fact.

"Maybe we're just too close to the election," Vincent suggested. "Maybe DeForest has a clearer of view of the outcome. Who knows? Let's toast anyway. Then maybe we can brave the street crowds."

"You mean let's be good sports. I'm all for that," Helen said, not certain if she even intended a sports reference. But she did know that she was nervous.

HUGHES WINS

The handwritten headline on a huge chalkboard at the side of the Times Square Building told the story. The festive public drunkenness suggested approval of the simple declaration.

A depressing outcome.

The evening was chillier than Helen expected. She pressed her head onto Vincent's chest. For some reason, it seemed easy—natural—despite having devoted so much energy weighing the possibilities. He drew his arm around her and gently pulled her closer. Both self-consciously concentrated on the sign that didn't require as much attention as they gave it. Neither wanted to look at the other.

"I wonder why so many people have come here tonight?" Helen asked. "Why *this* building?"

"Because this is where the latest results can be found, right here at the *Times*. Most of these people here gambled on the outcome. They want to know who won as soon as possible. Look around, Helen. Many are still betting with each other."

Loose circles of men stabbed their fingers in the air and at each other. They had adapted an improvised sign language that would replace verbal acceptance of bets whenever the surrounding frenzy overpowered their ability to hear each other. Newcomers to the circles quickly identified someone who would take the opposite side of a bet.

Helen smiled, enjoying watching the activity all around her. "It never occurred to me that people would bet on a presidential election. I must be very sheltered. Thanks for taking me out into the real world, Vincent." Helen looked around again. "Has this sort of *activity* gone on in other elections?"

"Yes, Helen. It started with George Washington's election and never stopped. Actually, it has been a very good predictor of the outcomes."

"How is that?"

"The favorite has always won. Hughes was a big favorite until this week. Earlier today he was just a small favorite. Do you know how that works?"

"I do have sports people in my family, Vincent."

He leaned down as she looked up. Their mouths opened and gently touched. He's so warm and strong, she thought, She was relieved *.It was easy. Thank goodness.*

They both glanced around, unfocused.

"It will always be difficult to understand what makes someone from a city as great as this vote for someone without a bit of flare or foresight," Helen said, reaching for a comment she thought might be appropriate.

Vincent agreed. "Yes, and I am always fascinated by people who vote against their own interests because they assume some personality trait in the candidate is more important than the issues."

"What do you mean?"

"Some people actually think they would rather have dinner with Hughes than with Wilson. Wilson is too intellectual for them. Even though the last thing in the world Hughes would want is to actually spend time with one of—"

"Kiss me again, Vincent." Helen stood on tiptoe and flung her arms around his neck.

"AS IF WE HAVEN'T been punished enough already, let's follow these happy penguins to their celebration." Vincent folded his topcoat around Helen and pointed east, following the surging crowd that seemed to know where the evening's next entertainment would unfold. "There's safety in numbers I was once told," Vincent added, leading her towards the East Side.

"Well, that is comforting to know," Helen said, allowing herself a flirtatious gaze directly into Vincent's eyes.

They walked in silence, the crowded streets slowing them. At Lexington Avenue, forward progress ended. Thousands had stopped, staring up at a blinking electric sign hung off the roof of the Waldorf-Astoria Hotel, reading simply, **CHARLES EVANS HUGHES**.

"This is where Hughes is staying tonight," Vincent said. "He's right to be here. This is his city, and he might as well celebrate the victory here. Everybody knows Wilson's low opinion of this town."

"You got that right, mister." A short man with a gray bowler had squeezed in front of them. He jerked his thumb over his shoulder. "They say the president's going to come to one of those upper windows in a few minutes."

"Wonderful. *Already* the president." Vincent said, returning Helen's amused glance with a shudder of his shoulders. "Enjoy yourself, pal."

Vincent took Helen's hand in his and turned down Madison Avenue.

She didn't know how it happened but suddenly they were in a doorway, embracing. They kissed. Vincent opened his heavy topcoat and unbuttoned her black cashmere coat. He drew their bodies together.

"I want so much for you to spend the night with me," Vincent said softly. "I hope you are not insulted. I know you are married. I just think about you all the time. Since you first walked into the Salisbury Hotel restaurant."

"I didn't think you noticed me." Helen laid her head on his chest. She was unaware of the cold. "I really can't do that, Vincent."

"I didn't mean to presume—"

"No, it's not that, Vincent—I want to—but Mrs. Donnelly shares the room with me. I don't want to lie to her. If I don't come back this evening she'll be worried. What would I tell her? The car broke down? A friend is in the hospital? She's a sharp old bird. I couldn't pull the wool over her eyes that easily."

"Mrs. Donnelly would be thrilled if we were together—she told me that several times, and in so many words." Vincent stroked Helen's hair back over her shoulder. "'You two would make a handsome couple'—that's what she told me in Boston. Tonight, she'll be staying at her sister's house in Queens."

"Oh my, Vincent. So you conspired with Mrs. Donnelly to—to shack up with me, I believe that is the vulgar expression. Is it not?" She slid her hand around his waist pressing him closer.

Vincent smiled. "I'm surprised a lady like you has heard it. But conspired? No. She commiserated with me. She said that she could feel the attraction between us, and that we were both too clever about it for our own good. That is exactly what she said—'too clever for your own good.'"

"I never realized we were on a stage, Vincent."

"Actually she told me"—Vincent could not finish his thought without grinning—"she told me, 'Don't stay in this hotel with her. You do have an apartment, don't you, Vincent. Well, use it!' That's what she said in the hotel lobby yesterday morning. 'People *will* talk. But I *won't* be one of them.' That is also what she said."

"So your friendship with the dear lady is not just old political stories, is it?"

"A personal relationship with one's colleagues often has unexpected benefits."

"So I see." Helen rose up to Vincent's lips again.

HELEN RAN THE PALM of her hand over the beige silk bed sheet. A silk sheet gentleman. A bit of a surprise. Everything the night before had been a surprise to Helen, even though she thought about it for weeks—she could now at least admit that much to herself. *We may have lost the election, but oh, my God. Where did he go? It would be lovely to be lying next to him right now. How exciting—standing over him while he undressed me. How he touched my breasts! Wrapping my legs around his thighs. How did we get to the bedroom? I can't remember.*

The front door opened, and then quickly snapped shut. She could hear Vincent putting a bag onto the kitchen counter, a few cans rattling.

"Where did you go? I thought perhaps you've already left me," she said, dreamily, knowing that to be an unlikely possibility.

"I went to the bakery downstairs. Helen, this is not over," Vincent announced from the sitting room.

"I should hope not. I do have some plans for you," Helen said, rolling toward him as he entered the bedroom.

He leaned over and pulled the cover down to kiss her breasts. "No, I mean the election is not over. Your Mr. DeForest got it all wrong. But so did the *New York Times*. So I can't complain only about you radio people."

"What are you talking about, Vincent?"

"The Hughes' victory forecast was far too premature. The later results show a big Wilson vote. Many states are *still* very close. It may take days for us to know the winner. This is rather extraordinary."

"Remarkable. Has there ever been an election this close before?" Helen said, stroking his check, still ruddy from the wind whipping off the East River.

"I don't know but I am grateful that *this one* is so close."

"And why is that? You sexy man." Helen pulled him by his tie onto the bed. He offered no resistance.

"Mrs. Donnelly thought that you and she should stay until there is a clear outcome. It was her suggestion. Everyone's going back to headquarters to await the Midwestern states' results, which might not be counted until later today."

"You already spoke to Mrs. Donnelly? I hope you didn't tell her too much. You both do gossip quite a bit, you know."

"I only told her, 'Thank you.'"

"I'll have to thank that dear lady, too," Helen said, drawing a deep breath. She undid his belt slowly and opened the buttons on his pants. In a smooth motion she slid her hand inside. "Now, Mr. Chelios, perhaps we can await those Midwestern results in this bed—"

24

NOVEMBER 11, 1916

GLENFIDDICH INN

NEW BEDFORD, MASS.

"SO ONE OF THE HEARST boys called Hughes's hotel room the morning after the election," Donald Townsend said. He began laughing as soon as he started the anecdote. "He wanted a quote about Wilson taking back the lead the next morning. Whoever answered the telephone said, 'The president is still asleep.' The Hearst guy tells him, 'When the president wakes up, tell him he's not the president anymore.'" He had told the story many times over the past four days.

"I only wish it had been one of my reporters," Donald added, sticking his fork into a large piece of Isaac's chocolate birthday cake.

"Imagine that." Beatrice looked around the table. "It took two and a half days to be certain of the outcome. We only heard the California results on Friday morning."

Agnes crossed the dining room with a coffee pot. "Someone said that if only one vote in every district in California had been for Hughes instead of Wilson, we would have had a new president. One town's results came in late at night on a snow sled and gave the state to Wilson. That's what I read. It might have been in a competitor's newspaper if I remember well, Donald."

"In time you will be forgiven, Agnes." Donald patted her on her wrist.

"How thrilling it must have been for Helen—" said Margaret—"being at the center of it all. She's finally coming home later today."

"We sold more newspapers over the past five days than we have in a long time." Donald motioned to Agnes for a coffee refill. "We should have a close presidential race every four years. Thank you, Agnes."

"I'm glad Helen had Mrs. Donnelly to keep her company," Beatrice said, cutting a sliver of the birthday cake. "Even a big city can be a lonely place after a few days. Especially if you don't have close friends or family nearby."

"Has Helen heard from Byron since he left?" Agnes asked. "It has been several months already, hasn't it?"

"He sent me a letter." Margaret looked away from the table. The corners of the dining room were dark, the candlelight on the table the only illumination. "I didn't bring it because, well, frankly Aunt Agnes, it was a bit too grisly. I know he fashions himself quite the war correspondent, but I would prefer to spare you the details."

Donald Townsend disapproved. "Margaret, you are from a newspaper family and one of our obligations is to provide details, *grisly* as they may be."

"But Father, you know that's not true. We are a family newspaper and you often excise these kinds of details," Margaret said, grinning, knowing her father was demonstrating his ability to be a 'bag of wind,' as her mother sometimes described him.

"At the moment this is a family gathering, not a family newspaper," Donald replied.

Margaret agreed. "So it is, Father. Dear Byron wrote about a Casualty Clearing Station, as they are called. They are usually located just a few miles behind the front lines. This is where they evaluate the wounded and send the worst cases onto military hospitals. They also do operations and whatever else is necessary. Byron also said that estates and castles are converted into these stations. Sometimes they use churches or factories.

"One afternoon he came over a hill with a wounded soldier in his ambulance. He could see the building that was being used as a Clearing Station less than a mile in front of him. He had never been there before. He was happy to see it because the wounded soldier with him was in great pain and the bumpy roads just made it worse for him.

"Without warning the hospital exploded from a direct hit by German artillery. The whole building just exploded. He could see the building shake and the walls collapsing. He heard horrific screams even from that far away. It was a beautiful sunny day and in one instant everything changed.

"As he drove closer to the destroyed building, he saw a sign that read something about Home for the Protection of the Children of the Frontier. Byron realized that the screams he heard were from the children—"

"I think that is enough detail," Beatrice interrupted. Agnes just nodded her agreement, her shoulders shivering.

Isaac and Hans Stitler entered, carrying a dented metal box. Isaac motioned to Agnes to clear off the marble-topped sideboard.

"This is what Isaac and I are developing now," Hans announced proudly.

"What is *this*, Uncle Isaac?" Margaret pointed at the box. "Or rather, what is it *this* time?"

"My dear, say what you will about progress, but you cannot stop it." Isaac enjoyed Margaret's teasing. "Remember dear, you have to contend with naysayers about your radio experiments, don't you?"

Margaret nodded, smiling.

"*This* is an electric dough mixer," Hans announced, pleased with their newly developed appliance.

Four thin metal strips molded into pear shapes welded onto each of two metal rods extended out of the main housing—a plain metal box.

Hans plugged the electric cord into the wall socket behind the sideboard. Then he pressed a button on the side of the box.

Isaac looked over his shoulder, beaming. "You put these rods into a large bowl and it mixes the dough," he explained, satisfied with still another creation—whether it had any practical use never seemed to matter.

The thin metal beaters rotated and whined.

"We will use it to bake the cake next time," announced Hans.

"Oh my dear Hans, perhaps you should concentrate on butchering," Agnes suggested. "I can just see the dough flying all over the kitchen."

Hans grunted his disagreement.

"Hans, do you and Isaac ever patent anything?" Donald asked. "This is a very clever invention."

"We've applied for several patents, but we haven't for a few years— that last one was for the—" Isaac said, looking toward Hans for a prompt. Hans shrugged.

"But don't they have electric mixers at bakeries already?" William was accustomed to their clever inventions never being quite finished. Never quite ready for patent approval. Inevitably someone else would put a refined version of one of their crude devices on the market first, and Isaac and Hans would just mutter to themselves.

Isaac picked up the box and held it over the table. "No William, they don't have these yet for the home. They do have industrial-sized ones."

"The problem is that this motor is too big for a housewife to use comfortably," Hans explained. "William, you remember, those motors you and Gunther brought to my shop? I think there is a very small one mixed into the lot of them. That one might work with this."

"Thank goodness the two of you cleared those motors out of here," Agnes said. "Why don't you tell our guests about the dough flying around the kitchen when you tested these beater gadgets last week?"

"That was a mechanical problem we are fixing," Hans said dryly.

Margaret and Beatrice giggled.

"Has everyone heard about the German submarine that docked at Newport last month?" Donald asked, concluding they had exhausted the mixing bowl discussion. "Judging from our circulation, there is a lot of interest in it. Our Navy men are still talking about the gadgetry on the U-boats."

"It sickens me to think of a German submarine in our ports," Margaret said. "It was even *escorted* into Newport. Imagine that? *Escorted by our Navy.*"

"We are not at war with Germany. We are neutral," William reminded her. "Not allowing them into our harbor would be denying our neutrality."

"What are you talking about, William?" Margaret asked, her face flushing. "I'm talking about a German submarine, just like the one that torpedoed the *Lusitania*. A German submarine killed your sister Louella and all of those innocent people. I don't care about neutrality. German U-boats, submarines, call them whatever you wish, don't have to be in our ports, do they?"

"And to think, all of our admirals and our Navy people went aboard to inspect it as if it would never be a threat to us"— Beatrice shook her head—"they even took their wives and children aboard."

"It was a good propaganda maneuver," Donald said. "They had a subtle message for us—*we can sink your shipping at will.* The government lawyers are still trying to determine if we should treat a submarine with the same laws of neutrality as we do regular sea vessels."

Margaret stared disbelieving at her father. "And while they were *determining* the legalities, that submarine left Newport the next day and immediately torpedoed five British ships."

"I read that some people don't believe a submarine could make it all the way from Germany without assistance—that they had to have help from somewhere," Agnes said, gesturing for Margaret to fill her and Beatrice's coffee cups. "Another ship to refuel it, perhaps? A *mother ship*, someone called it."

"According to everything written, it was a long journey and they were hunted by the Canadian Navy, who could have sunk them," William said, knowing he had good sources—his clients at Dexter Shipbuilding. "But the Navy's Morse code messages were all contradictory. Everybody knew they were around, but they couldn't agree on the submarine's exact location."

"George Creel told me those Morse code messages created chaos," Donald added. "The Navy censored most of them. That's why the U-boat just showed up in the harbor. Surprised everybody."

"I agree with Margaret. I don't like this at all," Hans said, removing the beaters from its housing. "I would be happier if they stayed away from our shores. I don't care what kind of modern devices they have. They can keep them in Germany for all I care."

Agnes gave Hans a table napkin to clean off the roughly welded dough mixer. "Everyone along the coast here is worried about those submarines. Remember, we're losing a lot of business here in New Bedford. People don't want a vacation at the shore knowing there are submarines sinking British ships on the horizon."

"Aunt Agnes, that sounds too dramatic for my taste," William said.

"Don't you read the family's newspaper, William?" Margaret asked impatiently. "Or *any* newspaper? There *are* German submarines sinking British ships right here—right off of Cape Cod."

Hans spoke quietly. "I'm afraid that even if we are neutral there will be big problems for us Germans if these submarines are nearby. Remember when that submarine sank the *Lusitania* and we lost Louella? The people in Liverpool burned the German shops. Even the Irish rioted against us—"

William shook his head, reluctantly agreeing. "Imagine what it would be like here if the Germans are winning the war. There'll be a lot of rabble in the streets—"

"—Henry Mendes believes that the Russian soldiers are mutinying on the Eastern Front," Margaret interrupted. "He says the Russians have no will to fight the Germans. If the revolutionaries take over Russia, they will ask for peace with Germany. Then Germany will be much stronger on the Western Front and maybe could win."

"Wilson's neutrality *won*, at least for us. We have a good chance to stay out of this." Donald took the bottle of port from Beatrice and absently gazed at the label. "All the Germans have to do to win the war is to not sink any of our ships. They seem too smart to want to drag us into this."

Four months later

25

"HELEN, IT'S BEEN A year since we last sat at this very table." George Creel spread his hands over the neatly placed dinner settings. "Actually, Mrs. Donnelly, you are the only one who wasn't here then. I'm very happy that you agreed to come down here with Helen to work for us—there is so much we have to do. Too bad Margaret couldn't join us."

"She's so busy these days working on radio receivers and transmitters." Donald Townsend said. Although he had newspaper ink in his veins, he had resigned himself to radio now having at least some potential to reach an audience. "The war has increased sales at the station. I know how much our newspaper circulation has increased over just the past year."

"There is still very little profit in the equipment but every sale gives us a few new listeners," Helen added.

"How do you enjoy living in New York, Helen? I still think of this as a most interesting place, regardless of whatever our president thinks," Creel said, his mood expansive—his work for Wilson had been receiving good reviews from his former newspaper colleagues. "I understand that Vincent was able to find a comfortable apartment for you and Mrs. Donnelly. Will he be joining us for lunch?"

"Yes, I agree Mr. Creel. New York City is a far more interesting place than I ever expected." Helen said thoughtfully and then glanced at the open menu laid out in front of her. "Especially after one is here for awhile."

"Vincent may come later." Mrs. Donnelly looked carefully at the menu, but for a different reason—this restaurant was a luxury for her, not a place she would choose for a workday lunch. "He has been spending so much time building out our new offices. I never worked for the federal government before—there are so many people involved in every decision, and yes, our apartment has a lovely view of the East River—and it's quite spacious. "

It was in reality now Mrs. Donnelly's apartment. The two women were far more likely to see each other in their office than in their sitting room. Helen would race to Vincent's apartment after work everyday. He lived only three streets from her.

Helen pointed to her menu and the waiter nodded. "Not well done *please*—I'm sure you would agree, Mr. Creel, this is not Denver, or Boston for that matter. Manhattan does seem to be an island unto itself." She knew that she and Vincent could never have carried on this torrid love affair in any of those cities. She had come to understand that New York allows one to— well, to just disappear.

She looked at Mrs. Donnelly having a whispered moment with the waiter, an amiable lean man with a shiny handlebar moustache. He pointed at an item on the menu with a bony index finger and smiled at her response. Mrs. Donnelly will always be a politician's wife—Helen decided—she has a word with everyone, and can certainly be trusted to keep a confidence.

Helen recalled an afternoon when Mrs. Donnelly admonished her loud enough so that Cynthia Havens, the office gossip, could hear her urging Helen to 'leave the apartment more often and take advantage of New York's magnificent attractions.' *Gilding the lily with Irish blarney.*

"I agree, of course. New York is special," Creel said. "I imagine that once we are in this war, I will be here a lot more."

Helen caught herself smirking. Margaret was so right, George Creel did have a bit of the blowhard in him. That's what Byron would call it, she thought.

"So you believe it's inevitable that we are entering the war?" Mrs. Donnelly asked. "There's still part of me that can't bear being on the same side as the British. Those feelings die hard, you understand."

"Indeed, Mrs. Donnelly," Creel replied quickly. "That's why we are thinking of organizing a massive educational plan to support the president. We know how many people in this country want to avoid the war at any cost."

"The Germans sank five of our ships two days ago. *Five of them,*" said Donald, shaking his head with disbelief. "They seem to want us in this war—against them? And after working so hard to keep us out."

"You know better than that, Donald." Creel handed his menu back to the waiter. "The Germans are sending more soldiers to the Western Front. Now they believe that if they starve Britain of American materials they can win. The only way to do that is to go after neutral shipping—that's us. They think we're not prepared for entry into the war and by the time we get ready, they can win. It's a rather uncomplicated strategy."

"Then it could happen—the Germans could win the war *that* quickly?" Helen asked, troubled by the possibility, one that she had never considered before.

"The Germans may be underestimating us, Helen," Creel said. "That's why the president wants us to be prepared for war. That's where people like Vincent, you, Mrs. Donnelly, and soon thousands of others, will be concentrating our efforts—in education."

"I hope that doesn't mean propaganda and not discussion, George." Donald had given thought to this concern many times before. "You know how easy it is for government bureaucrats to blur the thin line between information and their own propaganda. You had your own struggles with them many times, haven't you, George?"

"I certainly have had my battles with them." Creel took a deep breath and expelled it slowly. "Even our own bureaucrats can't keep it secret that the president will have to declare war within a few days. The Germans are giving us no room on this one."

"Here's Vincent," Mrs. Donnelly said, half raising her ample backside out of her chair. She waved in his direction. She realized her gesture was unnecessary; they were the only diners in the restaurant. He crossed the room.

"Has everyone ordered already?" Vincent asked, looking around the table.

"I ordered your usual, Vincent," Mrs. Donnelly said. She confided sotto voce to her tablemates, as if breaking a confidence; "the poor man asks for the same lunch everyday—a little bitty deviled egg salad. He could use more meat on his bones, if you ask me."

Donald rose to shake Vincent's hand. "You look very well, my boy. George was telling us that the president will ask for a declaration of war soon. *This* is what we call news—even though it has not exactly been a secret that we are moving in this direction. You have a difficult chore ahead of you, Vincent, changing public opinion. But like the rest of us, you have worked at it before."

"That's why I want Vincent here in New York." Creel never would let a conversation get too far away from him. "He's had plenty of experience with the Hearst people in San Francisco and they are masters at molding public opinion!"

"Vincent, I want to thank you personally—also from my wife," Donald said earnestly. "We disapproved of Helen's move down to New York. We would never allow her to live here by herself—despite how exciting and important she thought this work to be. It just didn't seem right, with Byron off on his fool's mission in Europe. I'm sure he wouldn't have approved of it either."

Donald paused, then turned to Helen. "Oh yes, Helen, I'm glad I didn't forget. I have that letter from Byron in my room. I'll send the bellboy up for it."

"I'm also certain that Byron wouldn't have approved if Helen was here alone," Vincent said. "I only regret that I don't have even more time to spend with her and Mrs. Donnelly. But they seem to be doing just fine."

He did manage to deliver his observation with sufficient candor—after all, Helen *was* 'doing just fine' in New York.

III

"It's a plague"

26

"I KNOW PRECISELY WHAT I would like for my birthday, William."
Margaret stretched over the workbench, pulling the wall telephone
receiver cord taut. It had just enough play for her to reach a small cardboard box. "—No. Wrong again. No cigar, as they say. I'll just have to
tell you—why don't we go to New York that weekend? Especially since
Byron won't be here to celebrate our birthdays together. I haven't seen
Helen for months. Now that we have a war on our hands she'll be busy
working for Creel. We can see a Broadway show—that Irving Berlin
one. Do say yes."

She turned the cardboard box over, examining each side. "—*Oh
no.*—No, nothing to do with you dear—I just noticed the transmitter
box says '1EX' not '1XE'—That's not very funny, yes it does matter,
William—*some people* do know the difference. I spent so much time
on the design and that senseless printer just changed the lettering—"

She pushed the box to the far edge of the workbench.

"I thought we could even surprise Helen and knock on her door.
But maybe we should ask in advance if she and Mrs. Donnelly even

want us to come to New York. Maybe they have too little time for us—I'll see you at the inn—tell Aunt Agnes that I'm certain dinner will be wonderful." She hung up, and glanced back at the box on the workbench.

Harold Power walked across the room. "Margaret, I was talking to DeForest yesterday. He sends you his best regards. He's still broadcasting music and a few news stories every day. I was surprised to know how fond he is of classical music. He doesn't seem the type."

"No, he doesn't seem the type," Margaret said. "Too bad there was no broadcast of the president reading his speech to Congress. Can you imagine how dramatic it would have been to hear the president himself ask for a declaration of war on the radio? *Everyone* would have listened!"

"I agree completely, Margaret, but that'll change soon. This war will be responsible for radio receivers in many more sitting rooms."

"Well, I hope whoever buys our equipment doesn't get one of these boxes." She pointed to the misspelling of the station letters. "William asked if anyone would know the difference." She shook her head in mock disbelief.

Power grinned. "Well, we certainly have spent a lot of time educating people about who we are. Let's hope that by now they know the difference between IXE and IEX."

Margaret watched the familiar Navy car stop next to the gravel path leading to the station. "I didn't know Chief Henderson was coming today."

"Maybe he's here to complain about the misspelling," Power suggested, amused by the possibility.

"Whatever he is here for, he brought a few other officers with him," Margaret said; three men in crisp blue uniforms walked alongside Chief Warrant Officer Henderson.

"Maybe they want the two-cent tour?" Power shrugged his shoulders. "After all, they *are* our best customer."

My, Harold, you are in a good mood today."

Margaret answered the telephone on its first ring. "Oh hello, Lee. So nice to hear from you—What? —That can't be true. No, I don't want you to read it to me—It was just issued today? —They are here already. They just arrived—let me get off the telephone—Can we talk later? —Thank you."

Power walked to the transmitter room with Chief Henderson; the other officers stood in the center of the laboratory, holding themselves ramrod straight as their unblinking eyes took in the banks of equipment.

Power read the document Henderson handed him. Henderson removed his hat, twirling it.

"Read it aloud please, Harold." Margaret already knew its contents. Harold looked up. "Margaret, this is Executive Order 2858—"

"Read it please, Harold."

Power complied in a dull monotone;

"'Such radio stations with the jurisdiction of the United States as are required for naval communications shall be taken over by the Government of the United States and used and controlled by it, to the exclusion of any other control or use; and furthermore that all radio stations not necessary to the Government of the United States for naval communications, may be closed for radio communication.'"

"This is *our* station, Chief Henderson," Margaret declared, a reddening of cheeks accompanying her indignation. "Why do you government bureaucrats have to stop our work? We have nothing to do with the war."

"I know how you must feel." Henderson's eyes searched the room. "Remember Margaret, we have been working with you for several years now. We intend to keep you busy perfecting transmitters and receivers. I hope—"

"I don't care what you hope." Margaret looked to Power for support.

"But Margaret, this is wartime," Power reasoned.

"What do you do now, Officer Henderson—to 'take over'?" Margaret asked.

"The men with me will be sealing and dismantling different parts of your transmitting equipment."

Margaret laughed derisively. "Would they even know what a transmitter looks like?" She shot a challenging stare at the trio—they looked away.

Margaret glared at him. "Perhaps you can help them if they need it?" Henderson's tone was gentle, conciliatory. Margaret glared at him. "I think not." She looked at Power once again. "I know *you* understand how important radio is, Harold. We could get information about the war out to the listeners instantly."

Power said nothing.

Margaret turned to Henderson. "Do *you* understand, Mr. Henderson?"

"Margaret," Power answered for Henderson, "Do *you* understand that the government does not want us to give just *any* information about the war to our listeners?"

27

JUNE 1917

THE PLAZA HOTEL

NEW YORK, N.Y.

"I DON'T CARE IF Vanderbilt was the first guest at this hotel—or if his family mansion has thirty-nine rooms just for the domestics." Margaret tugged at Helen's arm to alert her to an overflowing baggage trolley pushed by a hunched-over bellboy moving toward the front desk. They stepped around him, through the polished brass revolving door and out into the late June midday sunshine.

"Our office is just a few streets to the east." Helen pointed across Fifth Avenue. "Walking will probably be easier than a taxi, especially going *crosstown*, as they say here in New York."

Margaret hooked her arm around Helen's elbow. "So you've become immersed in the local culture, my dear? A *New Yawk* accent won't have the same charm as your old country Colorado manner."

Helen smiled. "I don't think I'll ever be a convincing New *Yawker*."

They turned toward the small plaza, cut out of the corner of Central Park South and Fifth Avenue. Couples in earnest conversation occupied the few benches, along with an occasional solitary soul contemplating the splashes of colors in the carefully clipped flowerbeds.

Margaret walked towards the bronzed statue of General William

Tecumseh Sherman, astride his horse, looking off heroically to a distant horizon. "You are aware that this little space of green required a newspaper man, Pulitzer, to donate the money for it?"

"Yes, I know. They finally turned the water on in the fountain just the other day."

"Yes. Grand Army Plaza, as they call this, is not so grand, is it?" Margaret said. "But it is charming. A modest tribute to the Union soldiers. Is your Committee already planning an appropriate tribute to our boys when they come back from Europe? Whenever that is."

Helen gestured toward the other side of Fifth Avenue.

They crossed the avenue toward a brown brick mansion stretching the entire city block.

"So, Helen, here is a mystery for you to solve. Perhaps it is something your new committee of thought-shapers can examine," Margaret suggested. "How is it that Alfred Vanderbilt was the first guest at The Plaza, where he had his own apartment, *un pied-à-terre*, so to speak, while his family mansion only two streets away has one hundred and fifty six rooms?"

"Not quite a mystery." Helen moved out of the path of a chubby little girl running away from her nanny. "He was a bit of a cad with his wife. Loved intrigue with the ladies. A simple story."

"I think that it would be a bit too close to home for my comfort," Margaret said.

Helen lightly guided Margaret away from a man strolling next to her, reading a newspaper, oblivious to the foot traffic around him. "I still find it remarkable that a man like Alfred Vanderbilt would act so valiantly on the *Lusitania*, knowing that he wouldn't survive. He was last seen tying infants to wicker baskets, hoping they would float."

"Yes. Yes, I know, Helen. The richest man in America, and he never learned to swim. When I think about the *Lusitania* all I can imagine is our Louella drowning and leaving Sarah almost an orphan in wartime Scotland. That should be our headline, Helen, not the heroism of a Vanderbilt."

"You must admit this is an extraordinary structure." Helen said, ignoring the suggested 'headline.' She stopped Margaret in front of the main entrance to the Vanderbilt Mansion. Three men in an animated, inaudible discussion, pointed up to the canopy overhanging the entrance.

Margaret turned to Helen. "For all we know, much that has been written about his last gasp gallantry is as full of hot air as is this clever press-agentry you, Vincent, and Creel are engaging in about the war."

"If you have time later, we can visit the office—but only after we go shopping on Madison Avenue," Helen said. "You seem a bit caustic today. Do you want to tell me what is troubling you, Margaret—or shall I take a few wild guesses?"

"I just want to talk to you without your earnest colleagues bumping into me with their colorful 'why we are fighting' signs."

Helen stopped. "Shall I be blunt? It's about Vincent, is it not?"

"Some of it, yes." Margaret moved towards the front of a clothing shop window to evaluate a blue and white silk dress draped over a pink mannequin. "I was, at first, quite surprised at dinner last night—but then I should have guessed."

"We weren't businesslike enough?" Helen reached for a lighter tone. "We sat too close to each other? A lingering touch, perhaps?"

Helen anticipated this conversation since Margaret and William met her and Vincent and Mrs. Donnelly at Turin, the restaurant that had become her favorite, just two blocks from the apartment she now rarely even visited.

"I was embarrassed. I wasn't sure if my embarrassment was for me or for you," Margaret said cautiously, trying to temper a confrontational tone. "It was so obvious. You both worked so hard to never look at each other. Quite unnatural, if you ask me. And you did appear a bit flushed."

"I was looking for the right moment to tell you about it. Byron being your brother makes the situation all the more—difficult." Helen lightly touched Margaret's elbow.

"And Mrs. Donnelly? Has she been a co-conspirator, so to speak?" Margaret looked a little closer at the rose and yellow dress in the window. "I do like it, don't you Helen?"

"Yes, she has known about it since the beginning. Margaret, I am torn. I don't really know what to do. Byron is so far away. He left me, remember?"

"Helen, Byron is an idiot for leaving you. We all know that. How evolved has this plot become, may I ask?"

"I don't know. It is all so new—and different." Helen turned to the shop window. "Byron's recent letter made me cry. He actually thinks that he is doing something that dozens of other writers are not doing. After a while all of the news is just dreadful."

Margaret grinned. "As soon as we declared war the Army made the volunteer drivers join the military. So now my foolish brother is a military ambulance driver. And even more restricted in what he can write about—not exactly the outcome he was looking for."

"Does William know about me and Vincent?" Helen asked. "It is— uhhm, sensitive. Did he say anything to you after dinner last night?"

"William is as aware of these matters as is the mannequin I'm looking at right now." They both giggled at the comparison.

THE HUMMING EFFICIENCY OF the Committee office surprised Margaret. She had expected a replica of the hectic campaign headquarters she had visited in Boston before the election. That she understood—it felt like her newspaper office as deadline approached.

The Committee for Public Information had only been funded two months before; but the New York office already had the feel of a company with focus—and purpose. Only one person imprinted this Committee. One with a vision, and the power to exercise it—George Creel.

Ironically, only two years before he was railing against corporations that exploited child labor, and had been struggling to keep a spotlight focused on it. Margaret remembered his concern that the United States would go to war and that his battles with corporate greed would be forgotten. Now he had a single directive from the president—*sell the war to the American people.*

"Margaret, so nice to see you." Vincent Chelios threaded between two desks, extending his hand. "Helen called to tell us you might stop by."

"Vincent, when I think back to that night we met at Father's dinner for Mr. Creel—" Margaret faltered. "That was just two years ago. Who would have thought we would now be in a war? Sending our soldiers over there seemed so remote then."

"We all now need to put our differences aside and find a common purpose," he said, his response measured and thoughtful.

Margaret's mouth curled into a wry smile. "Are you considering running for office, Vincent? That had the tired cadence of a speech someone makes from the back of a train, somewhere in the hinterlands of Illinois, perhaps."

"I suppose it does," he responded agreeably.

Margaret looked around the room. Artists huddled around large signs, applying color to rough charcoal sketches. A man sat at a drawing board, applying broad black strokes to a canvas; his foot rested on top of an opened lower drawer, exposing a faded plaid sock in need of darning. Probably a bachelor, concluded Margaret. *Most wives would not let him out in the street that way.*

"Could it be true the committee will be expanding to as many as one hundred thousand people?" Margaret asked.

"We are hiring people all over the country." Vincent gestured for Margaret and Helen to sit down at his desk piled with folders. "This is not unlike a newsroom—there is so much to be done. Educating the people about the need for unity after so much bitter disagreement will not be easy."

"You *do* plan for public debates—the way these matters were discussed even in Ancient Greece, according to my mother anyway—don't you?" Margaret asked. "Or will we just see one of these signs on every street corner?" She motioned to the large sign propped against a table, held securely by an artist, a stub of a cigarette in his mouth. The freckle-faced cartoon soldier wore a snappy military outfit and, looking earnestly at the viewer, pressed a finger to his mouth; the stylized copy warned **BEWARE, the Enemy is Listening.**

"Some of us feel that the time for debate is over," Vincent said. "Now we need unity. It won't be easy to beat the Germans. And don't forget, the war is far away. We need to fight them in France before we have to fight them here."

Margaret looked at Helen, seeking at least an amused reaction. She wasn't certain if she saw it. "Do I hear a slogan being honed by you, Vincent? *Fight Them There, Before We Have To Fight Them Here.* Fortunately, Vincent, and this may come as a surprise, even the government is allowing anti-war protests. We have permits to demonstrate our dissatisfaction next week. In Boston Commons. Fourth of July week."

"We?" asked Helen. She looked at Vincent, then at Margaret.

"Yes, *we*," Margaret said sharply. "Henry Mendes is one of the organizers. He's coordinating it with other anti-war groups. You do remember him, don't you? I'm working with him now."

"Henry Mendes?" Helen asked. "Oh yes, Byron's war souvenir from Mexico. Things must be slow at Harvard these days. I thought he came east to do research—or to lecture, was it?"

"No need to be so derisive." Margaret plucked up a cigarette from the bronze caddy. "Remember, there was a time, just a few months ago, in fact, that you, and probably Vincent, were as opposed to this war as some of us still are. Even though you are now getting paid to whip the population into a fervor, some of us *still* believe it is as wrong as it was five months ago."

"I'll be right back." Vincent started across the room toward four men huddled around a desk, turned quickly back to Helen, and then continued walking toward the group.

"He couldn't leave without one final look, darling," Margaret observed. "Love and patriotism are in the air."

"You can join us, Margaret," Helen said, flicking through a mound of rough pencil drawings.

"I think not, Helen. You do remember that the day after war was declared all radio transmissions in the country were shut down. In one day."

"This is war, Margaret." Helen motioned for Margaret to follow her. She looked across the room for Vincent. "You can still develop the receivers for the military. We know that they are being tested in the field. It may not be what we had hoped for, but there is still work to be done."

"That is loathsome. I'm late." Margaret walked toward the elevator. Helen followed at her side.

Margaret had a parting thought. "Helen, do you know what the latest innovation in radio is? You probably don't. You are so busy here filling people's mind with patriotic nonsense and dallying with Vincent. Radio receivers are now being built so that barbed wire can be used as antenna. Barbed wire."

28

I WAS—SMITTEN. WASN'T that Helen's remark when I first met William? Margaret had spent that afternoon right over there on the Frog Pond. Now she watched as a shirtless man trudged knee deep through the placid water. She had laughed so much when William imitated the quacking ducks surrounding them that day. And his leg—still pained from his slide the week before on that stupid baseball field. She remembered wincing every time he winced. *It still was a lovely day, just like today.*

Margaret refocused her attention back toward the speakers' platform— Henry Mendes stood next to it, greeting two men who she recognized from the last meeting at the Socialist Party office. She drifted again—why allow public speeches and then censor only radio? What are they so afraid of? Harold Power was right; the government does not want honest debate about something that only the Finnertys of the world are profiting from.

Surely Anne O'Reilly would be here—she had asked Beatrice Townsend for the day off. Mother must have felt a secret delight allowing Anne to go, she probably would have liked to be here as well.

Margaret was certain Vincent thought of her as little more than part of a throng of rich women carrying placards. What a pompous ass he had become—sadly, even William probably thought the same.

"Too bad the Red Sox are playing in town, Mrs. Morrison." Anne O'Reilly came alongside Margaret. "Billy couldn't get today off— he would have been here in a heartbeat."

"I understand the government is making it difficult for you Irishmen to speak out these days," Margaret said. "You're all subversives now."

Anne grinned, accepting the characterization. She wore a new jacket and blouse—modest, mass-produced garments sold in those stores in Boston. Filene's Basement, Margaret guessed. *She might have been without a job all this time, if not for Mother.*

Margaret felt a flash of anger. Those people around Helen and Vincent were even hinting that the Irish and the Germans in Boston had become subversives. Who? Anne O'Reilly she wondered, who wordlessly carries her burden daily? Or was it Hans Stitler?

"Henry will be speaking today." Margaret said proudly.

"This morning Billy and I talked about the Rising last April." Anne spoke solemnly whenever she evoked the plight of the Irish. "It was only a year ago. We will never know how many people were killed. Billy said that here at least we can have a peaceful demonstration without dying."

Yes, the Rising—The Rebellion. Margaret envisioned it as another stage for the Irish to show the world they can never be beaten into submission, and that they can endure whatever pain and suffering they are destined to receive.

"We're just lucky to have that real Irishman, James Curley, for a mayor—don't you think, Anne?" Margaret asked. "Who would have thought that possible twenty years ago?"

"Mayor Curley has been a bastard sometimes—even to his own kind—but he couldn't resist giving us a permit for today," Anne replied. "He loves to thumb that red Irish Catholic nose at the Protestants, doesn't he?" She enjoyed sharing that image with Margaret.

Margaret tracked people approaching the green field surrounding the wooden speakers' platform. They entered the Commons from Beacon Street, with more advancing from the Frog Pond path. Some carried red flags, and others, handwritten signs; a still beating pulse insisting, *don't send our boys to fight a King's war.* 'Bloody kings,' Uncle Isaac called them. He had often adopted curious British phrases that did not suit his New England accent well, but he uttered them with such impassioned charm their origins were never questioned.

Uniformed servicemen formed on the fringes of the field. They must be concerned also, thought Margaret. After all, they will be the ones on the Front, not the Finnertys of the world. *They must want to find a way to stop it, even at this late date.* Henry Mendes had told their study group once that the Russian soldiers walked away from the Eastern Front, and now are even close to overthrowing the tsar. Who would have ever believed that possible even a year ago? Many of these men must be having second thoughts about our government's new-found hatred of the Germans. Of this Margaret was certain.

Henry tugged on the lapels of his crumpled suit, looking almost as if he had slept in it. That's how William described his appearance when they first met. Margaret remembered appraising Henry that afternoon. She had concluded that his self-assurance was limited to his words and thoughts. *Not a strong, silent William. Or even a dreamy Gaspar.*

Henry had become a favorite speaker of the Greater Boston Socialist's Party. Margaret appreciated that Byron had introduced Henry to important people at Harvard and helped him get established so quickly.

Margaret scanned the fringes of the Commons. Now even larger groups assembled. Just waiting to see how the day would go, Margaret imagined. Yet, she noticed, they gathered too far away to hear the speakers—and not a sign or flag in evidence.

Cops weaved amongst the ever-growing crowd, swaggering, twirling their long batons.

A speaker mounted the dais. Margaret did not recognize him. There were now several thousand people on the grass. Margaret reminded herself how unsatisfying had been her attempt to judge the attendance at Fenway Park one afternoon; her only visit in the five years it had been open. She had said to Byron, "There must be at least nine thousand people here today." Amused, he instantly corrected her. "Not even close, Sis. The stands are full. There is standing room only. More than thirty-five thousand people."

The speaker had a tattered binder of papers in his hand. He squinted at the top page and looked up again. Margaret assumed the organizers did not foresee the need for a lectern—or any place for someone to fan out their papers.

"My name in Colin Quinn and I am one of you—I grew up right here in Boston. The most important thing you must know is that they are afraid of us. They want to silence us." His voice rose with greater force than Margaret anticipated. "Only last month they passed the Espionage Act. It is now against the law to urge those young men across the street to even think about whether they really support this war. We would be engaged in a criminal act if we discuss these grave issues in front of them. And yet, the same law says there is no intent to abridge our free speech."

Henry Mendes circled absently, his mouth moving, talking to himself. Jabs of his finger into the air informed Margaret that he was rehearsing his speech.

"—The government's attempt to penetrate America with pro-war propaganda is not working as well as they hoped. Much of the Midwest would vote for socialist legislatures if they held the election today." Quinn paused and, shielding his eyes from the sun, looked out into the distance.

Erratic movements distracted Margaret. A moment before, waving patches of red accented the summer greenery; now a struggle ensued to hold the flags aloft.

"—A German victory would mean that the industrialists here would lose the millions of dollars they loaned to the British. Is that worth—"

Shouts overpowered his question. Quinn stopped and stared at the disjointed movements of the crowd near the Frog Pond. Soldiers in crisp uniforms jostled Margaret as they shoved forward, pulling flags and signs from demonstrators' hands.

David, the muscular silver-haired ironworker Margaret had seen at the Socialist Party meetings, punched at the servicemen. They backed away. Two charged at him, one trying to tackle him. His balled fist came down on the back of his assailant's head. The sailor disappeared from view, evaporating into the crowd. David caught his other attacker with a wide, arcing right hook, directly in his face. Margaret thought of a batter hitting a baseball.

Then fear enveloped her.

The platform emptied of speakers, a blur of red motion encircled it as more servicemen grappled with flag carriers.

Three policemen on horses galloped into the disturbance. Relieved by their presence Margaret was certain they would quickly restore order. After all they did have a permit for the gathering.

A mounted cop maneuvered his horse's hindquarters, roughly pressing a demonstrator against a tree. Screaming in pain, the man wriggled to push himself free. The policeman swung his baton, barely missing the target—instead a hollow ringing issued from the tree trunk.

Shouts and curses from across the street; the onlookers, silent only minutes earlier, were agitated now, encouraging the cops and doughboys to press their attack.

Immediately, Anne sensed the changing pulse of the crowd. "This is awful. The police are anxious to get at us. So are these soldiers."

Margaret looked back at the platform. Three soldiers toppled it over. Demonstrators jabbed at them with their flags. *Where is Henry Mendes? He was right there. He must be part of this— riot. That's what it is.*

SUPERINTENDENT CROWLEY PUSHED TO the front of the now flattened speakers' platform, his passage cleared by eight young Boston policemen—each bounced a black sap on his palm, challenging the demonstrators.

"As directed by the City Council I am revoking the permit for this meeting." Crowley spoke each word slowly. "You are ordered to leave the Commons immediately."

"That's horse shit," Steven said, a mechanic who had once straightened the door on Margaret's car after it dented against an iron fence near Copp's Hill. Blood flowed from a gash on his forehead onto his greasy blue overalls. "Mayor Curley gave us a permit. This is a legal gathering—it's constitutionally protected."

"I don't give a damn *who* authorized this meeting. The City Council just closed you down. You are now in contempt of the law." Crowley, tufts of graying hair billowing from under a yellowed straw hat, moved towards Steven.

"James Michael Curley, the mayor, gave us the permit. Have him come and revoke it. You're just a fucking errand boy, Crowley." Steven turned to other demonstrators, now emboldened by his defiance.

Crowley pointed at Steven. Two policemen charged him. He had no time to react. They threw him to the ground. One held a baton tightly against Steven's throat with a strong two-fisted grasp. Steven's protests were just incomprehensible gurgles.

"Now then," Crowley said, snarling at the crowd. "Don't you think that a lawful directive should be obeyed on this fine Sunday afternoon?"

"You piece of shit," another demonstrator called. "Let him go, you fucking coward."

"Coward?" The policeman released Steven and rose up, swinging his baton wildly. A hapless demonstrator caught the blow on the side of his head, tumbling hard to the grass.

Crowley waved his hand, pointing aimlessly into the crowd, indicating that the police could arrest anyone in the crowd. Anyone.

MARGARET WANDERED THE COMMONS. The lush grass fields, once enticing summer strollers to lie down and gaze up at a blue sky, had become a trap. Marauding civilians and their military accomplices charged at stragglers who, buckling under the unrelenting onslaught, had by now discarded their banners and red flags. Random violence had rendered the demonstrators into glassy-eyed prey.

Margaret turned onto a narrow path shaded by elm trees. She remembered that William had once removed his jacket and laid it out on the ground under the largest of these trees. Today, it was different—

five men circled a demonstrator under the same spreading elm, a sailor jerked a red flag from his hand. They insisted he sing *The Star-Spangled Banner*. He resisted. The sailor jabbed him hard in his ribs with the blunt top of the flagstaff—and then again. He covered his face. Margaret couldn't see if he was bleeding. Or crying.

"Stop this now, I insist!" Margaret screamed, a futile gesture. Nobody noticed her.

A solidly built man in a dark blue suit and bowler appeared at her side. He wore a purple and white pin on his lapel. "Stay away, lady," he warned her, without any hostility. His face was cherubic—in an odd manner, she thought.

"Have them leave that man alone." Margaret's voice was as loud as she had ever heard it. "He has a constitutional—"

"—get the hell out of here, lady," he said, his tone changing quickly. He pushed her back onto the winding path leading toward the Frog Pond.

Four soldiers struggled with David Samuels. He had been in fist-fights all afternoon, knocking soldiers to the ground with pile-driver punches. Margaret had never seen someone being punched, except at a bloody boxing match Byron once insisted she attend with him. Today she had enough brawling for a lifetime.

Now the vigilantes had David in a tight grip. One attacker sneered, holding a shredded red flag. He grasped a clump of hair on David's writhing head with his other hand, intent on filling David's mouth with the flag.

Margaret hurried along the coarse gravel lane, nauseous, and certain that she needed to get out of the Commons. Anne stood alone at the fork in the pathway, tears on her cheeks, watching Margaret approach. They embraced, both exhausted.

Dejected, Anne reported the news. "Mayor Curley is in New Hampshire for the weekend so one of the bastards, who never wanted us to meet, cancelled the permit."

"Horrible," Margaret said. "These people actually want to go to war. Haven't they heard what that Front is *really* like?"

Then Margaret and Anne saw the smoke spiraling up from Park Square. The summer sky, so delightfully blue just hours earlier, now darkened in front of them.

"The Socialist Party offices are on Park Square." Margaret's voice trailed off. "The fire is probably there."

They hurried in that direction.

Margaret imagined those connected rooms; the narrow, haphazardly created aisles cutting into the overflow of magazines and books piled onto the floor. Perfect kindling for fire. Had Henry sought refuge in the offices? Is he in there now? How can he find his way out with all of that junk on fire? And those staircases—old dry wood. She quickened her step.

Two women ran toward them. Anne recognized one from earlier in the day.

"They're beating up everyone in the office," said the smaller of the two, frail, her brown hair matted with sweat, pointing toward Park Square. She gathered her breath. "They threw the books out of the windows and are burning them."

"Did you see Henry Mendes there?" Margaret asked, now frightened, imagining him cornered, being pummeled by athletic bullies. Or trapped by a fire.

"No, he was arrested as soon as the fighting started," the other woman said, gasping as she spoke. "I saw the police throw him in one of the paddy wagons with Alexander Dixon. They were both kicking and punching."

29

SCALLOPED MASSES OF MISSHAPEN steel and chunks of concrete foundations littered the racetrack. Not a splinter of wood from the private clubhouse had survived the fire; William would bet on it. Gracefully sculpted molding along the walls, and long, thick, polished floorboards had once appointed the dining room and plush lounges with a country estate's elegance. Now all ash.

William remembered that afternoon in the clubhouse with Finnerty's scoundrel stockbrokers only two years earlier; the day before the *Lusitania* sailed out of Pier 54—for the last time. Their stock pumping campaign worked smoother than they had anticipated. They could barely wait for the next opportunity to make easy money. It seemed like such a long time ago.

William stepped out of the taxi next to a pyramid of charred wood—remains of the row of kiosks where racing forms were sold and sleazy touts congregated, preying on the unwary visitors, promising winning bets that rarely materialized. Now all just firewood stacked for collection.

William congratulated himself for giving Finnerty an excuse so that he could ride out from Manhattan alone. His attention had drifted back to his triumph of the week: the confirmation of his sale of the copper Finnerty had schemed from Hiram Harris. His contacts at Dexter Shipbuilding offered to supply a contract later for whatever price was agreeable to Finnerty. Hiram's threat of private detectives didn't matter anymore. Dexter would smelt the copper as soon as they received it—there would be no accountings or appraisals.

Another fire, two weeks after the grandstand fire, killed thirty thoroughbreds and left only the charred concrete outlines of small structures and an unaffected walking ring. Still the racing season was on. Now everything at Belmont was improvised—wagering booths, food stands, toilets. William was impressed—nothing would stop this cash machine from taking a gambler's money. Whoever invented horse race wagering opened a gold mine. William had to accept that the new brokerage business was now on hold—Ennis and the other guys had all enlisted in the Army four months ago. He would now have to endure working for Finnerty—at least, he guessed, for the duration of the war.

"William, I suppose we're in luck," Finnerty called to him from a few feet away. "If there had been no fire, August Belmont would have donated this track to the military for bivouac, just like they did at Rockingham Park. Then we wouldn't have been able to spend this lovely afternoon in the sun." Finnerty looked around, surveying the damage. "Of course I would have preferred to be in that fabulous clubhouse. I suppose everyone has to rough it a bit these days—the war and all that."

"There are many people right now who wouldn't think this is 'roughing it,' Joe."

"I supposed there are *those* people. I just haven't communicated with them recently." Finnerty removed his straw hat, running his hand through his brown hair, and put it on again at what he probably thought a jaunty angle.

What a jerk-off. It's astonishing, thought William, how Joe Finnerty could make so many profitable deals even when everybody can see through him. *Now that is a rare talent.*

Five workers in heavy blue overalls sifted through the debris and stubby spines of steel once supporting the most beautiful racetrack grandstand in America. The smell of the charred grandstands now floated on a gust of wind to the track railing William leaned against.

"So Babe Ruth is meeting us here?" William looked at Joe. "Isn't he with the team on the road somewhere? I know they're not playing in Boston."

"They played yesterday in Detroit. Tomorrow they'll be in Philadelphia. He took the overnight to New York. Loves the races. He is a simpleton you know. Kids. Animals. He loves them all. Last year he bagged peanuts a few times with the kids who sell them at Fenway. A real imbecile."

"I heard the peanut story from Byron." William stilled his curiosity. *What was this meeting about? What was Ruth going to be used for?*

"No doubt, William, you're wondering what this is all about, being the curious sort you are."

"It never occurred to me." William's gaze followed the horses being led back to the starting line. The third false start. He hadn't even looked at the program to see which horse might deserve a few buck wager.

Finnerty waved toward a short, slender man, a shabby black hat tipped back on his head, taking money from two bettors nearby. He recognized Finnerty and pushed a wrinkled racing form toward him. Joe pulled a few bills from his pocket and stabbed at a name. The man took the money and disappeared into the crowd.

"To think, William, we just got back our right to gamble at the track only four years ago," Finnerty declared. "Those temperance people had the laws changed all over the country. Stopped racetrack gambling all over—now they want to stop us from having a goddamn drink. Do you know how many tracks went out of business? How many horse owners? Trainers?" William recognized one of Finnerty's random attempts to convey sympathy with someone, somewhere. He wasn't expected to respond.

"It took a lot of effort to get the laws changed back to where they were before those temperance idiots came around. Mark my word, William—they will make this a dry country before they are finished. I'd like to ship them all off to the Front in France, or wherever it is these days." William again found no need to respond.

The third race started. Excitement mounted as the horses approached the first turn. Shouts of encouragement—"That's it, 4," "Go to the outside, Golden Blossom"—encircled them.

It didn't matter that the stands had burned into rubble or that shabbily built fetid wooden booths had now replaced the toilets—the frenzy of the bettors still swelled, just as it had always done, until the first horse crossed the finish line, then evaporated immediately. William didn't watch the finish or know the name of the winner.

Babe Ruth appeared next to him. William looked straight into his eyes. Ruth wore a tailor-made blue silk suit. William knew the gossip about Ruth's hygiene; he wondered if it had improved. He reminded himself to ask Billy if Ruth had learned to change his underwear yet.

"Hello, Mr. Finnerty." Ruth removed his straw hat and held it in his hands. Ruth's casual recognition of Finnerty surprised William.

Ruth's moon-shaped face, as homely, friendly, and guileless as an English bulldog's, suggested hesitancy around men he thought of as educated businessmen. William knew that if he sensed this, then so would Finnerty, who would exploit it.

"This is my associate, William Morrison." Finnerty put his hand on William's forearm. "He has excellent contacts at Dexter Shipbuilding, so you might see a lot of each other."

What the hell did that mean? William ran through the possibilities of what his contacts at a shipbuilder would have to do with Babe Ruth.

Ruth looked around slowly, perhaps just realizing something was out of order. "This place is a goddamn mess, isn't it? With all of the money I dropped here last year couldn't they build a new grandstand?" Finnerty and William laughed with Ruth.

"Too bad Frazee bought the team. I know you wanted it, Joe," Ruth said. He nodded sympathetically.

Finnerty smiled wistfully. "That must have been the worse kept secret in town last year. Yes, William, wouldn't we like to be the owners of Red Sox? We could watch Babe here every day. He's having a great year. When he's not punching umpires, that is."

Everyone in Boston knew that Ruth had a few disagreements with the umpire the week before. Finally, he punched the unsuspecting umpire and the police took him off the field.

William agreed with Donald Townsend's conclusion that even if Ruth was 'a simpleton,' he was no longer the naïve boy who had arrived two years before from the workhouse in Baltimore. *Now he expected everything to go his way.*

"I always play as hard as I can," Ruth said, oblivious to Finnerty's humor. "I *am* having a great year. I hope I can keep it up."

"Well, we'll see what happens with the team." Finnerty flipped his losing tickets to the ground. "It looks like the press has something else to write about. Now with this draft they want to see all of you players in uniform—army uniforms, that is."

"So far, we're all right with marching around the field in formation," Ruth responded, nodding seriously. "We did that a few times. Frazee made us do it. Some of the guys said we're like chorus girls in one of his goddamn Broadway shows. Anyway, they didn't draft me because I'm married."

"If we lose as many boys as the British and France have lost, they will draft everyone. Probably me as well," Finnerty said, smiling. Ruth nodded gravely.

William watched the horses for the next race parade in front of the railing. He knew it was true—the losses in Europe were staggering, and the question was being raised louder with each day's news—why aren't these players in uniform? They looked so fit. Sliding into bases. Racing for balls in the outfield. The baseball owners tried to deflect criticism by have the players march around the field in formation before the games—and William observed their publicists work the angle that baseball was a moral boost for a country at war. *It's bullshit of course*—he was amused by the gambit—*but right now it's working for them.*

"Farmers and workers in shipbuilding and munitions will never be drafted. Did you ever think of that, Babe?" Finnerty waited for a reaction. Ruth nodded slowly, probably not clear himself if he had or had not 'thought of that.' William would have bet Ruth never thought of it.

William had tried to enlist along with the first rush of new enlistees when war was declared—he didn't care if Margaret would have been 'appalled.' He was conflicted but found himself on the long line nonetheless. Dr. Carlson had told him that he would be rejected as soon as a doctor saw the terrible gash on his right knee from the botched operation—Dr. Carlson was right.

Strangers driving by on the street had called William a 'slacker'. Yelling it out. Never saying it to his face. But he knew many people thought it to be true. Maybe it would be better if he could have enlisted. *A goddamn slacker. That's what they're calling these healthy baseball players now.*

"Every shipbuilder has a baseball team. Some of them are pretty good. Not professionals, but they can play." Finnerty had adopted an authoritative tone. "They're needed for the war effort. They're deferred from the military." He paused theatrically. "This war's going to get uglier for all of us. The newspapers won't be happy unless all of you are in the military. You may want to be in one of these shipyards soon— especially if you're making even more money than you do with the Red Sox."

"Babe, can I take a picture with you?" A man in his early twenties—about Ruth's age—moved in front of William, holding a camera. It was the same camera that Sarah had that afternoon at Margaret and Byron's birthday party. William winced. *A camera now lying on the bottom of the ocean. With his sister.*

"Sure you can," Ruth said. "Is she goin' to take the picture?" He motioned towards a gray-haired woman. She nodded and reached for the camera.

"I'm Mae—Mae Thurmond. We're fans of yours, even though we live here in New York," Mae said, thrilled to talk to her hero. Struggling to continue the conversation, she looked at the man with her. "This is Walter. He's my son. We go to as many games at the Polo Grounds as we can."

"That's nice to hear, ma'am." Ruth said politely. "Who do you like in the stakes race today? I'll bet your pick gets to the finish line before mine."

Ruth attracted attention. Bettors recognized him. They nodded toward him, pointing him out to strangers. Everyone had pencils ready for an afternoon of marking their racing forms. Now they were dangling them in front of Ruth for autographs. Finnerty had lost him to

273

the crowd.

Finnerty lowered his voice. "He's a valuable asset, William. Getting him on the Dexter team could be profitable for all of us. Babe loves to gamble and he loves to do favors for people. That combination can give someone an *advantage*."

William had another view. "I'm assuming you lost out on buying the Red Sox to Frazee, so you might as well see what you can do with his most valuable asset. Am I looking in the right direction, Joe?"

Finnerty led William a few steps away from the gaggle of fans swarming around Ruth. "If you can talk Ruth into joining the Dexter team, and also get *them* to see the benefits, you will be a hero. If Dexter doesn't want to pay his whole salary, we can throw in some money—what is he earning this year anyway, about five thousand dollars? Think of yourself as a broker in this."

"Is this to improve company moral at Dexter?" William asked, amused.

"Fuck company moral. I'm thinking of having Babe let us know when he will be not feeling so great. It's called the edge in some circles." Finnerty was happy with his insight. "You are managing the Dexter account with us, and doing a fine job, I might add. So let us reap the ancillary benefits. Don't you agree?" William nodded vacantly, watching Ruth pose with five boys, huge grins on every face—Babe's too.

Finnerty moved to the side as more bettors surrounded Ruth. "Let's talk about it some other time. For now, let's enjoy a great day with our sports hero." He paused, allowing himself a change of subject. "So, how is Helen doing down there in New York? I heard that she is working for that new committee putting out all that crap to support the war efforts. They even got old Mrs. Donnelly down there as a believer."

"I didn't know that you knew Mrs. Donnelly."

"I don't. I had a few dealings with her husband. A thieving Irish politician— we could all be proud of him. He got a few bucks out of me more than once. Died in his own vomit in an alleyway behind a tavern, I heard. And Helen is well?"

William struggled for a second to conceal his discomfort. "I saw her last month when we went to New York. She looked well—thanks for asking."

"It s appears she has found someone to keep her company." Finnerty awaited William's reaction.

"Yeah. It's lucky Mrs. Donnelly is down there with her." William watched the crowd around Ruth.

"No, I mean that Hearst newsman, Chelios. She's practically living with him." Finnerty waved again to the little man with the racing form.

"How the hell do you know?" William was more annoyed with himself than with Finnerty. Yes, of course Helen and Chelios are involved—those quick glances in the restaurant that night in New York. Margaret never said a word. Did she know also? *She must.*

"Mrs. Donnelly has a big mouth then." William was disturbed that he had to hear it from a gloating Joe Finnerty.

"No—Mrs. Donnelly despises me." Finnerty smiled broadly at the thought. "So did her drunken husband. She would never tell me anything—but she did tell one of the girls in that office who I know quite well."

30

SEPTEMBER 5, 1917

CAMP DEVENS, MASS.

STAGING AREAS CRAMMED WITH six-foot high stacks of freshly milled wood planks lined both sides of road into the camp. Workers and soldiers stripped to their waists consulted, pointing to buildings; some only frames, others just finished, each propped above the ground along the gravel paths, anticipating next spring's heavy rains. All efforts carefully coordinated.

They had to be.

Donald Townsend intended to run a feature when the surveyors had first paced off the land for Camp Devens earlier in the year. Even before the first axe bit into the nearby pine stands in this isolated Massachusetts countryside, the plans envisioned a camp for twenty thousand young men requiring sanitation, barracks, firing ranges, garages, kitchens.

The *Boston Examiner* story detailed the War Department goals: workforces would race to complete fifteen cantonments across the country for training the young men destined for the Western Front. Ten of these frame buildings were to be completed every day—at each camp. The workforce for these camps would be the biggest in American history. Neither stone facades nor decorative brickwork appeared in any blueprints for Camp Devens—only wood cut from the nearby pine and elm forests. At the last minute the military censors forbade publication of the story—it violated newly evolved secrecy standards.

Four rows of recruits in crisp uniforms accented by their pointed, wide brim khaki hats marched through the main street, led by graying mustachioed officers, mounted on white horses, well tended by their newly conscripted grooms. The first draftees had arrived only two months earlier and now there were already ten thousand, with more arriving each day.

"Donald, until one undertakes an endeavor like this, the challenges remain hidden," Dr. William Welch said, leading the others down a narrow path bordered by coils of electrical conduit. "Of course, nobody has ever embarked on a project as complicated as this—building fifteen cantonments around the country—all at once. I've already visited most of them."

Dr. Welch, recently enlisted in the Army, had immediately begun his assignment overseeing sanitary and medical conditions at military bases all over the country.

"There's the School for Cooks and Bakers, Donald." Dr. Welch pointed to a three-story building on top of a knoll. "*Someone* has to learn how to cook for twenty thousand people, three times a day. Who would have imagined that teaching country boys how to wash their hands before handling food would be an urgent need?"

Donald stepped around two soldiers unloading a long cylindrical cardboard tube from a truck parked on a grassy patch. "Dr. Welch, I remember you said that 'in every war more soldiers die of diseases than from battlefield wounds.' Has that been the case with the Brits and French so far?"

Dr. Carlson leaned in front of him. "Actually, Donald, there are problems getting accurate statistics from the Front. Everyone's afraid the Germans will get the information."

Dr. Welch stopped walking, breathed deeply and then continued. "Donald, one of the problems we didn't foresee only a few months ago is that these men would be in very close quarters. Many of them know only farm life; they have no immunity to the contagions rife in this group environment. Frankly, we don't know what to expect. Some idiotic congressmen don't even want us to take measures against syphilis. They are deathly afraid of those temperance people, who believe that if we contain syphilis, we will be encouraging promiscuity. Not an issue we need right now. But I, too, must be a politician at times."

"Then there's tuberculosis and measles, cholera, and small pox to worry about," Dr. Carlson added, taking a long stride over a stream of water seeping down an embankment from an open pipe. "Last year's polio outbreak is still not contained. And we are looking at potentially one million boys crisscrossing the country, from one camp to another. We have no idea what these boys will be bringing to these camps. We've never mobilized like this before."

These doctors had spent their lives developing what was now called 'public health.' Donald Townsend had championed their battles to get this concept accepted—the prevention and containment of communicable diseases. But government officials put this at the bottom of their lists of priorities.

Donald was certain that George Creel would have been the first to insist that the government keep the public informed of the dangers lurking at every turn as this massive mobilization gained strength with each passing day. How many times had he witnessed Creel berating government officials who hid even the simplest facts from the public? No longer! In a few short months, Creel had become the most fervent censor in Donald's memory. Surely Beatrice would have an appropriate quote from Plato. Why Plato? Why not Thomas Jefferson? Or Shakespeare? How did she settle on Plato?

"And what about cold weather?" Dr. Welch asked, continuing his litany. "These boys from the South never experienced a New England winter before. We have two thousand beds in this hospital. It's fully equipped. I insisted on it."

They had come to the entrance of the camp infirmary. It was the third building finished on the base.

"The Army has also built barracks and hospitals for the colored soldiers," Dr. Carlson said, touching on still another facet to the mobilization. "Keeping the coloreds and the whites separate is just one more hurdle. And we don't know if the coloreds have any unusual susceptibility to illnesses. We'll have to watch that carefully too."

"I hope our inspection today has not devolved into a list of bureaucratic complaints, Donald," Dr. Welch said, weary from the endless considerations calling for his attention. "But, so be it."

Carlson swung open one of the two large doors to the mess hall, steaming metal food counters lining the walls, long tables and benches forming precise lines across the canteen. Men in white undershirts and puffy white cooks' hats mixed and stirred food, anticipating the arrival of the soldier-workers Donald had seen all morning.

Dr. Welch regarded two cooks mixing a doughy batter. "Just a year ago we took it for granted that sanitary and health inspections would be done by qualified medical personnel," he said. "Now we have to rely on untrained accountants, truck drivers, even military policemen. Whoever will volunteer for the job. So not only, because of censorship, can't we communicate effectively from one camp to another, we now have no ability to identify threats in advance, even on the same base. Many of our inspectors could not differentiate measles from mosquito

bites"—he shook his head; Donald and Edward Carlson smiled grimly—"of course that is not their fault. We just can't train them as much
as I would wish. And I fear the worst is yet to come."

There is 'worse to come' and it isn't just Byron who put himself in
danger, thought Donald. *Margaret is also flying too close to the sun. She
will get burned.* Donald never could moderate her passions. Neither
could Beatrice. Radio, art, the Boston Museum. Girlish excitement
perhaps. He had seen the country's mood shift—everyday now he
was receiving virulent letters, many hysterical in their support of the
war. *Yes, when American bodies start to fall on the Front it will only get
worse—then Margaret will be in real danger.*

"It seems that we have to prepare for the very unexpected," Carlson
said. Dr. Welch slowly nodded, reluctantly agreeing.

Donald had known these doctors for fifteen years and he now heard
them clearly. *The amalgam of young men straight from the farm to
these close quarters all over the country will lead to problems impossible to predict. And then Creel's censorship will make communications
between the camps ever more difficult. This may not end well.*

31

OCTOBER 21, 1917

THE NORTH END DOCKS

BOSTON, MASS.

"NO, LITTLE DARLING. DON'T go over there." Since they stepped out of his chauffeured Packard, Joe Finnerty's focus on his daughter never wavered. "Let those little wretches play by themselves."

Joe enjoyed William's uncomfortable reaction. "Don't worry, William. She's too young to understand some of my harsher observations. She is, I suspect, just thrilled to be with Daddy on a Sunday morning."

Clarisse had wandered toward the train tracks, intent on a dozen boys in wool caps and ragged pants ballooning out from their dirty leggings. They formed an imperfect queue at the leaking storage tank; each had improvised a container to retrieve a pint or two of the thick molasses now seeping from pores at its joints.

Grinning, Clarisse looked back at her father, turned and pointed to the boys, wanting to enlist him in her current preoccupation. Finnerty crouched down, opening his arms, motioning Clarisse to come toward him. She started to run. He held his palms towards her, urging her to slow down.

"Yes, you are truly my angel." He embraced her as she crashed into his chest. He stood up, grasping her under her arms, lifting her off the ground. Then he swung her around, her little patent leather shoes pointed out, describing a circle, her frilly skirt ruffling as she turned.

"William, I really can't stay too long," Joe called over his shoulder. "We have a church function to attend. You know how I detest being late for them."

"Yes, Joe. You do have a reputation to uphold." William wondered if the men sleeping on the hay bales stacked next to the fire department stable door were the same ones he saw two years ago when he first came to inspect the molasses vat.

"William, I'm glad you could come today," Finnerty said. "I want you to know this may be the last time we see this monstrosity. The United States Alcohol Company made an offer for it. A generous offer."

"I thought you were going to keep the damn thing until the molasses prices ran up even further."

"I told you before, 'only a fool holds out for top dollar.' So let's get rid of it now. Wouldn't you agree?"

"Sure."

"This war is a very interesting endeavor, William. Making profitable deals for copper—even molasses. Their value goes up even as we stand here. Let the new owners make a buck also."

"Joe, I always knew you could be magnanimous."

Jell called over to them. "I put a few more security guards on duty, Mr. Finnerty."

"Give us a few minutes, Jell." Finnerty held up his hand for Jell to stop talking.

William watched Jell circle back toward the tank. Compensating for his abrupt dismissal, he moved toward the boys clustered around the tank, yelling obscenities. They must have known him well—they dispersed quickly.

"William, one of the executives at the Alcohol Company saw the molasses dripping down from the leaks. He had an idea that never occurred to either of us— certainly it never occurred to *him*." Finnerty gestured toward Jell, now making himself busy on the other side of the vat. William waved his hand, encouraging Finnerty to continue.

"The first thing he would do, if the deal goes through, is to paint the vat brown, *molasses brown*, he said. Then nobody would see the leaks—'unsightly,' was his word. Clever, wouldn't you say, William?"

William followed a rivulet of dark molasses, its source close to the top of the tank. It etched a course over the horizontal bands securing the heavy girth, and flowed around the thick bolts bonding the steel plates. The stream ended in a rusty pail.

William tired of Finnerty's deal talk. "Joe, remember at the race-track you told me about Helen and that Chelios guy? That they were involved with each other?"

"What about them?"

Clarisse tugged at Finnerty's arm, then she ran around the car. He peered over the hood playfully, catching her attention.

William absently watched Clarisse turn in circles. "Did your source ever tell you anything more about Helen? I was just curious."

"Just curious?" Finnerty asked, unable to hide a mocking tone. "You don't want details, do you? Not about your sister-in-law. She's supervising the production of magnificent original posters exhorting us all to greater efforts to support the troops. Is that what you're interested in?"

No—it was really Margaret who interested William. She refused to listen when he mentioned Joe's gossip about Helen. He had seen her indignation before, and had a good feel for when it wasn't honest. *This was one of those times.*

"I guess I just don't believe you happened to be poking someone sitting next to Mrs. Donnelly, and she hears something about my sister-in-law and runs off to tell you. That's all." William managed a relaxed recitation of his doubts.

"The truth is, William, you are right." Finnerty looked around, feigning someone might be listening. "How can I say this delicately—I hired someone to watch after Helen when she first went to New York."

"Who, a detective? Or is it part-time employment for one of the office girls you're screwing?"

"No, William, it's a professional, not a housewife," said Finnerty, relishing William's surprise. He waved at Clarisse, who smiled back.

"One of those Pinkerton cops who loves to beat the shit out of you Irishmen?" William asked, his annoyance poking through.

"Not that dramatic. Just someone I've used before for sensitive projects. In fact, the same gentlemen who our Hiram Harris hired to determine if we were, how should I say? Undervaluing his assets. I never did tell you what he discovered, did I?"

"No, you didn't."

"Hiram Harris, the heir to the copper business, that young man you were so concerned about, was all the while keeping the sale from his aunt. It appears that she owned half of the copper company. Hiram told her that he got much less than we actually paid him—he pocketed the rest. His very own investigator, our Herman Oliver, brought aunty the news of Hiram's infamy and now she is suing him. An ignoble sort that Hiram Harris is after all, wouldn't you say?"

"So what kind of *sensitive project* is Helen?" William already knew the answer. Byron would one day inherit an influential newspaper—he would never want his wife's little secret to be public. *Maybe Joe wants to get close to Donald Townsend—even if Donald loathes everything about him. Who the hell knows what he's thinking?*

"William," Finnerty said, "I could appear concerned for this small town girl's well-being in the big city. But I don't suppose you'd believe that's my true intention, would you?"

"I know your goddamn intention, Joe." William didn't care if Finnerty knew he was angry or not. "But so what if you know who's poking Helen? What do you think that will do, get your picture on the front page of the *Examiner*?"

"I prefer to look at it as a business expense," Finnerty said calmly. "I'm a betting man, and I will wager that if Margaret knew she wouldn't tell you."

"I suppose you'll never know what Margaret tells me."

"True, I don't know what Margaret tells you. But I do know she is up to her fashionable hats in that socialist bullshit. That's something you should think about. Don't you think?"

"Leave Margaret out of your spying. I don't know why you're doing this, but let's say it's not a healthy preoccupation."

Joe nodded slowly. "If it was anyone but you I would take that as a threat. It isn't, is it, William?"

"A warning. I just don't want to hear about your spying anymore. Understood? You should be thrilled, fleecing everyone for a few bucks. If I was you, I wouldn't have the time for tracking Helen around New York."

Finnerty's daughter, ever more impatient, ran toward him, pushing him again toward the car. "I'm sorry if you misunderstand, William. Perhaps my tone was not exactly right."

It had been of concern to William for months—*that little shit-heel, Henry Mendes. Was he bewitching Margaret with his socialism crap? Was he in her bloomers also?*

William watched the boys wander off toward the row of tattered wood frame houses, their full pails swinging lightly in rhythm with their stride. Other boys approached the huge molasses pot from a different direction.

32

WILLIAM PADDLED PAST TWO canoes drifting aimlessly, the flirtatious teenage girls in one playfully splashing the young males in the
other. William aimed his canoe toward a patch of grass on the bank of
the Charles River. He hadn't been to Norumbega Park since he was a
boy. It now seemed so small. How old was he when Uncle Isaac unex-
pectedly insisted that they go to the amusement park? *Uncle Isaac trying to explain how the gears worked on these rides—that metal horse whipping around in a circle frightened me. I didn't care how its gears worked.*

Margaret watched their canoe rise up onto the grass and then slide
to a gentle stop. "Aunt Agnes, we're so happy that you could tear yourself away from the inn," she said. "We thought it would be fun to take
you here—too bad Uncle Isaac couldn't join us."

The end of the amusement park season was quickly approaching. In
just a few more weeks, the men's rolled up sleeves and short vests would
need reinforcement with heavier jackets. The women had already dis-
pensed with their full-length, form-fitting summer white cotton wears
in favor of sensible wool plaid dresses. Both Margaret and Aunt Agnes

had wisely draped their shoulders with brown woolen shawls.

Agnes shook her shoulders. "There is a bit of a chill, isn't there? It's delightful to be here again—the last time was when William was very young." She stood up, steadied herself in the rocking canoe, and reached for William's hand. "Do you remember, William? You were so excited when you won that cowboy hat at one of these games. What game was it?"

William nodded, guiding her step onto a dry spot of grass. "Yes, I do remember, Aunt Agnes. It was one of those throw the-ball-into-the-little-basket games. I don't remember what it was called. It was great fun though." He reached for Margaret's hand next. She hopped out of the canoe.

William waved for the young attendant, his attention riveted on a lanky girl standing next to him; a single thickly coiled braid of brown hair ran down her back to her waist. He saw William and hurried over. William pulled coins out of his pocket and paid for the two-hour canoe rental.

Agnes shaded her eyes, looking across the crowded midway at a perfectly cylindrical stone tower with a window set halfway to the top. "I never could understand that ridiculous tower—it looks as silly now as it did last time." She shook her head with exasperation. "Isaac, of course, thought it was 'well constructed.' I told him something could be 'well constructed' and look ridiculous at the same time."

"Norumbega Tower," William said. "In school, none of us understood why someone here in Massachusetts would want to build a memorial to the Vikings."

"To the Vikings?" Margaret asked, amused and curious.

Agnes held Margaret's arm for support her as she stepped onto the duckboard straddling a patch of mud. "Yes, Margaret. Supposedly the Vikings came up the Charles River and—"

"*Supposedly?*" Margaret said. "And someone built a monument!" They both laughed.

Games of chance, and people willing to take a chance, crowded the midway—knock over a metal milk jug with an old baseball and get a prize; smack a wooden lever with a heavy mallet and if it propels a metal disc up a guide track to the bell fifteen feet in the air, take a raggedy cloth doll home. All nonsense games, William thought. But ones that thrilled every boy when he was young.

There was also, *supposedly*, new additions to the zoo, according to Joe Finnerty. Lions, tigers. Finnerty's reported that little Clarisse was 'absolutely crazy about the monkeys.'

William decided not to suggest a visit to the zoo; the crowded midway was oppressive enough, without voluntarily submitting to stale air and jostling people in that building.

They stopped at the entrance to the beer garden, its interior obscured by an enclosure of bushy potted plants. William motioned them inside.

"Agnes Morrison?" A thin lady in a white and black-checkered hat stopped in front of Agnes, her voice quivering. She leaned on a bamboo cane. Agnes gave no sign of recognition.

"I'm Florence. I owned the drapery shop on Union Street. I used to see you every spring."

"Oh yes. Hello, Florence. This is my nephew, William, and his wife, Margaret." William and Margaret looked at each other, both certain that Agnes did not remember Florence.

"Oh William, I remember you very well. Agnes, will you join Doris Duffy and me? We are at that table over there—" Florence pointed across the garden. An amply built woman in a bright red dress waved at them.

Florence started to lead Agnes away. "Of course, you both are invited to join us," she said over her shoulder.

"No thank you. You go, Aunt Agnes. We'll join you in a little while." William said. "Margaret and I have a few things to discuss anyway."

"WHAT EXACTLY DO WE HAVE to talk about?" Margaret reached for one of the large mugs the waiter brought to the table.

"Helen Townsend—*your sister-in-law.*"

"Does this have to do with—"

"Yes, with Vincent Chelios."

Margaret said nothing.

"I'm not certain how I feel, Margaret. But please don't try to talk me out of feeling betrayed."

"I didn't know what to do. Helen and I have had our talks and our secrets. I didn't—"

She saw his surprise. "No, William—*neither* of us had secrets like this before. I'm embarrassed, maybe even hurt; it is my brother she is cheating on—you do understand that, don't you?"

William nodded cautiously.

"How did you find out? Was it Mrs. Donnelly?"

William withdrew his hand from the table. "Nobody had to tell me. It was so obvious when we saw them in New York." It was certainly easier for him to say than to admit that Joe Finnerty had to tell him.

"I didn't know that you noticed. I did." Margaret seized William's lit cigarette and inhaled slowly. "I don't know if I should be angry, not just because of Byron but also for the work Helen is doing—she's immersed in that propaganda machine Creel has created."

"Your parents would be very upset if they found out."

"I know. Fortunately it may be over almost before it began." Margaret handed the cigarette back to William. He motioned for more information.

"Some of the people at that horrid Committee have misgivings about the lack of free speech they're creating around the country. Vincent has been outspoken. He is, I suppose, a genuine newspaperman and can't bear the censorship Creel is imposing."

"And Helen?"

"She's still excited about *her role* in the Committee. I tried to talk to her about the effect this propaganda is having on the country."

"And what does she say?"

Margaret arranged her answer, wanting it to be accurate. "She believes I'm still angry about the radio station closing. Actually, when we last talked about it, it was, how could I say it? *Acrimonious.* Censorship and fear tactics can never be good. She doesn't seem to share my views about that."

"I know how you feel, and you know how I feel, about those socialist creeps you are involved with, Margaret—even if I agree with some of what they say. There will be time after this war ends to speak out. If you didn't work for your father, you would be out of work by now—"

Margaret acknowledged Agnes's wave. "Let's join Auntie now."

33

"—AND THE TIME FOR US to act as one nation is now. We must fight the Germans in Europe before we have to fight them here, right on these streets in New York."

The brownish leaves of a New York Thanksgiving weekend swirled around the wooden podium, a sign reading **CPI PUBLIC SPEAKERS** perched in front. Helen huddled inside her heavy woolen coat. She had shivered throughout her speech the previous weekend, and it distracted her—this time she was prepared.

The audience spread out toward the trees enclosing the small field. Helen had spent hours at the office reliving her previous mistakes with others who also had volunteered to speak in public each weekend— today she would do better. She mapped out each line, building to the suggested finale. Luckily, the speeches could only be three minutes long. Creel had dictated that length believing that neither audience nor speaker could retain more than a few minutes of information.

"—You may ask yourself, why is a woman speaking here today? I will tell you why. Because we are the ones who will face the German

Pillage if they should reach these shores. We have documented stories of German violation of women in every country they have illegally entered."

'Documented stories?' Vincent Chelios asked himself. He had been at the same meetings as Helen while these speeches were rehearsed. Nobody could ever prove any 'violations;" yet these speakers still claimed they had documentation. *It was propaganda, nothing more.*

Vincent stood in the middle of the crowd, his arms folded.

He knew Helen believed it more important to energize the audience than to present *just* facts. He could not convince her otherwise. She had come a long way since her first day at the campaign headquarters—maybe too far.

"Lady, there are a lot of Germans in the streets here already," shouted a wide-shouldered man wearing a thick turtleneck sweater and a dark blue wool cap rolled down over his ears. "I'm one of those Germans. What the hell do I want with you? Or your daughter?" He searched the crowd for agreement. The two men next to him snickered.

"There are people all over the country asking our citizens to unify—" Helen tried to regain her momentum.

"Against us Germans who've been here for forty years, lady?" the heckler persisted.

"You goddamn Germans started the war!" a beanstalk of a man in a postman's uniform shouted at him. His head, mounted on a pale stick of a neck, loomed above the now murmuring crowd.

"And we also built your cities and are as American as you!" spat the heckler, pushing his way through the sea of bystanders toward the mailman. They wrestled each other wordlessly.

Another fight on the fringe of the crowd distracted Helen. Two men swung wild punches at each other, the crowd moving away, giving the combatants space to grapple.

The heckling and fighting surprised Vincent; he had noticed less of it over the past few weeks. He had concluded that the Committee had been doing its job—squeezing a consensus for the war out of the public. He reminded himself that he had told Creel that this is the same propaganda he would have once fought against—even if there had been a war going on.

Vincent needed to talk to Helen, and he knew where to find her. All the speaker's schedules were posted on the wall in the office, next to Mrs. Donnelly's desk. He wanted an answer that day. The moment she stepped off the podium, he moved in front of her.

"You may not know it, Helen"—Vincent groped for the first few words—"but Union Square has been a place where people have debated for over one hundred years. Even during the Civil War there was free—"

"I know what you're going to say, Vincent," Helen said, watching the crowd dissipate into the streets radiating away from the square. "I know you're not happy with what we're doing out here. I'm saddened that you no longer see the value—"

"Helen, I will never see the value in preventing other opinions. That's what we're doing now. I'm still a journalist. I would rather win people over—"

"—with facts rather than wild stories?" Helen turned toward the 14th Street border of the park. "I heard you say that several times already. You're losing that battle for good reason, Vincent."

"There'll never be a good reason for propaganda. That's what our message is now—propaganda." Vincent stopped Helen, turning her towards him. "I need to tell you something, Helen. Ask you something."

"Yes, Vincent. What is it?"

"I'm going back to San Francisco. My work is done here."

"Is that what you want to *ask* me?" Helen continued to walk, pulling her coat tightly around her. Vincent followed next to her.

"I want you to come with me. I know you love me. I know you are married to someone else. But I want to be with you. Someplace else. Believe it or not, there are many people out West who still believe we shouldn't be in this war. Maybe even your own family in Denver."

"Your work might be 'done here,' but mine is not. As long as we are fighting for democracy we must speak out."

Vincent took Helen by her arm, guiding her past women picking through cheap clothing piled onto pushcarts. He imagined that most of them had come up from the Lower East Side tenements on the subway looking for the bargains this street had long been known to provide. "Helen, you can believe whatever you want. I don't even know if I can get a job on a newspaper anymore—the way things are."

"What do you mean?" Helen asked, surprised. "You are a wonderful journalist."

"I need you with me. Will you come with me?"

"I can't leave now, Vincent. The war effort needs everyone in the Committee now. Don't you see that we're the ones who will ensure a united stand against the Germans? We have to fight those who want to undermine America."

"Helen—" Vincent paused, choosing his words cautiously. "This 'united stand' will be fine without either of us. But we won't be fine without each other. I know you know that."

"I can't think of personal needs now. I have to stay." She turned around and maneuvered through the women swarming the pushcarts.

34

"I HAD A SMALL EMERGENCY with Clarisse. Otherwise I would have been on time," Joe Finnerty said loudly, moving briskly toward William, the heels of his dark brown and cream shoes clicking off the polished marbled floors.

William examined a model of a Dexter-built merchant ship, long and sleek, with one smoke stack and two masts. Its fifteen-foot glass enclosure dominated the bank lobby.

"Dexter just set up this model here this morning," William said, adding an afterthought he hoped would be amusing; "I hope they don't consider this as repayment for the loan we gave them." A welcome bit of levity, William thought, after a morning of apprehension about the upcoming encounter.

Finnerty threw his head back and smiled. "To tell you the truth, William, I'm surprised this model is so public. I see those *The Enemy is Listening* posters all over town. And yet, right here in the middle of our lobby, is a model of the latest ship design. Shouldn't this be in a vault somewhere, protected by our Marines?"

"No need to concern yourself, Joe. The Germans already have the plans for all of our ships. Just like we do for theirs. But thanks for your suggestion. I'll see if I can get someone's attention at Dexter."

Finnerty had insisted on this meeting with William—and that Margaret should join them. She agreed, curious why William couldn't divulge the reason. William and Finnerty had decided two days earlier that they shouldn't tell her. If the meeting would have any effect on her, or even shock her, it had to be a surprise.

They would pick Margaret up at the newspaper building. She never even wanted to be in the same room with Joe Finnerty, and now they would all ride downtown in Finnerty's new 1915 Winton Six limousine. William knew that Margaret would not find a ride in a limousine enough to distract her from the discomfort of being so close to Finnerty. *She must have been very curious indeed to agree to this meeting.*

MARGARET STOOD JUST INSIDE the bronze and glass revolving door, her new assistant talking to her with exaggerated hand movements. William absently looked up at THE BOSTON EXAMINER etched above the brick and concrete entrance. He motioned for Margaret's attention.

They walked to the curb. Finnerty, in the back seat, held the door open. Andrews, the chauffeur, looked straight ahead.

"Margaret, I know you can't be happy to be in such close quarters with me." Finnerty's sincerity surprised William. "But this is a matter of great urgency for you—and also for William."

The limo's interior was outfitted with facing upholstered bench seats—Margaret and William sat looking forward, Finnerty opposite them. "Andrews, let's go to State Street," Finnerty said, craning his head toward the cab's partition window. Then he turned back to Margaret and added, "Margaret Morrison, this is Herman Oliver."

She hadn't noticed the other man sitting in the chauffeur's cab.

"Pleasure to meet you, ma'am," Oliver said, looking over his shoulder.

"Thank you, Mr. Oliver." Margaret loosened the collar of her fur coat.

Earnest, alert, William had first assessed Oliver when they drove over to meet Margaret. Maybe a lawyer—an athletic one; his suit did not obscure a well-muscled torso. His questions were pointed; he wasted no time with pleasantries. Then William had remembered the name, Herman Oliver—this was the same man who had 'helped' with the Hiram Harris business, and later spied on Helen. *Finnerty keeps him busy.*

"Margaret, perhaps I have given you no reason to believe anything I say," Finnerty said with a disconcerting gentleness. "So I thought I should take you to see something."

"Quite *dramatic*, wouldn't you say, Mr. Finnerty? *Mysterious?*" Margaret said, a bit taunting. Finnerty did not react. He turned toward the front cab and silently looked through the windshield.

Andrews guided the Cadillac through twisting Boston streets, emerging onto State Street. He pulled to the curb and stopped.

"Andrews, wait outside the car. Perhaps inside that doorway." Finnerty gestured toward the department store behind the Santa Claus in a threadbare red and white costume with his beard askew, Christmas shoppers detouring around him.

Finnerty closed the gauzy beige curtains on each passenger window. "Mr. Oliver, please?"

Herman Oliver half-turned to address Finnerty and the other two occupants in the back seat.

"The Espionage Act was passed a few months ago. It is now illegal to interfere with the operations of the military. We use that to charge a lot of people. Then they can try to convince the jury otherwise. They often go broke defending themselves—"

Of course, William realized, Oliver was a government agent. How did he not see it right away? *Athletic, and he knew how to use the law.*

"—Even that Anne O'Reilly girl who worked for your mother, Mrs. Morrison. How quick were they to put her on a troop transport back to Ireland? I know you're aware of that—am I correct?"

"How do you know what I am aware of?" Margaret asked, more curious than indignant.

"Because I came to a few of your meetings—those Socialist Party meetings."

"I can't say that you seem the type, but then we hope everybody would come." Margaret's attempt at breeziness was ignored. "You spied on us. For who?"

"I work for Mr. Finnerty."

"Margaret, let us not waste time," Finnerty said, his voice level. "Let me tell you what happened and you can decide if we are acting in your interests."

"Does William know what this is about?"

"Yes Margaret. We told him the other day." Finnerty nodded in William's direction. "We asked him not to discuss this with you until we could be present."

"We?"

"Mr. Oliver and I."

Margaret turned toward the shrill sound of the big bronze bell Santa rang with no particular rhythm.

Herman Oliver continued. "Mr. Finnerty asked me to attend your meetings."

"Why? I could have told you about them and spared you the inconvenience. All you needed to do was call." They ignored Margaret again.

"I listened to your colleague, Mr. Mendes," Oliver went on. "An impressive speaker. *Inspirational,* perhaps—if you are of that persuasion. I noticed that you and he had an extended conversation outside the meeting hall one evening. I suspected that the two of you might have been lovers—"

"—We are *not* lovers. We have never been *lovers.*"

"I think not also. I followed him for several days. Just intuition perhaps. I'm not sure what I expected to find. I even went to a lecture he gave at Harvard. Roman Orators. Interesting—for a few minutes anyway."

Oliver pointed toward the intersection in front of them. "Then one day he turned that corner onto this street. I would have bet my life then that I knew where he was going. I understood immediately."

"And where was that, Mr. Oliver?" Margaret asked, not quite concealing a genuine interest.

"To that building." He motioned toward a four-story office building across the street. Two mermaids embossed on the terra cotta entrance beckoned to passersby. Three steps led up from the sidewalk to the shiny brass door opening into the lobby.

"I followed him inside. I knew he was going up to the third floor. He did. He knocked on the glass window to Gehrer's Imports. I continued past him to an office that I knew was a travel agency."

"Convenient that you knew there was a travel agent on that floor, wouldn't you say?" Margaret strived for a more comfortable posture—challenging Herman Oliver. "How would you know that, Mr. Oliver?"

"Obviously I've been there before, Mrs. Morrison. I had been to Gehrer's Imports many times a few years ago. We joked even then that it would be ironic if a mob burned down Gehrer's, thinking it was a

German company instead of what it really is."

"You have *piqued* my interest."

"It's an undercover field office for the U.S. Attorney General's office. Your Mr. Mendes is a paid government informant, Mrs. Morrison. One of many in Boston, but I believe the one of most concern to you."

Now Herman Oliver's sparing with Margaret ended and they could move along.

"If what you say is true, then I would want a little more evidence than that he entered a government office. Is that not a reasonable question?"

Margaret looked at William. He shrugged his shoulders in agreement that it was indeed a reasonable question.

"I followed him to the building several times. The easiest person I ever followed." Herman Oliver grinned pleasantly. "He was a regular Little Nemo in Slumberland—lost in a dream world. I could have walked alongside of him for days—he would have never noticed."

Margaret was now thoroughly engaged.

Oliver looked at his watch. "I did organize a bit of a performance for today, a *drama* you might call it, Mrs. Morrison. Please pay careful attention."

Finnerty drew back the curtain on Margaret's window facing the building. They sat in silence for five minutes. Not a word.

Henry Mendes exited the building between the frolicking mermaids, falling into step with pedestrians walking briskly in the chilling wind.

"How did you know he would be here now?" Margaret asked.

Another reasonable question, thought William, one he had not asked Oliver earlier.

"He's been here the last three Tuesday mornings at ten AM—I did have help knowing his schedule. Otherwise it would have been hard for me to make this *drama* ring true."

A man in a blue suit and blue bowler exited the building. He stopped, lit a cigarette, crossed the street, and peered into the limousine.

"Hello, Herman," he said, acknowledging everyone else in the back seat with a nod.

"This is Michael Connors," Oliver said. "We worked together for years."

"Thank you for your assistance in this matter, Mr. Connors," Finnerty said. Then he rolled down the window facing Santa and motioned for Andrews to come closer. "Take us back to my office."

"MRS. MORRISON," HERMAN OLIVER began, "you have made proposals in front of Mr. Mendes that could be deemed violations of the Espionage Act. Are you aware of that?"

Like a prosecuting attorney, thought William. Oliver was firmly leading Margaret through an informal interrogation—but an interrogation just the same. Even the slight edge of menace beneath his 'Mrs.' politeness conveyed the tone of a government agent who knew he had the upper hand. William couldn't help being impressed, even if his wife was the target.

"I'm only aware that I'm doing everything possible to bring an end to a war from which a few profit and many suffer." Margaret looked at Joe Finnerty sitting at his desk. He listened motionlessly.

"Your reasons for wanting to end a war are of less interest to the Attorney General than is your violation of federal law." Oliver picked up Finnerty's silver cigarette lighter. He lit a cigar. "What you should know is that in a few months, President Wilson will pass another law that will make it a crime to use disloyal, profane, or abusive language about the government, or about the military during wartime. The post office can stop mail delivery to dissenters of government policy. Anybody can be sent to jail then—"

"Agents like Mendes will make sure people get charged and stay in court fighting charges for the duration of the war." Finnerty interrupted, leaning forward, resting his forearms on his desk. "Or that they stay in jail until the war is over—maybe longer."

"Are there no longer constitutional protections for freedom of speech?" Margaret asked. Nobody answered her.

"So where do we go from here?" William asked. "Is it—"

"Mr. Oliver, how do you know Mr. Connors, if I may ask?" Margaret's tone was now gracious.

"After I followed Mendes to that building I stood outside, down the street. I was surprised to see Connors walking down the street. You see, we worked together on a miner's strike out west some time ago. I hadn't seen him in two years—about as long as I have worked for Mr. Finnerty. He filled me in on the Mendes case once I told him of my interest."

"So Mr. Connors is a government agent informing on his informants? Is that correct?" Margaret observed, unable to resist a bit of sarcasm.

Oliver shrugged his shoulders, acknowledging the truth in her conclusion. "You might want to know, Mrs. Morrison, that I've seen you before—I stood next to you at that meeting in the Commons last July."

"You were following me then?"

"Once we found out about Mendes, Finnerty asked me to follow you to that demonstration. I would have protected you if you were endangered more than you were by that man who pushed you onto the footpath."

"I would have been much obliged if you had punched him."

"Why would I do that? He was with me. Don't you remember that man with the bowler?" Oliver laughed. "It was Connors, the man you just met. I told him to frighten you and get you out of the Commons as soon as possible. It was ugly. Did you notice the purple and white pin on his lapel? I wore one also—a sign to the police that we were, how would I say—friendly sorts." Oliver smiled. "It doesn't always work. We have to take our chances also."

"What about Mendes—why did the police arrest him, an informant?" Margaret asked, understanding there were subtleties in this conversation she did not grasp—and those subtleties were rapidly unfolding.

Finnerty lit up a cigar. "They got Mendes out of the way so that he would not get roughed up by the police or those soldiers."

"A courtesy to our informants," Oliver said jokingly. "Seriously, Mrs. Morrison, you are very exposed. Mendes of course knows of your relationship to the newspaper, and also knows that compromising you would be advantageous to the government. They can use your legal exposure to extract favorable press, to say the least. This has been done before, you understand. The other members of your group are quite—small potatoes."

Margaret studied Finnerty's familiar cat-that-ate-the-canary expression. "Joe, what is your interest in this matter?"

Finnerty shrugged his shoulders. "I hear they give out long prison sentences these days."

"So you are doing a good deed for me."

"Margaret, I don't want you in jail, and I don't like the government's tactics either. I'm still a feisty Irishman. Even sending that little Irish girl Anne back to Ireland bothers me."

"So, Joe Finnerty has a change of heart?" Margaret said, hoping to lighten the moment.

"Call it what you wish, but I will still make money from a war I never asked for."

"And what about Mr. Mendes. Does he come to a *dramatic* end?"

"No, nothing dramatic," Oliver said, amused by Margaret's question. "Let's just say he is of no further use to anyone here in Boston. After we chat with him he will be happy to get out of town. Trust me."

35

THE GERMAN ARTILLERY ROUND burst at the bridge's embankment; vehicles and men on the country road froze in the searing flash of light. Byron had been driving his ambulance all day and into the night, past soldiers wandering vacantly, slogging through ankle-deep mud, accumulated from two days of incessant rain that had mercifully just stopped. Horses strained, pulling carts loaded with munitions.

Another shell slammed in front of him. The ambulance lifted off the ground and squished down again into the mud. Byron pulled the steering wheel towards him, instinctively attempting to create distance between himself and the blast.

A lorry in front of him, and its two horses, took that direct hit. A handful of gooey flesh flew through Byron's windshield, its glass long ago knocked out by artillery blasts, oozed down his face. Bloodied pieces of horse's innards landed on his jacket. Body parts, human and animal, made the deeply rutted road even more difficult to traverse. He hoped this time he wouldn't vomit.

A mule stood weaving at the side of the road, gazed dumbly in Byron's direction, both its front legs twisted, unable to support its upper body. An approaching officer pulled his sidearm and sent a mercy bullet crashing into the animal's skull. The mule's legs buckled; its front quarters sank in slow motion as the rest of the body fell forward into the mud.

"Just my luck," Byron muttered, knowing there would be a wait to push the broken carcass off the road.

He quickly turned onto a side road he believed to be a detour that would eventually lead him back to this same road, further on towards his destination. He soon found himself lost in the country night and rolled to a stop at a tree line at the edge of a glen surrounding a distant abandoned farmhouse. The waist-high grass swayed in the frail moonlight.

The sudden quietness around him incited an uncomfortable nervousness. He was alone for the first time in days. Was anyone in the house? Maybe Germans sleeping inside? Or friendly soldiers? He knew that each bit of ground has been taken and retaken dozens of times by each side in this insane war. *Who knows who is in there?* He reached for his binoculars jammed under the seat. They were covered with cold mud. *I can't see a damn thing. Useless.*

He slid out of the vehicle and crawled toward a dank wooden hutch, stopping to evaluate the terrain. He estimated the fir trees on the far side of the glen to be five hundred feet away. He wasn't sure—it didn't matter anyway.

He wasn't sure of anything. Did the moonlight benefit him or not? The Germans could see him as easy as he could see them. Maybe they had an advantage; they patrolled every night, looking for Allied soldiers wandering in forests, blinded, maimed, or just crazed from a trench war that now had endured for more than three years.

Sudden movement in the trees to his left—a human figure. It

stumbled out into the clearing. Maybe not a soldier—he had no weapons. Holding his midsection, he lurched forward towards the empty farmhouse; then disappeared into the grass. *Did he fall or was he hiding?*

Byron decided to crawl forward to the small rise the soldier had disappeared behind. He parted the grass at the edge of a patch of mud; the man sat erect with his legs spread in front of him, his back supported by a tree stump. He stared straight into Byron's eyes, his head bent down to his chest, emotionless,

"Are you British?" Byron called to him, unable to distinguish the uniform beneath the covering of mud and caked blood.

"American, I think. What town is this?" The man spoke with difficulty in a raspy voice.

"What town is this? Damned if I know," Byron said. "I think they call it Just Another Shithole In France. I'm lost also. But I'm in better condition than you." Byron crawled closer to the man. "You're shell-shocked and I need to get you out of this field."

He looked toward the abandoned farmhouse.

THEY STAGGERED TOGETHER THROUGH the high grass, Byron firmly grasping his confused charge, keeping him from falling into the moonlit pools of mud and rainwater. Closer to the farmhouse, he understood why the farmhouse lights were out, why it appeared empty from far away. It was just a shell of a building. Only the front wall remained standing—the rest rubble. Curtains still hung tenaciously from the farmhouse windows as if ready to be drawn open at daybreak.

Byron guided the soldier around the side of the house, hoping to find the remains of the kitchen. He stepped around a toppled cupboard, and sifting through the debris he pulled out four tin cans, blackened shells offering no clue as to their contents.

Byron slipped them into the medical supply bag he had instinctively flung over his shoulder when he crawled out of his ambulance only minutes before. His companion started to wander off again. Byron guided him back to a tottering staircase now leading up to the clear night sky. He guessed that if there was a cellar it might be under the staircase. He struggled to move a bed frame that had crashed down, along with much of the second floor. The other man stood watching him, saying nothing, offering no help.

Byron found the cellar door under a toppled armoire and a carpet of white porcelain shards. He wondered if they would be cornering themselves in the cellar or if they should find cover in the forest surrounding the farmhouse.

He didn't have to make a decision. A cloud of dust and the hum of distant mechanized vehicles alerted him to the approaching convoy. He pulled on a rusted metal ring and opened the creaking door. Byron led the man down the narrow ladder, a wave of must rising to envelop them.

EARLY MORNING LIGHT SEEPED into their cellar retreat. They had both fallen asleep on sacks of potatoes, which, surprisingly, had not been found by one army or the other. Whoever had passed nearby the night before didn't matter now. They were gone.

"I'm from Kansas City in America," the man said, without prompting. "I've been here for two months or so. My head is still ringing from the concussions from that German artillery. It just missed me. Terrifying. I never would have imagined."

Byron estimated his new companion to be a few years old than himself. He wore a wedding ring on his left hand. He seemed coherent, his breathing now normal. There was no sign of a cut on his face—the caked blood might not have even been his.

Byron extended his hand. The man grasped it harder than he expected. ""Byron Townsend. I'm from Boston. I'm an ambulance driver. I came over with a group of volunteers from Harvard. I got here before Wilson declared war. They put us all in the Army. Now I'm just another doughboy."

"Sidney—Sidney Griggs. I'm a doctor. I got lost. Thank God I stumbled onto you. Thanks—Byron."

Byron offered him his canteen.

Dr. Griggs drew the water in deeply. He stretched his legs over a potato sack and stood up. "Now I have to take a piss. A long one, if you don't mind."

"Help yourself, Sidney. Just don't piss in my flower pots upstairs."

The doctor looked at Byron for a few seconds and then laughed. "Yes, let's do keep our wits about us. Very witty."

Dr. Griggs pissed on two dust-covered bottles of wine lying in a corner that had survived the artillery. "That's in case the Germans find them and drink them."

"What happens if it's us Yanks who find them?" Byron asked.

"Well, fuck them also." Dr. Griggs laughed. So did Byron.

"Are you a field surgeon, Sidney?"

"No, nothing as glamorous as that. Actually I'm here on special assignment. I'm doing public health research, evaluating the conditions in different forward regiments."

"You mean like seeing the effects of men standing in freezing water, shit, and blood for weeks on end? See if they get a disease?"

Dr. Griggs grinned at Byron's light-hearted summary of his assignment. "Yes, something like that."

Byron scanned the cellar for an implement to pierce the misshapen cans he had found the night before. He reached for a pitchfork hanging from a wooden beam. He braced a can against a wooden block and plunged one of the long prongs into it. Then he twisted the pitchfork, widening the hole, and handed the can to the doctor. A yellowish squash bubbled out.

Dr. Griggs shook some into his cupped palm and swallowed it. "Not as bad as I expected, although the presentation is a bit crude. It's probably tastier when heated. What do you think, Byron?"

"I think a public health doctor should wash his filthy fucking hands before he pours food into them. Even putrid food. Especially after he takes a piss."

"Hand washing—we do teach that practice to the soldiers." Dr. Griggs pulled a broken cigarette out of his shirt pocket. "I forgot I had this."

"So, you're with a public health survey." Byron rolled onto his side and pulled out a small box of matches from his pocket. "Couldn't you have figured out how to stay away from the Front? You look like a smart guy. And you volunteered—but so did I. So what the hell am I talking about?"

Dr. Griggs thought for a moment. "The truth is that I was hoping to come here, spend some time talking to the soldiers, write a few reports, and then have a career in public health. This crap hole was supposed to be a great opportunity for me."

"And so how did you get lost at the Front instead of on your way to the commissary at a hospital?" Byron asked, reaching for the lit cigarette Dr. Griggs handed him.

"As soon as I got off the boat in France I saw miles of ambulances, stretchers, amputated men held up by their buddies, and doctors who looked like skeletons. That same day I forgot about my career and have been in the trenches ever since. If these men can do what they do every day, so can I. I hope that doesn't sound too heroic,

Byron—there's nothing heroic about what I do. I just do what needs to be done."

So while Sidney Griggs talked I realized that I have done the same. So have many others. We all just do what needs to be done! That is why there have been no more 'stories from the Front' from me. It now seems so self-ish, sitting on the fringe of this terrible conflict and writing about it, hoping for another byline. Or so that I could show Father and Mother that I am independent. I am here now, alongside everyone else, working for a victory.

Right now all I can say is that I am proudly serving my country.

I hope you can forgive me my past selfishness.

Love,
Byron
November 1917

Helen laid Byron's letter on the coffee table.

"'For a man to conquer himself is the first and noblest of all victories.'" Beatrice's Platonic quote penetrated the silence in the inn's sitting room—not a word, or even a sigh, had been uttered during Helen's reading of Byron's account of his harrowing night in the abandoned farmhouse.

"I had to read the letter to you as soon as I could," Helen said. She took a deep breath. "I needed time away from the Committee. New York is not a place for quiet thinking."

"Well, we're always glad to have you stay with us. It is so rare to see you." Agnes looked up from a crimson and sky blue woolen sweater she knitted. "And it seems like we will have a lot of empty rooms here as long as the German submarines are right here, off the coast. And Beatrice you, of course, are always welcome anytime."

"It's as much a death warrant for a seaside hotel as would be food poisoning." Isaac said, sorting clusters of wires with his bony fingers. "But we've had rough times before and managed to get through them. I imagine we'll get through this one also."

"Uncle Isaac, I once asked William how you decided to call this Glenfiddich Inn," Helen said, picking up her coffee cup. "He said I should ask you but I never did. He did give me a hint—no one in the family is from Glenfiddich in Scotland and that probably no Morrison would even know where it is."

"Now that is just not true. I know exactly where it is. So does William by now." Isaac nodded toward Agnes. "And she knows too."

"*She* may know but *she* doesn't care." Agnes rested her sweater-in-progress on the chair next to her. "Before you get a wild story from Isaac, let me give you the facts. He can dispute them later."

"Oh, thank you, Aunt Agnes," Helen said, smiling, knowing that a fanciful refutation by Isaac would soon follow.

"When we opened the inn, it didn't have a name. We had a dinner celebration with our first guests. One of them, I think it was Mr. Penn, had just returned from Scotland. He brought back several bottles of whiskey from a distillery that had just opened in a town called Glenfiddich. I don't think Isaac ever tasted it, or any other whiskey that I am aware of. But he insisted on naming the inn after the town and the whiskey."

"Just like that?" Helen asked.

"Not only '*just like that*.'" Agnes looked over at Isaac's web of wires. "But he even asks anyone visiting Scotland to keep an eye out for *anything* that has the name Glenfiddich on it."

"*Anything?*" Helen enjoyed the light moment. "He still does?"

"Of course he *still* does." Agnes waved her tiny hand, offering the walls as proof. "Haven't you ever wondered why there are photographs of streets in Glenfiddich, of one of its mayors, and my favorite—a picture of a graduating class of youngsters from a school in Glenfiddich? My goodness, I would expect that at least one guest would have asked who we knew in the photograph. But nobody ever did. Remarkable— maybe they all know Isaac is just a bit daft."

Isaac ignored Helen and Agnes. "Beatrice, I'm glad to hear that Margaret is involved again in your circulation department. She is so competent. I know William was concerned about her running around with those socialists. Not that they don't have a point, mind you."

Beatrice gazed at the photographs on the walls. "I think once that Henry Mendes character left town everybody moved on to other things—good riddance, anyway."

"I didn't know that he left Boston." The news surprised Helen.

"Yes, he left." Beatrice peered, squinting at a photograph of a circus troupe posing acrobatically on the steps of the Glenfiddich town hall. "Apparently there was a sudden death in his family and he had to return to El Paso—I think it is—to handle family matters. Margaret says that he plans to come back for the fall semester."

36

MAY 17, 1918

CRYSTAL LAKE

NEWTON CENTRE, MASS.

"THANK YOU FOR INVITING me to your lovely home." Dr. Griggs followed Donald Townsend down the steps to the lakeside table. "Byron described this so well. He even mentioned that strange tree growing out of the middle of the lake."

"It's nice of you to join us for Byron and Margaret's birthday party. You will be a most suitable *temporary* replacement for our son." Donald pointed to the bench, indicating a place for Dr. Griggs. "We feel like we know you quite well by now."

Margaret held out a bottle of wine, offering to fill an empty glass for him. "That *strange* tree, as you call it, Dr. Griggs, has been a curiosity to this family for years. We have no idea how it survives."

"How did the lake come to be called Crystal Lake?" Dr. Griggs asked.

Margaret assumed it was chatty small talk but was delighted to share the history. "Ice harvesters moved in some years ago. They thought a change of name would allow them to call their product Crystal Lake Ice. That would be more appealing to their customers than would Baptist Pond Ice—"

"Baptist Pond?" Dr. Griggs asked, amused, happy to engage the family of the man who saved him just a few short months before.

Margaret appreciated the doctor's easy manner despite his nervous adjusting and readjusting the wire-rimmed glasses on his narrow nose as he sat in the armchair next to her mother. She estimated him to be bulkier than her brother, probably needing a larger shirt than Byron.

"The local Baptist church used to use the lake for its baptisms. And hence the old name," Margaret answered cheerfully. "Father has often said that he would rather look at that straggly tree than fools being baptized any day."

Donald Townsend nodded vigorously.

"Dr, Griggs, I think it an extraordinary coincidence that you met Byron in a forest, in the middle of the night," Beatrice said. "And to think that you work with Dr. Welch. We know Dr. Welch and his work. So does Dr. Carlson—he's on his way here now. He is so looking forward to meeting you and to hear about your adventures at the Western Front. Byron's wife, Helen, will also be here soon. She certainly wants to meet you as well."

"That poor Helen was under such a strain in New York. I'm relieved she has her family around her now," Mrs. Donnelly said, two ledgers closed in front of her. She found herself conveniently within her short arm's length from a dull orange colored pottery bowl filled with large boiled shrimp.

Donald wondered if he had made a mistake giving Mrs. Donnelly the bookkeeping job for the newspaper. Too conscientiousness, he concluded with amusement. Unlike a few of his writers who didn't always embrace his fidelity to facts—men he had to keep under a tight watch. She however seemed incapable of deception. He was relieved that Mrs. Donnelly had been in New York with Helen. Women out on their own—damned war, he had muttered to himself many times. *What a relief they both left that propaganda cesspool Creel is creating.*

"Mrs. Donnelly, we're grateful that you could stay so long with Helen in New York. It has been equally wonderful to have you back here with her—and with us," Donald said. "Besides, in my thirty-six years in the newspaper business I never heard some of those stories before. Your husband was an interesting man."

"Most people had other names for him." Mrs. Donnelly laughed.

"So did I," Donald confessed. "If the truth be known."

Dr. Griggs reached into his scuffed black suitcase. He handed a package to Margaret. "A birthday present for you, from Byron. He chose it himself."

"With all due respect, Dr. Griggs, I can tell you that this package was definitely wrapped by a man," Beatrice said. "Why is it that men have so little appreciation for gift wrapping?"

"Please call me Sidney," Dr. Griggs suggested, looking around the table.

Donald grunted his acknowledgement.

"I suppose it does look like poor Byron wrapped it in the dark—while wearing boxing gloves." Dr. Griggs said, reaching deeper into his case. "Actually, I have two more inadequately wrapped gifts—one is for you, Mrs. Townsend, and the other"— he raised his voice so that it carried to the steps—"is for you, Helen. I recognize you from the picture Byron carries with him."

Beatrice turned toward Helen who held her full-length beige and red dress tightly at her knees, carefully descending the stone staircase. "So glad you could join us, Helen darling."

Margaret had undone her package and held out a black cashmere shawl.

"Oh, it's lovely. Thank you so much for bringing it all this way,

Dr. Griggs—Sidney." She looked at the label. "It's from Paris. The Champs-Élysées. Even during a war."

Dr. Griggs swirled the wine in his glass. "Margaret, a surprising facet of this war is that the streets of Paris are filled with British and American soldiers buying gifts to take back home. I was quite surprised. Of course everything is extremely expensive."

"Hello, everybody. Happy birthday, Margaret." Edward Carlson descended, carrying a paper bag, holding it carefully. "A few bottles of French wine I found the other day. Don't ask where."

"Marvelous. France seems to be the motif for the day." Margaret held out the scarf toward Dr. Carlson. "A present from Byron."

Dr. Carlson stepped over the bench, maneuvering his legs under the table. He looked around at the tureens of food. Donald nodded towards a covered bowl. Carlson removed the porcelain lid. "Oh yes, my favorite stew—lamb and potato. How did you remember, Beatrice?"

"Hasn't it has been your favorite stew for thirty years, Edward?" Beatrice raised her eyebrow. "Why would I, all of a sudden—forget?"

Dr. Carlson shrugged his agreement with Beatrice's logic.

Margaret smiled. *It's hard to believe Mother had another—involvement with any other man—let alone with Dr. Carlson. Mother and Dr. Carlson? She must have broken the dear man's heart.*

Carlson turned to their guest. "Dr. Griggs, Dr. Welch tells me that you're one of his most capable staff at the Front."

"That is a nice compliment, even if I often have to be a doctor and put aside my work on his research team. Byron didn't mention that his family knew Dr. Welch when we first met. But then again, it didn't come up for several weeks. We were both, after all—*in the war.*"

"I read your report on influenza at the front lines," Dr. Carlson said. "Curious, isn't it, that it seems to have traveled across the Atlantic? We monitored it at Ft. Riley in Kansas last May. The troop trains carried it to the East Coast—and then to France. That's the state of our thinking anyway. Especially given the censorship restrictions."

"Do you also find it curious that it's affecting young men more than anyone else in the population?" Dr. Griggs asked. "Not children or the elderly, and they are usually the most vulnerable."

"We don't have proper statistics yet but that does seem to be the case. There was also a higher degree of pneumonia amongst these patients," Dr. Carlson added. "The incidences appear to be diminishing. Flu is a cold weather disease, so maybe the worst is over."

Donald moved his hand abruptly. "Oh, I forgot, I need to show Margaret and William a legal document in the study. It is time sensitive and I would like a response." He looked around the table for approval. "We'll only be a minute."

DONALD TOWNSEND LOOKED OUT the sitting room window. He watched Dr. Griggs charming Beatrice, Helen and Mrs. Donnelly at the table below.

Margaret sat on the velvet sofa, gesturing to William to sit next to her.

Donald turned from the window and walked in front of them. "We should only be away from our guest for a few moments. So let me get to the point."

Margaret cautiously urged him to continue.

"Why is it that I don't quite believe the story that Henry Mendes left his own Bolshevik Revolution here in Boston to care for a sick aunty in New Mexico—or wherever she is supposed to be?"

He looked at them. No response.

"I understand that neither of you may be able to shed light on this matter." Donald looked over at William. "I thought that perhaps you, William, would have some views, given your antipathy toward Mr.

Mendes. A benign antipathy to be sure."

"DR. CARLSON, I REMEMBER the lecture Dr. Welch gave at Harvard two years ago." Helen wrapped her new turquoise cashmere shawl around her shoulders. "He said that in every war more soldiers die from communicable diseases than from battle wounds." She turned toward a squadron of ducks quacking their presence on the lake.

"That has always been the case." Dr. Carlson followed the ducks' progress across the lake, as he had so many times over the years. "Two times as many soldiers died from infections and communicable diseases than from wounds during the Civil War. That's why we're studying this conflict so intensely."

"Influenza will be the communicable disease of this war—some of us were on the lookout for small pox and polio," Dr. Griggs quickly added. "There were some outbreaks but they disappeared. The problem is the overcrowded camps. I understand that some have two times more than the number of conscripts originally intended."

"Another problem is that idiot Creel is not allowing any mention of this—no mention of illnesses," said Beatrice, disappointed with an old family colleague. "It makes the words *public health* a joke—the idea is for the public to join in to prevent disease from spreading. Not to keep it secret."

"Mr. Creel believes that it would give aid and comfort to the enemy," Helen said defensively.

"Helen, I'm afraid you've gone overboard with this *Creel*." Uttering the man's name, Beatrice's face soured. "I remember Creel from years ago—when he fought for freedom of the press, regardless of consequences. Now he is censoring everything. It's probably against the law for me to even say this much now. Are you going to report me, Helen?"

"That is a hurtful thing to suggest." Helen looked away.

"*Democracy passes into despotism,*" Beatrice said, refilling Helen's glass. "I'm sorry dear, it is just so difficult for us to watch this censorship unfold. Please forgive me."

"SO JOE FINNERTY PULLED your chestnuts out of the fire? He defrocked this Mendes character." Donald Townsend looked at his daughter, his tone thoughtful, gentle. "This war will never stop producing surprises, will it?"

"Herman Oliver is right about the crackdown on all dissent," William said. "Margaret would be arrested now just for questioning the war—and they would use that to influence your newspaper."

"That son-of-a-bitch Creel could shut me down any time." Donald tossed a key chain he had absently twirled in his hand onto the low coffee table. "Or any damn newspaper in the country, for that matter. All he has to do is tell the post office that we're sending seditious material through the mail—they pull our mail certificate and we're no longer a newspaper. After struggling every day for thirty-five years to keep it on newsstands, he can shut us down in one day."

"You may be able to remind him of how he always fought government censorship, Father," Margaret suggested. "He respects you."

Donald settled into an armchair next to Margaret. "I called Creel last week and told him he never would have stood for a government agency demanding that newspapers publish its press releases. That's what they're doing now, and a lot of papers are running them as if they are *news*. He told me that I was an unpatriotic so-and-so. Then he hung up on me." Donald leaned back smiling. Then he paused for another thought. "I wonder what Byron and Helen know about this Mendes character."

"Byron knows nothing about this," Margaret replied. "That man who works for Finnerty, Herman Oliver, said that Henry was also a government informant in Mexico. He just used Byron as a passport into the Boston *intelligentsia*. He used that word," she said, trying to laugh, "—*about us*."

"Why does my skin crawl to think that I am indebted to Joe Finnerty for this Mendes situation?" Donald Townsend asked nobody in particular. "It's not as if there's space for his picture in the paper these days." He grinned and shrugged his shoulders in resignation.

"Finnerty may be doing it because he's as disgusted by the government as we are. Or, it may be me he wants payback from," William said, considering the possibilities. "Not you."

"What kind of payback could he expect from you, William?" Donald asked.

"Maybe with the government wanting baseball players to fight or work, these guys will be looking for jobs in the shipyards. I think Joe would like to get close to Babe Ruth—and use my contacts at Dexter to help him."

"Why would he care about that?" The investigative journalist still beating within Donald Townsend sensed a story, even if it was one he could probably never publish.

William grew pensive. "Gambling. The racetracks are closing down because of the war. Gamblers now try to fix as many baseball games as they can. The government keeps threatening to shut down the baseball season. Every player in the league thinks he won't get paid if the season ends early. So they're looking around for any money they can get. Finnerty has his eye on Babe Ruth. He didn't tell me that but it's not hard to see. At least that's my best guess."

"Bribing Babe Ruth to fix games? He does aim high, doesn't he?" Margaret asked.

William smiled faintly. "I suppose, but to tell you the truth, I do feel I owe him for you—and who cares about fixed baseball games anyway? I mean it isn't taking money from an orphans and widows' fund. Its just gamblers beating each other. I'm meeting Joe and Babe Ruth tomorrow at the bank."

37

"COME IN." JOE FINNERTY responded to the light knock on the door.

"Mr. Finnerty, *Babe Ruth* is in the lobby. He's here to see you," said Gladys, the new receptionist, barely stepping into the room.

"Please show him up."

"Can I ask him for an autograph?" Gladys inquired cautiously.

"Sure, why not? I'm sure he'll be delighted."

Gladys leaned into the room a bit more. "He's very interested in the model ship in the lobby."

"Thank you, Gladys." Finnerty waited for the door to close, then shook his head. "That woman has a terrific body, William."

"I knew you wouldn't miss it, Joe."

Finnerty grinned. "Babe Ruth—I can imagine him looking at that ship model in the lobby from every angle, trying to figure out how you get the people onto it. You know he is a simpleton, don't you William?"

"So you have said, Joe."

"NOBODY'S COMING TO THE games this year," Babe Ruth said dejectedly. He sat at the edge of a chair next to William with his tree-trunk
legs sprawled out, holding a straw hat in his hands, his thick fingers
running around the brim. "We don't know if we'll even get paid."

Finnerty feigned interest in the predicament. "Surely, Babe, the
Red Sox will be in the Series and you'll earn money then."

Ruth nodded slowly. "It's a long way 'til the Series. The War Department wants to cut the season short. Some of those fucking fans
are yelling 'slacker' at me, and saying, 'why don't you go fight like my
brother did?' Sons of bitches."

William supposed that he had a role in the drama, and he guessed
this was a good moment for a proposal. "I already talked to the Dexter
management. You can sign and play for them right now. They have
a Fourth of July exhibition game. Everybody would come to see you.
And didn't you say even if there is a World Series there would only be
chicken feed for the players?"

"That's right." Ruth stood up and pulled his pants out of his butt
and sat back down. "Yeah, the owners are talking about giving the
Series share to the first four teams in the league. Some crap like that.
That leaves only a few bucks for the guys who play in the Series. They
just want to spread the money around to keep everyone quiet."

Finnerty swiveled in his chair to face Ruth. "Most of the players
are making more money on the shipbuilders' teams than in the major
leagues." Then he leaned in closer. "Even you, Babe, with all the betting on the games, can make more than Frazee gives you."

"What about the contract I have with Boston? How can I play for
Dexter too? Wouldn't the Red Sox sue them?"

Finnerty lit a cigar. "Actually, Babe, the shipyards' teams are not
part of the company. The workers in the yard organize the teams
themselves. The Red Sox would have to sue the workers—all Dexter

330

is doing is giving you a job in the yard."

William observed the deal unfolding. A simple one. One that would bring Babe Ruth within Finnerty's grasp.

Ruth drew his eyes into a squint, trying to evaluate the new option.

Finnerty calculated that he needed to draw the point a bit sharper. "Imagine the Red Sox suing the workers in a shipyard because a baseball player wants to join the war effort. That wouldn't look too good, would it, Babe?"

If Ruth never played a single game for Dexter, Finnerty could now have what William understood he wanted. Access. Action. A star player who could help Joe gain an edge with the gamblers especially when Ruth went back to the Red Sox—which would inevitably happen.

"That's pretty goddamn smart," Ruth said, his bulldog face blooming into a jowly grin.

"Thank you," Finnerty said, reaching for a modest tone.

"You see, Joe, it's just that a lot of the guys are worried about not getting their money." Ruth recounted conversations on soot-ridden trains transporting the team from one American League stop to another.

Finnerty listened to each story with whatever degree of compassionate he could muster. "I imagine every player is looking for a way to earn a few bucks on the side before the owners stop the season but I wouldn't really know." Finnerty threw back his head in one of his trademark laughs—a self-satisfied bray from his gut—always intended to ingratiate himself with his mark. "I heard a few of the guys bet on their own games. Sometimes even on the other teams." He laughed again to keep the suggestion a casual observation.

Ruth laughed too. Uncomfortably. "Yeah, that's right. Maybe we want to fix them more now that the owners are chiseling every dime they can from us. It only takes one or two guys to throw a game."

38

JULY 21, 1918

THE TOWN OF ORLEANS

CAPE COD, MASS.

HELEN WAITED FOR WILLIAM and Margaret to smooth out the green and black plaid blanket they had stretched on the grass incline. "Margaret, I felt so comfortable with your parents from the moment I met them. They never required Sunday church. I must admit that was a relief." She unbuckled her shoes and knelt down onto the blanket.

"Father always rolled his eyes whenever the subject of Sunday church came up. He still does." Margaret said, placing the wicker basket at one end of the blanket as if to anchor it from a rogue wind, an unlikely occurrence on this humid Cape Cod summer morning.

"I was surprised he never asked me what church I belonged to." William uncorked a bottle of wine and secreted it in the wicker basket, intent on not provoking the disapproval of the other weekend guests in the cottages on the gravel road above them, overlooking the inlet.

It was, after all, Sunday, *the Sabbath,* on Cape Cod. He nodded toward a couple walking along the shore. "We'll never know if they are churchgoers or just coming home from a late night party."

Margaret laughed. "I doubt a late night party here in Orleans."

William watched a tugboat, and then the four barges hitched to it, stream into view from behind a dense stand of trees at the water's edge. He could just barely read its name, *Perth Amboy*. Surprised to see women and children on the barges, he guessed they were related to the crew, all on a Sunday outing.

"I agree, Margaret—they are churchgoers, and not too keen on our bottle of wine on Sunday," Mrs. Donnelly said. She had already pulled out a baguette and evaluated the rest of the basket's contents with hungry zeal. "Not that I have ever been here before, mind you. The only Irish here are working in those big houses on the other end of the Cape."

"Glad you could join us for the weekend, Mrs. Donnelly," William said, leaning back onto the grass, supported by one elbow. "By the way, I didn't hear the story you were telling last night about your late brother-in-law."

Mrs. Donnelly pulled a hunk of deep yellow cheddar cheese from the bottom of the basket. "Oh yes, that story—My dear husband Thomas had a brother, Matthew, a detective with the Boston Police. One day Matthew tells me that he wants to leave a valuable ring to my first grandson.

"'Thank you, Matthew,' I said, 'and where did you get it from, then?' I asked. He said that he and his partner were at a murder scene—a famous Boston gambler, I forget his name now. Well, Matty tells me that he looks down at the body and says to his partner, 'Now that's a beautiful ring.' So he gets it off the dead man's fingers. His partner says, 'this stiff is my size. Judging from this house, I bet he dresses better than I do.' So he goes into the poor man's closet and finds a silk suit. It fits him perfectly. He hangs his old shabby suit in the guy's closet and puts on the silk one.

"Just then their new captain walks in. They think he saw them pilfering the dead man's belongings—and they don't know him that well—so they're a little nervous. But instead the captain points to the big carpet on the floor from one of those Arab countries and tells them to roll it up and put it in the paddy wagon. He wants it for evidence— he tells them."

"—Marvelous! Joe Finnerty would love that story," William said. His shoulders shook as he laughed. "Even though you might want a different source for your grandson's inheritance, I bet if you told the boy that story when he is older, he would enjoy it as much as I do now."

"I already told him, and he loves it." Mrs. Donnelly smiled at the irony. "He is an Irishman after all."

"I know I told you that I would read Sarah's letter, but I left it back at the cottage—oh well." Margaret shrugged her shoulders. "But I can tell you the two most important points."

"You have more of our attention than the minister in that church we past by before would have," Helen said cheerfully. "Sarah will be nineteen? I just thought of her."

"That's right. Next month is her birthday—she left three years ago." William weighed her absence. So much had happened to her since they last saw each other. Her description of that terrible day aboard the *Lusitania* still awakened him some nights.

"Sarah married a Scottish lieutenant," Margaret continued. "They didn't have a grand celebration; there is so much to *not* celebrate there, I suppose. His name is Andrew Williamson. She sent a photo of them. He shipped back off to the Front. And she is working all day in a military hospital."

"I didn't know that, Margaret," William said, disappointed the news waited a day or two. "What is the other important point?"

Margaret looked at him, not understanding.

"You said there were 'two important points,' didn't you, Margaret?"

"Oh yes, sorry, William. Byron writes that influenza has been sickening a lot of the soldiers. It just started over the past two months. Many are dying. Their bodies turn bluish. *Absolutely frightening.*"

"BYRON IS COMING HOME at the beginning of September." Helen gazed around the blanket, happy to share the news. "He's now part of Dr. Welch's public health project. He'll be working in the Boston area."

"I'm glad he's doing that. But to work with Dr. Welch—wouldn't he need to be a doctor?" William asked.

"No—Dr. Welch wants a written history of their public health efforts," Helen said. "No doubt Dr. Carlson had something to say about adding Byron to the team—so to speak."

Margaret glanced over at William, lying back in the grass, looking at the clear summer sky. People on the gravel path higher up on the bluff were motionless now, staring at the ocean.

Margaret turned, following their focus. Then she screamed.

William raised himself to one knee. "It's a German U-boat," he said, responding to Margaret's unspoken question.

They stood up. The conning tower of the submarine had just punctured the ocean's smooth surface. It rose slowly, displacing seawater from its deck, to reveal a U- boat's sleek body, one seen by all of them in newspaper photographs many times.

A woman wandered down from the gravel path above them and stopped next to the blanket. "Oh my God," she said, almost whispering. "What will they do?"

Nobody answered.

They followed the linear ripple issuing from the U-boat as it closed on the tugboat. The stout little craft shuddered on the torpedo's impact; a plume of smoke drifted into the morning air. The cries of panicked women and children on the barges overlaid the silence on the bluff. William raced towards the water's edge.

"William—don't," Margaret pleaded, but not certain what he should do. He didn't hear her anyway.

William's feet sank into the water, his heavy shoes planting him deeper into the murky bottom. From the water's edge he could see a Coast Guard station inside the inlet from where the tugboat and barges had appeared only minutes before. Sailors were racing toward their launches.

Another torpedo hit the tug, fire now consuming its helm. Three crewmen on the barges struggled to loosen the towline, hoping to free themselves from the sinking tug.

Another shell shattered against the cliff, sending jagged clumps of rock splattering into the air. William ran chest high into the water and rolled himself onto a small boat being guided by two fishermen toward the threatened vessels.

Three more rounds from the U-boat hit the barges; the children and women's screams grew louder.

Precision Coast Guard rowers dispatched from the Coast Guard station angled their boats alongside the barges. A guardsman dove into the water, anticipating that a frightened woman holding onto a barge rail would lose her grip and fall. A shell burst nearby. The woman did fall—almost on top of the guardsman. He grabbed her.

The roar of propellers disoriented William. They couldn't be from the boats circling him—none of these Coast Guard rowboats had motors. The now deafening sound came from above, not from the water's surface. William looked up just as the military planes passed directly above him—sent, he assumed, from the Chatham Air Force Base that had luckily just been built up the coast. The planes swept in toward the U-boat, dropping bombs. Two bounced off its hull. Duds.

More U-boat artillery hit the shoreline.

William boarded the barge closest to the slowing sinking tug. He grabbed a screaming boy wearing a pressed white Sunday school shirt and handed him to the fisherman balancing himself in the bobbing rowboat with his long arms reaching out.

William then straddled a metal lip on the barge at water's level and the rail of the rowboat, grasping a woman tightly as she cautiously hopped onto the rowboat. She quickly clutched the boy to her breast.

Both U-boat and tugboat disappeared beneath the water. Guardsmen dived into the water. The women, children, and crew were soon on the rescue vessels, everyone accounted for.

The rowboat William had rolled onto just a half hour earlier headed back towards the inlet and the bluff where now hundreds of people stood silently, watching the return of the flotilla of life savers.

WILLIAM DROVE THE THREE, now hushed women passed a row of storefronts on the street leading out of Orleans. The sign read HEINRICH'S DRY GOODS above the jagged plate glass window. Five men stood on the street, watching them. Locals with wool caps.

A long-limbed teenage boy threw a brick high into the air. It crashed through Heinrich's second floor window. "Hun bastards," he shouted.

Margaret stroked William's hand as he shifted gears. "When you were out on the water did you think of Louella and Sarah?" she asked, just above a whisper.

"Yes, I did—for a moment. What it must have been like to be that fearful. Drowning. Defenseless." His voice low.

"You were heroic, William." Mrs. Donnelly leaned forward. "All of you boys were—with those bombs going off all around you. Everyone was saved."

They heard the speculation on the bluff after the attack; there must be Germans spies along the coast guiding the U-boats to easy targets, maybe at night with fires, maybe using secreted Morse code machines. How else could these U-boats operate with such impunity along the American coast?

Mrs. Donnelly decided to spend the night at the inn. A choice William welcomed; he needed a few minutes alone on the familiar inn porch, not a drive to Mrs. Donnelly's small frame house stuck into a Boston side street.

"YOU MUST HURRY, WILLIAM." Agnes ran down the long driveway. "I know something terrible has happened to Isaac."

"Where is he?" William moved quickly towards the inn.

Agnes stopped him. "He's not here. He went to Hans' store. Hans called. There's a crowd around the store. They can't get out. People are yelling at them. I can hear it when he called me."

"Did Hans call the police?" William asked.

"I don't—"

"—Never mind. Call the police, Aunt Agnes. Everybody stay here."

"William—don't," Margaret said for the second time that day. "Let me go with you."

William didn't hear her for the second time that day. He raced to his car.

Two blocks from Hans Stitler's shop, he could see the crowd spreading out onto the cobblestone street; flames leapt out of the store's upstairs windows.

William inched through the crowd and jerked to a stop. He jumped out, pushing two men to the side, not certain what they were yelling through their cupped hands.

Hans Stitler and Isaac stood in front of the shop, wavering between defending themselves and being wary of the anger of the crowd. A teenage boy, squat and muscular, already cursed with too much hair for his simian body, stood near them, yelling at the crowd. William couldn't understand him. The boy pointed at Isaac and Hans.

A rock crashed into the display window, spraying shattered glass onto the sidewalk. William struggled to assess the danger.

"They have spying equipment in the back," the squat boy announced. He pointed a fat accusing finger at Hans and Isaac. "It must be to contact the German U-boats with."

William recognized him—*Phillip* that was his name; he had delivered an order to the inn recently.

"I've been watching them," Phillip yelled out to the increasingly agitated crowd. "They're always moving these machines around back there."

"They are motors—*old* motors, you idiot!" Isaac shouted. "You must be the most stupid boy ever to work for Hans."

Trembling with rage, he advanced on the youth, pumping his balled-up fists in the air. "How could you be so stupid, boy? I'll ring your foolish neck!"

William grabbed his arms. "Uncle Isaac, stop now. Let me talk."

Isaac pushed William's hand away but said nothing more.

"German spies—both of them," a woman yelled, leaning into the semi-circle tightening around the shop. She was Agnes's age. William thought he had seen her before; he was certain that he knew everyone in town. Still. Even after living away for several years.

"Shut up, lady," William said, barely suppressing his anger.

He turned to Phillip, the delivery boy. "Don't you know goddamn rusted motors when you see them, boy? I brought them here myself."

"They have wires, like radio equipment, and they're hidden in the back," Phillip said, turning to the crowd for approval. They gave it to him. The shouts and murmurs were incomprehensible to William but he had no doubt about their hostility.

"Don't you know the difference between spy equipment and broken down motors, you idiot?" William wanted to slap the boy. Instead he threw up his hands to quiet the crowd.

"I've known most of you for my whole life." He found a strong firm tone that rose above the murmuring. "You used to be reasonable people." He pointed at Hans and Isaac. "You know these men too. They have been here longer than most of you have. How could they be—"

"—Don't call that boy an idiot. He's a patriot!" someone shouted out. A rock flew from the crowd now animated again, hitting Hans Stitler on his shoulder. Hans turned away from the blow, grabbing his arm. He bent forward.

Fire in the back storage room fanned out, illuminating the angry faces. William knew that their only exit was straight forward, into the crowd.

Isaac fell to the ground, clutching his chest. William moved toward him. A muscular man in a white undershirt dashed forward, his fist cocked back, looking for a place to land it on William's face.

William swung first. His big fist struck the attacker squarely in the chest, crashing through ribs and settling in softness. The man collapsed straight down, both knees hitting the pavement at the same time. He gagged heavily, and then he toppled onto his side.

The crowd gasped and moved back, creating a larger space around the inert Isaac and William's fallen assailant.

Two policemen pushed through the crowd—one grabbed onto William's jacket, throwing him against the brick wall at the side of the butcher shop. The other stood over the attacker, now silent.

"Help my Uncle Isaac, damn it." William looked at the policeman holding him. "Bathgate, what the fuck are you doing?"

Officer Bathgate awkwardly handcuffed William. "I'm arresting you for felonious assault, William."

"Take him in, he's a goddamn slacker," someone yelled. "And a German lover."

"My uncle, get him an ambulance, Bathgate." William's voice was more imploring now. "Is he alive?"

The other policeman, kneeling over Isaac, looked up. "A heart attack, I think." He yelled at a fireman pushing his way through the jeering crowd. "Haggerty—get an ambulance, quickly."

He motioned toward the other man, lying face down. "That one's dead."

"You killed him, William," Officer Bathgate said quietly.

39

JULY 24, 1918

BOYLE, TODD & SIRKIN

BOSTON, MASS.

"WILLIAM COULD HANG for murder." Stacey Sirkin measured the reaction around his polished rosewood desk. "If these were other times, the prosecutor might submit a manslaughter charge, if any charge at all. He might have gone along with our self-defense claim. But this was a soldier on leave—a soldier just days from shipping out to France. And there is not a single friendly witness. We really don't know what to expect."

Margaret cried softly. "And all we have is a German shopkeeper for a witness."

"And his friend, who is now dead." Donald Townsend touched Margaret's arm gently. "I am truly grieved about Isaac. He was such a decent man."

Margaret regarded Sirkin's owlish eyes and his long torso, clad in a blue and white striped seersucker jacket. "But Mr. Sirkin, isn't it clear that this *was* self-defense? William would never attack someone."

"The prosecutor has become a patriot." Sirkin stretched across his desk to the stack of documents piled neatly in one corner. He shuffled through them. "For him, this is a case of a young soldier stepping forward, out of a crowd, with the sole intention of helping to defuse a confrontation. Then in a blind rage, William struck him, breaking bones in his chest, killing him instantly."

"And what about the delivery boy?" Margaret gazed out the arched window onto Beacon Street at dusk, people and vehicles moving homeward on the still steaming pavement.

Sirkin ran his finger down a document. "Here he is—Phillip Miner. The boy who claims to have seen no threatening motion by the soldier."

He motioned toward the hefty marble cigarette box to Donald Townsend and then to Margaret. Both declined. She quickly glanced at the lid, upon which a pair of Scottish terriers had been etched in great detail.

Sirkin continued. "As William's defense attorney, let me point out that juries are often uncomprehending of subtleties—this boy, Phillip Miner, could be a very damaging witness. In this case, a manslaughter plea—"

"—How dare you even consider it, Mr. Sirkin?" Margaret snapped. "We must fight this. We can't have William in these horrid jails just because he wanted to protect his uncle."

"I didn't suggest that we agree to a manslaughter plea. I was merely going to say that it is an option."

"It is *not* an option." Donald Townsend spoke with assertiveness comforting to Margaret. He had readied himself for this battle. "We'll find a witness willing to state the truth no matter how long it takes. Someone must be able to offer an opposing view."

Sirkin leaned over the side of his swivel chair, and pulled a file from his briefcase on the floor. "We have already begun the process, Mr. Townsend. We intend to interview everyone on these police reports." He slid the file toward Donald. "Here are the names. Someone must have known William personally. Let's review them with William."

"He may not remember their names, who knows?" Margaret said dejectedly. "Aunt Agnes would be of help but she is so distraught. She is even talking about moving to Ohio to live with relatives she doesn't even know."

"There is another problem," Sirkin said. "That Miner boy, unlike most of the crowd, had the clearest view. Was William's assailant's demeanor angry? Conciliatory? The others didn't get as good a look. So every witness will not carry the same weight in a courtroom—unfortunately."

"I feel comfortable with you as our attorney." Donald glanced at Margaret's blank face but could not confirm the same assurance. "We will look carefully at each of our options."

"Thank you for your confidence," Sirkin said.

"To think that my son-in-law's life might be ruined by a patriotic errand boy." Donald shook his head. "I'm glad that Joe Finnerty recommended you. Frankly, my knowledge of criminal defense attorneys is not that extensive."

Sirkin tried to laugh. "Neither is Mr. Finnerty's. He knows his way around the courthouse the same way as you do, Mr. Townsend. Frivolous lawsuits and, on occasion, ones with actual merit. I imagine there is a special irony for you, seeking his legal recommendations—he has been a bit of a pariah to the local newspapers, as if I need to tell you that."

Donald motioned to Margaret that the meeting was over. "Mr. Sirkin, we already owe Mr. Finnerty a quiet debt of gratitude, for other reasons. Who would have thought you would have heard me say that even one year ago?"

40

SEPTEMBER 7, 1918

PENNSYLVANIA RAILROAD CAR

CHICAGO TO BOSTON

IDIOTS. BUFFOONS. HERMAN Oliver watched the two men grapple down the aisle of the cramped train compartment, cursing joyously—oblivious to the discomfort of the other players and passengers who moved their shoulders and ducked their heads to dodge an elbow, or a body slam to the seats in front of them—or on top of them. Both wrestlers stopped and turned suddenly towards Oliver, as if his presence had been announced only to them.

Oliver elicited a curiosity in Babe Ruth; at least whatever curiosity Ruth could muster for anything other than the child's game that was making him famous. Oliver resented Ruth's oafishness; he didn't know why—but he was sure that he could take Ruth down. He recalled the tough miners he had to slug it out with years before—he was certain that this Ruth guy wouldn't know what hit him. *Someone in that industrial school should have taught him manners—my father would have kicked the shit out of me if I wrestled in a crowded train car.* But he was on an important mission for Finnerty and he couldn't dwell on someone's manners.

Just that morning Oliver learned that the Army would no longer

347

give intelligence tests to its recruits. The reason amused him—Northern coloreds scored higher than Southern whites. So the military immediately stopped the tests. He was sure that if the military gave an intelligence test to this baboon Ruth he would score lower than a colored man—any colored man—anywhere.

"Ain't you that guy I met with Finnerty once? With some other guy too? I'm supposed to talk to you, right?" Ruth asked, his white shirt a sponge of sweat, his big ham of an arm curled around Walt Kinney, the other semi-literate grappler. Men on the train followed Ruth's every movement; despite his intrusiveness, he was still the most famous person they would ever see up close. Something to tell their families about.

"What happened to that little guy who Finnerty used to send around?" Ruth pushed Kinney away and signaled that their romping was over—at least for a few minutes.

"Devin Keane? He's gone. Nobody has seen him in a while. I think he got on Finnerty's wrong side," Oliver said, shrugging. "Maybe he pocketed a few too many extra bucks."

"What about that guy with the shipping company? I really wanted to play for them for a few games." Ruth was earnest, almost apologetic. "But Frazee broke my balls and I didn't. Maybe all of us will be playing for shipping companies soon."

"You mean William Morrison. He's in jail, charged with murder. I don't know the whole story, but he says it was self-defense."

Ruth took no notice of Morrison's plight. He leaned in closer to Oliver; his breath stank of cheap beer and he belched up the aftertaste of hot dogs. "This is the time to talk with the Cubs. They're really pissed off about the few bucks they're getting for the Series—we're pissed off too."

Oliver stepped back to distance himself. "From the way you guys

348

played the other day I would think you would be fighting with the Cubs on this train instead of rolling around with your own teammate. It looked nasty on the field to me."

Oliver surveyed Walt Kinney, a third-rate pitcher on the Red Sox, big and strong like Ruth. Kinney and Ruth enjoyed nothing more than knocking each other to the ground. Kinney was just happy to get the attention of Jidge, a nickname for George, Babe's real name. His teammates would never call him Babe—they left that for the fans and writers.

"Nah—none of the players gives a damn about what happens on the field. That's an old story." Ruth looked around, caught Kinney's eye and again motioned for him to wait a few minutes. Kinney grinned a slow-witted acknowledgment. "The guys know the only chance we can make a few bucks is to put some money down on the Series. This fuckin' war might never end, for Chrissake, and we might never play again."

That Ruth even knew about the war surprised Oliver. Finnerty had offered to bet him that, even though Ruth spoke German, he couldn't spell "Kaiser"—or that he would even know which country Kaiser Wilhelm II ruled. Oliver laughed whenever he thought about that.

"Look, Babe, I don't want to bullshit around. There is very little action on this World Series. You know that." Oliver wanted the deal done so he could go to another passenger car—any other car would do. "We can spread a lot of small bets for you guys around the country. The Cubs are favorites so we can make some money if they lay down."

"The winners are supposed to get $2,000 each. Hooper told us today that it might even be less than $1,200," Ruth said.

Ruth had thought about the numbers all day, Oliver concluded. "Finnerty can guarantee each of you will get the difference from him. He told me to let you know that."

Oliver was satisfied with his short presentation. He knew that he didn't have a man with a long attention span in front of him.

"Claude Hendrix is the guy on the Cubs we've been talking to." Ruth waved toward a sturdy farm boy leaning out a window, ignoring the soot flying past him into the car. "He, and Douglas, fixed a few games during the season." Ruth gleamed with delight. "We'll be talking to him in a few minutes—before he gets too drunk. Just make sure that Finnerty comes through like he says."

Herman Oliver turned away. *It should be a crime—a federal one—that someone this stupid could have such a carefree existence.*

41

"NO, BYRON. IT'S WORSE than that." Donald Townsend hesitated, uncertain where to begin. "I received calls from Creel's lackeys three times last month. They pick out sentences from the editorial page and insist I'm undermining the war effort. Me!" He stabbed at his chest for emphasis. "Can you imagine that? Half of them wouldn't know what a war was like if you dropped them in the middle of France."

Donald turned to Helen, her gaze lowered to the silverware in front of her. "Helen, I know you work for them." His voice softened. "I don't suppose everything they do is wrong, but they should never censor the newspapers. We know better than to mention troop movements. We don't need twenty-five-year-olds telling us about that."

"Helen told me that when you talked to Creel, he hung up on you," Byron said, nodding his head and laughing silently.

Donald smiled, carefully pouring wine into each glass. "Yes, he did indeed hang up on me. Well, that about does it for the *vin Français*. What better way is there to celebrate your safe return, Byron?"

"I second that, Mr. Townsend," Dr. Sidney Griggs called out from the foyer. Eloise, Beatrice's recent hire, showed him to the table. "To be honest, Byron, I prayed every day for you to get out of that hellhole safely. I told your family many times about how you saved me—just an undeserving physician."

Byron circled the oval dining table to embrace his friend. "Save the speeches for later, Sidney. It's so good to see you. From what I've heard we now have a nightmare on our hands in the Army camps. That might be a reason for censoring the newspapers. I don't know. I would probably be scared to death if I read about *mysterious illnesses* first thing in the morning."

Donald greeted Dr. Griggs. "Just for the record, Byron, I did have another encounter with Creel. This one in person."

"And where was that?" Margaret asked. "Are *you* censoring the news now, Father?"

"Not hardly, dear. It is more likely plain-old forgetfulness rather than censorship," Donald said, then pausing to recall the circumstances. "I went to that newspaper publisher's dinner a few weeks ago. Creel spoke. I heard that his organization went through the guest list and dumped everyone who didn't support his censorship crap. I don't know how my name got through."

"And what happened?" Byron asked, smiling again, ready for an interesting story.

"While he was taking those craven powder puff questions, I got a chance to ask him if he favored Thomas Jefferson's belief that if he had a choice between a newspaper or a government, Jefferson would always choose a newspaper. Creel was uncomfortable, but glib as always. 'We can't indulge ourselves with quotations from our Founding Fathers these days. You should be amongst the first to know that, Donald.'"

"I told him, 'There was a time when you, as much as anyone else, would have championed that quotation.' I felt like punching him, very hard. An urge, one of several, I haven't felt for a while."

"Maybe you should work on some of your urges, Donald," Beatrice suggested with a tauntingly raised eyebrow. She patted his forearm before he could protest.

"If you struck him, Father, we would have visited you in the cell next to William." Margaret rested her elbow on Byron's shoulder. "Anything can happen in that prison—that is my nightmare. You mentioned a nightmare 'in the camps' a minute ago, Brother—mysterious illnesses?"

Byron nodded, no longer playful as he was just a moment before. "We have, potentially, a deadly epidemic on our hands. Nobody knows how devastating it will ultimately become. Or where it came from—or even what it is. But it is killing soldiers on both sides of the Front. They are dropping very fast. Now we have clear signs of it right here in Boston."

Helen was incredulous. "They don't know what it is? Or how to stop it? And it is 'right here in Boston?'"

"No, we *don't* know what it is," Dr. Griggs said, agreeing with Byron's assessment. "In two days Dr. Welch is coming up to inspect Camp Devens. Byron, Dr. Carlson, and I will be going with him. The reported cases there are mounting quickly. "

"WHERE SHOULD WE START, Byron? Shall I fill you in on the past two years of my life?" Helen wasn't certain if she meant to be sarcastic or conciliatory. She poured a whiskey for him. She opened the gauzy white curtain, allowing the fading sunlight to bathe their sitting room in an autumnal gold. "I must confess that I actually had hatred for you when you left. I can't feel that way any longer. Your letters were very moving—your bravery, your selflessness; a far cry from the boyishness of Mexico."

Byron looked through the bay window, tracing the stand of trees and intertwining gravel paths, a comforting view he had not seen for a long time—he was finally back in his own home. Helen brought her glass over to the sofa; they toasted. He took her hand gently, and guided her to sit down next to him.

He twirled the glass, watching its liquid swirl. "I haven't thought about a drink of real whiskey for the past year. A few bottles of rancid wine worked fine. I hope I haven't gotten used to it."

Helen had thought of this moment since he had left. How awkward would she be? What should she say—exactly? She understood that the words wouldn't go according to plan; they never do in these circumstances, she reminded herself.

"Byron, I couldn't wait to come home with you today. I was going to scream when your mother quoted Plato the second time. A dear woman, but not today. I was glad to leave." Helen ran her hand along Byron's arm. "Unblemished. Despite the heroics that your new admirer, Sidney Griggs, told us about so many times."

Byron pivoted on the sofa to face Helen. "Please don't ever say 'heroics' again, darling. The only heroes are the ones who died. Even the Germans."

She ran her finger down the sharp pressed crease of his pants.

"I had an affair with someone while you were gone." She didn't expect the words to come out effortlessly, but they did. "Do you want me to tell you about it?"

He touched her lips. "Maybe some other time." He thought for a moment. "This war has been terrible for all of us." He looked out the window again. The parlor fell into shadow as the sun sank against the blood-red sky. "Do you want to be with me again? I guess that is all that is important right now."

She leaned over and caressed his neck, her mouth opening as their lips came together. He slid closer, let his hands explore her soft body and then gently pulled away.

"Helen, it was frightful over there. I don't think anyone—"

"Bring the drinks with you, darling." She took his hand, and motioned towards the staircase. "The bedroom is where it has always been. Nothing has changed."

NOT A CURVE OF her body had changed. He kissed her breasts. He ran his hand slowly up her thigh to the tuft of blonde hair. She rolled unto her back, spreading her legs.

"Give me a few more minutes, dear," Byron said. "It has been so long. I missed you so much."

"Of course." Helen ran her hand casually through his hair.

Byron reached over to the bed stand for his whiskey glass. He handed it to her. She sat up.

"There is so much I want to say. I know Father and Mother wanted to avoid most of it." Mother no doubt orchestrated this reunion. I can just hear her: 'Let's give Byron time to adjust.' Am I right?"

"What does it matter? We are here now alone—just us, Byron."

"It's so hard to imagine how our lives have changed," Byron said. "William is in prison for *murder*. Louella drowns in the Atlantic. Uncle Isaac dies in front of a mob of patriots. We lose the post office license for the newspaper."

"That hasn't happened yet, dear." Helen put her hand to his mouth.

"It's only a matter of time. If this war goes on we *will* be out of business. Just like dozens of newspapers already." Byron raised himself off the pillows and sat up on the side of the bed. "Ironically, somehow the news that affected me most was that Joe Finnerty's daughter died of influenza. He is crushed. Beyond consolation. I know how you loathe—"

"Stop, Byron. We would never wish this on him or anyone. That was terrible news. Your mother was right; 'nobody gets immunity from this war.' Who knows, maybe she really is quoting Plato. And it finally makes sense."

Helen smiled, laying her head back on the pillow. She opened her arms and beckoned Byron to her.

42

WILLIAM WOULD NEVER DESCRIBE the conditions to Margaret: vermin in his cell, layers of dead flies cemented into the ceilings, opiated men wandering in the courtyard, the noxious odor of piss on piss. Every day horrific. He tracked Margaret across the visitor's room—its metallic green paint peeling back, blackened water stains spread across the ceiling.

The week before a syphilitic man moved into his cell. Otis. William recalled that night. Otis—what was his last name? The shriveled man had spent the next two days moaning, fending off rats nipping at the pus running from his open sores. Then he died.

"You dressed down for the visit, darling. Am I not worthy of your best efforts any longer?" William forced a smile.

"Oh, William—"

"—I'm joking."

"Father wants to know if you're being harassed because *they say* you killed a soldier."

"I'll be all right. How is Byron? Tell him I said hello."

"He's adjusting. He had to admit that he's disappointed because he can't publish either of the two stories he is involved with."

"What are they? Tell me again." He wanted to hear something other than his own plight. His fate rested with a softening of the witnesses—*especially that stupid errand boy*. A discussion about the case with Margaret would change none of his dire circumstances.

"Byron claims he has proof the Cubs and the Red Sox fixed the World Series. He heard it from a few of 'his sources.' That's what he calls them. Billy O'Reilly also told him what he had overheard in the clubhouse during the last few games. But he could never publish it because the censors would say it hurt morale—that it would be injurious to the war effort."

"It's a story made for Byron. Of course, he could never go to another baseball park in his lifetime," William said, grinning at that prospect. "That would probably cure him of baseball, if the war didn't do it already."

"And it was Finnerty who set the *fix* up," Margaret said, her tone betraying a trace of conspiracy, not her condemnation of the past. "Byron said 'that a guy named Herman Oliver' was Finnerty's agent on the deal. I was shocked to think that it was the same gentleman we met."

"Gentleman? All right, if that is what you think he is, Margaret. By the way, Stacey Sirkin was here yesterday. He told me the grim details of Finnerty's daughter dying. Joe did love that little girl—"

"—That's Byron's other story."

"What? Clarisse dying?"

"No, influenza. The overcrowded Army camps. Soldiers getting sicker every day. They don't even know what it is. Strong men show symptoms of the flu and a few hours later they're dead. The censors won't let *that* story out either—for obvious reasons."

"Sirkin told me doctors are asking the military to stop the troop trains from crossing the country. But the military doesn't want to stop the war effort," William said, turning his attention to the ceiling. "Some of these patches of damp are quite artistic, wouldn't you say, darling?"

Though tears rolled gently down her cheeks, her voice remained steady. "That is an amusing observation, darling." She tried to smile, but instead just sighed. "There are so many things going wrong. I can't bear the thought of you in this place. I would do anything to get you out. It is so—*unjust*."

"Unjust it is, Margaret. But the world is unjust—and it always has been. Maybe it's just more so now than ever." He looked at her; perhaps waiting for a response, even though he didn't think it was a profound observation.

"I don't care about the world being unjust. I care about you. We all care about you right now—not the world."

William nodded. "I'm thankful for everyone's support. I'm also glad you're going back to Tufts. I'm sure radio is going to be in demand after the war—and it's not that I didn't agree with some of that socialist crap. Anything that would end this war would be a step forward. Who knows?"

"I can't stand that our transmitters are being sold to the military. But I know one day we can inform the listeners without policemen pushing us around in a park."

"Maybe you can broadcast a baseball game once in a while for the rest of us."

Margaret returned her husband's playful smile. "We'll keep that in mind. I'm sure when our engineers return from Europe they can apply themselves to making a broadcast from Fenway."

"I hope I'm around to hear it."

43

SEPTEMBER 24, 1918

BOSTON, MASS.

HELEN SPREAD HER HANDS out over the dining table. She had just arranged the Lenox china Beatrice Townsend had given them—and had never before been used—into two place settings. Byron's favorite breakfast awaited him: smoked salmon, scrambled eggs with chives, and toast.

"Thank you, dear," Byron said, entering the dining room and running his hand lightly through his still-wet red hair. "Ah, blackened toast—the only way it should be eaten."

Helen grinned lopsidedly. "I never *claimed* to be a good cook."

"Good in the kitchen—you're not. But you excel at other things."

Helen smiled and motioned him toward the table. Byron sat down and poured coffee.

"I had intended to breakfast somewhere with the doctors," he said, blowing on the hot brew. "Somehow you are far more exciting to me. Does that surprise you?"

"That's quite a relief to know," Helen said, adding a flirtatious gaze into his eyes. "They won't be here for another hour. Maybe we should go back upstairs." Before he could answer, she took his hand, her tone serious. "Byron, I can't tell you how thrilled I am that you're writing for Dr. Welch now. I remember how much I had hoped—" Her voice trailed off. She didn't need to finish the sentence. It didn't matter anymore; Byron was home.

"FATALITIES ARE INCREASING EXPONENTIALLY at Camp Devens." Dr. Welch half turned to face Byron, sitting next to Sidney Griggs in the back of Edward Carlson's car. "Our medical teams cannot evaluate this, at least with any certainty. Every patient has symptoms of pneumonia—and in almost every case, it's fatal. But the pneumonia is occurring too quickly for it to be the result of the flu. We just don't have good vision on how this is unfolding."

Dr. Carlson steered carefully on the country road, slick from the light, but insistent, rain that began at sunrise. "There is another consideration that might especially interest you, Byron," he said. "We dodged a bullet—a frightening one."

"What bullet is that, Dr. Carlson?" Griggs asked, leaning forward between Carlson and Dr. Welch in the front seat.

"A bullet Byron is familiar with—the World Series. Those games that were played here two weeks ago"—Dr. Carlson slowed, yielding to a boy on a bicycle, oblivious to the car, his basket still filled with the morning newspapers, a ragged piece of burlap covering them from the light rain—"If those last few World Series games were held here in Boston this week instead, the influenza incidents would have been far greater. Every soldier at those games would have been an incubator. We're lucky they cut the season short."

"Yes, Edward, we are lucky the season ended early," Dr. Welch agreed, glancing out the window. "But I have a feeling our luck has run out. We may be working against something we have never seen before."

soldiers stared at them, their eyes glazed and recessed. More despairing, Byron thought, than even those poor souls standing in the fetid trenches in the freezing French winters.

Dr. Carlson's car rolled slowly past other troops marching in tight formations—men with seemingly no understanding of the deadly disease in their midst.

Dr. Welch realized his worst fears as they turned a corner off Main Street. Two stacks of bodies formed grotesque pyramids at the back entrance to the morgue, attached to the hospital. Soldiers with white masks laid still more rigid corpses onto the ghastly piles. Nobody in the car said a word. Drizzle misted the windshield.

A sickening stench rendered their breathing difficult as soon as they stepped into the mud in front of the hospital. Unshaven soldiers stood in line, staring vacantly. Others lay on the wet ground, wrapped in moldy blankets, all with a bluish cast to their skin. Horrific deep purple lesions burrowed deep into the cheeks of other sullen faces staring into oblivion.

Dr. Welch immediately diagnosed lung failure from a still unknown contagion. He expected these eyes listlessly now watching him would be shut for eternity by nightfall. No medical procedure could change that bleak reality.

He remembered the barracks constructed for the colored soldiers. Were any coloreds standing around him now, he wondered? The gruesome skin discolorations erased distinctions between the races.

"Major General Henry McCain?" Dr. Welch asked the officer waiting to greet him. "I am Dr. William Welch."

"Lieutenant Colonel Welch"—McCain snapped a salute—"I was told to expect you today. Conditions have deteriorated considerably since my report earlier in the week."

Dr. Edward Carlson introduced himself and extended his hand. "This is Dr. Sidney Griggs, and Byron Townsend."

General McCain focused on the raggedy line of deathly ill soldiers, and then turned to Dr. Welch. "No battlefield is as grim as this. We had sixty-six deaths yesterday. And forty already today."

Dr. Carlson recalled his visit to the camp a little more than a year before, the sense of progress—of forward motion. The building out of an efficient military facility had impressed him then. Now only a nightmare existed.

"Can't we stop transporting conscripts around the country?" Dr. Griggs asked.

Everyone in the small circle standing in the rain, surrounded by the walking dead, knew that Dr. Welch's pleas to stop the military trains crisscrossing the nation had been ignored—the military needed to move troops to the East Coast for embarkation to Europe. Nothing would change that simple imperative.

"They're sending these men to certain deaths in these camps— even before they get to France." The doctors ignored Byron's irony. Thousands of young men were carrying *something* highly contagious, a fatal illness oddly affecting mostly young soldiers, physically the strongest segment of the population. And the tight censorship stifled any warning from being uttered in any public forum.

"We need to do an autopsy immediately," Dr. Welch ordered. "At least we equipped these cantonments for autopsies. Some of those Washington sons of bitches didn't think we needed morgues." Dr. Welch grimaced. "'How many young men will die in a training camp?' That's what one of those dolts asked me."

BYRON RETCHED OVER THE porch rail as soon as Major General Mc-Cain opened the hospital's front door. How could the doctors walk calmly into its midst? He wondered. He followed them inside, the stench searing through him.

Men lay two on a cot, others shivering on the floors. Dr. Welch had once campaigned for a two thousand-bed hospital. His requests denied each time. Now there were now over eight thousand patients.

An orderly in a once white gown opened the double doors to the morgue; this time even the doctors stepped back, distancing themselves from the unbearable smell of the putrefying, discolored bodies.

Dr. Welch walked to the far end of the morgue and spoke to a physician cradling a soldier's head in his right arm. The physician gestured toward two orderlies who immediately lifted a body onto a metal table. They spread steel cutting tools onto a mobile autopsy tray. Dr. Welch removed his jacket and slipped into a gown already smeared with darkened patches of blood.

He cut into the cadaver's chest. The doctors surrounding the table gasped. Their reaction frightened Byron, but he had to inch forward anyway for a closer look. The exposed lungs appeared to be more like a liver—a liver bulbous and strangled with bluish foaming bile.

"This soldier was brought into the hospital just yesterday evening," Gen. McCain said.

"We would expect this kind of pneumonia after a long battle with influenza, not overnight," Dr. Welch said, barely audible beneath his mask. He paused before offering a chilling diagnosis.

"This must be a new kind of infection—or a plague."

"THEY ARE REPORTING THOUSANDS of cases all over the Eastern seaboard." Donald Townsend stood near the fireplace in Byron's sitting room. "They allowed a march in Philadelphia to take place last week, even though there were cases of this—whatever it is—on the docks there already. It was a war bond sale rally and they wouldn't stop it—even though they knew the risks."

"Don't get worked up, Donald. We're all exhausted." Carlson slouched into the sofa, stretching his legs out onto the rug.

Donald sat down next to his friend. "I'm sure it was a terrible day at the camp. Byron looked exhausted when he walked through the door. I'm glad Helen put him to bed. What's your best guess, Ed? Why it is just the young who are afflicted?" He managed a wry smile. "By the way, I don't expect a definite answer."

"Dr. Welch thinks it may be because we old-timers were exposed to that influenza outbreak thirty years ago. Maybe it gave us some immunity. We don't know for sure."

"There really is no way to stop this, is there, Ed?" Donald waited for an answer he already surmised.

"We have no idea what can affect the human body this quickly." Dr. Carlson turned toward the foyer. He heard Helen descending the staircase, still out of view.

She ran into the room. "It's Byron! Foam is coming out of his mouth and his skin is pale. Something is terribly wrong."

The two men raced up the stairs.

Dr. Carlson entered the bedroom first, recalling the last time he was in this bedroom—Helen's miscarriage. He knew the moment he saw Byron that the outcome this time would also be tragic.

44

THE HEADLINE READ: **ARMISTICE IN EUROPE**.

The newspaper had lain upon the coffee table for three days, next to the colorful pamphlets promoting New Bedford tourist attractions.

Agnes glanced at it as she gathered her overcoat and the two stuffed suitcases. "Who would have thought it would ever end?" she asked herself, more than of the others in the sitting room.

"I am still numbed by the news," Donald Townsend said. "*Overjoyed—but numb*. That would be my personal headline. I can't think of another description."

Beatrice helped Agnes with her coat, usually a simple procedure, made difficult this time by Agnes's absentminded balancing of two leather shoulder bags in her hands. Beatrice took them from her and set them on the table.

"Thank you, Beatrice," said Agnes. "It will be harsh without my dear Isaac—and this inn." She looked at the photographs on the wall once again. She smiled gently.

Margaret recalled the day Aunt Agnes, with amused derision, satisfied Helen's curiosity about Uncle Isaac's preoccupation with everything Glenfiddich. It had been a wonderful day. And this day, so terribly sad.

"I don't know if I will ever come back. I'm not young anymore. I just can't stay here—too many memories." Agnes studied the room, tears flowing. "It's unbelievable—William is in a cell with such an uncertain future. But I'm glad you will move into the inn and wait here for him, Margaret. I will come back whenever he, or you, needs me."

"Of course, Aunt Agnes. We know you will." Margaret composed her response as evenly as she could manage. "William will be found innocent. But dear, dear Byron—I miss him so much, I can't imagine life without him. To be taken like that—and so many others as well. And we will never know why, will we, Father?"

Donald shrugged his shoulders, unable to look at his daughter.

Beatrice stood in front of Agnes, regarding with tenderness the dear friend she perhaps would never see again. "It seems like we just put dear Helen on the train back to Denver. Now we are seeing you off to Ohio, Agnes."

Margaret embraced Agnes, a few tears forming. "Helen promised me that she would return as soon as she could. We both still want to be part of radio."

Donald Townsend settled for a comforting assurance. "Margaret will take excellent care of the inn, Agnes. She loves this place as much as William does."

Margaret watched the large touring car pull into the driveway; they would accompany Agnes to the train station for still another sad farewell. "When I told William I would wait for him here at the inn until he came home, he seemed as overjoyed as one could be in that disgusting jail."

Agnes smiled sadly.

"We will paint this room a pretty color in the spring, Aunt Agnes—maybe orchid," Margaret said smiling, remembering William's account of the orchid paint explosion on the inn staircase when he was a young boy.

"Margaret, I hope you are not moving to the inn just to keep it open for my sake," Agnes said as the family grouped around her.

"Oh, no. William and I can both build up the inn now that the war is over— and after William is proven innocent. It won't be easy for him to get a corporate job, not with all this publicity. And there is always room for you to come back, dear Aunt Agnes."

Agnes glanced again at the photographs over the fireplace mantle and nodded.

Donald picked up Agnes' scuffed leather valises. "The taxi is waiting," he reminded them, his voice cracking.

EPILOGUE

WILLIAM TURNED TO VIEW his profile in the closet door mirror. He adjusted the derby, tilting it to a jaunty angle. Then he held the hat in his hands, admiring it once again.

Ruggiero nodded approvingly. "It was meant for *you*, Mr. Morrison."

"It's sad and funny, Ruggiero. When I bought this hat, I thought I should have bought my brother-in-law a hat instead of binoculars. It was his birthday just a few days before I gave the hat to you—I don't know what makes me think of that now."

"Well, now you can give him this hat for his birthday. It must be coming up again soon—that was the beginning of May, wasn't it? The Kentucky Derby, right?"

William twirled the derby. "Byron died in September from the flu. He would have been my age—twenty-nine."

Ruggiero looked out the window. He had read somewhere the influenza pandemic had claimed more than fifty million souls worldwide. Nobody would ever know for certain. More that even the deaths in the war. By the grace of God, he had been spared from both horrors.

"Right out on that pier, there must have been two hundred empty coffins one day," Ruggiero said shuddering. "I never saw anything like it. Some of the guys on the docks said it scared them to death. They went to MacPhail's Tavern afterwards for a few more than usual."

"Yes, I heard the flu was bad down here also—I guess it was everywhere," William said softly.

"And you know what, Mr. Morrison? It started to go away once the war ended. Well, sort of anyway. Nobody ever said why it came or why the damn thing stopped—" Ruggiero turned toward the knock at the door.

"Someone with another hat for me?" William asked. "Only one head, sorry."

Ruggiero laughed. "Good joke, sir. We can always use one these days." He opened the door.

Joe Finnerty looked past Ruggiero. "Hello, William. Nice to see you."

William waved Finnerty into the room. "Thank you again, Ruggiero."

"Good luck, Mr. Morrison." Ruggiero moved toward the open door.

"No—wait a minute, Ruggiero." William picked up the binoculars from the windowsill. "Take these—it's a long story. Just take them." Margaret had insisted William have them when she cleaned out Byron and Helen's house. "Maybe these will bring you luck also. Thank you, Ruggiero."

Ruggiero hesitated, not certain what to say. He took the case and closed the door behind him.

"I gave him this hat when I came down here for the *Lusitania* sailing. He just gave it back to me now. He said it brought him good luck——he won a few bucks on the Derby that year. He wanted me to have some of that luck too."

"Nothing like an Irishman who wants to share his good luck, I always say."

"Uh, Joe—*Rug-gi-e-ro*? I think that makes him Italian."

"Oh, those bastards should keep anything that brings them any luck at all," Finnerty responded quickly, and then laughed. He slowly regarded the room. "William you always were attracted to the seamier side of life. I image this provides a *frisson* unavailable at the fine hotels uptown. That is *excitement* of sorts in French?"

"Oh I didn't know that because you robbed the French on a few deals during the war that you learned their language."

"All the better to rob them with, William—if you must be so cynical."

They both nodded, smiling.

Finnerty pointed to the bottle of Glenfiddich on the tray. Ruggiero had left it behind. "My, William, you've changed." He poured two drinks. "And all this time I thought you were basically a temperance type like me. Not a whiskey bottle at midday kind-of-gentleman."

"Joe, I thought you didn't drink because you never wanted to give anyone the edge. That you'd rather they be less sharp than you."

"I didn't need them to drink for me to have the edge. I rarely drink or smoke because I want to be the first Irish Pope." Joe Finnerty flashed his big toothy grin, satisfied with his joke.

"Fat chance, Joe. But as far as I'm concerned I owe my liberty to you, not to those papists in Italy. I'm glad I can thank you in person. I know I didn't get the whole story from Stacey Sirkin. All he said was that the charges were dropped—the key witness, that little errand boy prick, changed his testimony. He believed that I acted in self-defense after all."

Finnerty walked to the window. "Let's just say that the end of the war made everyone a little less patriotic—and a little more reasonable."

"And that means?" William moved next to Finnerty at the window.

It was almost time to go down to the pier.

"It means that the boy's father needed a good-paying job and I found one for him up in Maine. Something to do with a nature preserve. A healthful existence, I suppose. Moved the whole damn family with him, including that 'little prick,' as you so unkindly characterize him."

"And that district attorney who was howling for my scalp?"

"The war ended. He didn't need to wave the flag anymore. And I promised him *sufficient* help. He's running for Congress or something. A step up the ladder of success for another Irishman. It makes me so damn proud to help."

William nodded. "Thanks, Joe, that's all I can say. What brings you to New York?"

"Boston has some painful memories for me. Little Clarisse and all that. I thought I would move my operations down here. New York is the heartbeat of America, you know—if you'll allow me that poetic turn of a phrase—and I thought I would come by today to see if you wanted to relocate down here too."

"And no doubt your sources told you where to find me?" William asked, amused by the remote possibility that Herman Oliver was following him around the city.

"You might say that, William. I did find out that your darling niece, Sarah, her husband, and their little baby will be strolling down that gangplank in just a short while, am I right? I'm happy for you, William."

A moment of graceful sincerity; devoid of sarcasm, William concluded.

"And about moving to New York?" Finnerty arched his eyebrows expectantly.

"No thank you, Joe." William looked out toward the Hudson River. "I'm going back to the inn. Margaret and I will make it grander. There's plenty of room to build it out. We'll be ready for a new era of tourists—and young Sarah and her new family will be with us now."

Joe nodded, understanding.

"And Margaret can still stay close to that radio station. Helen will be returning in two months. The two of them have an exciting idea for a radio program," William added. "I think there's a great future in those broadcasts."

"So do I," Joe agreed. "That's another reason I'm down here."

"What does that mean?"

"There is a great future for radio. I may even invest in it with that guy."

"What guy, Joe?"

"That DeForest character. He's looking to partner with someone, I heard—I'll be talking to him this week."

"Well, be careful, Joe. I heard he is a bit of a con man." William feigned concern.

"I'll do my best to watch out for myself." Finnerty attempted a serious frown.

William smiled. "Come on, Joe. Walk with me over to the pier. You seem to have some time on your hands today."

They walked down the narrow staircase into the lobby, three guests readying themselves for the cold. Maybe, thought William, perhaps also going out onto the pier.

"Molasses Storage Tank Explodes in Boston!" A gangly boy, all mouth and curly blond hair flowing out from under his gray cap, shouted the headline of the newspaper he held in front of him. "Read all about it! Twenty-one dead!" William grabbed at the paper from the hawker and shoved a coin in his palm.

He read aloud, jumping from paragraph to paragraph. "Half-inch pieces of steel plate shoot through the air—unseasonably hot day heats filled-to-capacity tank—21 people killed, including children playing near the tank—firehouse destroyed, three firemen among dead—20-foot wall of molasses surging through streets terrifies onlookers."

William turned quickly to Finnerty, who shrugged his shoulders. "William, remember, we haven't owned that storage tank for, what is it—almost two years."

William nodded slowly, then he pulled his fawn derby a bit tighter so that an errant wind wouldn't knock it off, and shuffled through the faded wooden door.

The End.

Photo by Joe LaRusso

ALAN GEIK has an M.Sc. from the London School of Economics & Political Science. World War I has been a subject for his research and interest, especially the profound effects of the emptying and virtual disappearance of a generation of young men from the cities and hamlets throughout the British Isles during WWI. France, Germany, Belgium, Russia and the other combatant countries, of course, also willingly offered their young as cannon fodder as well.

He has written about the ongoing collusion between money center banks and politicians throughout the Western World to enrich themselves under the guise of "banks are too big to fail—they never were "too big to fail without the economy crashing" (a banking lobbyist's deceit) and never will be.

Glenfiddich Inn is his first novel.

His next literary effort is set in his youth, in an extended family involved in both organized and freelance criminal pursuits, including, but not limited to convictions for mail fraud, police corruption, labor racketeering, and income tax evasion. The title *Uncle Charley Killed*

Dutch Schultz refers to a kindly Murder Inc. assassin (who was also convicted and served twenty-three years for the deed).

Alan grew up in the Bronx, NY. He graduated from the City College of New York. He has since given up the intolerable winters on the east coast for the intolerable summers of Nevada where he now resides with his wife, Yvette.

Proof